By Desire Bound

By Desire Bound

Thea Devine

Zebra Books
Kensington Publishing Corp.
http://www.zebrabooks.com

ZEBRA BOOKS are published by

Kensington Publishing Corp.
850 Third Avenue
New York, NY 10022

ISBN 0-7394-0019-3
Zebra and the Z logo Reg. U.S. Pat. & TM Off.

Printed in the United States of America

For John, Thomas and Michael, the most patient of families, for all the reasons they know . . .

And to the ladies in Corporate Travel: Becky, Sally, Maureen, Angela, Jane, Charlotte, Ann, Ingrid and Marlene, and Sue and Mike . . . for your friendship and encouragement, bless you all.

Prologue

Goole Abbey, Croxfordshire, England—1895

She had fallen in love with the face in the portrait the moment she walked into Goole Abbey as a new bride.

"That's the good brother," Roger had said mockingly. "The dead brother."

The brother who had been the heir of the house of Pengellis, jewelers to the Crown.

The brother whose face was rugged and ascetic both, with piercing dark eyes and a firm carved mouth, who carried himself like a king.

The brother who had died in quest of a legendary diamond nine years before, his exploits documented in a hundred sepia photographs that were kept enshrined at the London town house and at Goole.

The brother who was mourned and revered and almost canonized.

The brother who was still alive.

Not only that, but Roger and his mother had known that Connack Pengellis was alive all those years they were publicly mourning his death.

And now she knew, dangerous knowledge for which she was locked in the tower at Goole Abbey like Rapunzel.

And at the door, Gorgon, in the form of her malicious malevolent mother-in-law, Lavinia, just waiting for the moment to pounce.

And the only thing that was keeping her alive was the thing Lavinia coveted most: she was carrying Roger Pengellis's child.

One

He lay sprawled on the thickly tufted sofa, grizzled, touseled and naked, just another anonymous male body in a brothel full of them.

"He's new," the madam said. "Just brought in last night. He's . . . asleep—but very willing, as my lady can see."

Oh yes, she saw: he was long and lean and strong and beautifully made. His body was canted at an angle so that one of his legs was supporting his torso, and the other was crooked up on the sofa in a seemingly unconscious pose that put him deliciously on display.

He looked utterly knocked out; he could have been unconscious or drugged, or maybe he was just playing coy.

She couldn't tell.

But she knew who he was. Instantly and shockingly she knew, the way she tended to know odd things, and she believed it was he, and she immediately understood that she had to keep them both safe at any cost.

Any cost.

How much did she have? Her hands shook. A wad of banknotes she had stolen from Lavinia, and in her bag, an armload of unmarked silverware she had taken from Goole Abbey.

Enough to keep the dogs at bay for how long—an hour? A day?

She had to tread very carefully because she knew the madam had recognized her from a half-dozen forays she had made to the brothel when she was newly wed and skirting the thin edge of ostracism with the fastest social set in London.

She had been good at pretending. She had always been good at pretending. Roger hadn't cared what she was doing; he had only cared about the gold her father had dowered to his quirky only child to buy a baronetcy, which was as close to a title as Leonard Boulton would ever come.

Not that she had cared. She had been his willing partner in complicity, eagerly reaching with both hands for the title, the money, the freedom. They had done it before, she and her father, only this time, he had required she make a lifetime commitment to an indissoluble marriage and unending privilege.

What obedient daughter could refuse such a request? Especially one who had been as avaricious as she?

"My lady?"

The madam knew not to show her impatience, but it was there, a thin thread in her sharp question.

Her heart was pounding wildly but she didn't hesitate; you didn't, with these people, and she needed to get out of Madame's sight as quickly as possible. Too much had happened too quickly. She needed to act quickly, *now.* She could think about it later. "I'll take him."

"As my lady wishes. For how many nights?"

Oh lord— She drew herself up. "We'll see how he works out. And since he's new, I will of course expect a more favorable fee, since I will be the one breaking him in."

Such daring . . . but she had always lived on the edge of disaster . . . it was the only way she knew.

The madam eyed her skeptically for a long moment. This one had never bargained for anything a day in her life, she thought. And never in a brothel. She knew this one: this one had never ever chosen from the menu in all the times she had ventured into the house.

It was amusing, really. "Very well," Madame said. "And payment will be arranged how?"

She calculated quickly, but she already knew she could not give up her banknotes. "I have silver."

"Indeed?"

"Which you can convert easier than I."

"You think so."

Awful woman—but still, the safest place she could think of with Lavinia in pursuit—she had no choice; she had to convince her.

"Unmarked, Madame. Who is to know?"

Now the madam was curious; it showed plainly in her eyes.

"My lady surely has money."

She gritted her teeth; she had to gamble, and her bluff was cloud thin. "I will buy this gentleman for the night with silver. Let me say that I know you are probably aware of its origin. Therefore this will be my only offer, Madame. Take it or leave it."

"Let me see."

She opened her bag and removed a silver sugar bowl and handed it to the madam who held it to the light and examined it thoroughly.

"If you have the entire set, my lady, you may have him for two nights."

"I have the teapot and cream jug, and I must be assured I am buying your discretion."

"If you add in the tray and trivet, I believe we may have a bargain."

Any cost . . .

It was all she had of the silver, and she thought how sharp it was of the madam to understand exactly what the whole comprised and to bargain accordingly.

Madame knew she had no choice. But Madame *was* willing to bargain; she had picked up on that right away.

She handed them over reluctantly, with the madam examining and nodding over each exquisite piece.

"We have a bargain. Two nights. And of course you may be assured *I* know that such a one as my lady would never venture forth to such a place. I have never seen you. I don't even know who you are. Is that satisfactory? Good. Then I will have him transported to a more private room."

Madame clapped her hands and two burly men appeared with a pallet onto which they lifted the inert body of her would-be lover, and then they proceeded to a more private room on an upper floor of the brothel.

It was a very utilitarian room—with a bed, a washstand, an upholstered chair, an armoire for clothes, and carpeted floor. A fireplace for warmth, which was crackling with a banked fire, and nothing in the way of decoration except for fabric-draped walls in a neutral color.

Good enough for her purposes. And isolated in the back of the house.

Any cost . . . did it matter now?

She watched as the porters unceremoniously rolled their burden onto the bed, and exited the room.

Alone at last . . .

She locked the door with shaking hands, marveling at her bravado and her reserves of sheer nerve.

Or was it the familiar rush of triumph at having outwitted an adversary yet again . . . ?

But then—it was *him* . . . his face, thinner, longer, gray with fatigue and something else, and buried under a bushy growth of beard and hair—but *his face* nonetheless.

And that body, that unimagined body that she had looked at every day, three and four times a day, in his portrait at Goole Abbey.

That painted body, clothed as plain as a priest, with no clue to the sinew and power that lay beneath.

It was a body made to be touched. Even in repose, even with him unconscious, she felt the awful urge to feel the texture, the heat, the muscularity of him.

. . . the him of her dreams . . .

Really him? Or just a demon of her imagination?

She stretched out her hand and laid it on his shoulder—and jumped back. His skin was hot, burning hot.

Like a demon . . .

. . . oh, God—this wasn't real . . . it couldn't be—she wasn't in a brothel with the man who had been canonized by his family who had known all along he hadn't died . . .

—and she hadn't just buried her husband of five years and escaped from her tower prison . . .

. . . dear Lord . . .

The stuff of gothic romance . . .

Even she didn't believe it.

But there he was, on the bed, naked as a baby and burning with fever, and she was his sole lifeline, even if only she knew it.

She took a deep breath to slow her drumming heart and calm her jangling nerves.

What to do now, with a complication she could never have envisioned in her life?

Except she hadn't planned anything, not the how, the where, the what, not even Roger's unexpected death; all she had was the amorphous dream of killing Lavinia—yes, destroying La-vinia—somehow, and escaping.

But then Roger had died instead, suddenly and inexplicably, and as his grieving widow, she had had to put on a public show, which had given her time, precious precious time, to act on her impulses.

And to this moment, she didn't know how she had done it, how she had had the rational thought to overpower Lavinia, steal the money and the silver, and to escape with her life and her lies.

And escape to this . . . the unforeseen, inconceivable, unbelievable coincidence of finding Connack Pengellis in the very last place anyone would expect or look.

And naked and for sale.

How likely was that?

And yet, the brothel had been the first thought that came into her mind as she fled the grounds of Goole.

She reached out to touch him again just as he shifted and rolled onto his side.

She had been meant to find him.

No!

Unthinkable.

Her hand shook as she laid it against his bearded cheek. He was hot, hot as the devil, consumed in hell.

She had known somehow he was here.

Irrational . . .

Inconceivable.

Maybe.

Not.

But she didn't want to consider the incomprehensible and the implausible. She liked reasons, explanations, and possibilities grounded in reality.

But there was no explanation for this.

For him.

Who had been thought dead.

Or somewhere in South Africa.
At the very least.
And who was where he wasn't supposed to be, with her who was somewhere she wasn't supposed to be—
And both at the mercy of Lavinia who wouldn't scruple to kill them both.

She lifted the edge of the bedspread and draped it over his naked body.
She wanted to climb into bed with him—
Dear God— That was insanity.

She sank wearily into the chair, and rested her head in her hands.

There wasn't a sound except the crackle of the fire in the hearth.

She couldn't hear the wind, or a guest, or a mouse.

There was nothing—just her own injudicious thoughts as she rummaged through the events of the last twenty-four hours.

She was safe—for the moment.

And so was he.

She had known Roger was going to die. She knew the way she always knew things—a moment before and a step ahead.

She had watched him from the slit of the window in the tower where they had imprisoned her; everyday she had watched him careering over the fields of Goole Abbey until the fatal day he had tried to jump a downed tree trunk and his horse didn't make it.

And neither did he.

The funeral was lavish and overcrowded.

Lavinia chained her to her side, and everyone commented on how devoted they were and how fortunate it was that there would be an heir to carry on the family business and Roger's name.

Only there was no baby. There would be no heir.

And it would not have been too long before Lavinia found out and her life would have had no value.

Lavinia would have killed her without blinking an eye.

And so, in that infinitesimal moment when Lavinia was distracted by the intricacies of unlocking her manacles before incarcerating her again for the last time, she attacked her, disabled her, and managed to elude the servants, steal the silver and money, and escape.

And all on a tide of driving fear and sheer gut instinct. She had no reserves left.

She couldn't think beyond the next minute.

She had no idea where next to go or what to do.

She had two nights.

And the limp naked body of Con Pengellis to burden her down.

And she wasn't going to leave Croxfordshire without him.

Everyone knew the story of Connack Pengellis, Bart., head of Pengellis-Becarre Company. He was the man who had mined a fortune in diamonds and then left the company at the height of its production and expansion to devote his life to pursuing a legend.

No one knew if he had ever found the mythic diamond they called *The Eye of God.*

Everyone thought he had died seeking the fabled Valley of the Diamonds.

Only Roger and Lavinia knew he had survived.

And then her—long after Roger had inherited his brother's wealth, his mines, his title, and his properties.

They couldn't take the chance she wouldn't tell; they knew she hated Roger and, since she had her own money in a trust set up by her father, that she felt no loyalty to him either.

She knew they would have no compunction about killing her—but she saved herself by giving Lavinia the one thing she wanted above all else—a child of Roger's blood.

And with that quick-witted, brilliant and inventive lie, she bought herself some time.

Two months and two nights.

She felt as if the whole of her life were compressed into that time. One more month and Lavinia would have wondered why she did not show. One more night and she would have been condemned forever.

And she couldn't begin to think what might have happened to *him* if she had not escaped.

She was meant to find him.

She shuddered at the thought, but she felt it to the very marrow of her bones.

That, and the loss of everything. Just everything.

First her father, and now this. And she could count her money gone as well.

Dear God—all that money . . .

Her share of her father's initial profit from his partnership with Roger: he had banked it in Funds before his death, and now she couldn't risk trying to get hold of it.

All she had was the silver and a fistful of banknotes. And an unconscious naked man who didn't know that she was his savior.

She didn't even have a plan.

No . . . she had the barest sketch of a plan: she had bought two nights, so they would stay there the two nights.

Beyond that, she couldn't think.

She couldn't move, she wanted to stay immobile forever and never have to make another decision. Her body felt heavy, constricted. Tight, as if something were squeezing her very vitals.

She jerked awake in panic, unable to move, unable to breathe—choking, choking, choking on her words, her breath, her life.

He was behind her, on his knees, his muscular arm around her neck, pulling back on her throat to almost the point of no return.

He had tied her up in the thin bedspread with which she had covered him, and she felt the murderous anger emanating from him in waves.

He was going to kill her. A wild naked man on his knees was going to finish what his family had started.

He increased the pressure on her throat. She felt her helplessness in the face of his strength, his fury, his heat.

She couldn't see: there was only darkness and his panting breath and her futile gasps for air.

She felt the life going out of her. Another minute . . . and then darkness and gone—she would be with her father, soon, to eternity—

She welcomed it, she did . . .

"Who the hell are you?"

The pressure against her throat eased—just enough so that she could gulp some air.

"Where are we?"

His voice was savage with an explosive frustration.

She heaved against him in an impotent attempt to loosen his hold.

He clamped her against the back of the chair more tightly, the tension in his body palpable.

"Jesus God, who am I . . . ?"

Two

Red . . . bright, burning, liquid . . .

In her eyes, her mouth, clotting in her throat, constricting in her veins . . . no help, no hope . . . he was too powerful, and fueled by pure animal rage . . . she was losing, losing to his strength, his heat, and his savage instinct to defend himself.

All the answers—she had all the answers . . . if he would just—she couldn't breathe . . . agonizing—smelled his fear, felt the beast roar, felt her body giving up, going limp, words gagging in her mouth . . . last gasp—last ounce of strength . . .

She twisted her body wildly against the encroaching darkness . . . such a puny defense against a lion . . .

. . . and yet—

. . . she gasped for breath as his arm eased away from her throat . . . coughing, rasping, inhaling weakly, her body shaking, gulping air now as she felt him release the pressure just enough . . . just—

Not an animal then; *something* had broken through the fury, the fear.

He wanted those answers. Maybe.

She swallowed convulsively. *He might kill her anyway.*

He would, if he didn't like the answers.

She didn't like the answers.

The silence took on a heavy sentient quality. He waited

with the patience of a predator, his muscular arm around her throat, tense, taut and hot.

She swallowed again, just to feel the movement in her throat.

And he waited, his body alert, poised as if he were marking the passing moments by a dozen other senses.

The silence became elastic, stretching just to the breaking point of his patience and her fear.

And when he finally spoke, his voice was deep, rich, and rough with the hard edge of a man who was on the knife edge of sanity.

"Who are you?"

And she thought, she didn't have the answers, not even that one. What could she say to vanquish a lion?

"My name is Darcie Boulton," she said finally, her voice raspy from the tightness in her throat.

He ingested the information. There was no other word for it. It was as if he took every word and turned it over and examined it to see if it had any meaning.

She could feel it, the long slow parsing of that one sentence.

"My name is . . ."

Liar. Cheat. Thief. Relation by marriage . . .

He locked his arm against her throat again in a sudden sharp move.

"Who are you?"

She choked. "I—"

"Goddamn it . . . !" He pulled tighter.

"Darcie . . .

Tighter still.

"Truth . . ." she gasped.

He moved his arm—just a fraction. "Why should I believe you?"

"Tell you . . ." she panted, between deep gulping breaths, ". . . everything . . ."

"I live to hear it—Darcie. Boulton."

"Stop . . . please . . ." she whispered, and he eased the weight on her throat, but his arm remained like an iron bar across her shoulders.

"Talk."

She felt the aftershock immediately. Her body quaked like she was in a firestorm. Her throat cramped up. She couldn't think of one coherent word that would make sense or that he would believe.

Her throat was so raw, she sounded like a croaking frog.

"I know who *you* are," she whispered.

Tension: immediate and palpable. She felt as if she had a knife at her throat; his arm inched threateningly closer.

"Tell me."

"I—"

"Tell me—"

Pressure just at her collarbone; she coughed violently, then she caught her breath and choked out: "Pengellis—your name—" Another spasm of coughing and then: "Connack Pengellis . . ."

Again she had that sense of him absorbing the sound, the texture of the words. His hold loosened slightly and his body shifted.

"Tell me more," he commanded, his voice guttural and hard.

She heard just the faintest wariness in his tone. He didn't know. He had meant it: he really didn't know. And so how could he believe *her?*

She drew in a long shuddery breath. "Please . . . don't— I'll tell you everything—just don't . . ."

"Don't what? Strangle you? Attack you? I'm to believe a stranger—Darcie? I can't tell the truth from a fairy tale. I wonder what lies you'll spin to gain your freedom."

"I'll tell you the truth," she said desperately.

"Whose truth? Your truth? How can I know it when I don't even know that name."

"Let me tell you what I know." She wasn't pleading; God, she hoped she didn't sound like she was begging. But even so, what she would tell him was the stuff of a penny novel. He wouldn't believe her anyway.

She felt a swamping hopelessness. His situation was fantastic, incredible, improbable, and she had been rash and imprudent. He could kill her as easily as believe her.

But he *needed* her. And she had to make him understand.

"Let me tell you," she whispered, "and maybe something will strike you."

"Tell me who you are."

She thought about it—one beat, two, how much, how little, the details, the omissions.

He is real; he is here. He must have found the diamond. The biggest, most legendary diamond on earth . . . he knows where it is. And if I could get a piece of it, I could be free forever—

"I told you—my name is Darcie Boulton. I was married to your brother. I'm your sister-in-law."

His arm tightened. "My . . . *brother* . . . ?"

She closed her eyes against the inevitable. "You have . . . had—a brother. He inherited your wealth, your companies, your title. He died in an accident not a week ago."

"And his wife wound up—*where?*" His voice now was dangerous, silky with a kind of repressed anger.

"In a . . . whorehouse," she whispered. "A *male* brothel."

That silence again. Long and rubbery, thick with all the conflict within him. His arm moved closer to her throat.

"And what exactly am I doing here?"

"I don't know."

"And you—"

"Hiding . . ."

"Hiding," he echoed. "Hiding. You buried your husband and you're hiding."

"From your mother."

His arm tightened again. "Jesus God—my *what?*"

"Mother—" she choked out. "Dead. They said—dead . . . you. Died. Years ago. No one knew. *No one.* I found out. Dangerous. They wanted to kill me."

"No—no . . . I don't believe you—God, are you a liar—"

And she was. She knew it. Just not about this, which sounded, even to her, like the biggest lie of all.

She swallowed raggedly. "Roger—your brother—he took over everything. He ran the companies, the mining operation, the store. He . . ."

"Liar."

"They made you a saint."

"Really?" he sneered. "And on what altar was I sacrificed?"

"You gave yourself up to *The Eye of God.*"

He went still. A tight eerie stillness as if he were obliterating himself. As if he recognized *that* in some deep recess of his forgetfulness.

"Go on," he hissed.

"Nine years ago—*they* said. You disappeared. *They* said you'd died. Somewhere in India. It was in the newspapers—everything. You gave up the company, the day-to-day operation of the diamond mines. You wanted *The Eye of God.* You went after it. And you never came back. *Aghhhh . . .*"

He jerked his arm against her throat again.

"Jesus God . . . what hell is this? What kind of shit is this? Who the hell are you?"

She gulped a precious mouthful of air. ". . . married your brother five years ago . . . I—father . . . money, gold—Roger wanted . . . to fund company—"

"What company?" he growled.

". . . Pengellis-Becarre . . . mining . . . jewels—diamonds . . ." she gasped out.

He went dead still again.

She had a moment, the merest moment, to persuade him that her story wasn't a fairy tale, that it was real, *he* was real, and *she* could save him.

"My father—looking for investment and a title. Roger needed the money. Knew you were still alive. Knew it, and he and your mother, kept the secret for years. I found out. Couldn't risk my telling. Imprisoned me. Everyone thought you were dead. *Everyone.* Roger took everything—years before I came. And then they thought—they knew—I would tell everything. They locked me up. They would have killed me."

"They didn't," he said flatly, coming out of the silence and filling in the one detail that could puncture her story.

And now, and now—the biggest lie of all. She sagged against the chair, rolling the phrasing around in her mind to find the way to say it that wasn't a lie and didn't bend the truth.

"I told them I'm pregnant," she whispered.

He listened to the words and the tone of her voice closely, too closely, as if he were weighing every nuance.

"Are you?"

She chose not to answer that. "Lavinia—your mother—wanted the baby. I was to stay locked in the tower at the Abbey until it was born."

He heard that too. He *heard* it.

She took advantage of his hesitation as he absorbed the information.

"You need me." Brash of her when he could choke her to death in one abrupt motion. But he had eased the pressure, and considered her words even as he dismissed them.

"Hardly," he said sardonically.

"No—somewhere inside you know it's true, and you need me."

"I know *nothing*, Darcie Boulton, except you are a consummate liar."

"I know," she said with a hint of desperation. "It sounds impossible. But I paid the madam with the silver from Goole Abbey to have you for two nights."

Another hard pull against her collarbone.

"What a sweet detail, Darcie," he growled close to her ear. "You just can't stop yourself, can you? What kind of woman are you?"

"It's true. All of it."

And she thought maybe he felt it, viscerally, because he hadn't killed her—*yet*.

"So let me summarize what we already know," he murmured, his voice icy now with danger and distrust. *"My name is Connack Pengellis, and I am believed to have died nine years ago in quest of something called The Eye of God.* But my family has known and kept secret that I am alive, and meantime, my brother took over my business properties, but conveniently died last week, and his pregnant wife, who had discovered I was still alive, escaped from a tower where she was kept prisoner in order not to reveal to the world the mesmerizing secret that I had survived, and somehow wound up in a brothel in order to hide from my nasty—I guess my mother *now*—who allegedly wants to kill her . . . have I got it right, Darcie? Is that what I'm to believe?"

It sounded awful. It sounded spur of the moment, out of her mind, ridiculous, crazy, absurd, impossible.

Insane.

"Yes," she whispered. *"Yes."*

"Bravo, Darcie. Bravo. You're good. It's a fabulous tale. *Fabulous.* A tale out of *A Thousand and One Nights.* You made it all up. Am I right?" His arm tightened. "I have to be right, Darcie, because nothing else makes sense."

"It's the truth," she muttered. "It is. I swear it. I'll take you to Goole. You'll see. It's all there. The scrapbooks, your portrait. Yes—the portrait. That's how I knew. There's a painting of you in the entrance hall at Goole . . ."

He pulled against her throat and choked off her words.

"You're good, Darcie. You're very good. Take me to Goole—it sounds so authentic—what the hell is Goole? No!—don't answer. Someplace you'll make sound impossibly plausible that has a portrait that looks amazingly like me . . . how clever of you, Darcie . . . how damnably clever of you . . ."

His hold loosened. She felt his hands on her shoulders as he rose to his feet and came around the chair so that his hips and his blatant nakedness were level with her gaze.

He was a big man, bigger than was evident when the porters had lifted his unconscious form to carry him to this room.

He scared her. She could never have imagined the reality of him from her pristine daydreams about his powerful figure in the portrait. Nothing she knew about him had prepared her for the sight of him, and the scent of him, as he knelt beside her so that now his face was devastatingly close to hers.

That face—she had studied that face forever, in pictures and in his portrait. She thought she knew that face, she thought she loved that face, but he looked older than in the portrait, and his face was pale from lack of sun and carved with lines from years in the field. His brows were thick and well defined, and his mouth, sensual in the portrait, was thin with impatience and frustration both.

"Take a good look, Scheherazade."

His eyes bored into hers; they saw into her every lie, her every deceit, and straight into her soul.

And then he lifted his hands and touched her face. Moved his fingers to feel the shape of her eyes, her nose, her lips, the curve of her jaw, the line of her neck.

Cupped her cheeks and moved his head still closer, as if he were about to kiss her—

—but he didn't.

Instead, he settled his hands lightly around her neck, exerting that slight threatening pressure that told her clearly and firmly who was in control.

And then she understood: those eyes that looked so clearly and frighteningly into the deepest recesses of her mind saw nothing.

He had not only lost his memory, he was also blind.

And now she had the power.

And she didn't need to state the obvious. He needed her, and he had known it all along. He wasn't going to fight her: he would use her, just as she would use him. And nothing more needed to be said.

The silence lengthened.

"You're a real terror," she said finally. "You ought to untie me."

"I ought to kill you."

"I can help you."

"I don't think so."

"I'll be your eyes."

"For the five minutes it takes to get out of here."

"Why did I save you?"

He looked down at himself, his naked body, his turgid member. "For just the reason you said, Scheherazade. For two nights, no questions asked."

"Damn you. Don't you understand—if she finds you, she'll kill you."

"I thought that was your story," he said nastily.

"She wants Roger's baby."

"Roger . . . my brother, do I have it right? Roger's dead. They should welcome *Con* back with open arms."

"They heard you'd escaped, that you were on your way to England. I overheard them . . . they were going to find you first—contain you, kill you if they had to—"

"And Roger died first," he interpolated. "Or maybe *Con* killed him?"

"Don't do this . . . Lavinia will kill you. She inherits everything. She wouldn't stand for anyone getting in her way."

"Or maybe they're trying to smoke *Con* out?" he suggested with a note of irony.

She froze. *Oh, my God . . . he thought it was a joke. He didn't know, he didn't remember—anything was possible, anything, with Lavinia, even such a bizarre scheme to find Con before he found them. It was so likely, so like Lavinia.*

And Roger.

But she had seen Roger fall, seen him in the coffin, attended the lavish funeral . . .

Insane that she was even considering the ridiculous theories of a blind amnesiac . . . they were both insane because she could almost believe it.

She would believe anything to stay safe and keep him alive long enough to lead her to The Eye of God.

And maybe Lavinia wanted that too. She was evil enough, and devious, and cold-blooded.

Anything was possible.

Anything.

"You—*you*—are Con Pengellis, and if they want to get to you, they will get to you. You need me. You're as helpless as a baby."

"I got here," he pointed out.

"And you don't remember how or from where. You have no clothes, no money, no papers, no eyesight. Exactly how do you expect to proceed?"

"I'll figure it out."

"You need me."

"What's in it for you?"

"You won't kill me," she answered imprudently.

He smiled nastily and cupped her neck again with his large callused hand.

"So you'll kill *me* instead. Or turn me over to the dreaded Lavinia. I don't think so. Maybe *you're* the trojan horse. Maybe you'd better make up a better story than this poppycock about a baby and a wicked stepmother because I'm going nowhere with *you*, Darcie Boulton."

He leaned into her menacingly, and for one moment she could have sworn he saw everything. And then she thought, he would be a millstone, a drag, he would load her down, and pull her back. She was crazy to consider going on the run with him.

But without him, she would have nothing. And with him, with his memory, with the most legendary diamond in the universe, she could own the world.

She considered the ramifications of being totally honest. Always, always, it was a delicate balance of how little to say, how much to withhold to accomplish her purpose.

She was skilled at it; she and her father had dealt with the incongruities of fate for all the years they had sifted for gold. But Con Pengellis blind and naked was a proposition she could never have conceived of.

How much truth, how much lie? What would convince him to go with her, to let her be his eyes, his memory, his motive power?

Honesty. And on a point he couldn't remember. Maybe that was a plus. Maybe.

She had another moment to decide.

He smiled knowingly, almost as if he sensed her struggle. "Give up, Darcie. It was a good try."

She made up her mind.

"I want a piece of the diamond," she said abruptly.

"—the diamond—?"

"The Eye of God."

"The thing that Con Pengellis supposedly died for—?"

"I think you found it," she interrupted relentlessly. "I think you know where it is, and I think Lavinia thinks you know where it is, and they want it, and that's why they want you."

He started clapping. "Scheherazade is back in form again. Excellent story, Darcie."

"Roger said you thought it was real, and that you knew where to look. And that's why you gave up the company, the mines, everything."

"Just like that? Some businessman I was."

"Or a romantic," she said, and the words dropped like falling stones between them and settled into the sudden, startling silence.

She met his steady gaze, and it was so eerie to be looking into his eyes that could see nothing—

Or was it nothing?

Was he that clever? Was she? She still had the sense that he could see everything. Or was he learning to use his power in other, more disconcerting ways? God, he was formidable, but without his sight, he was defenseless, and that was the endgame.

He needed her. And he knew it.

"An eye for an eye," she said softly, "My eyes for a piece of the diamond."

"And she barters too; what a splendid trade, Darcie, and all on the strength of your belief I'm this Con Pengellis. Who are *you*, I wonder."

"I'm a gambler," she said bluntly. "I always have been."

"Or maybe you're a bigger fool," he said roughly, "and much more of a romantic than I."

His words hung between them, truths she didn't want to admit.

A romantic? No . . . a pragmatist, maybe, doing whatever was expedient to get what she wanted. She wasn't accustomed to viewing herself through someone else's eyes; she sounded like a madwoman. Worse, her scheme sounded like a hoax.

His hands tightened gently on her neck. She felt as if her skin were singed by his touch. His dark eyes bored into hers. His skepticism was palpable. "Why should I believe you, Darcie Boulton?"

But he had no choice. She might be a lunatic, but she had a plan, whereas he had no memory of anything prior to waking up in this room. *Not anything*.

A crazy woman. But she meant it about the jewel. That was real, and he felt her intensity, and the underlying greed to possess it, in her words.

"You have to trust me," Darcie whispered, watching as he considered every angle. This was the throw of the dice, and he had no idea what was at stake. "You can't leave without me. And I can't go without you."

He rolled it over and over in his mind. But she *could* go without him. She would be stronger, move faster, go further without a blind man hanging onto her skirts. If he let her go, she could disappear in a minute, leaving him at the mercy of any stranger.

His gut knotted. This wasn't a duel of wits. He either put himself in the hands of a madwoman, or he fended for himself. That was his only choice because he didn't know how to reclaim his life.

Yet.

He moved closer to her, sensing a desperation in her. There was something more here, but she wasn't ready to tell him. For the moment, he could trust her. She needed him.

"*I'll* be your memory," she whispered. "I'll be your eyes."

"What else will you be?" he murmured, leaning into her so that again, his face was inches away from hers. This was the way. Maybe the only way he could tell anything about her motives and her desires. He needed her irrevocably bound to him and he would do what he had to do to insure it.

He knew women; he felt it viscerally. And she didn't fight him, she didn't plead for her virtue. She stayed still as stone as he felt for the soft lush lips he had touched with his fingers.

And then his mouth settled on hers with a surety and possessiveness that jolted him. She opened to him with a keening little sigh of surrender that sparked a spiralling need deep in his belly. The taste of her was electrifying, and almost catapulted him out of control. He wanted to live in her mouth, surround himself with that hot wet heat forever.

It told him everything he needed to know, and more. Miss Darcie Boulton had feelings for this Con Pengellis. And that suited him just fine. He was perfectly willing to be Con Pengellis until he got back his memory.

He pulled away from her slowly, softly before he drowned in her honey. "We have a bargain, Darcie Boulton. An eye for an Eye."

A kiss for a kiss. He felt her relief, her surge of energy, and suddenly everything became clear. Darcie had more than feelings for Con Pengellis.

She was in love with him.

She had thought she had another whole day to plan out their escape. "But the first thing we have to do is get you some clothes."

He had untied her, and she was massaging her wrists as she talked. "There has to be a laundry in this place. Those men didn't arrive here buck naked. And we have to get some food. I'm starving. Being nearly choked to death gives you an appetite." She stopped abruptly. "Con?"

He didn't respond.

"Con?" she said more insistently.

He turned then, with the sheet wrapped around his lower torso. "I have to get used to your calling me that."

"It's your name," she said briskly. "Listen. I'm going to find the laundry, we're going to eat, rest and in the morning, we're going to get out of here."

"It's a plan," he agreed, eyeing her warily as he eased down onto the bed. *She loves Con Pengellis; she won't abandon me now.*

She slipped out into the hallway and down the back stairs. She heard laughter, voices, moans; inhaled the scent of whiskey and musky sex. Found the door under the stairs that led to the basement.

Heard the pounding at Madame's front door, and froze.

"Open up! Open! Now, Madame!"

"Yes?" Madame's smooth continental tones. "What can I do for you?"

"We are looking for this woman."

A silence. Darcie edged toward the basement door and opened it a crack.

"I do not know this woman," Madame said.

The door banged against the wall, as if her questioner had thrown it open and entered without Madame's invitation. And what could she do? She could not call the police.

"And what's this?" a burly voice demanded.

"Payment," Madame said, but her voice was less certain now. "Silver."

"You know whose silver," the voice said.

Darcie fled down the stairs, as Madame told them, "A young woman like the one you described, came and left in one night. She did not give me her name, I did not ask. Indeed, my clientele trusts me to be discreet. She paid for the evening with the silver."

Madame's lies might buy them an hour, Darcie thought in a panic, but if she had to give back the silver, she wouldn't scruple to give them up altogether.

Suddenly, she had no time at all and she had no idea where to find him clothing. She whirled, racing from one end of the belowstairs hallway to the other, and almost knocking down a maid who had emerged from one of the doors.

"Where's the laundry?"

She must have sounded crazed; the woman opened her mouth, closed it, and pointed to one of the doors.

No time, no time. Lavinia's henchmen were already climbing the stairs. They wouldn't find *her*, but they might recognize Con.

Oh God. She burst into the laundry and scanned the room. A fat old woman lounged by the washtub. In the corner, a maid was fitfully ironing a shirt.

"I need . . . I need—" She raced around the room, piling clothes into her arms. And shoes. Where did Madame store the shoes?

"Where are the shoes?" The younger maid looked up from the shirt, her eyes wide as saucers.

"In the cupboard, my lady," she whispered, pointing to a built-in cabinet along one wall. Darcie threw open the doors to find shelf upon shelf of shoes and boots of all shapes and sizes.

She grabbed the largest pair of boots and ran.

Down the hall. Up the steps. Easing into the parlor hallway and around to the back staircase. Not thinking.

Acting on pure instinct. Frantic that Lavinia's men had already found Con and had dragged him from the room.

She raced up the stairs, flattening herself against the first floor landing wall as she heard a loud thumping on a nearby door.

"Open up!"

The same authoritarian voice. Protests from within the room at the untimely interruption.

Darcie jumped and took the steps two by two. There was still time. Just a little time. She almost fell into the room, weak with relief that Con was still there, and that his expression mirrored her own.

She had come back for him, she had kept to the bargain.

"We have to hurry," she whispered, tossing the clothes at him. "Lavinia's men are after me. I brought you some clothes."

He rummaged through them quickly, picking out a shirt, trousers and a coat, and began dressing hurriedly.

A kiss for a kiss. An eye for an eye.

She had meant what she said: they were in this together, for better or for worse, and the journey had already started.

Three

Goole Abbey loomed up in the darkness like a monster, a hulk of a building set on a dreary crag, surrounded by winter-weary trees with branches reaching to the sky like skeletal fingers. Her prison. Her nightmare.

She shivered at the sight of the tower outlined menacingly against the light of the moon, the dead stillness, the frigid cold, the soulless windows, dark and shuttered.

Lavinia was not at home.

Danger lurked, she felt it in her bones. The price of saving Con Pengellis was already too steep. She wasn't sure at the moment she wanted to pay it.

And yet, she had planned to bring him to Goole before he had shocked her with the fact of his blindness.

It could still work, she thought. They could hide in the tower—no one would think to look for her there. Not now.

She could retrench, take stock. Try to jog his memory with the smells, the sounds, the familiarity of Goole. She could steal food and clothes and more things to sell, and then, in a few days, they could be on their way.

It didn't matter where. Anywhere. Until he got his memory back.

India, perhaps, where he was alleged to have died . . .

An owl screeched above them, and she jumped. He

felt the movement and grasped her arm tightly. "Where are we?"

"We are at Goole," she whispered. "Can't you tell?"

He breathed deeply and all he inhaled was the cold night air and the sense of eerie dislocation. This was the devil's own quest, and he was still wondering how he had let her talk him into it.

Diamonds. Death. Dust.

The stuff of a thousand and one nights, just as he'd said.

And yet—*yet* . . .

He was disturbed by it, an indefinable something that felt familiar and just skimmed the edge of his consciousness. It was within reach, and he cursed his sight, his memory, his clumsiness, his stupidity that he couldn't quite . . . *quite* . . . grasp it.

In the dark, there was an obliterating nothingness, and he *hated* it; he would die before he gave in to it. He was certain he had been a man of action once; now he was a creature of the senses, as weakened as Samson without his hair. And he had no idea how it had happened— how he had *let* it happen.

The woman was insane. But he was in no position to disclaim a savior. Even a lunatic.

And then there was that simmering sense of familiarity.

She slipped her arm around his waist. "There doesn't seem to be anyone around. We can go to the tower now. It's tricky here, in the dark."

He cursed the fates that had killed his sight as he slipped and tripped down the path beside her. Her body was almost too fragile to support him; and he could feel how elegant her bones were. Touch was a marvelous thing. He had imprinted her face, her shoulders, her throat, in the very tips of his fingers.

And yet he knew the tensile strength in her too, in the way she bore the burden of him, and in the way she had fearlessly stood up to him and gotten, in the end, what she wanted.

What had he to lose, after all? He couldn't remember a thing, and she offered a momentary safe harbor.

An eye for an Eye . . .

The owl screeched again, and this time both of them reacted; she slipped and he pulled her back against him tightly.

"Not much further to go," she breathed, almost as if she were afraid to disrupt the night with even a hint of noise.

But it seemed to him that this night had been a succession of torturous time-warped passages to nowhere. He was feeling edgy, as if unseen entities were all around him. He wanted sanctuary, out of the endless night, away from the cold dank air.

"Shhh . . ."

He sensed they were in the shadow of the building now. But he felt the blow of the wind and an eerie openness beyond. He heard the scrape of a key. The squeal of a hinge, and then there was a deep enfolding feeling of darkness.

He reached out a hand. Cold stone walls. A straw-strewn floor. A sudden lighting, as if she had lit a torch or a lamp.

"Come . . ."

Into a narrow confining space then, a stairwell. Up the stone steps, their footsteps echoing unnaturally as they climbed to the tower room.

Another door, opened this time without a key, and then they were safe inside.

Safe—? No one was safe anywhere . . .

And this place—it felt hollow, it smelled musty, and he felt a palpable aura of danger.

"Here . . ."

She guided him downward; he sank onto a mattress, and he sensed her beside him.

"This is the tower room," she murmured. "I extinguished the light. Soon, I'll forage for food and—" she broke off, and he sensed, in his darkness, what she did not say: clothes. Items to barter. Money.

She was, after all, a thief, and it was how—if she were to be believed—she had paid for him.

"—water," she finished. "You can't move away from this place."

"How could I?"

"You have to believe me," she added urgently.

"I'm here," he said mordantly. God, he hated the darkness.

"I'll be back soon."

A rustle of clothing. A step, two, three toward the door. The subtle latching of the door.

Alone again.

Alone . . .

The thought struck a chord somewhere.

Alone. He had known aloneness. An absolute crushing loneliness. A bottomless emptiness. His skin prickled, and he rolled onto his knees in a defensive movement.

This place reminded him of something.

*Not some*one. *Some* thing.

He reached out his hands. Stone floor. Stone wall. Mattress on a platform. Thin cotton coverlet. A pillow.

He moved forward on his hands and knees. And fell off the bed.

Dammit, dammit, dammit . . . goddamn dammit—

He had scraped the palms of his hands, but he pushed

forward, crawling past the bed, and all around the perimeter of the room.

It was larger than the empty place in his consciousness. It was furnished with a clothes press, a table and chair, a washstand. A palace in comparison to . . . *what?*

Where he had been—

What? Mist. A moment of clarity, and then that goddamned everlasting mist. And he couldn't see through it. Just the musky edge of something— Dark. Dirt. Dank. His memory playing tricks.

He stood up, and inched his way back to the bed again.

Nothing familiar.

And yet—yet . . .

Maybe it was the feeling of helplessness; and the sense that he'd fallen headlong into a pit . . .

. . . a pit—

Something about that . . .

He sank onto the bed.

Deep—

Something about that . . .

To hell and gone—

Hell—life without sight was hell on earth . . .

It was a puzzle with pieces that didn't fit, and a flirty sense of familiarity that beckoned him like a lover. Goddammit, *why* couldn't he remember? He pounded the mattress. No memory even of the moment before he woke up in the brothel. Just a thick fog, and a mind-numbing sense of desolation.

He shrank back against the wall as if something were threatening him. *Fool. He was falling headlong, suddenly, into an abyss—helpless, hapless, furious, in his mind, with his body, dizzying, endless—*

REAL . . .

"NO-O-O-O-O-O!!!!"

Dead . . .

He jerked awake violently and opened his eyes to the isolating darkness. Sweat poured down his face and he gripped the edge of the mattress, trying to shake off the bone-jarring sense of tumbling into nothingness. He felt as if he were weightless, mindless, and he was the only soul in a sea of oblivion.

It scared him all to hell. He couldn't conceive of it. Someplace in the blankness of his mind, he knew—he *knew*—he had had a life before the nothingness. It was like a blank canvas with shadings here and there that might form into recognizable shapes. But his brain refused to fill in the shadows or the colors. There was just the dark, the indefinable, shapeless, hopeless *dead* dark . . .

"I'm back."

Reality . . . he swam up up up toward the voice, Darcie's voice, an anchor in the void.

"Here." Her touch. He wasn't dead, not yet. He grasped her hand and felt something cold spill onto his leg. "Water."

He sipped, the elixir of life. *He lived.* He drank greedily.

"Lavinia isn't in residence." She spoke in a whisper. "The servants . . . we have to get by the servants so I can take you around the house. I think our best chance is to do it tonight. We're risking a lot just by being here. We have to get out by tomorrow. I brought you something to eat." She pushed something into his hands.

Bread. *Staff of life.* He tore off a piece and stuffed it into his mouth. His stomach growled. *He wasn't dead yet.*

"And what exactly are we trying to accomplish on this midnight foray?" *We* . . . he thought of them as *we.*

"I'm not sure. I thought something might jar your memory." *It has to, she thought; she was counting on it, depending on it, on him, and his strength and his ferocious will to remember. He would remember.*

She would make *him remember. And then she could forget that devastating kiss.*

"And we need things . . ." she went on.

"*. . . we . . .*

"Things we can wear. Things we can sell. We're going to need money. Papers, if we travel . . ."

. . . we . . .

She had thought of everything. *We.*

"When?"

"Soon." It had to be tonight. Lavinia could return at any time. A servant could be keeping watch. She would have to be very clever with him. Take him to the areas of the abbey that Con Pengellis would have lived in. The entry hall with the portrait. The great long parlor with its beamed ceiling and massive fireplace. The dining room. The library. She was sure that he, of all of them, had used the library . . .

She shivered. This was the biggest gamble she had ever made: staking both of their lives on his regaining some of his memory.

"I want us out of here soon. I spent too much time here after . . ." After she had found out the truth. After Roger had caught her listening, and hauled her into the dining room for a thorough cross-examination.

She hadn't understood what she was dealing with, that *they* had been holding him prisoner for nine years while they tried to coerce out of him the location of the diamond.

And now it was only Lavinia. Unless . . . unless they had plotted and planned the unthinkable ruse that *he* had suggested.

It was too complicated to even think about. Roger wasn't that devious. He had just wanted his brother's wealth, his title, his life.

But Lavinia was . . .

She shivered. Lavinia was evil, and she had felt the force of it all around her as she prowled the house to-night. How did you escape the evil? What if Lavinia already knew she was there?

"After . . . ?" he prompted.

"This is where they put me after I found out you were still alive."

"Con Pengellis was still alive," he amended.

She didn't argue. Time was going slowly enough without engaging him in a war of semantics. And so much tonight depended on time. Where she could take him, what she could appropriate that she could turn into money, if she could swipe some of Roger's clothes for him. Whether they could stay safe and undetected in the tower for just this one precious night.

She couldn't let herself think of the alternatives. It would work. It *had* to work. Something about Goole would rewaken a memory in him. And then they could go on from there.

A clock somewhere in the distance struck midnight.

He reacted, an involuntary movement in response to sound of the sonorous gong.

"What? . . . What?" she whispered urgently.

"I don't know. I don't *know.*"

She heard the frustration in his voice, felt the tension in his body. "You've heard this clock."

"I don't know. I don't remember." He sounded angry, confused. There *was* something—and once again, it curled around the edges of his body, and then just drifted away.

"We have to go."

He wanted to go, he wanted to *do* something tangible and concrete to help him grasp the wisps and turn them into something real.

"I have a candle. We don't need much light."

No, a blind man didn't need light to *see*, he thought angrily, as she led him slowly down the tower stairs.

"There's a way to the house from the tower. Down some steps and underground."

It was noticeable instantly. He stepped down into the dank cold air, five steps down, ten. And then there was grit and water beneath his feet, wet, icy cold, and their footsteps echoing faintly against the moist walls of the tunnel. And the sound of hinges squeaking, his foot hitting a stone step, and her band carefully guiding him up and into warmth and sanity.

A long long moment while she listened for other voices. There was only a dead stark silence and then the scrape of a match as she lit the candle.

"Come." He heard her unlatch another door and then she took his hand and pulled him forward.

And then she stopped.

"Where are we?"

"In the reception hall," she whispered barely above a breath. "I'm looking at the portrait. It's *you.*"

He stood as tight and still as if he were paralyzed. Something about this place was familiar. He had a sense of soaring space, and a scent that pricked his consciousness—but he had felt that about the tower too.

He couldn't trust his senses. Darcie wanted him to be Con Pengellis too badly and it would be so easy to fall into that trap.

Bong . . . the clock struck the half hour and he shuddered.

He knew that sound.

No . . . !

She propelled him forward, into the parlor.

Here . . . here—soft deep carpets, he knew them. The edge of a sofa, deeply carved and curved. He knew it. The stones of the massive fireplace. Familiar.

And always, always, the scent in the air, lurking in some hidden place, waiting for him to identity what it was, what he remembered.

The dining room was next, and it was the same, just that spiralling feeling of something familiar but unidentifiable, something pushing the edges of his consciousness, waiting for one particular connection. Like turning up the flame on a gas fixture, and illuminating everything that had been in the dark.

But no matter if he remembered, he would still be in the dark . . .

A door slammed.

"Oh my God," she breathed. "Lavinia's home." She doused the candle, and pushed him behind the thick dining room draperies. "Stay here."

And she was gone. He grasped the thick damask curtains just to have something to hang onto. He knew these curtains; and the scent that was so familiar seemed to be caught in the folds.

As he was caught in Darcie's fantasy. There wasn't a sane man alive, blind or sighted, who would have fallen for her story the way he had.

Or had he just fallen for her?

He gripped the curtains as he heard footsteps. And then the voice:

"Salit!"

Her voice.

Whose voice?

"Mem?" The liquid tones of her butler at the door of the dining room.

"I trust all is quiet."

"Just as you would wish."

"She has not returned?"

A flash in his mind: obsidian eyes . . . glittering, greedy,

*her hands holding a large unprepossessing stone—she says it's
not that one, not the one she wants . . . and he doesn't care—*

"We watch and wait, mem."

. . . he is dressed in white and always wears a turban . . .

"See that you do."

*. . . she slaps a quirt against her thigh . . . always impa-
tient, always filled with dark dreams . . . no, that one is not
her . . .*

"She has not come." The voice of Salit, gently empha-
sizing her well placed trust.

Salit—

That was why . . .

*He understood now . . . he almost had it . . . and then,
and then—everything went dark and slipped out of his grasp.*

"Shhh . . ."

He was on the floor; somehow he had slipped down
on the floor and Darcie was beside him, behind the
curtain which was suffocating him with its scent.

He almost had it, the scent, the voices, everything . . .
and all he remembered was Darcie and her leaving him
behind the curtain, and it was as if that curtain had
closed off his mind entirely.

"Come. We have to go."

He crawled to his feet, and let her lead him.

"We have to chance it—one more room. I don't think
they'll come back again yet. She went up to her room."

*She. Yes. The voice. And something else he had remembered
that now had slipped away.*

He followed, edging after her as best he could in a
fog of disorienting feelings.

"In here." She opened another door and guided him
into another room.

He knew this room.

A different scent this time. Leather. Parchment. Something else.

He didn't resist when she took his hand and brushed it over the thick tufted chairs; the leather desktop; the glass inkwell; the leather-bound books, the ladder that ran on a brass track around the room.

He knew it—and he didn't.

And maybe she wasn't hoping for any epiphanies tonight. It was too dangerous to linger with that woman in the house.

"We have to go."

A nightmare passage back to the tower, as they edged their way back to the tunnel in the dark, desperately trying not to make a sound.

We watch and wait, mem.

Where? Where were they waiting? Who?

He had a bad feeling about her going back to the house again.

. . . Salit . . . bowing his turbaned head—he could see it, and then the picture was gone.

"Stay here. I'm not done. We need food and clothes, and whatever I can find that we can sell."

"We'll find some other way to do it."

. . . we . . . he had said it without thinking.

"There is no other way. How else can I get food and money? I'll do that now, while they sleep. But you—you *have* to remember. I think you did, a little."

"I don't know . . . I think I recognize something, and then the thing just slides away from me. The whole thing is too crazy, Darcie. It's too chancey for you to go back to the house."

"I'll be back soon. Just . . . just don't do anything but think about what you felt, what was familiar. You *are* Con Pengellis. You just have to find the thing that will trigger your memory."

She slipped away from him again. Holding onto her

was like trying to grasp the wind. She was so determined, and it worried him that the whole of her plan depended so heavily on *his* memory.

No, Con Pengellis's memory.

But . . . but—something flashed in his mind and spiralled away. The scent. *The scent . . .* he felt himself reaching for the idea of the scent. That was something real and tangible, something that connected somewhere inside him.

And all those pinpricks of recognition. Suggestion because Darcie wanted it so much?

. . . The clock . . .

Faintly, in the distance, the sonorous gong—once, twice . . .

. . . leather-topped desk, his hands pressing down, facing the back of the leather chair . . . I'm going—you're crazy, but I won't stop you; we want it, if you find it, you'll bring it back—you won't have it . . . obligation to the company—our money—my money, I made it—I made the company . . . bong, bong, bong— late late late so mother wouldn't hear . . . between him and his conscience and—and . . . and . . . turn the chair around— speaking to who who— Who? Scent of . . . what, permeating the room? Inhale, think—I know that smell . . . I can just just just—taste it . . .

Taste it . . . bong bong bong bong argument endless . . . he's eating—that's what . . . white turban—arguing . . . company the company all the time the company . . . And the smell . . . What is that smell?

He shifted, rolling this way and that on the narrow bed, enclosed by the silence and the dark. It was all around him now, the scent, immersed in a dream.

It *was* a dream, he thought from somewhere in the depths of it, but it was someone else's dream. And somehow he had to find a way to make it his own.

Four

Bong . . .

"Hurry . . ." Someone shaking him, whispering in his ear. "Shhh . . ."

Dark, dark, dark . . . he emerged from the dark suddenly, violently, utterly disoriented, groping for the location of the voice. *The voice . . . but it was a woman's voice . . . a different voice—the clock . . . the voice, the smells, he was eating. He remembered that much—in the dream, someone had been eating.*

"Con—" *her* voice, not the other one, barely above a breath.

. . . watching and waiting . . .

"We have to go." She grasped his arm and he shook her off. Not that voice, the one in the dream. Another voice, a different dream. . . . *the company, always the company . . .*

"Con . . ."

"What?" he answered ferociously, full voice.

She winced. Dear God, if he failed them now . . . *but he had answered to his name . . . !* "We have to get out of here—then we'll talk."

"Who are you?"

"I'm Darcie, remember?" Her patience was running out. This was a bad idea. He'd obviously had a dream, and he had no idea who he was or the danger of the situation. "Please come."

"Is *she* coming?"

She managed to maneuver him to his feet. He sounded, he acted almost as if he were inebriated.

"No. But she will. We have to get away from here."

"Good idea," he muttered, and swayed against her containing arm around his waist.

"Quick now; don't think. Be quiet. They're watching and waiting . . ."

. . . watching and waiting . . . the turban had said that to the voice . . . yes, this voice was right—they had to get away from her . . . even he knew that—

The scent followed them, and the incessant *bong* of the clock.

Bong, bong, bong, bong, bong . . .

"It's almost dawn," she whispered as they stumbled down the tower steps.

The scent was everywhere, in his consciousness, in his pores. *He was eating . . . no, the other one was eating. And the company, he had made the company—yes—*

The image faded; the scent remained.

"Quick . . ." She thrust open the door and shoved him into the cold night air.

He hated the dark, God, he hated it. Like he was swimming, drowning, pushing up up up for air, and there was no air, only the numbing reality of the dark, and death.

She pushed him forward and he collided with a wheel.

"I stole a cart and a horse. Hurry."

He fumbled for the step, feeling her hands guiding him, cursing his inadequacies. The horse was restive, dancing, moving, he couldn't get purchase to hoist himself up and into it.

And he was so confused, so bewildered. Everything

was fuzzy, indistinct; he didn't understand about the cart, the horse, *her.*

But the scent was gone, and the ominous *bong* of the clock . . .

She pushed him and heaved him up, face first, into the cart, and clambered up and over him. He heard the snap of the reins and the cart lurched forward, and he pitched backward onto a pile of *things.* And then he lay very still.

She glanced back at him quickly, but she didn't have time to tend to him. She didn't have time for anything but getting as far into the woods and out of sight of the Abbey as possible. And she had chosen the oldest, the calmest of horses, the one who wouldn't get spooked, unruly, or disturbed by a blind man fumbling all around it. One that would stand still, and respond to her unfamiliar commands.

But it was the slowest animal on God's earth, and it plodded at a sedate pace that was as nerve-racking as watching a child's first steps as the first light of dawn rimmed the horizon.

Her heart pounded like a sledgehammer. *Dear God, what had she done? Made things worse was what. And now he was in a stupor, and so disoriented, her every plan was shot to hell.*

It took too much time to reach the shadow of the trees, and she grit her teeth as she pulled hard on the reins and brought the cart to a stop. There was no shelter here. She twisted around to check on Con; he was sprawled across the bag of clothes and food that she had appropriated, and he looked either unconscious or asleep.

Maybe this was better. He could only be a hindrance in his present condition, and she had a half-dozen decisions she needed to make right now. For both of them.

He was hers now for real, she thought, though her dream of acquiring *The Eye of God* was beginning to seem like the fairy tale he thought it was.

What if she had damaged him with her precipitate return to Goole? What if he never remembered anything more than he knew now? She'd have to come to terms with it. She'd lost the gamble. She let the words sink in slowly. *She'd lost.* Only she didn't feel as if it were over. Something told her it wasn't over.

But if Lavinia or Salit had seen them . . . it *would* be over.

Fear shot through her. She jumped down from her perch and edged out toward the open field, trying to quell her panic. Thank God, *he* was still as limp as the morning laundry; that was a blessing right now. She needed to concentrate, to think logically and to see if she could sense anything.

She took a deep cleansing breath. Reasonably, it was too early for anyone at the Abbey to have found the horse and cart missing. But she had to get moving. Daylight was creeping over the horizon, and the stablehands would be about soon. And when the thefts were discovered, Lavinia would know she was the culprit.

Lavinia wouldn't give up looking for her. Lavinia wanted the child.

She flattened her hands against her belly. The danger wasn't over yet. She felt that as clearly as if it were a spoken thought.

But at this point, it didn't matter where they went, but maybe it made sense to go as far from London as possible. Maybe toward Portsmouth, she thought, where there would be places to sell the items she'd stolen and obtain papers if they should need them.

Yes, Portsmouth. It felt right in her bones, and she always listened to those feelings. The threat she sensed was still beyond—and far away. She would not be able to outrun it. All she could do was find a place of safety and security and consider what next to do.

He slept. Through the whole horrible excruciating journey, he slept and she worried, about the stamina of the horse, about Lavinia following them, about his memory, the course she'd chosen, and she berated herself for her folly, her gambler's nature, her feckless soul.

She sat in a slipper rocker beside his bed in a small inn at Savernake, and rocked gently back and forth, feeling for the moment safe. And guilty for telling the innkeeper a storehouse of lies.

Con was her brother, she told him. They had driven out to the country for a picnic. He'd fallen. He was conscious, but he had fallen asleep, and she couldn't travel with him in this condition.

They needed a doctor, and a doctor was duly summoned to lend credence to the lie, even though it cost her a precious couple of pounds. It was worth it, to maintain the fiction.

And Con had slept, through the bouncing and jouncing of the cart all those long miles, through the awkward lifting of him into the inn, through the doctor's perfunctory examination, and now, as her demons receded into the darkness, he slept through the night.

An owl screeched outside the window and she jerked awake. She'd slept. What a fine thing, to find a moment in the midst of her turmoil to sleep. She'd thought she would never sleep again.

She leaned over and checked on Con. He looked so peaceful, as if nothing had disturbed him in the past twenty-four hours. She wished she could penetrate his mind and unlock his memories. All it would take was

one connection, one detail recognized, and she would
have the key to a fortune.

All she could do was keep trying, she thought. But
that was her nature. She had learned long ago how to
keep moving and chase the dream.

They had to keep moving, she amended her thought,
even with a lumberous horse and a rickety cart, and she
had to believe his memory would return.

*I'm funding this myself, he told them. This has nothing to
do with the company. You'll have no claim on it. You won't
get a piece of it—*

If it exists. Roger, skeptical, petulant.

It's my risk. And it will be my gain.

*Roger hadn't liked that. Roger was too eager to take over the
Company and everything else. But even having control of
Pengellis-Becarre in South Africa was not enough for him.*

*It would have to be enough. He had decided that long ago,
when he had first decided to undertake the quest. It would be
all his, something apart from Lavinia and Roger and all the
Pengellises before them.*

*Bong, bong, bong. The clock tolled the hours of their secret
meeting.*

*A knock on the door—Lavinia, barging in, followed by Salit
carrying a tray. Always there, Lavinia, never leaving a soul
in peace. Playing the mother when she really wanted to play
God.*

And food was the excuse.

*Salit set the tray down on the leather-covered desk and un-
covered the plates. The scent of cumin wafted up from the
tray—*

. . . the scent . . . the scent—

He bolted upright, his heart pounding. *The scent,*
Spices. *Spices.* He swallowed, almost as if he could taste

them. Spices, always a part of the meal. The cooks Lavinia had imported on the advice of Salit to recreate the food of her childhood.

Spices. Oh my God.

But he remembered nothing else about the dream except the spices.

Maybe it was enough. One tenuous thread linking him to the fantastic tales of Scheherazade.

He groped his way around the bed. The scent was different, the sense of his surroundings. The bed and its coverings. The wall—smooth and plastered. This was a new and different place, and he couldn't remember how he'd gotten there.

Where is she?

He slipped to the edge of the bed, and reached out a hand, blind, blind, blind. She was there, in a chair beside the bed, her skin warm to his touch.

Reassured, he eased back against the pillow and closed his eyes.

Spices. The thought flowed away from him like a stream.

The last he remembered, they were in the tower.

And the clock. *Bong, bong, bong, bong . . .*

. . . The longest journey of his life . . . plotting, planning, digging . . . disappointments. Thieves. Lies. Loss. Pursuit. Scenes speeding past him like a train gone out of control. And then into a tunnel, a dark dank dungeon, crashing into the wall. Dead and gone, as if he never existed.

Bong, bong, bong, bong . . .

Another clock, a lighter more musical sound now, and somewhere below. But there was no below; he was below, deep deep deep in a hole that only God could find . . .

No! He wasn't going to think about the hole . . . and the putrid food they threw at him as if he were a dog . . .

Animal; he'd become an animal. Everything he remembered,

everything he was, he subjugated to the rage to survive and escape.

Bong, bong, bong, bong, bong . . .

He jerked awake again, his arms flailing.

"Con?" Her voice was soft as rain.

"Where are we?" It seemed like he was always asking that question.

"Far away from Goole."

He swung his long legs over the bed, and rubbed his face. He felt as scruffy as a chimney sweep, and his mouth was thick with an unholy thirst.

He looked focused, Darcie thought, he looked . . . *there,* and she felt a huge swing of hope. *It wasn't over.*

"There's food," she said. "It's cold, but it's edible. There's some wine. There's water to drink and in the basin. It's cold, but it'll do for a quick wash. What do you want to do first?"

"Damned if I know."

She poured him some water. He drank it greedily and gestured for more. Then she helped him wash up, and set what was left of dinner in front of him.

He tackled it with a gusty appetite that was heartening to see. She studied him carefully as he ate, trying to discern what was different. He was alert and fully awake now, and she thought there was an attentiveness about him that there hadn't been before.

"Con?"

He looked up sharply, and her heart leaped. *He had answered to his name again. It wasn't over . . .*

She cleared her throat. "We're going to Portsmouth."

"Why is that, Miss Darcie?"

"It makes sense. It's away from London, and we can get anything we need there. And I don't think Lavinia will think of looking for us there. She'd more likely try Dover."

"It sounds like we're going someplace," he murmured. "Where would that be?"

"Wherever the diamond is," Darcie said sharply, "whenever you remember."

"Ah, the diamond . . ." *The diamond* . . . the minute the word struck his consciousness, he felt himself falling. *The diamond—not meant for man to find . . . he'd held it in his hands, the weight of it almost insupportable . . . he saw himself lifting it, marveling at it . . . the myth, the story, the tale of a thousand years—and then somewhere outside of it, alone, on the ground as if he had been blasted from its very presence . . . He'd dreamt it. He knew he'd dreamt it. And then they put him down the hole . . .*

He shook himself, pulling himself out of the blackness, and away from the splendor. He sensed her watching him.

"An eye for an eye," she said softly.

"I remember." His voice was rough with frustration.

"What else do you remember, Con? I know you're starting to remember."

He didn't answer. He didn't want to remember. Who was this Darcie Boulton who was forcing him to remember? Roger's wife. The perfidious Roger's wife. The *dead* Roger's wife, who was carrying his child. How could he trust *her*? All he could trust was his sense that she was in love with him. No, with Con Pengellis, the man in the portrait.

And that wasn't him. He was a shell of the man he'd been. A husk, hollowed out by forces out of his control. Blinded by greed, youth, fame, and the need to always be in the spotlight. Arrogant Con Pengellis, setting off on a quest that was worthy of the *Arabian Nights*.

A legend in his own time. The story read well, though it didn't quite go the way he had planned. What did that matter? Con Pengellis had died for a madman's dream. It was only fitting that he should be brought back to life by a madwoman in love with that dream.

How much of what she told him was real? Even he couldn't define the line because he didn't know what was real and what was the dream. All he could see was the darkness. And now, imprinted in his memory, in his touch, the weight of the jewel he'd died for; the taste of the greed that had saved him.

A fairy tale, without the ending; her kiss would not turn him into a prince.

"Some of it," be said finally. "Some of it's coming back."

"Then you know you *are* Con Pengellis."

"I'm someone named Con Pengellis," he corrected. "I'm not the man in the portrait."

But he was, she thought. He was. Only older and more dangerous, especially as be honed his senses against his frustration with his blindness. She had to bring him back on course, make him understand that the threat from Lavinia was real, and that he could not renege on the bargain. Nothing could get in the way of that. *Nothing.*

"You're the man who knows where to find a legendary diamond," she said pointedly. "And that's close enough for me."

"We're going to sell the horse and cart, and hire a coach to take us to Whitechapel," she announced after he had finished eating and she'd called for a pot of tea. "It would take us a week to get there otherwise."

"That's rather profligate," he commented.

She shrugged. "It's Lavinia's money. And I don't think you are taking her threat seriously. You understand, if you turn up alive, you are a hero. You can claim

everything Roger took from you, and you'll still know
where to find the diamond. Do you think for one moment that Lavinia will stand for that, if she and Roger
kept you incarcerated all those years because you
wouldn't reveal its location? Do you think she'll let you
live now that she's running the company? Or that you'll
die this time without telling her?"

Lavinia. The other voice locked in his memory. He shook
his head as if he were trying to grasp something. *Something about the voice . . .*

"Lavinia wants the baby," she whispered. "We have
to protect the baby."

*. . . the baby . . . yes, she'd said something about a baby—
and it was all jumbled up with the voice, and his flooding
memories . . .*

"I saved your life. I want my share of the diamond."

*Always the diamond, always the greed and the desire for
power . . .* he hadn't been immune himself, he thought,
but Darcie Boulton was something else again. And what
was the diamond? He knew that now: it was something
to balance out the fates, exactly as nature intended.

*All the pieces tumbling around in his mind like dice. Luck
and the throw of the dice—he'd played Hazard and gone down
the hole, just like Alice, into a dark upside down world where
nothing made sense. And now, the Queen of Hearts was after
him, and he was years too late. And anyway, the thing probably
wasn't even there . . .*

*There—where? That was the question . . . and the price that
had bought his life. And now he was fully aware that Darcie
was waiting to collect.*

"I have no memory of that," he said into the darkness. God, he cursed the darkness. He needed to see
her eyes, her face. He couldn't sense a thing except her
stillness.

"But you will," she said finally. "And we'll go there,

and you'll think about it, and you'll remember. We'll wait in Portsmouth until then."

It would take a day to get to Portsmouth by coach and by train; he stared unseeingly into the darkness as their carriage careened down the connecting roads from Savernake to Whitechurch, and a tide of memories careened through his mind.

Think . . . he'd had enough of that for a lifetime. How many years in a dungeon, with the rats and his ferocious determination not to lose his mind and keep his secret? All they wanted was the location of the diamond. The biggest, most valuable uncut octahedron ever discovered. A legend no one believed existed except him, and from the moment he believed, others did too.

He'd known he was being followed as he made preparations for his journey. Roger, certainly, because Roger had been enraged that his quest was not all for the company. Roger had been a company man, and insanely jealous of him. He had known Roger would usurp everything when he was gone.

But Roger wouldn't appropriate the diamond. The diamond was his, if he could find it, if he could claim it. If, if, if . . .

He closed his eyes against the crushing memories that were as real as if they were happening right before his eyes.

They'd caught him in Delhi, on one of his sojourns into the city for supplies. And they had no mercy. They wanted The Eye of God, *and nothing less would appease them. And he refused to tell.*

They thought isolation and imprisonment would loosen his tongue. They thought the beatings, the torture, the moldy food would debilitate him, and instead he became more determined more indomitable, able to withstand the most heinous cruelties, ready to die rather than divulge the location of the diamond.

They wanted to kill him.

Some powerful hand stayed his execution. The barbarians

could not gnaw on his bones, and until his captor possessed his knowledge, he knew he would live. But how he escaped, he couldn't remember. And how he got from where he'd been to a bordello in London was a complete blank in his mind.

No matter. The important things were still there: the sharpness of mind, the decisiveness, the hunger, the memories. He ought to have been grateful he'd only lost one of his senses.

But if he were planning to go after the diamond, he thought, he might have lost them all . . .

They had an hour layover before they changed for the train to Portsmouth. They arrived at dusk and Darcie stepped out first into the crisp night air and stopped so abruptly that he walked right into her.

She felt it there, on the platform, that sense of lingering evil, suffocating and aware.

"Oh my God," she whispered, clutching his arm. "Oh my God. We can't stay here, Con. I can't explain it, but it's not safe—*I swear . . .*"

Five

It was the worst of hotels, but the best she could do with the furies following them. When she finally closed the door of the room, she still felt the pull of amorphous lurking evil, and that somehow he might be a part of it.

But how so? She had found him; no one else knew he was alive. And she'd left no clue to their whereabouts at Goole—and yet all around her, she sensed a foulness that didn't bode well. Lavinia could not have known they were coming here, but she couldn't take the chance.

"We have a lot to do in the morning," she told him briskly. "We're going to France before Lavinia finds us."

That shocked him. It was too soon. Too fast. And he was deeply suspicious of her desire to move quickly. "You've assured me time and again, Lavinia knows nothing about us."

"I'm not so sure now."

He felt a chill. They were on the edge of nowhere because of her certainty about Lavinia. He didn't like this new permutation at all. "The story suddenly changes? How convenient, Darcie."

"It would be more convenient if you remembered the location of the diamond," she snapped. "That's all

I care about; that's all the payment I want for saving your miserable life."

"And if you hadn't, you'd probably be exactly where you are now. Roger's widow and on the run from Lavinia, if your story about the baby is even true. What difference is a chip of a legendary diamond going to make?" he asked venomously.

"All the difference in *my* life. And maybe yours."

"I'm better off dead," he said brutally, "and the diamond left buried."

"Unless someone else finds it," she retorted. "Someone else could find it. Roger caught *you*, so they must have some idea where to look."

He went completely still, every nerve in his body on alert, cursing his blindness, and his inability to *see* what should have been obvious before.

She was either his savior—or his assassin, and she could be his whore. But there was more than one side to this equation, and it was time to dig out more.

He smiled mirthlessly. "That's right. Roger's men caught me. I remember now."

He was slipping away suddenly, and she didn't know what to do to contain him. She couldn't tell him about her feelings; he wouldn't understand them, or believe them. She had no leverage at all except his waning gratitude for her saving him. And right now it sounded as if he wished she hadn't tried.

"Stop it! You couldn't recall a thing until I took you to Goole. You need me and I need you."

"I was probably better off," he muttered.

"That diamond is worth a bloody fortune. And you found it. You have to claim it before someone else does."

"So you can exact your tithe for saving me."

No use lying. "Exactly," she said. "What's wrong with

that? What would have happened to you otherwise? I might still have come to Portsmouth—but you might be dead. And if you survived all those years in captivity, you don't want to die. Or to have your secrets to die with you."

She was so so clever. Everything she said was designed to galvanize him toward the goal of retrieving the diamond. She didn't know what she was asking for. He was staring to remember, piece by piece, bit by bit, all dredged up from that dark place in his soul.

The darkness was the key to everything. Even a diamond could be buried in darkness.

"If we go to France, there's less of a chance we'll be followed," she said.

"If anyone is after us at all."

"Don't do that, Con. The danger is very real. You don't know Lavinia."

"I'm staying here for the moment," he said obdurately. "You can go on without me."

"What will you use for money? How will you get around? Are you insane?"

"Hell, I probably got from Portsmouth to London by myself. I'll just do it again."

"You'll be killed before you leave Hants. Why are you doing this?"

He was amused he ever thought she would abandon him. "Just trying to get a fix on who you are, Darcie Boulton. And how much I can trust you."

"You can trust me," she whispered, her voice breaking.

It was an excellent touch, so sincere. A man could melt under the throbbing emotion in that voice. He hardened himself against it, against her. She was a gambler, playing the odds and taking the risk that he was only testing her. And she was good, very very good to have gotten him with her this far.

And she was smart enough to know when to stop pushing.

Who was Darcie Boulton, really? He had only one card to play, and he decided right then and there that they weren't going to France until he found out.

How did everything get so out of control? She didn't like it that suddenly everything seemed out of her grasp. But she knew why: he was remembering more and more, he thought she was a liar, and she had to make him trust her again.

How stupid of her to say anything when they got off the train. That had only aroused his suspicions about her motives. She shuddered to think what this layover would cost them. But she would work around that. She always did when she was confronted by an obstacle.

"All right," she said finally, "we'll stay in Portsmouth for a while. We have a lot to do anyway."

That roused him. "Really? Do let me hear."

"I have to sell the—" she broke off.

"Sell what, Darcie—the jewelry you stole from Lavinia?"

"How did you know?"

"Deduction—what else is small, portable and valuable enough to pawn? And why isn't a diamond necklace enough for you, Darcie Boulton? You could have taken a fortune in jewels from Lavinia any time in the last five years. Why does it have to be *The Eye of God*?"

How could he understand? She had been born seeking castles in the air, weaned on the sacred quest for El Dorado. She didn't know anything else. And this one was for her father as well.

"It's the next big strike," she whispered fiercely, "and I want it."

He wasn't shocked; she saw it in his all-seeing eyes. He comprehended it perfectly, because he had wanted it too. And he had almost died for it.

He sifted through the impact of her words. They were too alike, he thought mordantly. She had thrown him completely off-balance by giving him something he completely understood and making it sound real. She'd found the one thing he might respond to, the craving and the greed.

"And you're starting to remember more and more," she added, "and you don't want anyone else to have that diamond but you."

He didn't respond to that; what he remembered, what he wanted were his only leverage right now. "What did you take from Lavinia?"

She recognized a distraction when she heard it. She had made her point, and now she had to convince him to continue on. "Nothing too obvious. A couple of diamond rings, a diamond bracelet, three necklaces, a choker. I'm sure you know what's in her jewel box better than she does. She'd buried these at the bottom. If I had to guess, I'd say she hadn't seen them in years."

"Likely not," he agreed, but he wished he could see them. He could tell her their worth, their price. He felt the frustration rise again, and then shift. *He could tell her . . . if he could goddamn see, he could—he could—remember . . .* "Give them to me. Let me see if I can figure out what you took."

He heard rummaging sounds, and then he felt her take his hand and place something cool into it. A bracelet, by the feel, all edges, sixteen stones, flat-planed and faceted, with gold-pronged settings and clasp.

He could just picture it, and then, in a wash of memory, his mother at dinner, and his father handing the narrow velvet box across the table. Mother's long clever fingers opening it, her mouth rounding into an "oh," as she saw what was within. Father coming around the table and fastening it to her wrist. That bracelet. That warm wonderful time before he was old enough to become greedy and saturated with the day-to-day running of the Company and the lack of adventure in his life.

That bracelet in the hands of a charlatan . . . he crushed it in his hand, feeling the prongs prick his palm. "Don't take less than fifty pounds for it," he said, keeping his voice neutral. "Those diamonds are perfectly matched, and set in a custom design. A gift from my father. Probably everything you took was one of my father's many gifts to her."'

"*Lavinia?*"

"Lavinia," he said flatly.

His reaction bothered her. He couldn't understand about Lavinia. She wasn't soft or lovable. She was as avaricious as the rest of them. More so, because she had been the driving force to keep the secret that Con was still alive. But obviously, from the expression on his face, the bracelet had aroused some deep cozy memory, and if he had a choice, she thought warily, he wouldn't let it go.

But he had no choice; Lavinia would kill him if she could find him, and they had to get out of England as soon as possible.

"Not less than fifty pounds," she echoed. "And the necklaces proportionately more, I would guess. Do you want to . . . ?"

"No," he said abruptly. "I don't want to know."

"But you remember," she persisted. "And you know we have to go."

He hesitated before he answered. How much, how

little to tell her. She didn't know it, but she had, with her words, aroused in him again the instinct of the hunter. And she had said it more than once: he didn't want anyone else to claim *The Eye of God*. He had found it, and it was his, and while it remained hidden, he still owned it.

But now, without a doubt, Lavinia was searching for him, just as Darcie said. And Lavinia wanted both of them, to claim different treasures.

No one will have The Eye of God *but me* . . .

Darcie had called it. He was every bit as much the mercenary as she.

"Sell the bracelet," he said, his tone firm and devoid of emotion. "We'll go to France."

Dark, dark, dark . . . time meant nothing to him. It could have been morning or midnight when Darcie left him, and he railed against the darkness that held him captive. He was helpless as a baby in the darkness, much more so than he had been in any prison when he'd had his sight.

To depend entirely on Darcie . . . a liar, a cheat, a thief. A woman married to one man for privilege and power, and hopelessly, impossibly in love with another—

Darcie, who'd given him back his life . . . and he, like a genie, could grant her fondest wish . . .

"Con . . ." Darcie, at the door.

"How much did you get?"

"More than your estimate," she whispered. "Shhh . . . the walls are thin as paper." He felt her weight depress the mattress where he lay. "Listen, everything is arranged. In two days, we can sail for Le Havre. I have the papers, I bought suitcases, and some things we'll need, and I figured out a disguise. We're going to be a nurse

and her elderly patient. No one will think to question it.
I don't suppose you speak French?" she added hopefully.

Her efficiency was stunning. "As it happens, I do,"
he said dryly.

"I should have known," she murmured. "Well then,
I've got a wheelchair down at the front desk. You'll pretend to be old and ill, and we'll just wheel you on board,
keep to our cabin, and any time we go on deck, I'll take
you in the chair and no one will think we're anything
but nurse and patient."

He was shaking his head, and she felt her heart plum-
met. "Don't you think it's a good idea?"

"I forgot: we're not safe in Portsmouth, whatever that
means. What does it mean, by the way? And I think
you're crazy if you imagine anyone's going to think I'm
elderly."

"But you haven't seen yourself. Your hair and your
beard are longer than St. Nicholas's. All we have to do
is powder it and you'll hunch over, so you don't look
so tall, and you'll wear this hat—" She put a slouchy
felt hat in his hands, "—and no one will know the difference."

He pulled the hat over his ears, and slouched down.
"Like that?"

"Absolutely. That's very good, Con. Have you done
this before?"

"In another life," he muttered, removing the hat.
"God, I *hate* the darkness."

"Con—" she touched his arm. "I don't think Lavinia
knows we're here, but I felt something ominous when
I stepped off the train."

"That's too nebulous for me," he said, a bad feeling
settling in his gut. *Something ominous* . . . he had a feeling he was about to *hear* something ominous.

"They're trying to get a step ahead of you. They're

after *The Eye of God,* and if they can find you, they think you'll lead them to it."

And who had him so obviously in tow? Who conceivably could be working for Lavinia? Whose every word could be a lie? Who was in love with Con Pengellis? And how badly did she want a piece of the prize?

"So why exactly am I going to do that, Darcie?"

"Because," she said emphatically, "you want it for yourself."

She lay beside him on the rickety bed, her body stiff as a board so that she wouldn't inadvertently touch him. God, if she touched him . . . if he even knew, even had a hint about what she felt about him—

It was all she could do to keep the goal in sight. *The diamond. Her father. What he lived for. What she could die for.*

She could do it. She was strong enough for both of them. She had taken care of her father all those years before, now she would take care of Con. She saw it as a simple extension of what she had done all her life.

Only now, so much more was at stake.

What would she have done if none of this had happened? If Con had really died? How long could she have evaded Lavinia?

Her heart pounded painfully. *An easier task than eluding her with a blind man keeping pace behind her.*

It didn't matter. She could do it. And no matter what happened, it was still easier to travel with him than to go on by herself.

She hadn't forgotten that kiss. She had a feeling he hadn't either. But it had been a kiss to exert domination. She had understood that and reacted accordingly.

She hoped.

What could a man tell from a kiss?

What kind of dreams had she woven around the feelings from that kiss? Impossible dreams. Dreams she had tamped into nothingness because she had no right to have them.

But *she* was the one lying next to him in a seedy hotel on the edge of oblivion. *Fate . . . ?* She had thought that when she'd found him. She didn't trust in fate; fate was capricious. Anything could tip the balance.

If she moved one inch, it would tip the balance. One inch and she would fall fast and hard into the darkness, and welcome it with open arms.

Thank God, she had kept them moving so she could defy the darkness. But moments like these scared her. She felt his heat, his skepticism, his need, and she didn't know what she feared most.

She feared herself.

She shifted slightly, unable to maintain the rigid tension of her body.

And he knew it.

This wasn't supposed to happen.

What could happen? Another kiss? What was a kiss in the scheme of things? A moment two people were moved to connect with each other, nothing more, nothing less. What could he tell from a kiss? Even she, who had flirted with lovers in the course of her marriage, knew a kiss meant nothing. She had learned to be as hardhearted as the rest of her set during her marriage to Roger. She could handle Con Pengellis.

She shifted again toward the edge of the bed. Easy. She could put all feelings aside in pursuit of the dream.

Con Pengellis had been a dream, she reminded herself.

. . . A nightmare, given his blindness—but if she hadn't found him, she might be settling down in some small village

in Ireland or France, using Lavinia's jewelry to maintain a modest and circumspect lifestyle.

This was infinitely better. It was like her days on the trail with her father through Colorado and Nevada. Over the hill to the next big one. Around the pass to the place where no one else had ever thought to look.

Familiar territory even though she was a thousand miles away from it, and her father had realized his dream of becoming a respectable gentleman.

All that gold . . . they found it—one big strike, one huge profit from the takeover by a mining company in Colorado. And then her father's last dream: marry a title. Marry money. His itinerant daughter set for the rest of her life; himself aligned with an honorable, giving luster to his otherwise vagrant family tree.

And somewhere the future, he expected her to appropriate a piece of The Eye of God, *whenever it would come into Roger's possession. It had been all he wanted before his death; she could do nothing less than oblige him as she'd always done. And then fate handed her Con Pengellis . . .*

She woke with a start . . . oh God—she was backed up tight against his chest, the last place she wanted to be. And she had slept, when she'd had no intention of doing so. Why on earth hadn't she stayed in the bedside chair, as she had last night? You couldn't get into trouble if you slept upright and as far from temptation as possible.

Or had she unconsciously wanted to provoke something? Oh, nonsense. They were conspirators, he waxed hot and cold about her motives anyway, and she was making more of this than it was.

He was sleeping; he needed his sleep after their strenuous trip and his grappling with his returning memory: his breathing seemed regular, she thought, there was no reason not to be at ease with the situation. This was not a scene for seduction.

She couldn't relax. Her body tensed up. Her muscles contracted as she tried so hard not to make an untoward movement. *He mustn't ever think* . . . She'd make sure he didn't think . . .

The hours stretched on, punctuated by the sound of a foghorn, the squawk of a seagull, her pounding heart, the feeling of his arm around her waist, the touch of his mouth against her hair.

What did he *see?* She could be anything to him, *anyone.* She could look exactly like his deepest fantasy. He could be hers. He had been hers in her dreams, but it had been the Con Pengellis in the portrait, who could be anything *she* wanted.

But in the portrait he hadn't had this world-weary face, or that mouth with its harsh words and ingrained cynicism. His lips had been, in her dreams, soft, coaxing, obedient, teasing her, tempting her, letting her lead him to the places where dreams were made.

His arm had not been hard, veined and muscular. His hands, in her dreams, were not rough, callused, hot. His body didn't pulse with that raw heat that was so disturbingly male.

In dreams, he was cool, elegant, aloof, and he pursued her with an ardor that placed all the power squarely in her hands. And yes, she did show him mercy, she did. She allowed him to touch, to kiss, to command.

The man beside her would allow no such thing. The reality of him was different, dangerous, *hell.*

How far into the darkness did she want to leap?

. . . *as far down as I have to go to* . . .

No! She made a restive movement, and regretted it instantly. He shifted closer, and now against her buttocks she could feel the thrust of his erection, thick and hard as wood.

. . . that far down . . . and he could take her and break her and she wouldn't care . . .

A slight lift of her head, a wiggle of her derrière, a twist of her body . . . she could have him. He was awake, aware, his hand tensing as he grasped her hip.

This wasn't part of the bargain.

Maybe it was . . .

She was an adventuress, after all—and her father had taught her by words and by example that no sacrifice was too great for the bigger picture. And how many times had he used charm and guile to get them food and lodgings and transportation. She wasn't stupid—and she had known exactly what the whole entailed, even when she agreed to marry Roger.

And she'd kept her side of the arrangement, submitting all those bloodless, passionless nights that Roger had taken her, doing his duty, a lackluster lover, and earning the gold her father had stuffed into his coffers.

But Con—oh, but Con . . . all she had ever longed for, in his hands, within her sight. Maybe she was a creature of the senses after all.

But—she felt it instinctively: a bargain with Con, would be something else again.

She had to decide if she was willing to pay the price.

"Con?" Her voice was barely above a breath, pulling her back to him magnetically. She wanted no words; words would disturb it, disperse the fog of heat and need.

"Yes or no, Darcie?" She liked that; a man who knew what he wanted, would take what he wanted if it were offered.

"Yes," she whispered, and the word floated in the air, as firm and fragile as a bubble. She twisted her body toward him. She felt his hand skim from her hip to her shoulder, to her neck and her chin, and she shuddered.

The touch of a sightless man, feeling his way in the dark. Unfamiliar territory but for her traitorous mouth. That he knew, and he hadn't forgotten. She *had* given too much, and it was too late to backtrack now.

He cupped her chin firmly to position her mouth for the devastating press of his lips, faintly moist, against hers. The sensation spiralled all the way to her toes, and she parted her lips and invited him in.

The dark enfolded her. She felt as if she were an island, alone with him, a part of him, and that nothing existed outside of him. Hot, wet, hungry: she couldn't get enough of him; she was neither mistress nor slave to him. She just *was*, drowning in his heat, her need, the taste, the feel and the sensation of him living in her kisses.

He had all the time in the world; he explored her mouth as if it were a new world, as if the taste of her nourished his soul. She took him greedily, feeding on her dreams, her unacknowledged desires.

She had thought she could hide in the dark, that nothing would be visible that she didn't want to show. But he knew everything, just from the taste, the touch, the ache in her. And then, it was too much, and too late to refuse him anything.

She stretched against him like a cat, her body swelling with a shimmery longing that settled definitively between her legs.

His had nestled between her breasts, feeling the contour, the shape, caressing one stiffened nipple beneath the soft worn bodice of her dress.

Heaven . . . luscious heaven, as if that hard peak were the only pure pleasure point of her body. His kisses drove her; the nebulous feelings in her took shape into something more potent and powerful as his fingers shaped her nipple in concert with her moans.

But the contact was not real, not strong; in a frenzy, she ripped her dress, her underclothes away from her breast to bare her nipple to his stroking fingers.

And she almost convulsed when he touched it, circling it gently and enclosing it in his long callused fingers. And she wanted it; she never knew how badly she wanted it. Her body sunk into a morass of voluptuous sensation. He knew just how to touch it, how to play with it and stroke and squeeze it. Never too hard, never too little. Always just the right amount of pressure and delicate massage.

She arched herself against him, lost in his kisses and the keening excitement of his manipulating her naked nipple. She never wanted him to stop.

His hot mouth, her feverish kisses, his knowing fingers, her frantic body writhing beneath his expert caress of her hot hard nipple—she wanted more and more and more. Both nipples at the mercy of those fingers, both at once. Her mouth, her body, her soul, he could have everything if only he never stopped the movement of his stroking thumb.

The pleasure was too sharp, too necessary for her very being. And it was building, steeply, deliberately, deliciously to a hot hard peak that she willingly ascended if only to ask for more.

He gave her more. He deepened his kisses, and the pressure of his fingers against her nipple. Just that much more feeling, just that much more sensation. It crashed over her like a wave as he squeezed her naked nipple deliberately hard.

Her body convulsed, she pushed against his invasive fingers, seeking the last hot spasm of pleasure, and he gave it to her. He wrenched his mouth from hers and squeezed her nipple hard between his lips that were wet with her honey, and she bucked against him like a gun as her body fired off one exquisite sensation after another deep between her legs.

On and on, he wouldn't give up her nipple. He wanted it, and she pushed him to squeeze her, to suck it, until she was hot and dry.

But she was wet, sopping wet, with her tumultuous climax and sobbing now it had ended, because that he had gently let her go.

More . . . more than she'd ever dreamed—how could there be more? She was insensate with the pleasure of it, and the way he pulled her against his chest in the dark.

She made a motion toward him, and he pushed her hand away.

"Next time," he murmured.

Next time. She savored the words and curled up against him, awash in the lingering scent of her sex, and the heat of him.

Next time. He smiled faintly in the darkness. Next time. A world of promise in his consideration and his skill.

He had done what he had planned: tonight he had made her his.

Six

Next time.

Everything had changed. The next morning she felt satiated and raw. And she didn't know quite how she was going to face him.

But of course, she thought ruefully as she tugged at her torn bodice, it wasn't a case of him *looking* at her. It was her shame, her need. If she hadn't crept into the bed, if she hadn't rolled against him, hadn't turned . . . if she hadn't let her fantasies override the reality of the situation . . .

She needed a needle and thread, instead of recriminations. It was all of a piece. They would find the diamond, Con would reclaim his life, his position, and his mercenary sister-in-law would probably have to find another place. Why not take her pleasure where she found it?

Oh my God—next time . . .

He was still asleep, doomed to the darkness forever. *Poor Con.* She leaned over and stroked his face. *The pleasures of the night would always take place in the darkness,* she decided. *If there were a* next time. *If she really were that weak. That needy. That bold.*

She threw a cape over her shoulders and went out into the brisk morning air.

There was nothing like a seacoast town. The smell of fish, the fishmongers already hawking the first catch of the day, the caw of the gulls, the stiff wind off the water, the sun burning hot by contrast.

She sensed no threat today. She felt awake and alive, and everything she saw touched her awareness as sensitively as he had touched her last night.

She really had to stop dwelling on that. It had been a moment, cut out of many more moments to come where things like that would never happen. She wouldn't think about it. She wouldn't hold him to a promise he might never keep.

Next time . . . she could make it happen, she thought, as she hunted up a seamstress from whom she could purchase a sewing kit, and then bought some bread and cheese for their breakfast. Did she want to make it happen?

The innkeeper had already provided morning tea and a pitcher of lukewarm water for washing, but little else, and he had brought both items to the room, which saved her the exertion of fitting her purchases around the pot and cups, and going back downstairs again for the wash water.

She set the tray on a table. "Are you awake?"

"Very," he said dryly, and she understood exactly what he meant. *Next time. He wasn't going to conveniently forget last night.*

"There's tea, and I have bread and cheese."

He swung his legs over the bed. "That will do. Can I wash?"

"Yes. On the other side of the bed, there's a stand with a pitcher of water."

She watched him as he groped his way across the room. He was no less powerful and desirable for his blindness. Perhaps he was more so, because he was vulnerable.

But a man like Con Pengellis would hate that. He would trade on his strength and his intelligence. He was a man who had conquered a universe and made a legend real. And he had possessed *her* last night. He had taken her need and her lust and made it his own. He had given her pleasure and worshipped her like a queen.

Who wouldn't dream of a next time with one such as he? Her heart constricted just thinking about it, and she wheeled away from him to pour the tea. Useless thinking like this. He had probably come to his senses, and she was still out of hers.

"There's tea."

He inhaled deeply and moved toward the scent, letting her guide him to a chair beside the table.

"Do you take sugar?"

He shook his head and she placed the cup in his hands. *His hands. That hand, an instrument of pleasure.* He sipped, and she watched his lips jealously. *Those lips, savoring her sex or liquid heat with equal pleasure. Either. Both. Next time.*

Her breath caught, and she poured herself a cup and went to sit on the bed. She couldn't think of a thing to say.

"The ship sails tomorrow?" he said finally.

She swallowed hard, and wrenched her mind away from the image of his hands caressing her. "At the tide. The booking is made. The papers are in order. The bracelet bought us time and money."

He listened to the nuances of her voice. For the first time since they'd begun this journey, she wasn't thinking about Lavinia, Roger or the diamond.

Just what he'd wanted. Just what he'd hoped. She was

thinking about him, and the explosive demands of her body.

Even he wasn't immune to them. He'd been isolated and removed for so long. He had thought he was dead, dry, dust; he had suppressed every urge and all emotions, pushed every thought of a man's desire as deep into the pit as he was.

But a man never forgot. A man never lost the capacity to rise to the occasion. His ferocious lust to possess her shocked him. And this morning: he wanted her. He hadn't nearly had enough of her. He wanted to explore that passion and that driving need with which he sent her plummeting over the edge. He wanted her to erupt like that always and ever only for him.

And he was staggered by how deep and hard the feeling went.

This was something he hadn't planned. Something he needed to think about. He folded his hands around the hot cup and lifted it to his lips to sip.

One didn't sip a woman's body . . .

Jesus . . . he slammed the cup down on the table. "There's bread and cheese?"

She bit her lip. *That was a violent reaction. What was he thinking? What was he sorry he had done?* "Right by your elbow."

He ripped off a piece of bread like it was the neck of his worst enemy and bit into it aggressively.

"All right," he said finally, after he'd demolished the bread and several chunks of cheese, "so—we sail tomorrow. And what did you plan in the meantime?"

"I didn't." *Uh-oh. Better clarify that.* "I thought it would take longer to arrange things," she amplified.

"I see." Did he? *He saw her naked body writhing in his hands. Next time. Now? Never? He had to decide. But he had promised—those very words—next time.* "So all we have to do is . . . ?"

"Pack," she said, distracted by the movement of his lips. "Remember."

The air thickened. "Remember what, Darcie?"

"You . . ." she started and couldn't quite get out the rest of the sentence. Not when he was looking at her as if he could see her, and as if he wanted her again.

"*I* remember," he said softly, and the decision was made, had been made since the moment he discovered she loved the demon adventurer whose portrait launched a thousand dreams.

He shook himself. One dream. Darcie's dream.

The distance between her sex and a legendary diamond didn't seem so remote now. He could almost taste the secret yearning in her, so excellent to use to his own advantage.

And what about all his secret appetites, dredged up from the grave?

"It was a mistake," she whispered, her heart pounding. *He remembered. This could be—next time. And more . . . And an even bigger mistake.*

She didn't care. She wanted him to counter her hesitation, to give her a reason to willingly give herself to him.

What about your swollen lips, your aching breast, your own dreams and desires? She could subordinate them, she could.

No, she couldn't.

She felt the sweet ache between her legs that had nothing to do with reason or respect.

"Let's see if it was," he said softly, and her whole body twinged at the note in his voice. "Take off your clothes, Darcie."

Her breath caught. He wouldn't see a thing. He would go crazy imagining it, and she wanted that. She wanted him hot and melting at her feet, where there was no mercy for a man who could make her feel like that.

"Darcie . . . ?" There was a catch in his voice.

Next time . . . "Come and get me," she breathed, and backed against the bed.

He came toward her as surely as if he could see her, and she didn't know how. How he knew, how he reached out and unerringly found the torn flap of her dress, and then just ripped it from her trembling body.

"Now, Darcie."

She wished it were dark. Even knowing he could see nothing, she wished it were dark and that she were more perfect, that it was a love more perfect—but in absence of all of that, she would willingly take this much from him, and maybe even more.

She peeled off her underclothes, unhooked the unwieldy corset, tossed off her shoes, wriggled out of her underslip and stockings, and finally her drawers. God, how long it took to get ready to sin. A man could lose all his heat in the time it took a woman to divest herself of the props of civilization.

But once they were gone, she felt as primitive as Eve. "Con . . . ?" she murmured, and she knew he heard the excitement in her voice.

"Come."

She walked into his arms and lifted her mouth to his and surrendered to the darkness.

And in the darkness, there was light: he nestled himself against her hips, so she could feel his length, his pride, his power. He lifted her against him, and she wrapped her legs around him and ground her hips against his driving erection.

Oh God—she wanted him. All of him buried to the hilt deep within her. All that heat and power contained in her . . .

She pulled her mouth from his mesmerizing kiss. "Do

it now," she whispered, wriggling her derrière against his questing hands and his thrusting member.

"Soon." A breath against her swollen lips, and then he claimed them again, while his hands stroked her and probed her from behind.

Her body jolted against him as his fingers slipped into her slick wet folds and deep into her very core.

"How many fingers?" he murmured against her lips.

It didn't matter; they felt hard and thick and full sheathed in the heat and velvet of her, and she didn't want him to move, ever.

"Three? Four?" She licked his lips, seeking his tongue. "I love what you're doing. I love what you did yesterday."

"I know." He moved to the bed and sat, still holding her wrapped around him. "Don't move. I want to feel you just like this."

"I want you inside me."

"Not yet. Do you feel my fingers?"

She drew in a deep breath as he stroked her. "Yessss." She made a sound as he probed deeper. "Oh God— Con . . ."

"I know you like that. I'm going to find out everything you like and I'm going to give it to you, Darcie."

She squirmed against his fingers. "I want you to." A groan. A wave of sensation as he pumped his fingers between her legs.

"You love a man there."

"He's not there yet," she whispered pointedly, grinding down on his fingers.

"Oh, he's there. Give me your tongue, Darcie. We're not nearly done yet."

She arched against him and gave him her tongue. Gave over her naked body to his expert fingers as they stroked and felt between her legs, prodding her, priming her, teasing her. He never touched her nipples. His free hand explored her buttocks, and found the hidden place at the small of her back that turned her into a wild woman.

"Oh God, Con—I'm so wet—"

"Good. I want you wet and hot, Darcie, and only for me."

"Ohhh . . ." she sighed from deep in a haze of swamping pleasure. Those incredible fingers . . . she rode them like a stallion, whipped into a frenzy by his words, his caresses, his desire.

She felt every spurt of his penis. It was like an untamed animal waiting to break free. She wanted to mount it high and hard and deep inside her and keep it there forever.

But she was losing it, to him. His fingers worked inside her, pulling her inexorably toward the edge.

"Con . . . !" she cried in anger.

"Come to me, Darcie, come . . ."

"I can't . . ."

"You don't have to . . . come—"

"Con . . ." She was trying to hold it back.

"I want you. I want you to come—" His voice was so soft, his fingers were so hard, so coaxing; they wanted her fire. They wanted *her* draining her juices into his hand.

And she came, climaxing on a long soft sigh into the light. Into glitter and gold. Into a spiking pleasure that attacked her very vitals and drained slowly slowly slowly from between her legs. Just like that. Just there.

Into silence as he held her tightly against him.

He had seen everything.

"Shhhh . . ." he laid her reverently down on the bed and curved his body around her. "Shhhh . . ."

And then she slept.

* * *

And now he knew her. He knew her luscious mouth, and her responsive nipples, the special place at the small of her back. And in the heat of her woman's flesh, her gorgeous wanton sweet spot.

He lay with his fingers gently inserted, just there. She spread her legs slightly to ease his way, and from time to time in her rest, she wriggled erotically against him to let him know she was awake and aware.

There was something so voluptuous about lying with her like this. He had forgotten those small delectable pleasures. His every nerve ending pulsated with the need to possess her. His penis was as stiff and heavy as stone; he wanted to penetrate her, embed himself in her, and drive them both to completion.

But the waiting . . . the waiting heightened the intensity of his need, he liked that. He was accustomed to waiting; there was something very potent about it, when the imagination conjured up pleasures and delights for the taking. And he liked having her waiting, naked, and yearning, naked, just for him.

He felt her restive movements beside him.

"Con . . ." There was a slight thread of supplication in her tone.

"Tell me what you want, Darcie."

"Where do I start?" she murmured, wriggling urgently against his fingers.

He pushed deeper. "I need to hear one thing you want."

"Don't make me beg."

"Tell me, Darcie."

She shimmied desperately on his fingers. "Con . . . you know—"

He pushed again, to give her a taste of the pleasure to come.

"Say it, Darcie. How else can I know?"

She grit her teeth. "I want you—you *know* I want you between my legs . . . oh! Don't . . . don't take away your fingers . . . you beast—that's what you wanted to hear . . ."

He loomed over her. "I needed to know you crave *my* penis."

She stretched out her hands and grasped him. Oh dear God—he had forgotten this too—what it was like to have a woman take him purposefully with both hands, surrounding him, feeling him, pumping him, lavishing him with caresses and murmurs until he was out of his mind with rocketing need.

"Oh God, Darcie . . ."

"No, *no*—I have you now, and I'm not giving you up. You're mine now, do you hear me? And you'd better not move."

He couldn't move; he was braced on his hands and knees over her slender body, poised to penetrate and sink himself into hot velvet. And instead, instead, she had brought him to worship before her, with her pure erotic possession of his throbbing member.

She caressed it, she felt its length and thickness; she played with it, sliding her fingers all over it, tapping the lush slick underside of it, and then finger walking back down to the base of it to entangle her fingers in the crisp hair, and finally to cup the taut scrotum below.

And then the attention she gave his scrotum—sliding her palm under it, stroking it, stroking him deep between his legs and almost to his crease . . . his knees went weak. His arms trembled. He tried to kiss her and she wouldn't let him. She wanted to watch his face as she caressed and pumped every long inch of him until he was ready to explode.

And then she began feeling around the very tip and sensitive crown.

"Darcie . . ."

"I'm going to bring you down, Con . . ."

"Darcie . . ." he managed before she began the steady rhythm just at the crown, on and on and on, her relentless hand taking him as no woman had ever taken him before.

She licked her lips as he began thrusting in concert with the movement of her hand. She held his scrotum with her one hand as she pumped and pulled with the other. She brought him close to her mouth and licked and sucked at the turgid tip of him, and when he reared back for that one last roaring thrust into her circling fingers, she caught some of the cream of his desire on her breasts and tongue.

And he was gone—spewing himself all over her body in concert with her ecstatic moans.

And when it was over, he collapsed on top of her and she held him lightly, tightly, possessively as if they had always been lovers, and she would never let him go.

"Con?" It was dark now; they had slept, but he wouldn't know the dark from the daylight.

"Ummm."

The dark was better, she thought, sliding her hand down to cup his quiescent penis. It immediately leaped to attention. She liked that, she liked how things were more explosive in the dark and how she was hungry for him all over again.

"Are you awake?"

He grunted.

She rubbed him with both hands, moving them lightly in opposite directions.

"Ah, Darcie . . ."

"Are you hungry?"

"I am now."

Her body twinged. *Next time. As many next times as she could desire. Anything she wanted, borne of his celibacy and need. As many times as she wanted, as many ways as they could invent.*

"Do you want me?"

"Don't be coy, Darcie."

"I'm naked for you, Con. What are you waiting for?"

"I like the waiting. It makes everything deeper, more powerful."

She loved this game. She loved him talking rough in counterpoint to her caressing his potent manhood, and she reveled the power of her touch when he couldn't suppress a groan.

"I think you want me," she murmured, her fingers squeezing and working up and down his quivering length.

"Spread your legs then."

"Do you want me?" She twisted the palm of her hand around his shaft.

"You know what I want, Darcie. You want it too, so spread your legs."

"How much do you want it?" she asked coquettishly, her hands still working her erotic magic on him.

"I've had all I can take of your silly game. I don't want to talk, I want to cram myself into you . . ." he wrenched himself out of her grasping hands . . . *"now . . ."* and he pushed her legs apart and rammed himself into her, deep, oh so hot and deep and just when she thought he was totally embedded within her, he drove himself deeper still.

"Oh God . . ." Who said it . . . one or both . . . the raw nakedness of him penetrating her so deeply, so immeasurably, so darkly; he almost rocketed out of control.

"Darcie . . ."

She whispered against his mouth, "Take me *now* . . ."

"I don't want to move."

"Do it—"

He'd never had a woman like this, who shimmied and writhed and spread her legs and pushed down demandingly on him and commanded him to give her everything he had.

"I'm never going to let you get dressed again," he growled in her ear. "I want you naked so I can take you whenever I want."

"Do it, Con . . ."

He shoved himself deeper. "I can't wait for it now . . ." and he pulled himself back, so long and strong and thick that his withdrawal made her feel bereft. And then he rocked back into her with deep, hot thrusts, one, two, three, withdraw, thrust, a rhythm that made her whimper with need. He was too far away too far; she reached for him desperately when he removed himself. She needed him deep inside her. She needed to feel him, to squeeze him, to know he was hers.

Short, stiff thrusts, suddenly, hard against the flaring center of her heat. No kisses. No caresses. Just his potent power lunging and plunging and driving her home.

He felt her body seize up and her resistance to it. "Come for me *now,* Darcie—"

"No. I want you to work for it."

"Do you?" He could go on forever, a machine, pumping and thrusting into the encompassing heat of her. He was hot for her, out of his mind for her. *She* was the light in the darkness and he drove into her wildly to appease her, to pleasure her, to bind them even tighter so that she would stay.

"*Now,* Darcie . . ."

She made a sound at the back of her throat, almost a whimper. She didn't want it to end, but they both wanted it too badly; five thrusts later, she careened out of control, sliding down the shaft of his power, and riding him to oblivion, triumphant at last when he followed her into the darkness and satiety.

Seven

They lay side by side, exhausted. She thought at one point she slept because there was a short spate of time in which she was not thinking about him, and his sex, and their explosive coupling. And then she was awake suddenly, stretching her body luxuriously to just touch his, to experience what feeling his bare skin did to her.

There was something so illicit and delicious about knowing he was there, naked and hard, and waiting for her.

"Are you awake?"

"I'm here."

Did she dare . . . ? "How *here?*" she whispered, her voice trembling just a little.

"As *here* as you want me to be," and there was no doubt what he meant. She reached out her hand to grasp him and he groaned and rolled toward her.

His heat enveloped her as she welcomed his weight and parted her thighs. His mouth settled on hers, feeding off the intensity of the desire that had aroused them both quick as a flame. He slipped inside her, thick as a cloud, and they moved in unison to her rhythm.

He was the man in the desert who had found an oasis, and he didn't want to find out if it were an illusion. All he knew, all he could feel was *her*—soft and slick and enfolding a starving man as deeply as his aching soul. Slowly and softly, she moved with him, coaxed him, adored him. His sweet discharge, when it came, spiralled them endlessly outward toward oblivion, and then she held him tightly while they slept.

When she awakened again, it was still dark. She reached out to touch him and he wasn't there. She panicked, scrambling over the side of the bed and reaching for the lamp on the night table.

"Con . . . ?"

"I'm here." His voice, strangely disembodied, from the other side of the room.

"What are you doing?"

"Thinking about you."

She liked that. She sat back on the bed and considered his words. "Tell me what you're thinking."

He wanted her again. He was rigid and rampant with it and he didn't understand a need so consuming it kept him awake and hot and throbbing for almost a day and a night. If he took her now, he would want her again in an hour. He didn't like feeling that out of control after so many years of denial. But—her craving for his sex was every bit as strong as his desire for her.

He had accomplished what he had set out to do—he had enslaved her, only he had ensnared himself in the process. But at the moment, it didn't seem to matter. There was something about the dark and her untamed response, and the sense that he could say what he wanted, he could do what he wanted—in the dark—and somehow it would all be absolved.

"I can't get enough of you," he growled.

She loved that. "Tell me how much."

"I want you now."

She swallowed. His words made her breathless, made her body quicken with desire. She loved the idea of coming to him in the dark; in the dark, they were equals. In the dark, they were the same.

This was time out of reality. It didn't count when it was in the dark and filled with such devouring pleasure. They didn't have to acknowledge the things that they did in the dark. And she could hold those memories in her heart forever.

She felt her way across the room to where he was sprawled in the chair, and she knelt between his legs and placed her hands on his knees. She loved this, feeling for him in the dark, where every sense was heightened by the scent of their sex, the knowledge of everything they had done before, and the drive of their mutual desire.

She rubbed her face against his penis, loving its texture, its length, its rigidity, its power. And then she buried her lips at its base, in his hair, her mouth taking him at the root in a ferocious love bite.

"Get up here."

"I like it better down here." She nipped him again, a little further up his shaft. And then another and another, until she encircled him at the ridge and pulled on him in a long wet sucking kiss.

His body jolted against her rapacious mouth. "Je-esus . . ." he groaned. He felt himself spinning, pushing himself into her mouth, and he didn't want to let go, not now, not there. Not yet. *"Darcie . . . !"* he reached forward and grasped her arms.

"I'm hungry," she protested.

"Me, too. Get up here." He pulled her onto his lap and she straddled his legs, spreading her thighs and settling herself precisely on his rigid length with appreciative little murmurs of delight. "I like this; I like sitting on you like this."

He cupped her breasts. "I like it too."

She arched her back inviting a caress.

"You're very hot, Darcie."

"It's because I'm pressed down on you. Make me wet," she begged, bracing her hands against his shoulder and pushing her breasts closer to his mouth.

He pushed her breasts closer together, and then he brushed her nipples with his lips, first one, then the other, back and forth equally, one and the other, in a lush erotic rhythm that made her writhe and moan.

She ground her body down tightly against his hard length as he started kissing her nipples, one and the other with deep wet sucking kisses, over and over, licking, pulling, sucking until she almost couldn't stand it. And then, without breaking the rhythm, he began concentrating on each hard pointed tip, swirling his tongue, cushioning, pulling, squeezing with his lips, pulling, pulling, pulling, one and the other.

She arched up against his mouth in an erotic haze, begging for more, bracing herself against his knees, and feeling for his length, so she could stroke him there in concert with his relentless sucking.

The minute she touched him, he was ready to blow. Her nipple was tight and taut in his mouth, wet and hard from his sucking; he felt her fingers rubbing him, caressing him, feeling him. He pulled harder just at the sex-engorged tip in a dark ferocious sucking kiss.

"Ahhhhhhhhh . . ." She threw her head back and bore down on his manhood as her climax broke and streamed all through her body, a river of hot silver skeining down down down and exploding between her legs.

And then she melted against him, pressing her aching breasts against his chest.

He took her mouth in a soft soft kiss, waiting, waiting, until she was ready, waiting even though he was stoked to the bursting point. Waiting, with every one of his senses screaming for release.

"Let me come inside you."

"Please . . ." she whispered, rubbing her lips against his mouth.

She shifted to her feet, and then she slowly climbed back onto him; he held her hips, guiding her as she grasped his penis and positioned it at the point of penetration, and then she just sank onto his jutting length with a muffled groan.

His hands moved upward as she bore down; he covered her breasts, he cupped them, he caressed her nipples as she set the primitive rhythm, her whole body centered on her two most pleasure points: her tight taut nipples and the precious flesh between her legs.

There was just nowhere else for a woman. He fingered her nipples and let her move, and she thought she would just explode. But he came first, erupting into her with one volcanic thrust that lifted her from her erotic seat as spasms racked his body and finally made him complete.

His dreams were suffused with visions of sex and surrender, but the thing that held him captive were the memories surfacing from someplace down below, from beyond all conscious remembrance.

He couldn't quite grasp what he wanted to know. It was all tangled up with tunnels and pits and diamonds and trains and the Con Pengellis he used to be. The darkness mattered. Sometimes he thought he could see more clearly in the darkness. And sometimes he felt like he had to fight it like a demon, and blast his way up and out.

He remembered the diamond, remembered touching, lifting it, feeling the weight of it in his hands.

. . . leaving it . . .

Where?

No—it was the slender weight of Darcie he lifted in his hands . . . and then he was falling, top over tail, through the tunnel, down the pit, into the darkness, his eyes focused on the brilliant light beyond . . .

. . . wait . . .

He had waited. Patiently he had waited. Wait. A train. A tunnel. He was running. Wait. He knew what Con Pengellis knew. And The Eye of God was following him . . . The Eye of God saw everything and cast out a sinner . . . wait—

. . . the single largest octahedron ever found . . .

. . . balancing fate—

Darcie was fate.

And he would remember because he felt the hunger of the hunt all over again. The hunt for sex. The hunt for riches. And he would find his way to the tunnel before somebody else did.

And now he had Darcie to help him.

She never wanted morning to come. She wanted to curl up in that seductive fog and warm herself against his heated skin forever.

Instead, she was up and about before him, packing what few clothes they had, and seeing to breakfast.

It felt strange, this morning, to be folding away the memories of this room, where no one and nothing could touch them, but dreams couldn't last forever. They would never be as safe again, she thought. And she would never be as free.

Risks—they both had taken risks, and now it was time to go beyond the walls. And they couldn't turn back, he wouldn't turn back now, and let someone else claim it all.

She had gotten him a shabby old suit to wear, in the guise of her elderly patient. But she wondered, as she laid it out at the foot of the bed, how she thought she could contain his intense masculinity with any kind of disguise.

Well, he would find it, and know what to do with it. She needed to take the pitcher downstairs to bring back some hot water.

"I trust my wheelchair is safe," she said to the inn-keeper.

"Yes, mum. We was hoping the mister would recover some, as you said."

"He can sit up, and he seems well enough to travel. I'll pay the bill now and then I'll need some help bringing him downstairs." She hadn't told Con that part, but her senses were so disordered, she felt she needed to take every precaution. The charade had to begin, now.

"Ring the bell, mum, and I'll come."

She entered the room to find him half dressed, and groping toward the table. "That's right, you're almost there. There's tea and pastries, and I've just brought up some hot water."

He sat down heavily in the chair. "You sound disgust-ingly chipper this morning."

She pushed every other consideration aside, like his warm bare chest, and her rising desire. That was over now. It *was.* "We *have* to go."

"I'd rather stay here." Even he was feeling it, the reluctance and the need.

"We're going. There's a suit at the foot of the bed. And after you've eaten and washed, I'm going to pow-der your hair."

"Jesus." She really meant it, he thought; she was going to make him into an invalid. But he was already feeling like one now that the magic of darkness was gone.

"Everything else is packed and I've paid the bill," she said briskly. "I've asked the innkeeper to come help me take you downstairs, by the way."

He put down his cup hard. "Why is that, Miss Darcie?" he asked, his tone just a little dangerous.

"The play starts here, Con. I can't take the chance no one is watching us. I haven't been out and about in two days. I don't know what's going on out there. So we have to start play-acting now."

She knew he wasn't going to like that. She felt his skepticism clear across the room. But it didn't matter. She'd put the whole thing together in her mind the first day and she wasn't going to deviate from it.

"The story is, you've been recuperating for the past couple days from an attack of some kind, and now you're better and ready to travel. We have . . . oh, maybe two hours, and we'll need at least an hour to get you dressed and down those steps. And don't glower. It has nothing to do with anything else."

"It has to do with a fool's quest, and your stupid determination to find this damned diamond, that I still goddamned can't remember where or if I even found it."

"But you will," she said confidently, ignoring his frustration and his outburst. "You know what's at stake, and I know you will."

It was over, so abruptly he couldn't quite comprehend it. But it was nothing he hadn't expected, he thought. Darcie was eminently practical. She had spent the money for tickets to France, they were going to France, no matter what magic they had created in that room.

He couldn't afford to fall for her. Above all else, she wanted her share of the diamond. In one corner of that sensible mind, she had never forgotten the endgame. Nor would she ever let him forget he owed her his life.

And now he had made sure he had bound her to him like a wife. And he couldn't ever forget that had been his plan.

She eyed him like an artist surveying a masterpiece. "You wouldn't want to see yourself, Con. You look— fifty." She jammed the slouchy hat down on his head. "Perfect."

"I feel fifty," he grumbled.

"It's time to go." She jerked the bellpull. "I think I have everything. We have two suitcases, one each, and I tried to estimate what size clothes for you. I think I did all right. I didn't want to take too much, in case we had to move fast."

"Darcie—no one is after the diamond."

"You can't know that."

"And Lavinia has probably given up looking for you."

"I doubt it," she said, and she felt a rush of heat. Oh dear God, in all that happened, she had forgotten about the baby; how could she have forgotten about the baby. "I told you, she wants Roger's baby."

He felt like he'd been kicked in the gut. *The baby. The baby had utterly slipped his mind. She was carrying a child in that beautiful flat belly.* How *far along was she?*

There was a knock at the door so he couldn't pursue that thought; she opened it to admit the innkeeper.

"If you'd just let him lean against you, and I'll take our bags—I think we'll be fine."

He felt himself being heaved up roughly against a tall

male body. He felt Darcie lifting his arm on the other side, and he let it drape around her neck.

"That's good," she said brightly, wrapping her left arm around his waist and pinching his side. "That'll be fine. Just down a flight of steps, darling, and you won't have to walk again."

"Mmmph," he grunted, as they shuffled into the hallway.

"He's deeply appreciative," Darcie said, as they carefully descended the stairs.

"Grrmph," he growled when they reached bottom.

"And he couldn't have done it without you," she added, as they settled him in the rickety wicker wheelchair she'd bought on the cheap, and she dumped the suitcases in his lap.

She flashed a smile at the innkeeper as she slipped him a couple of pence. "Thank you so much."

"Good luck, mum."

"We'll need it," Con muttered.

"You never can tell," she whispered hotly. "Come on now, hunch your shoulders. Look *old.*"

She wheeled him into the sunshine, swerving around objects with the skill of a lorry driver. He felt the sun in a burst of light against his eyes. He heard the raucous noise of an afternoon in a coastal town: mongers and drays, and gulls and dogs, and voices and horns, all meshing together in one indelible picture in his mind.

And Darcie, determinedly wheeling him toward the dock.

"How many days to Le Havre?" he asked, his voice muffled because he had crushed his chin against his chest.

"Two days," she said, jerking the chair around sharply to avoid a cat, before her step faltered. She hadn't thought about that.

Two days. Even out in the bright fresh air, the words sat between them, a bridge between pleasure and promise. *Two days.*

But no—she wouldn't let it happen; that part was over. They had things to do now, and memories to resurrect. By the time they stepped foot in Le Havre, she had to know where their course would take them.

She wheeled the chair around purposefully, and bumped it up onto the gangplank, and pulled it up the slanted walkway from behind.

"Jesus, Darcie."

"Shhhh," she whispered fiercely. "Be quiet. You don't *know.*"

What didn't he know? he thought, and he almost fell out of the chair as with another clump and bump, she pulled the wheelchair onto the solid foredeck of the steamer *Rossignol.*

"We're here."

"I can tell." The sea-scent was more pungent here, the cry of gulls, the sound of voices as the crew shouted orders back and forth in preparation to sail.

"We just have to go through checks and ticketing. Act *old.*" There was an odd note in her voice.

"There's something wrong."

"No. Everything is fine," she said. But she wasn't sure. She didn't feel any aura of evil. There was no palpable sense of danger. But something wasn't right, and she couldn't quite put her finger on what.

Better to say nothing. Better to just get him to the cabin so they could settle in.

She felt all of her senses start to tingle. She would allow nothing to distract her now: the real journey had just begun.

* * *

The cabin was small, dishearteningly small, with two berths one over the other, and the top one folding up against the wall so the lower could be used for seating.

Darcie was appalled at the cramped space. Admittedly, she had bought a single cabin, but still—a pullman car on a train was roomier than this. Well, it was too late now, and there were at least a hundred other passengers, which meant there probably would not be any other space available.

They would make do. She was good at making do.

She asked one of the mates to help them down the narrow stairs to the lower deck over Con's furious protest.

"Shhh . . . you're infirm, remember?"

Oh, he was infirm all right, but it had nothing to do with age. He felt like throttling her. He didn't like this plan. He didn't like the mate settling him into the bunk like a baby while Darcie cooed instructions on the side.

He was amazed he had the patience to wait until they were alone in the cabin before he exploded. "What the hell was that all about?"

"That was about appearances," she said loftily, pulling a blanket over him against his struggles to sit up. "I'm going to leave you for a while. All you have to do is remember you're an invalid, and stay put. I have to arrange to have food delivered to the cabin. And you need to stop fighting me and—*think.*"

"Damn it to hell, Darcie—I . . ."

"Con, there isn't anything else you can do right now."

"I can think of one thing."

She patted the blanket. "We don't have time for that now."

Just as he'd thought. Practical, sensible Darcie. Put it all in a compartment and store it neatly away.

He heard the door close softly, and he kicked off the

blanket. *Goddamn darkness. Goddamn everything a stupid black blank . . . God, he hated it, he hated it . . . there weren't words for what he felt, how helpless he felt, how crazy he felt depending on a mercenary adventuress who turned her desires on and off like a faucet.*

He swung his legs over the edge of the bunk. A man needed to scout things out his surroundings. He'd been pinioned between Darcie and one of the deck hands, so he'd gotten no sense of where he was, and he knew how dangerous that was. He'd been careless once and—

What . . . ?

. . . careless—once . . . ?

—And what? What? *What couldn't he remember?*

He got up and began groping around the cabin. The berths were on the wall opposite the door. There were built-in drawers on either side and two doors, one of them leading to a minuscule water closet. There was a fold-down table, and two chairs tucked under the lower bunk. Neat for sleep and very little else, he thought, feeling his way back to the bunk. A tribute to Darcie's thrift. Nothing more or less than they needed for the short trip across the Channel.

. . . short trip . . .

That struck a chord somewhere.

He eased himself back against the wall. *Where had he been when they'd gotten to him?* His eyes narrowed. *Not with the diamond.* He closed his eyes. *He remembered that. Not with the diamond. So they'd been after him then. Roger would not have left it alone, just as he recalled. His memory had not failed him: Roger would have wanted it too, a coup for the company. An expansion into other realms. All of that was clear to him now. All the arguments, the anger, the recriminations. What he didn't remember definitively was what came after. That was just a grab bag of odd jagged pieces, a jigsaw puzzle in his mind.*

Think . . . As if he could wave a magic wand and con-
jure it all up. But the lulling movement of the ship reminded him of something.

A short trip. Precautions not taken.

. . . careless once . . .

*He had known there was danger. He would work back-
ward—or forward—from that.*

She stood topside at the deck railing, watching the
commotion on the dock, and being jostled by late
boarding passengers and deckhands wheeling their luggage alongside.

They were a half hour away from sailing into calm
waters against a cloudless blue sky. Overhead, gulls
screeched and dove for food. She watched as one
wheeled and swooped down low over the dock and toward the boat, toward her, she thought in shock as she
moved to dodge it. But then at the last minute it veered
nose-down into the water.

She could have sworn the thing was coming after her.
But that was ridiculous, she chided herself. It was all of
a piece with her feeling of disquiet. Everything would
seem threatening underscored by that.

She did trust her feelings. She and her father hadn't
gotten where they were by following the rules. There
were no rules. The last two days had proven that.

But even though she'd given in to her feelings, she
had learned long ago never to have regrets. Never to
be afraid to be wrong. There was always another love.
Always another strike.

Always someplace else to go.

Well, Le Havre was the first place they would go. And
from there she would study how to get them to India.

And somewhere between those two points, Con would remember all about the location of the diamond.

It was too late to back out, she thought. The die had been cast with Roger's death.

But the thing was to remember the details. Lavinia. The baby. The legends. The lore.

The game.

The game—the undefinable game against an opponent who wasn't there. And rules that didn't exist.

She stayed at the rail until the lines were cast and the ship moved out of the harbor and she could see the gulls no more.

Eight

She had arranged for tea, and breakfast and dinner, to be brought to the cabin. So she was expecting the knock at the door shortly after she returned to the cabin, and she opened it without cautioning Con to pull up the blanket.

The deckhand who had helped them when they boarded was at the door, the tea tray in his hands. She took it from him, mesmerized for a moment by the burning look in his eyes. But he wasn't looking at her; he looked beyond her, at Con sitting on the bunk with every evidence of physical vigor.

She grabbed the tray and slammed the door in his face, and she turned to face Con, her eyes wide. "He was looking at you."

"So what? He was just one of the sailors—didn't I recognize his voice?"

"He was the one who brought us down here." She folded down the table and set the tray on it, and then pulled out the chairs and set them up. "Come." She held out her hand. "I didn't like the way he was looking at you."

He fumbled his way across the room. "What could he have seen? I was sitting on the bed."

"You don't look old." She guided him to one of the

chairs, and took the other opposite. "You don't look *slouchy.*" She poured him a cup and put it into his hands.

"I hate this."

"Well, we all know that, but we're committed now."

"You know, I don't feel quite the same urgency you do."

"And I'm feeling it more."

"You don't think, if Lavinia were after you, that you would have seen some evidence of it by now?"

She shook her head. "She's very subtle. She and Roger managed to get to you, right?"

"I can't remember that."

"What do you remember? You remember the diamond." She was as certain of that as her life.

He nodded. "And all the arguments before I even set out on the expedition to find it. They wanted it for the company. They wanted this great big huge diamond that they didn't even know if it existed, and they wanted to cut into it and turn it into a fortune in crown silver. I left the company because of it, probably the only noble thing I've ever done, and all in service of this *grand guignol* gesture which was pure selfishness. *I* was going to find the thing, and be the mythic hero."

"And you found it."

"I found it. But I don't know where, and I don't know how, and all I next remember is being in a deep dark pit for an endless amount of time. And nothing after that until I woke up in the brothel."

She sipped her tea thoughtfully. All that was encouraging, she thought. "You touched it."

"Yes."

Very encouraging. "You held it."

"Yes."

"You didn't remove it."

"No."

"Why?"

Why? Maybe he hadn't been asking himself the right questions. Why?

He gave it a long moment's consideration. "I don't know."

"Think—maybe you knew they were after you."

Maybe . . . had he known? He must have known . . .

She saw his confusion. "Roger and Lavinia told everyone you'd died in India in search of the diamond. Long before I married Roger. It had been announced in the papers. They had a memorial service for you at St. James. They even put up a tombstone on the grounds of Goole."

"Was my funeral well attended?" he asked sarcastically.

"I wasn't there—more's the pity. I thought you were dead. This was the deepest buried secret, Con. No one knew."

"*They* knew," he said darkly, "—and you found out. I remember what you said. You found out. But you never said how."

"You escaped."

He slammed down the cup. "Jesus, Darcie—that's the most important point. I *escaped* . . . ?"

"You don't remember?"

"I keep goddamned telling you . . ."

"All right, I believe you. This is what happened: A messenger had come during dinner—something urgent. Roger was absolutely panicked. I heard them say they would talk later, in the library, after I'd gone upstairs, and I was desperate to know what had happened. I hid behind the curtains . . .

. . . *the curtains that were redolent with the scent of spices . . .*

". . . and I heard the whole thing, that they thought

they'd had you contained, they thought that the latest torture had weakened you to the point that you might be ready to tell. They wanted the diamond, they wanted it over, and they wanted you dead. And somehow you got away. Does any of this sound familiar?"

He shook his head. "You're chasing after ghosts."

"Lavinia knew I was there. How did she know? I understood what was at stake. I didn't move a muscle. I didn't breathe. I didn't make a sound. And still she knew I was there."

He tried to envision it. Lavinia, stalking around the library, in a rage because he had somehow escaped. Roger, placating, shaken, agitated. The two of them, plotting and scheming all to naught: they didn't know how he'd gotten away or where he was.

And then what? Darcie in the curtains. Lavinia dragging her out from behind, and pushing her in front of Roger.

Can't you control your wife?

Darcie said the words out loud even as they formed in his mind.

"And of course, I was so righteous about it. Roger looked about ready to kill me."

We can't let her run around loose, Lavinia would have said.

What are we going to do with her? Roger had asked. *How can we contain her? You know she'll tell the world.*

We'll—we'll lock her up, Lavinia decided. *In the tower. She always thought she was a fairy-tale princess, now we'll make her one. And then we've got to find Con. Do you understand, Roger? We* must *find Con.*

"And then what?" Con asked.

"They couldn't find you. She was living in dread fear you'd walk in the front door and accuse her of attempted murder, and she couldn't see any reason why they shouldn't kill me—that would be one more threat out of the way. But there was the baby. And then Roger died and I got away."

Yes, he remembered her telling him that. And now he remembered Roger. Greedy lustful Roger grasping for something to placate Lavinia that would draw him out in the open.

If I have to, I'll die for the company.

He remembered Darcie's stillness when he'd suggested it. He could just see Lavinia considering the possibilities.

That's an interesting idea, my boy. That's a very interesting idea. He might fall for that. He might come and reclaim everything, and then we'll have him.

They'd safely put Darcie away so they could concentrate on finding him. What better way than to lure him with everything he'd renounced.

"I think Roger's death was a ruse."

She didn't answer for a long few minutes. "You shocked me when you said that before. And I thought maybe you were right, that Lavinia and he could have pulled it off. But I was at the funeral. I saw him in the coffin . . ." her voice trailed off.

"Anybody could play a corpse in a coffin," he pointed out, defining the thing she didn't want to say.

"They buried him," she whispered.

"The coffin was closed . . ." He knew it even without her confirming it.

"Yes." She could still see it in her mind's eye: the gray day, the naked branches bending in the wind. The crowd. The coffin. The gaping hole. The prelate sonorously extolling Roger's life.

Herself, chained to Lavinia, playing the bereaved widow to the hilt. Lavinia who hadn't cried, who'd been as tight and controlled as an automaton, who must have

been desperate to preserve the lie and still come away
with the prize.

She shook her head. "I don't know now. Anything's
possible."

He sent her a speculative look that was so direct, she
was shaken by it. He saw too much, she thought. And
he saw too clearly.

"It all sounds ridiculous, doesn't it?" she whispered.

. . . And then Roger died and I got away . . .

He rolled that detail over in his mind.

She got away.

It sounds ridiculous.

Anything's possible.

How much was real, how much was illusion?

*Clever Darcie. She was Scheherazade, who could spin a thou-
sand tales over a thousand nights and one night.*

*She was Helen who launched a journey of a thousand miles
on the strength of his quest for a legend.*

*She had the audaciousness of an adventuress, the guile of
a gambler, and the confidence of a queen.*

Who was Darcie Boulton, really?

And when did he stop playing the game?

"It sounds insane," he said bluntly.

"But if Roger's alive—?"

He didn't answer, and she got up and began pacing
agitatedly. He heard her impatient footfall, the swirl of
her skirt, her abrasive breathing.

"This is crazy," she said finally, explosively. "We don't
know that Roger's still alive. We don't know anything
except that you found the diamond and that somehow
you were caught and imprisoned so that they could torture the location out of you. And we know that Lavinia
said you'd died in India. We have to assume that's where
they kept you isolated, and maybe even where the diamond is."

"I don't know that, Darcie. I still don't know that."

She ignored him. "That's why we're going there. It will help your memory, just like my taking you to Goole. You started to remember."

He didn't deny it. He had a lot of the pieces of the puzzle now: he'd been a strutting cock who'd tried to pull off the exploit of the ages. It hadn't been enough to own diamond mines in South Africa worth a million pounds. It hadn't been enough to be the head of Pengellis-Becarre, jewelers to kings, queens, and the wealthy of the world.

No, he'd wanted the intangibles—adventure, glory, notoriety. Risks and rewards. Slicing close to the edge, and sliding through. All of that. And more. The admiration. The envy. The women. The wealth.

It hadn't been some mystical quest. It had been greed, pure selfish greed, and an arrogant desire to annoy Roger and provoke his mother.

He'd been blind to how much was at stake. He never thought it was critical. And he'd been wrong. Dead wrong.

. . . *careless once—*

Words to live by.

. . . *careless twice—*

A man could die.

He had to exercise caution on every level. He knew nothing about Darcie Boulton other than what she told him, and for all he knew every word was a lie.

And now he was thinking like Darcie, he thought mordantly as he lay wide awake in his berth that night, and maybe it was better than being distracted by her.

It was too easy to slip into her body; she was so hot and too willing, a Circe at his beck and call, and if she climbed on top of him now, he would sink himself into her without a second thought.

"Con?" her voice was a whisper above him, shaping the wish into reality. "Are you awake?"

He hesitated a moment. "Yes." He heard the soft sound of her feet hitting the floor, and then he felt her hand on his arm as she knelt next to the bunk.

"I can't sleep." But she couldn't tell him why. It was the excitement of the hunt coupled with her heightened sense of him in this tiny cabin. He filled it. He heated it. He heated *her.* She wanted him, simply as that. "Con?"

"I don't think so, Darcie." The willpower it took to say that, when his body leaped to contradict him. She was a siren, tempting him in the dark.

"Then—just let *me* . . ." she whispered, fumbling with his clothes.

She had him at the point where he couldn't say no. He closed his eyes as her hand closed around him, enveloping him in pure pleasure in the dark.

She held him like a lover, her lips nuzzling him as she covered him with hot little kisses. Cloaked in kisses. Drowning in kisses and the heat of her mouth. Feeling both of her hands containing him, and her tongue slick and knowledgeable defining his length. Feeding off of her excitement as she pulled him into her mouth and begin rhythmically sucking on him.

There, there, there—his whole world was centered at the point of light surrounding her avid mouth. Right there. He could see it; he thrust into it, feeling its heat, its wet, its need. She pulled him toward the light, slowly, lusciously, inexorably, until it exploded behind his eyes and he soared into the incandescent light.

He fell back slowly, luxuriously, soft as a cloud, into the dark, into her hands, into the tight wet mystery of her femininity. And he was the core, the hot center, and she worshipped him. She adored him. And she erupted all around him in a shimmering spasm of radiant light.

And still it was dark. But he needed no other illumination to see her body. He took her with his hands, with his mouth, with every sense tuned to her lust and her longing.

The way he had defined her face, he delineated her body—the fragility, the strength, the long legs, the curve of her buttocks that fit so neatly in his hands. The texture of her skin. The contour of her breasts. The sweep of her belly that nurtured another life.

He lay his head against it, listening, trying to sense the quickening and the flutter of new life. He moved down her taut belly, swiping her navel with his tongue before he settled his relentless mouth between her legs.

The essence of her, the embodiment of Eve; he could take her with his mouth and create the chaos of fulfillment. On the tip of his tongue, he positioned her, poised for him to possess her.

She hovered above him, her hips grinding and writhing against him, seeking to envelop him in the perfume of her need. And suddenly she was sitting on the tip of a star, its center shining and golden, and without warning, she slipped and she plummeted into a backwash of sensation that furrowed through her body and down down down to break sumptuously at the precious point between her legs.

And then it was dark again, it always ended in the dark. It was better that way, he thought. Promises didn't exist in the dark. Time stood still, and threats receded, and the only thing that counted was the one forbidden moment of pure uncomplicated pleasure.

And the danger was, he thought warily, as he folded her against his chest, a man could get very very used to that. And it could be the very thing that Darcie was counting on.

They debarked at Le Havre the next day. It was late in the afternoon under an angry gray sky. The deck mate with the burning eyes came to help him maneuver the narrow interior stairs.

Darcie watched him with a vigilant eye as she followed behind with their suitcases. There was something about the man, even though he had been nothing but courteous and prompt during the trip. Still, the way he looked at Con worried her. He was too solicitous to a stranger, and he had the wheelchair, which had been stored above deck because it was too wide to go below, waiting as they emerged onto the foredeck.

"I'll wheel 'im off for you, mum," he offered, in that same respectful voice he had addressed her the last two days. "He is a heavy man, I can manage better and make sure all is right and tight. That is, if you want."

She took a surreptitious look around her. Passengers were streaming down the gangplank, deckhands with their luggage in tow. It seemed reasonable enough, she thought. It would cost a ha'penny, maybe two.

"I'd appreciate it," she said, bending down to Con who was once again hunched over his chest. "The deckhand is going to wheel you down. Do you think you could hold one of the suitcases?"

"I'm not dead yet, girl," he snapped in a crackly voice that made her smile. She placed his case on his lap and

nodded to the deckhand, and he wheeled the chair into
a queue of passengers advancing toward the gangplank.

"Have you got transportation, mum? Or a place to
stay?"

She looked up at him sharply. He was staring straight
ahead, minding the steps of the people in front of him,
and keeping the footrest of the chair at a precise foot
from the person in front of him.

It was an idle question, in aid of procuring another
few pence for a recommendation. Nothing more. Nothing less.

"Thank you, yes."

"That's good," he said.

They shuffled forward another foot, surrounded by
the hum of conversation, and the cry of screaming gulls
swooping overhead.

The gray sky enfolded them as an unexpected wind
blew up, whipping the waves.

They waited at the head of the gangplank for the
next knot of passengers to pass below. The mate lifted
the chair onto the walkway ahead of her and stopped.
She wasn't watching, and she bumped into him, and
that jarring movement seemed to make him relinquish
his grip on the chair.

She watched in horror as the wheelchair pitched
down the gangplank like a drunken sailor, gaining mo-
mentum and speed.

She screamed his name as it hit the dock and hurtled
a hundred feet beyond.

He heard her in the throes of the nightmare where
everything was pitch black, and nothing was real except
the fearsome sensation of falling down down down into
a pit.

He had to get out of there, even if he died. He
wrenched sideways, felt himself suddenly flying through

the air. He couldn't hang onto the suitcase—he couldn't hold onto his life. He was falling like wind-driven rain, his past spinning and spiralling before his sightless eyes.

He hit the dock with a sickening thud, his head glancing off a piling. For one fulminating moment, his vision cleared, and the light flooded in. He saw angels all around him. He saw Darcie and *him.*

Far above him on the deck, rooted there as if he were made of stone, the mate with the burning eyes, watching, watching, watching as Darcie flew down the gangplank to kneel by his side.

"Con . . ." she cried, and he looked into her beautiful tear-filled eyes.

The danger was real; the danger was *there.*

"I can see," he whispered, pulling his gaze from her to look toward the top of the gangplank.

He saw what he expected: the deckhand was gone.

And then his eyes clouded over and he could see no more.

Nine

He swam slowly up from the bottom of the pit, feeling as if he had been fighting wind and ice and fire and all the reigning evils in the world.

He opened his eyes to the darkness. "Darcie!"

"I'm here."

He felt the panic in spite of the calm tone of her voice, and he fought to come to the surface. "Where?"

"Shhh . . . this is the hospital of Dr. Rivard. He's been taking care of you."

"What happened?"

She hesitated. Even she didn't know, and what she felt and what she had seen were two vastly different things. "The deckhand . . . he let go of the chair. It fell. You fell. The doctor tells me there are no broken bones, and that the blow to your head caused minimal damage. He expects you will have a vicious headache at the worst. But he foresees no permanent damage."

"I saw you," he said suddenly, unable to comprehend anything she was saying because of the sharp pain behind his eyes. He waited, to see if it would materialize into a vision, the vision of Darcie.

But there was only the dark, the awful, deadly, godforsaken dark.

Her eyes swelled with tears. He couldn't have seen

anything, but she wasn't about to point that out. "What did you see?"

"Black hair. Blue eyes. Tears. A gray sky. Heaven."

No—careless twice . . . he licked his dry lips. *That close to death he had come . . . down another pit, across another lifetime.*

The danger was real. The danger was there.

Darcie grasped his hand and he held it fast. "This is the doctor's infirmary. We'll be safe here."

"Will we?" he asked, his voice raspy.

"As anywhere. The mate—"

"I saw him."

"You dreamt it, Con. The doctor says you couldn't have."

"I saw him—I saw you."

"You need to rest."

"Will you stay?"

"There's nowhere else to go," she said gently. "The wheelchair went into the water. The one suitcase is wrecked. I salvaged what I could. Everything else is safe. And we'll be safe here for the moment."

"That sailor . . ."

"I don't know, Con. I don't know if he just let go or if it was an accident. How can anyone tell?"

"He was watching you, just the way you said he was looking at me when he came to the cabin."

"You could *not* have seen that."

"I saw it," he said adamantly, and she started to protest, and then decided it would be better not to agitate him.

"I just remember screaming and running down the gangplank," she said finally, reliving that horrific moment in her mind. "God, I couldn't believe it. But you're all right. We can go on."

"And everything's safe."

"I made sure of it. I tied pouches all over my underthings. And there are places I can convert what we have to francs."

He closed his eyes. No difference in the darkness. It felt heavy, weighting him down. He would pull her down if she had to carry him across two continents. "You know how long a trip it is."

"I know. And we'll go. As soon as you're able."

"Tomorrow," he murmured, rousing out of his lethargy one more time before allowing himself to float.

"Tomorrow," she agreed, squeezing his hand.

It took a week, time in which he battled the demons in his dreams. The sailor led them all, dancing tantalizingly just out of reach of his memory, and goading him to the edge of sanity.

The danger was there; the danger was real. All he had to do was get one step closer, and all the answers would be clear.

He lay in a fever those first couple of days, and Darcie feared for his life. But she felt safe in their sanctuary as she tended him through the night.

The infirmary was quiet as a church. The doctor moved among his patients like the most holy father, stopping to lay his hand across Con's hectic brow, and nodding reassuringly as if his touch could heal.

"He progresses," the doctor said.

He was a sweet little man, with the most serene of faces, who spoke fluent English and she felt the utmost confidence in him and she didn't know why.

"He is delirious," she contradicted. "He thought he could see."

The doctor smiled. "So many things we cannot know between earth and heaven, my dear. Maybe he did."

Maybe he did. He knew her eyes were blue. He thought he'd gone to heaven . . .

The doctor touched her shoulder. "Stay with him again tonight, my dear. Tomorrow he will be fine."

She sat by his side in the dark in the silence. She felt surrounded by the darkness, as she saw through his eyes. Imagining hurtling blindly, plummeting through space. Praying for your life and calling on every one of your senses to save your soul.

She didn't know how he had survived with so little bodily harm.

I can see . . .

Or maybe he was delusional. Maybe this one accident was a portent of the end.

Oh dear God—all for nothing? All to end in some blind alley?

There was a part of her that couldn't stand the thought. The gambler in her that would take every risk, walk every line. And without him, there was nothing. She needed his memories; he needed her eyes. The bargain was the bargain, and she couldn't let anything stop them now.

She'd carry him on her shoulders if she had to, she thought fiercely. She'd carry him to hell and beyond for a piece of that diamond.

And what about a life with him?

Which is more important to you, Darcie?

She bit her lip. *Conscience couldn't enter into it at this point. Did it have to be both or neither, with no middle ground?*

That wasn't even a question for consideration right now. She didn't know why she was thinking about it. Maybe it was because she was nestled beside him, enveloped by the dark. The dark did funny things to you; erotic things, forbidden things, and it made you think about things that were buried deep in your soul.

All those things in the dark . . . *his* dark.

And now she had made it hers.

She stayed by his side for the succeeding three days. Dr. Rivard moved a bed into the cubicle for her, and every day, he came by to check, to murmur, to approve.

"He progresses," was the only prognosis he would give her. "He will be fine."

How did he know? What did *he* see? She saw no appreciable difference in Con's appearance. He was still pale, still feverish, delusional with visions of monsters and madness.

"Another day," Dr. Rivard murmured. "It will all come clear."

She fed him soup, water, crackers, barely eating herself.

"He needs a different kind of nourishment," the doctor told her. "You keep doing as you are doing. He will be fine."

She slept. They slept. The next two days drifted by.

Dr. Rivard came to see him. "He is well," he murmured, laying his hands on Con's head. "He is fine. Another day and you can go."

Five days' delay, she thought. And all they had was faith to propel them on. Well, she had enough for both of them. And today they were free to go.

She left the nurses to dress him while she got their things together and then went to find Dr. Rivard.

But the head nurse didn't understand English. She kept shaking her head and spewing words that Darcie did not understand. Finally in frustration, she went to get Con.

He hobbled into the lobby of the infirmary between the two nurses who had tended him, and cocked his head questioningly at Darcie.

"Ask them about Dr. Rivard," she said. "I want to see Dr. Rivard before we go."

He relayed her request in a spate of fluent French that really impressed her, and the head nurse answered in kind. They went back and forth for a moment, and then Con turned to her.

"She says there is no Dr. Rivard. This is not his hospital. Or his infirmary. She says she's never heard of him, that there is no such a one."

They took the afternoon train to Paris. Con slept. Darcie ruminated on the mystery of Dr. Rivard.

. . . no such a one . . .

And yet she could picture him so clearly moving among the patients, touching, soothing, listening.

Healing?

She sat bolt upright at the thought, and then sank back again.

Always in the dead of night he had come, she thought suddenly. *Always after the witching hour—always in the dark.*

And she had better stop making more of these incidents than they warranted. Both were merely a case of a careless deckhand and a kindly doctor who perhaps was doing a good deed in secret. Nothing more.

Nothing more.

They were going to Paris because Con remembered going there after sailing from Dover. Paris was a start, a good start. They had money, he spoke French, and he was slowly slowly remembering the details.

She was content with that. She put out a calming hand as he moved restively in his sleep. He felt her touch, he heard the clickety-clack of wheels, the wail of the whistle. He had come to Paris by boat and by rail, he felt the memories in his bones.

The swaying train. The vitality of the city. All of its extremes. A good glass of wine. A view of the street and the baudets gawking at whatever was the exhibition of the moment. The wealthy flitting back and forth between the hunt and the Opera; coutouriers and concerts; Biarritz and the Bois de Boulogne.

They used to send for him in the summer to come to Chatelguyon to display the latest in diamond jewelry . . . Roger would go sometimes, and sometimes he, because there was so much in the way of entertainment in France. And their hosts would foot the bill, no small amount of francs in order for them to have the exclusive right to purchase the latest creation from Pengellis-Becurre.

"We'll find a pensione near the Bois," he said. "A few days there . . ."

A few days here—five days gone—she felt itchy with the urge to keep moving. She had to give him time to heal, and curb her awful impatience to keep ahead of their enemies.

They didn't even know who their enemies were.

She felt them out there, closing in, coming closer and closer. *That deckhand had been their enemy. He had deliberately let go of the wheelchair. It had not been an accident . . .*

She shook herself sharply. Every suspicion had the substance of fog and air. And then it dawned on her what he had said. *Near the Bois. As if he were that familiar with Paris. Details. He was starting to remember the details.*

"We'll do that," she said. "We'll stay a few days and figure things out."

"We'll take Lavinia's things to Poiteau's. We'll get a fair price there, at least. I used to know everyone there—but that was years ago. We came over often in the eighties."

Details. One after the other, spilling from him as if he were reliving them in a dream.

"Did you?" she murmured.

"Pengellis had a designer of jewelry, a man named Valery, whose pieces were coveted all over the world. Every year, they would summon us to Chatelguyon or Biarritz or Nice for the newest display. And they would buy, lavishly and open-handedly, cost no object as long as the thing was one of a kind. We made our reputation on those pieces. And they *were* exquisite."

She got the connection. "Are the pieces I took the work of Valery?"

"I think so. I don't want to know. We'll just sell them."

"We still have some money," she told him.

"We're going to need a lot of it," he said, turning his blank gaze toward the window.

That sounded as if he were committed, she thought. And as if he were planning ahead. "We're coming into the station," she said.

"I know. I feel the train slowing down." All the telltale signs by which he was learning to negotiate his way without sight. Did a man ever get used to it? Could he, after that one heaven-struck moment of seeing his attacker and his savior?

He felt like he was reining himself in, that if he let himself, he would explode all over everything and everyone around him.

One step at a time, he told himself. *Methodical and well-planned, step by step as he started to remember. And just put the two incidents out of your mind. The whole thing with the wheelchair was an accident. And Darcie must have misunderstood the doctor's name. Simple and reasonable explanations. He hadn't been seriously injured, and now they were finally on their way.*

On a damned long trip.

The thought popped up from nowhere.

To where?

He tried to recall the previous time he'd come through Paris. From Dover. He knew exactly where to go because he'd been here before. He'd conserved money by staying at an inexpensive pensione. He had been at the beginning of his journey. *That* journey. But what he'd done next utterly escaped him. And he couldn't remember for his life where he had been going.

And that was crux. *Where.*

"We're here." Superfluous to say it, when the train had heaved into the station with a huge burst of steam and come to a lurching halt.

She guided him off of the train and onto the platform where dozens of hansom cabs vied for passengers.

"Where to now, Con?"

He shook his head, and then: "Rue Mirbeau, I think."

She signalled and one of the drivers pulled over. *"S'il vous plaît—"* she began, and then she looked up into the driver's face, and into the dark burning eyes of the deckhand of the *Rossignol;* into the evil smile and dark malevolence of their enemy, just as the horse reared up and the carriage shot toward Con.

And he could see! In that mind-flashing moment, as Darcie shrieked and tackled him and he fell heavily to the ground, he saw everything clearly and concisely: the horror of the faces in the crowd rushing forward, the deckhand working masterfully to get his horse under control, and then the fiendish rictus of his triumphant grin.

And then in a split second the man vanished, and the dark came on again.

* * *

He kept insisting he was all right, and he didn't tell her what he had *seen*.

"Well I'm *not,*" Darcie said tartly. "I didn't imagine that. Everyone saw it. It was the same man . . . the deckhand of the *Rossignol*. I'd know those eyes anywhere."

"He won't find us again."

"How do you know? How do we know anything?"

"It's a coincidence," he said, but he knew it was a half-hearted excuse. "No one will find us here."

"We're not there yet," Darcie grumbled. "Rue Mirbeau—suppose he heard you tell me that."

"He didn't hear." He didn't know how he could sound so confident. The incident had shaken him badly, far more so than the accident at the dock.

Two occurrences since they'd arrived. And in short order too. But he wasn't going to think about that. It had to be a coincidence, just as he'd said; it was easier to believe that.

Meantime, they could only go one step at a time. First, the boardinghouse he remembered on the Rue Mirbeau. Then a good night's sleep and Poiteau's tomorrow.

They had walked a good number of streets beyond the train station.

"I think it's safe to call a cab here," she murmured, lifting her hand to signal. Immediately, one came rolling over, handled this time by an older cabman who was courteous and kind.

"*S'il vous plaît—*" she began, and Con interrupted, "*A la Rue de la Croix, et vite.*"

He pushed her into and climbed in beside her.

"What was that about?" she whispered.

"I decided not to take the chance. We'll be close enough where he's taking us."

Close enough. Details. Memories. Little by little. Piece by piece.

The cabdriver set them down on a broad avenue that skirted the Bois, and Darcie paid him.

"Now what? It's getting dark."

"Across the boulevard on the far side, and down that street. Rue Mirbeau is down that way. Hurry."

They hurried as much as they could with her having to guide his every step.

Details. As if he'd had a map in his mind.

"Left down Mirbeau," he said, when she hesitated. "You'll see, there'll be discreet signs advertising rooms."

Details.

Ten more minutes before they made their way slowly down Rue Mirbeau in the oncoming twilight and she tried to find the signs.

"Ah! Here . . ."

"No. Keep going."

Details. What did he sense? What could he hear?

They continued on.

"Here's one."

"What does it say?"

"The sign says *restez ici.*"

He thought about it a moment. "Yes."

She would have questioned it, but it was getting too dark too fast, and she felt as if they were alone in a vast unknown. She stepped down to the basement entrance and rang the bell.

A pretty maid answered, and Con spoke for them, quickly, concisely, and several minutes later, she led them up into the hallway while she summoned the concierge. He made the rest of the arrangements with equal brevity, told her how much money the room would require, and to sign the register as husband and wife and in her maiden name.

She didn't question it. He had his reasons, obviously. The place seemed well kept, the gas-lit corridors were narrow, with two rooms to the side and one each front and rear as they came up the steps.

They were allocated a front room on the third floor. Darcie took the key and closed the door after them gratefully.

It was a small, small room, with a large bed tucked under the eaves, and a dresser, a washstand, a table and chair, and a closet.

"Do you think we're safe here?" she asked as she swung their suitcase onto the table and began to unpack.

He sank onto the bed. "I think we have a place to stay for the moment."

"And you remembered it." *Details.*

He considered that and nodded. "I think I did. And I saw the driver of the cab."

She stopped what she was doing instantly. "You didn't."

"I swear to you."

"Con—this is getting crazy."

"I had my sight, Darcie; I'm as certain of it as when I found the diamond. I saw him."

"Do you know him?"

He hesitated. "No."

"But you're remembering other details. Like Poiteau and the trips to Paris. So you're bound to recall things as we get deeper into the journey."

"Maybe." *But who needed him to do that more—their nebulous enemy as embodied by the deckhand—or Darcie?*

The answer was obvious, and it disturbed him even more that he was leaping from the mysterious deckhand to *her* as the source of his disquiet.

She felt the change in him instantly, sharply, like the connection between them had broken off somehow, and she had to reestablish it quickly or she'd lose him forever.

"Con . . . you don't think . . ."

"What, Darcie? What don't I think?"

He'd gotten up and he was moving toward her as unsteadily as if he were walking on quicksand.

". . . he has some other way to track us—to follow us?" *Uh oh—wrong question.* She saw it in his eyes.

"Maybe he does, Darcie."

"What are you thinking?" she asked, suddenly scared. He was too intense, too wary. And she couldn't back away and let him fall on his face.

"I just keep thinking there's one person who has a greater stake in this than anyone else. Someone who very easily could be helping my so-called enemies track me. Us. One person, Darcie."

"No . . ."

"You."

"No." She put up her hands protectively against the hot wall of his chest.

"How do I know?"

"You *have* to know, Con."

"I don't know. Tell me again, Darcie."

"I've told you—every way I know how," she whispered.

"A woman's way," he said scornfully.

"It's the only way I know." *She just couldn't believe what he was saying.* She felt brittle, like fine china that could fracture into a hundred pieces.

"You do it well, too. Who put you up to it? Lavinia? Roger? Who, Darcie? Your father?"

She broke. "My father's dead, Con. He died before he got to be an esquire. He gave over my dowry, he saw me married to Roger, and then he was gone. It's just me. My dream. My quest. And yours, if you still want to go."

"I don't goddamned know what I want to do," he snarled. She'd got him off-balance again. Her father was dead. To whom could she have allegiance then? Was she that good an actress that she could pretend to hate Lavinia so?

"Your secrets, Con."

"Till I die, Darcie."

"Then we'll make sure you don't die."

"Darcie—" It was so dark, and he was so alone.

"I'm here."

"Goddamn you," he growled, and he swept her into his arms and into the roaring tide of his heat, his rampant sex, and his punishing kiss.

She melted against him. His anger was potent and swift. He tore off her clothes and she helped him. He pushed against her and pushed against her until she backed up against the door.

Secrets. Hard driving secrets. Against her back. Against all reason.

She wrapped herself around him, her arms, her legs, her naked body pressing against the hard edgy core of his desire. He was like lightning, bolting into her without priming or preparation, and pinning her against the door.

It was absolutely what she needed from him: a storm of emotion binding him to her, and obscuring everything she didn't want him to see.

She clung to him as he pounded her toward the precipice; she climbed—slowly then, slowly, drawing him out, pulling with her.

And then she fell into the breakwater as he emptied himself into her, and she opened herself to him and, in that bone crackling moment of surcease, she gave him her soul.

Ten

They lay together on the bed, silent, quiescent, spent.

She felt liquid, satiated, golden, loving his hands playing on her bare skin and the feel of her naked body against his clothes.

He trailed his fingers down her shoulder, her arm, her hip; and then he slipped his hand to her belly and spanned its width.

She recoiled instantly.

The baby . . . she kept forgetting the baby. But that was the thing—it hadn't even been that long. Not nearly enough for her to think in terms of it being real.

Her body tensed as she waited for his question, but it wasn't the one she expected.

"When did your father die?"

She took a deep breath to calm herself. *He'll get to the baby, I know he will.* And it seemed to her that all that lust and sex evaporated in the face of his question.

"About six months after Roger and I married."

He sensed the reluctance in her and she cursed herself for letting that emotion show. She brushed his hand away and reached to pull the blanket up over her naked body, a movement she knew he would read correctly.

But it didn't matter; her father's death was still a sore point. And she didn't want to tell him why, even though she knew exactly what his next question would be.

"How?"

She tried to keep her tone neutral, but she couldn't keep out the slight tremor. "The doctor said it was a heart attack."

"So soon," he murmured, his response instinctive and quick. He wondered about it immediately. "He made the next big strike, he came to England, he sold you to Roger, and then he died."

"That's just how it happened."

"And Roger did what with the money?"

"Paid operatives to search for you," she said tartly, "because *The Eye of God* is more valuable than gold, jewels, diamonds, life—if it's real."

"It's real," he said succinctly, but that was all he wanted her to know. "And once Roger had the money, your father was expendable, and probably you were too."

"And you," she said bluntly.

"And yet, we're both still here," he pointed out.

"How can you believe I could betray you?"

"One wonders," he said, levering himself up and away from her and swinging his legs over the bed. Only he didn't know where he could go in the dark. Always always, he had to consider the dark. He wanted to pace, he wanted to *see*.

What did he see? Everything she didn't say. The breadth of his family's duplicity, and the lengths to which they would go to possess The Eye of God. *Their greed. Their gluttony. Their viciousness and immorality.*

Inherited traits, all. He had them. He'd had no compunction about using them.

Darcie's father had been sacrificed on the altar of the Pengellis greed.

The quest had killed him.

The Pengellis curse.

He had to decide now: did he continue to take the risk or did he walk away?

Balance. It was always a question of balance.

And trusting what he couldn't see.

A woman. A baby. His desire. Her motives. His memories.

Tenuous things, with all the substance of the dark in which he was immured. He had to come to terms with it: the dark was a place from which he couldn't walk away.

"We'll go to Poiteau's in the morning," he said, and the decision was made. "We're going to need all the money we can get."

Details.

She'd pulled away from the cliff—this time. She could see him weighing the details, determining their lives.

One misstep. One wrong move . . .

Forget it. She'd dealt with things like that before. The only tricky part was the death of her father. It was the only thing about which she thought there was something more.

They were past it now, she thought, as she dressed. She shouldn't have to defend her deceased father. She needed to focus on the baby. It was still early enough, and the baby would be fine. She just had to remember to consider the baby.

She was down to one dress, one skirt and one shirt-waist now. Two sets of underclothes, excluding the corset which he had ruined last night, and the little bags of jewelry, no bigger than sachets, that she pinned to her camisole and her waistband.

She buttoned the high collar of her dress and she was ready to go.

"We won't come back here tonight," he said, and she packed what was left of their belongings in the suitcase, they signed out with the concierge, and then they made their way back to the Rue de la Croix.

"Let's walk," he said suddenly.

"You're being awfully cautious," she murmured, but she was not immune to the feeling that someone could have followed them.

But there wasn't anything remotely suspicious along the sun-bright avenue.

"Which way shall we go?"

"The opposite direction where the cab left us last night."

They walked; he held onto her, which he hated, and he listened to the burgeoning morning sounds. It was early. There was only the intermittent rumble of a dray or cab along the avenue. A certain sense that there were no crowds and that they were alone. The heat of the sun beating on his face. Her sure step as she guided him along.

Her impatience grew with every step. They were wasting time, she thought, and she had no idea where she was going.

"I wish I had a map," she said fretfully.

"We'll get one." That was a problem he could solve. "The store is on the Boulevard des Anges. I think it's safe to find a cab."

Still, her hand trembled as she signalled one and another of the few hansoms canvassing for passengers along the avenue, and she didn't like that. She couldn't let herself be intimidated by anything. They were both counting on her strength, and she lifted her chin haughtily as the driver looked askance as Con gave directions.

They looked like paupers, she thought. They didn't look like anyone who would patronize the elegant stores along the Boulevard des Anges. People who shopped

there were blessed by the angels, and dripping with diamonds.

Nevertheless, the wealthy knew, as Con did, that Poiteau's was one of the few stores where they could dis-
creetly dispose of those assets, and no matter what they
looked like, no matter who they were, they would not
be turned away.

As the cab slowed before the tall golden double doors
of the entrance to Poiteau's, Darcie was gripped by a
sudden fear. "What if they recognize the settings, Con?
What if they know it's you?"

"It's been ten years or more. Who could still be there
who would care?"

"I don't know." It was stupid; she was being an alarm-
ist. Evil could exist on the beautiful Boulevard des
Anges.

She pushed open the golden door and they entered.
A gentleman in formal clothes immediately came to
greet them.

"Con?" she whispered. "There is a gentleman here
who probably would like to know what we're doing
here."

Con nodded and made their needs known. "He says
to wait in one of the salons at the rear of the store."

She took his arm and followed the man as he led
them past counters of glittering jewels set enticingly on
gold-corded creamy satin pillows in locked display cases.

Their gentleman indicated the first door along a hallway of doors the same creamy color with moldings picked
out in gold. Darcie opened the door to a room that was
papered in cream and gold stripes and furnished with
an upholstered bench, an elegant escritoire and two
chairs.

"Someone will come," Con told her, "and will ask to
examine the stones. You'll give him one piece—a ring,

if you have one—and he will determine the cut and grade of the stone, the value, and what Poiteau might be willing to pay."

"Sounds like a lengthy process," Darcie said. She was getting very nervous. She reached under her waistband and fished in one of the pouches for a ring. She'd taken two. Or maybe three. Or maybe she'd forgotten already in the heat of all that had happened during the journey.

She slipped it on her finger and stretched out her hand. The ring had a filigreed band and a round stone that flashed rainbow colors in the artificial light.

The kind of ring she would have liked: simple, elegant and visible. But it was Lavinia's ring, from a time when someone had loved her.

She felt Con's hand touch her and then slide down her arm to feel the ring. She saw by his face he knew which one it was, and that there were memories. Always memories.

"Monsieur, madame—" Their gentleman at the door.

"He says to follow him," Con murmured. "The appraiser will see us now."

She took his arm and guided him back into the hallway. The gentleman was moving toward the sales floor, and she turned in that direction.

"At the rear of the store," Con directed.

She turned to the right and maneuvered them past the sparkling display cases where customers were already on the sales floor. She could just see where to follow; Con slowed her up just ten steps behind.

"Where is he going?"

"There's an area back there they can evaluate gems. At least that's what he told me.

"Did you tell him what we have?"

"No."

That was quick and to the point. She only had time to wonder why when they reached the end of the aisle. There was only one place to go: she pushed him to her left where there was a smoky glass door through which their gentleman had gone.

"I guess this is it." She grasped the brass knob and opened the door.

Another man stood with his back to them across the room and their gentleman was nowhere in sight.

Darcie tapped on the door. *"Monsieur . . ."*

The man turned.

The deckhand . . . ! Trussed up in formal clothes, brandishing a loupe, his smile as malicious as a shark. Dear God, what was he doing here? How could he be here?

He took a step toward her and she screamed, "Con . . . !" And she grabbed his hand and she ran.

Down the aisles, through the store, knocking over tables, chairs, customers, pushing aside salespeople, oblivious to the shouts and screams that followed them. Con, lumbering blindly behind her, his one arm outstretched, crashing against everything in his path.

Oh God, oh God, oh God . . .

She smashed through the doors and into the sunlight, hauling him with her. *They're coming, coming, coming . . .* Her fear was monumental. They had to escape, she didn't care how. She bolted across the avenue, oblivious of vehicles, horses, pedestrians, curses following them as she ran interference for him.

She heard them shouting behind her, but she was oblivious to everything but getting them out of sight of the store.

"Con!" She was panting so hard she could barely get out his name.

"Jesus God." He was right with her. "What the hell . . . !"

"Can't . . . talk—" She didn't slow down, wasn't aware of the stares of pedestrians who saw a frenzied young woman and a blind man racing like furies down the street. "Can't . . . stop—"

Another block and another. She would never get far enough away. But she was running out of breath. She had a stitch in her side, and she was suddenly aware that she'd left their suitcase in the little salon in the store, and that all she had with her now was the money and jewelry pinned under the clothes she wore.

Oh my God . . . She slowed her pace to a walk, and waited as he fell in step beside her.

"God almighty, Darcie, what the hell was that all about?"

"Are you all right?"

"I don't know." He felt dizzy, disoriented, and dependent on her. And he hated it. Hated, hated, hated it. And more than that, he despised her eyes. And he was so intent on that, he almost didn't hear what she said.

"He was there."

He shook himself and tried to concentrate. *"Who?"*

"The deckhand. In the store, in the appraisal room." *"What?"*

"We have to get out of here. He's everywhere. He was even in the store, and for all I know, he's somewhere out here." Now she was panicked; she sounded close to hysteria. "We have to get away from here. Right now. Before he comes after us."

He felt himself going calm in the face of her agitation. Something he could *do,* he thought. He could focus and direct her and get her back in control. They had nothing, if Darcie couldn't maintain control.

"All right," he said with more composure than he felt. "We'll get out of here now; we'll take the first train, no matter where it goes."

* * *

Details. A train rocketing through the night. Arrangements made by telegraph for him to be met in Switzerland. In the dead of the night. Money exchanged. Confidentiality assured.

Another long night in transit. Munich next. Change trains. Board for Vienna. Another two days beyond that to Budapest. He's busy, mapping and plotting where he has to go.

No interruptions here. He's alone in the railroad car. Money buys that, and luxury. He's too used to it. His mother had told him. Money doesn't buy everything. It buys him the where-withal to travel in luxury. To purchase silence. To buy loyalty. To possess a legend.

His mother's voice, always in his ear . . .

They were going to Munich, economy class, surrounded by passengers who knew to travel with picnics and pillows.

"We can buy food; it doesn't matter," he said, and he knew he was speaking with the voice of a man accustomed to having all the money he ever needed at his command.

"What if he's on the train?"

"He's not on the train."

"Next you'll say he wasn't in the store."

"No. I believe he was in the store. Just like I saw him, on the dock and in the street. Maybe he's a figment of both our imaginations."

She shook her head. "You're remembering more now, aren't you?"

"I think so. I goddamned hope so. I hate being blind."

Balance. Always a question of balance. He had to maintain the balance, to stay calm and clear, and focused on the result. He couldn't allow himself to think about whether his blindness was permanent.

"Do you speak German?" she asked idly.

"A little. I learned just enough of everything to get me whatever I needed."

She could envision that. Con Pengellis was definitely a man who would always know exactly how to get what he wanted.

He got me.

She shook away the thought and turned her attention to the screaming children of the family across the aisle. A tidy middle-class family with two young ones, two older ones, a weary mother and autocratic father who portrayed a semblance of normalcy, direction, home.

Things she'd never known.

She felt a crushing sense of loneliness. *Father . . . I want my father—Her need slicing as keenly as a knife through her heart. Daddy—*

How awful—in the midst of bedlam . . . tears streaming down her cheeks; she wiped them away impatiently, thankful that he couldn't see them.

They came to Munich in the dark, and she refused to take a cab, go to a hotel, be stranded in the dark; nothing except stay in the station until the next connecting train arrived in the morning.

In the station, there was light. They could see everything, everyone—and they could blend into the crowd.

They bought food from vendors who came to the station, and she slept with his shoulder cushioning her head.

Late in the morning after most of the crowd was gone, they bought a ticket for a private car, and they boarded the train for Vienna.

As the train rolled through the countryside, she counted the money. Too little money. Not many more pounds and francs, and they had so much more to travel, and supplies to fund.

"We have to get some money."

"I know. We'll just have to take what we can get."

She closed her eyes wearily. It sounded more and more hopeless. There were too many factors operating against them. They were running out of money. They needed gear. His blindness was an obstacle almost impossible to overcome.

Crazy, crazy, crazy . . .

Finally, she slept.

They came into the Western Railway Terminal in Vienna early in the morning, and emerged from their car rumpled, tired, and cautious in the extreme, something they'd discussed the whole of the trip.

"We've taken the obvious route all along," Darcie kept saying irritably. "I want to know now—are we on a wild-goose chase?"

He wondered that himself. Things were going too slowly; he remembered moving fast when he had been alone, by steamer, by train, by horse and wagon when necessary, with all the Pengellis money paving the way.

Now they had near nothing, no gear, no clothes, no money, and an outside chance of selling Lavinia's diamonds for anywhere near what they were worth.

And all for *The Eye of God*.

He closed his eyes and he saw the grotto, the altar of ancient stone, the light pouring down as if from heaven . . . oh yes it was real, it was a dream, it was his, and he was going to claim it.

"For all you know, Lavinia has sent her operatives back to India just to wait for your return."

"Probably," he agreed, a little shocked that it didn't worry him.

"They're probably on this train."

"Don't get delusional, Darcie. We have work to do."

They found the Ringstrasse, which was like the center of the world. Here, on one side or the other of the cobbled boulevard, were the parliament and city hall. The university, the museum; the opera house, all built in grand gothic scale, and overlooking a seemingly endless stretch of malls and esplanades.

There were clubs and theaters, the woods and wine gardens. There was life in this place, teeming, rollicking, vigorous, and they walked right into it and lost themselves in the crowd.

The quest for a mythical diamond seemed like a fairy tale here, in a country that had lost its fairy tale prince to an operatic tragedy.

But Vienna was not only the Ringstrasse. It was also the Ottakring district, where they headed on a horse-drawn streetcar an hour later. Here the working class labored and their wives ran the anonymous boarding-houses that they sought. Here they could find a way to dispose of a diamond ring without approaching the better known dealers or stores.

He felt insanely hampered by his sightlessness. He felt like a ventriloquist's dummy, speaking only when Darcie needed a direction, an answer, a translation in his raw German.

But it was enough: enough to procure a room, enough to buy food, and to find a tailor who had some ready-made clothes in his store.

And nobody asked questions. It was the part of the city in which you could disappear like air. They bought food and maps and melted into the fabric of the poorer quarter as if they'd lived there all their lives.

"We can stay here for a day or two," Con said.

"I hate wasting time."

"Time is all we have. No one else knows where to look for *The Eye of God.*"

She eyed him across the narrow table where they had spread their dinner.

"Do you?"

Do you? Studying all the myths and legends. Separating the wheat from the chaff; pinpointing the reality in the fairy tales; the concrete from the dream. Poring over maps and directions. Did he know where to look? Did he remember?

Did he?

"Yes."

One word and he gave her everything she wanted to know. He felt the tension ease out of her, heard her pour some wine, felt her press his glass in his hand, heard her move things from the table and then the rustle of paper as she unfolded a map and spread it out.

"How do we go?"

Now he had to give more. "Just the way I originally went: by express through Budapest to Bucharest, and then a connecting train to Varna. We take a steamer across the Black Sea to Istanbul, and then it's by horse and camel across to Baghdad . . . and then over the Zagros Mountains to Isfahan and on to Lahore."

Her throat went dry. So many days. So many miles. So much time. And he needed his eyes. She had had no idea how much he needed his eyes. Hers were just not enough for the rough trip ahead.

She was silent for a long time, studying the route on the map. It wasn't enough, she thought, not his dream, not her desire, not their sex, not their greed. Nothing was enough to compel her to go on from here. It was too much, and they had too little. And even his confession that he remembered the location of the diamond was too little too late.

He couldn't do it without his sight. And she couldn't do it leading him blind. And she didn't know how they could do it altogether.

He sensed her withdrawal. "Darcie?"

"What?" She knew she sounded terse, unsure.

"You need a bath and a good night's sleep. It might be the most you get for the next three or four weeks."

"That's not funny, Con."

"It's truth. We're halfway there, you know."

"I don't know. I feel like we're halfway from anywhere."

"Like you felt travelling from—say Colorado to New York?"

She felt an instant flash of recognition. *Narrow gauge railroads and five car trains. Wagons. Dust. Dirt. Mountains. Rain. Flash floods. Dangerous crossings. Mules, sometimes, or horses. And other times, on foot.*

Nothing had ever stopped her or her father. Not weather, not impenetrable wilderness, or lack of money. Or thieves, outlaws, or dead dry claims.

They just stepped right over the bones of their losses, and kept on looking.

What was different then? And what did the obstacles matter when the next big strike was just over the hill? Or over a mountain. Or across the Black Sea.

"Halfway there," she echoed softly, moving her finger across the map and following the route he had outlined. Halfway to India, she thought, and riches beyond her wildest dreams.

There was a knock at the door, and she started.

"Probably the bathwater," Con said coolly. "Don't panic."

It was a little luxury she had paid extra for, and they both were going to use it. She opened the door to admit the landlady caring two pitchers of steaming water, and her husband and son carrying a narrow copper tub.

"Just in the middle," she said, and then she pointed. The landlady said something, which Con translated. "She'll be back in a moment with soap, towels and some more water."

But it took three trips to fill the tub. Darcie locked the door behind the landlady and stared at it doubtfully. "I guess I'll go first. You don't have to turn your eyes."

"I guess not," he murmured, settling back on the bed.

She watched him for a moment, and then she began stripping off her clothes. It was easier without corsets and hooks; she unpinned the little pouches of jewelry and set them on the dresser.

How long ago was that when she had stolen through Goole Abbey to search out those pieces? It seemed like forever ago.

She pushed away the thought and slid out of her camisole, petticoat and drawers. And then she was naked, and she trailed her finger in the steaming water to test the heat.

The water looked so inviting, but he looked even more enticing sprawled out on the bed, attuned to something that she would never be able to share.

She wanted to know suddenly if he wanted her still, or if he still thought she could be his enemy.

If he knew she were naked, would he come to her?

She needed to know. She wanted to explore her power and test his potency. She walked slowly to the side of the bed, watching his body, watching his face.

His body reacted first, spurting indelibly to life before her eyes.

This was power. She loved it. She reached out her hand and touched him. Hot. Thick. Hard. Yes.

She climbed onto the bed and straddled his legs, and

she was absolutely certain by the look in his eyes that he could see everything.

She wrenched apart his trousers decisively, mercilessly ripping the cloth that impeded her way. And then his penis was free, springing into her hands as if it were home.

"Is that what you want?"

"Bathe me," she whispered, sliding her hands all up and down his erection.

"I'll drown you in it."

"Do it," she breathed.

Her hand worked harder, faster, slower, lightly, tightly; his eyes closed, his body undulated beneath her, his breathing came fast, his hands reached for her nipples as she bent forward into his pleasure.

It was coming. Slowly it was coming, building volcanically underneath pumping of her hands.

Her excitement escalated. She wanted him now, all over her, every last drop of his desire, she wanted.

"Come to me," she goaded him. "Come."

She rose onto her knees and bore down on him. He was just ready, so ready. She held it all in her hands: his strength, his vigor, his power.

She grasped him tightly, pushing him, pulling him, bringing him on. She felt all his muscles contracting, she felt him gathering, and he jacked himself up and thrust against her encircled fingers, and erupted in one mighty blow.

He spewed all over her, on her breasts, her face, her belly, her hands. And still he came, his ejaculate spurting with each convulsive spasm. She held him until his last shuddering climax, and even then, she didn't let him go.

"I'm covered with your essence," she whispered. ". . . do you see me?"

"I see you," he said hoarsely. "I feel you." He reached up and grasped her at the waist. "I want you." He pulled her down to him and rolled her over onto her back.

This he was sure of—in the dark. Her body was a landscape he could negotiate, in the dark.

"The water will get cold," she murmured, as she welcomed his weight and parted her legs.

He positioned himself to breach her heat, slanting his mouth down within a breath of hers.

"It can't quench my thirst," he whispered against her lips.

And he drove into her like a drowning man who had finally reached the shore.

Eleven

In the Ottakring, it was simple to find shops catering to every need, and brokers anxious to buy or sell, or to lend you money. What they liked best of all was collateral, and they examined the ring that Darcie wanted to sell, one broker after the other, and made their unacceptable offers.

"And then they'll resell to whatever jeweler with which they have a connection and make a profit of a hundredfold," Darcie said disgustedly, as they entered a pawnshop on the Schloss Alee.

"We don't have a choice now," he told her in an undertone. "We're too conspicuous. What do you think they see? Two vagrants hawking a diamond ring—we don't have the option of going to one of the bigger stores. They'd have the authorities after us before we could count to three."

She looked at the shopkeeper, who was old, with papery skin, and dressed in a long black frock coat, and she could have sworn he understood every word. And his eyes . . . his knowing eyes as he took the ring and examined it under a magnifying glass and with his loupe.

He made her nervous as he turned the ring over and over and tested it every way possible, and then he looked up at Con and made his offer.

"It's a little more money than the others."

"It's not nearly enough," she said, knowing how she sounded.

He handed her a stack of gulden. "Come on now. It's just a little setback." He said some words to the shopkeeper, and motioned Darcie toward the door.

She took his arm and turned back to look at the man.

He was old and stooped and losing hair, and he looked as if he were gloating over the bargain he had made. And then he looked up at her, and his eyes . . . his burning, knowing eyes—

She slammed the door behind them as they stepped into the street.

"That man . . ."

"Darcie . . ." he said warningly. "I didn't sense anything."

"You didn't see him. His eyes—"

"Forget his eyes. I have a plan. We're going to use the money to dress ourselves like gentry who might be stranded and in need of cashing in some valuables. You said it yourself: we have to *pretend*. This is just the first step."

Her senses began to tingle. "All right. You're right. We had to accept less so we didn't have to explain things. I understand. But that man's eyes . . ."

"Let's go shopping," Con interrupted her. "Find a cab."

She was even leery of doing that. She could still see those eyes that had followed them from Paris to Vienna. Those eyes could be anywhere, even in a pawnshop. Or driving the next cab.

"The driver says we want the Kohlmarkt," Con said, climbing into the carriage after her. "And Rosteck's for gold and gifts. I think we'll do very well with our stake."

And that was what it was: a stake, and she didn't think

they'd do well at all, but by late afternoon, they had accomplished a lot. They found in the Kohlmarkt stores that sold clothing ready to wear. She purchased an elegant dove gray suit over an underdress of lavender satin, and they fitted him out in a severe black suit which emphasized his height and gave him an elegance that belied his blindness.

They were able to buy one outfit each, with underclothing, and toiletries, and a suitcase that didn't look as if it had weathered a war, and they had left a handful of kreuzer.

"That might buy us a pastry for lunch," Darcie grumbled as she guided him along the boulevard.

"Then it's time to find Rosteck's and proceed to the next step."

Rosteck's was the equivalent of Poiteau's in Paris. An elegant shop that sold gift items and jewelry. A place where nothing was advertised and everything was understood.

"We need to sell a necklace this time," Con said. "We're going to need a lot of money."

They were taken once again to the rear of the shop, straight to the appraiser's office. Darcie removed a pouch and handed it across the desk. Con did the talking, and she could tell he was playing on the gentleman's sympathy.

They had concocted the story before they even reached the store, and it was paper thin to begin with. They were on their honeymoon. They ran out of money. They had no family to turn to. The necklace was a wedding present, an heirloom, but they were willing to sacrifice to continue on their journey. They were young and gay and so much in love.

Darcie rolled her eyes. The appraiser took the necklace and began his examination.

He spent a nerve-racking half hour, going over each of the stones, calling for consultations, and excusing himself at least twice to confer with another appraiser on the premises.

"They are calling the authorities is what," Darcie fretted. "They think we're thieves. We don't look like people who would own such a piece."

"They will pay the price," Con said, but even he was a little unnerved by the amount of discussion that was going on about the necklace, and he resolutely pushed the picture of Lavinia wearing the necklace out of his mind.

He had been—what?—five or six . . . ? He couldn't quite remember. But there was his father, with an oblong velvet box which he had not placed under the Christmas tree.

My dear . . .

Oh my darling—as his father lifted the necklace from its satin nest and held it up in the light.

It might well have been that he had fallen in love with diamonds that night. He remembered how they glittered and shot rainbow light down to the floor; how they sparkled like ice as his father's long fingers slipped the necklace around Lavinia's neck.

She stroked the center stone. It looked smooth as water, deep as the ocean, and bright as a star . . . her voice soft, murmuring her appreciation at the thoughtfulness of his father.

That Lavinia . . .

"*Mein herr . . .*" The appraiser, an hour later, the necklace spread across his hands like a waterfall.

He jerked out of his reverie. The amount the appraiser was offering was beyond even what he had estimated. He nodded his head in agreement.

"We have to sign a paper that says we are free to sell the item, and that it wasn't stolen or obtained by illegal means. They want all kinds of assurances about it."

"I suppose technically you *are* free to sell it."

"Technically." He wished he could see her face as he told her the sum. "It's a lot of money."

"Is it enough?"

Even he didn't know. "It's enough . . . for now."

They bought the tickets on the Direct Express that afternoon. "I think we need to leave here as soon as possible" Con said. "Even if this is the most obvious route, once we reach Istanbul we can make modifications. And at least we'll travel in comfort."

They would leave the next morning from the Southern Terminal, which meant another night in the Ottakring. She wasn't happy about that, but she agreed that their money was better spent purchasing more clothes, sturdy shoes, personal items, a small stash of dried food, and another suitcase, for him.

It was like starting off on the next adventure, Darcie thought, as they bought packages of roast pork and vegetables from a vendor to bring back for their dinner.

She felt the growing excitement that always preceded the thrill of the hunt. And the fact they now had money eased some of her fears.

There was always a way to get money if one had something to sell. And the further away from Europe they travelled, the fewer questions they would be asked and the less trouble they would have.

She felt reassured by the thought. And she decided she'd imagined the man with eyes, and she had better stop feeling so overwrought.

No one was following them. Lavinia could not have known where she had gone from the brothel. And if she were still after Con, she probably had operatives searching all over India for him. And she had a business to run on top of that. She couldn't be everywhere. She couldn't be in Vienna at any rate.

And Con's blindness hadn't hampered them all that much, she thought, as she laid out their dinner on the small table in their room. They'd bought some beer and wine as well, and she poured the beer into a glass for him and handed it across the table to him.

"Let's toast the fact we've done well," he proposed.

"Certainly," she said before she could stop herself. "We'll congratulate ourselves on the fact you were almost killed—twice—and that we sold a flawless diamond ring for no money at all, and we were that close to having the authorities arrest us at Rosteck's."

"Pessimist." He sipped his beer and made a face. "I hope the food is better."

"This is the Ottakring. What do you expect?"

"You adapt well," he murmured, feeling for the food and lifting a piece of pork to his mouth. "That's not bad."

"Con—we should be moving faster . . ."

He shook his head. "Do you know it's almost seventy hours by train to Istanbul from Paris? And that includes the ferry from Varna. If you were travelling alone, you still wouldn't get anywhere any faster, Darcie, so just shelve the idea of going on without me. You'd wind up dead, and you couldn't tell them where to bury you."

"I didn't mean that."

"Sure you did," he said, setting aside his beer and pushing away the pork. He lost his appetite suddenly. Sometimes . . . sometimes, he forgot about the blindness and it almost seemed a condition he'd lived with all his life. And he didn't want to get used to it. He wanted to remember when it happened, because he hadn't always been blind. And that meant there was a chance he could regain sight at some point in his life.

There was always the hope. Always the next dream. Darcie had lived her life that way, and to some extent, so had he. Only he had always had the advantage of money, and all she had had was faith and guile.

Sometimes he forgot they were only partners in a game to outwit an unknown enemy. Unholy partners, he thought; both of them rapacious, hungry, and bound by desire.

A perfect trinity. A blind man. A greedy woman. And *The Eye of God.*

Their compartment was in the fifth of seven sleeping cars on the Direct Express, and one of the smaller ones at that. But it did have its own lavatory, and a small closet beside the door to the room.

On either side of the car there were berths that folded up against the wall during the day; and there were seating benches beneath, and a clever table that pulled up from under the window.

Darcie guided Con to the tufted bench on the left hand side, and sank into the seat opposite by the window. She would unpack later, she thought, as she watched the porters hauling piles of expensive luggage toward the rear car. Their two small suitcases suddenly seemed awfully meager when she measured them against what other people were bringing on this trip.

Or maybe she was feeling the weight of the gloomy weather. They were leaving in the rain, and rain was always a bad omen, although they had arrived before it had begun. Others were just now scurrying down the platform, ill prepared for the weather, and covering themselves with whatever came to hand.

The train would leave in an hour, the next stop Budapest. And meantime, they would dine royally in the dining car, have the luxury of a porter making up their beds at night, and the diversion of new acquaintances in the bar car.

Con sat very erect, staring straight ahead. The darkness today seemed overwhelming, especially on top of the chaos of the departure he sensed beyond the compartment door.

Things he used to be able to *see*—

Things he couldn't remember. When he'd escaped; how he'd gotten to England; what happened to his eyes . . . blank spaces in his mind, as black as the vista in front of him.

And Darcie . . . what did he see? The softest of hair, long and flowing down her shoulders; smooth silky skin, magical hands—but not a face or figure came to mind when he pictured her. She was a presence, ephemeral by night, and solid practicality by day. The sum of the parts of her body that he now knew as intimately as his own.

Even the thought of her aroused him.

He didn't need to see her to want her. It was a continual ache in his groin. He was suspicious of it. He hated his dependence on it. And worst of all, he never stopped wanting it. But he couldn't live a life obliterating himself in a sexual void.

It was too easy.

She was too easy.

It was the thing he couldn't quite get around, at night, in the dark, when he couldn't sleep.

A man with no eyes could see more clearly in the dark.

But a man with no eyes, he thought warily, was also a very easy mark.

She saw the man with the eyes as the train pulled out of the Southern Terminal station. On the platform, beside an empty luggage cart, staring up at her, smiling, smiling smiling, that evil knowing smile. The face of the deckhand, the cabdriver, the money lender. He was all of them—and none.

And then he vanished as quickly as a ghost.

But when she turned her head and looked behind, she thought she saw him again, swinging up onto the steps of the last car as the train left the station.

Oh my God . . . oh my God— She rose from her seat and then slumped down again. She'd imagined it. She had. The train had been going too fast. Even if he had been on the platform, he wasn't strong enough to jump on a train moving at full speed.

Her imagination was playing tricks. How was she going to tell Con?

She wouldn't . . . It was a threat he couldn't see, and there was no purpose at all in telling him.

She would have to take all the precautions.

If she had seen what she thought she had seen.

I'm going crazy now. Just when I think things have calmed down, that there is no threat. That everything's behind us . . .

She was trembling. She was shaking like a belly dancer.

. . . and the baby—she mustn't forget the baby, it was too easy to forget the baby . . .

She stared out the window as the train rolled through the outskirts of the city. She would have to bring their food to the compartment, and she would have to scrutinize every stranger.

And every stranger would look like the man with the burning eyes . . .

She jumped at the knock on the compartment door.

"Who is it?" The first words Con had spoken since they entered the car.

"A porter." She could see his face through the window, benign, respectful, smiling. Nothing to be afraid of. "I'll get it." But her legs were shaky as she got up and went to the door.

And then impossibly, before her very eyes, he changed, his face metamorphosing from the elderly porter to the man with burning eyes, evil personified, bent on getting through the door.

She threw herself against it, shrieking, "Con!" and he bounded up, and, with his arms stretched out, fumbled his way toward her, and the thumping sound of something trying to enter their room.

"Con!" She wasn't strong enough, and he wasn't fast enough. "Hurry!"

The man with the eyes had superhuman strength, and he was beating her; slowly, inexorably he was forcing the door, and she just didn't have the power to stop him.

And then Con heaved himself against her and his weight in combination with hers enabled her to slam shut the door. She fumbled with the lock. Click. Click. The most welcome sound she'd ever heard. She ripped the curtain across the window, effectively closing out their nemesis.

But for how long? She was absolutely certain that if she pulled the curtain he would still be there.

She swallowed hard as he started pounding on the door, and Con looked questioningly at her.

"Don't open it, Con."

"Darcie, what the hell's going on?"

"You won't believe it."

"You sounded scared to hell."

"It was the man. And I don't know that this isn't him."

The pounding grew louder.

"Ma'am . . . Ma'am—is anything wrong? Can I help you? Let me make sure you're all right. Ma'am? Ma'am? If you'd be so kind—open the door."

"That's crazy," he said under the pounding.

"I know." She cursed the fates that Con couldn't see him, and that he couldn't see how scared she was to open the door, "What should I do?"

He was so logical. "See who's there."

"But he looked—" she started to say, but what the man looked like made little difference to him. He'd seen him twice—if he had seen him at all, and he wouldn't be able to see the evil beyond the window.

No one could, except her. If it existed. If she could believe her eyes.

She drew the curtain slowly, slowly, her hand shaking, her breath shallow with fear.

The elderly porter outside the door looked at her quizzically, and mouthed, "Are you all right, ma'am?"

"Stay close to me," she whispered to Con as she unlocked the door and opened it a fraction of an inch. "I'm fine, thank you," she said to the porter.

"Could I bring you some tea, ma'am?"

He was a kindly man, she could see it in his eyes, and she would have loved some tea. But she couldn't trust anything, not even him.

"That's fine, thank you. I'll see to it myself. Later."

"As you wish, ma'am."

She eased the door closed and locked it again. And looked up once again to see the man with the burning eyes, laughing at her gullibility from beyond the window of the double-locked door.

"We're not going to eat. We're going to spend two days on this train and we're just not going to eat."

She knew she sounded delirious, but she didn't care. She was shaken beyond anything she cared to admit.

He, however, was practical. "We paid for the food, we're going to eat it."

"And how, pray tell, if we can't go to the dining car and we can't trust a porter to deliver it?"

"Darcie, you can't fall apart now."

"You didn't see that man."

"I saw him twice."

And that was the thing. Had he or had he imagined he could even see at all?

She decided not to comment on that. "I'll make arrangements to get some food," she said finally.

"And I'll lock the door."

Con alone and in the dark in their compartment? No, no, no. She couldn't leave him. If the man could transform himself from a porter into a portent of evil, Con would have no defense against him. None. And he'd already tried to kill him twice.

"That won't work either. We'll have to starve. I will not leave you at the mercy of that fiend."

"If you want to find a diamond, Darcie, you'd better feed me."

"I don't think you should even say that out loud."

He heard the note in her voice and cursed the darkness. "God, he's got you terrified."

"He's stalking us, Con."

He felt as helpless as a fly. He remembered looking up at the eyes, seeing the evil, and the lustful grin. Malevolence rising from the dust and dirt of a thousand years, provoking fate, disturbing the balance.

Sometimes death was the only solution.

"Then we have to destroy him," he said, as if he were pronouncing a sentence. "And you'll have to find the way."

They'd eaten some of the dried food they'd packed for the trip, fruit and beef, washed down with water, a makeshift dinner at best, and now she lay in her berth, staring into the dark, seeing what he saw every moment of every day.

Nothingness. Dark blank nothingness.

. . . I'll be your eyes . . .

And anything else you ask of me . . .

How could he live like that, staring endlessly into the dark, depending on someone else's eyes?

She turned restively in the narrow bed.

What if the man with the eyes was at the compartment door now? What if he watched them all night long? What if she couldn't get out tomorrow to get some food? What if, what if, what if?

She slipped down from the berth and folded up the bed. She wasn't going to get any sleep tonight. Instead, she was going to prowl the room and chew on the *what if's* until night turned into day.

She drew back the curtain on the door. A muted light filled the window from the sconces in the passageway. No shadows. No sense of a lurking presence.

She had no idea of the hour. She unlocked the door and opened it, and stepped out into the passageway. Not a sound but the rhythmic click of wheels on the rails. Not a breath intruding on the silence.

She inhaled deeply to calm her pounding heart. No one was about. There was nothing to fear. Maybe this was the time—her stomach was growling—she could just make her way to the dining car, and procure something for them to eat.

She heard Con stir in the bunk behind her. If she slipped out now, she could be back before he was ever aware.

And then she wouldn't feel utterly terrorized by that man.

The dining car was between the third and fourth

sleeping cars. She carefully locked the compartment door and slipped down the passageway, surrounded by silence and enfolded by the dim light.

Late as it was, there were still a couple of passengers sitting in the dining car, and one tired waiter waiting patiently at a table at the far end of the car for them to finish.

He got up wearily as she approached. Five minutes later, he returned with a tray; she took it from him, waving away his polite offer to carry it back to the compartment for her.

Another couple of moments, she would be safely there. She pushed her way through the first of the connecting doors into sleeping car number four.

He jolted awake suddenly as the train rounded a sharp curve.

Goddamned dark; can't see a goddamned thing. Shit. Hell. Bloody blast . . .

He toppled off of the bunk, his arms flailing, shouting her name.

No answer. He got up off the floor and groped his way around the room. No Darcie.

He felt his way to the door. Locked.

Damn and blast.

The key—taken. Where the hell had she gone?

He ripped open the locks and eased into the passageway.

No help there. No point in him going one foot further.

He had never felt more useless. He slammed the door furiously behind him.

And then he heard Darcie scream.

Twelve

He jumped her from behind between the cars, catching her totally unaware. She screamed as his arm wrenched her neck, and everything on the tray went crashing to the floor.

Careless. Her sole coherent thought before he pulled her backward into the darkness. She heard his animal panting in her ear, and she pulled and twisted, trying to get purchase to resist him, holding the tray in a death grip, her only weapon to defend herself.

But he was too strong. He dragged her toward the door, toward the steps, wrestling her as she fought him, as she hooked her feet in the doorframe, as she grabbed for the door.

He was choking her; she couldn't swallow. She could barely summon the energy to fight. He yanked her backward, and she relinquished the door and he forced her toward the steps. She heard the ominous clack of the wheels and felt the cold night air.

She was that close to death. He would kill her to get to Con—

Nooooo . . . !

She went limp against him, making him drag her full weight as he jerked her toward the steps.

Last chance—no room to turn, can't breathe . . . tray—

Both hands, no strength—
In the name of The Eye of God . . .

With both hands, with the last vestige of her feeble strength, she lifted the tray backward over her head and bashed it against him.

She didn't know what she hit—his arm, his shoulder, his head . . . but immediately his grip loosened; he fell, and she fell on top of him; she scrambled to her knees, and lashed out at him blindly, crashing the tray over his head, and breaking it in two.

He lay bleeding, his head propped against the second step from the bottom. Moaning. Limp. Vanquished.

. . . we must destroy him . . . and you must find the way—

She didn't think twice. She lifted his legs and pushed, tumbling him legs over shoulders down the steps and off the train.

She managed to salvage some of the food, as the porters came running, and one of them summoned the train manager to report the accident.

They'd paid for the food, she thought practically, as she gathered the basket of croissants and fruit. At least they would eat. Thank God she was still alive and she could eat.

A porter brought tea to the compartment, where Con was pacing like a caged tiger, and was just setting it on the table when she entered.

The train manager, she saw, was already there.

"Now madame . . ." he said, his voice calm and respectful, and Con translated.

She had determined her story as she made her way shakily back to the room, and she was going to stick to it. No one could prove it happened otherwise, and, she thought, she did not need to attribute a motive to the man with the eyes. He could have been any lecher seizing an opportunity to seduce an unchaperoned woman. And anyway, the fewer details the better.

"There isn't much to say. The man attacked me, and in the course of my defending myself, he slipped and fell from the train."

The manager made a tcching sound. "Did madame know the man?"

"I never saw him. He came at me from behind, his arm around my neck. I was coming from the dining car with a tray of food. I hit him with the tray. He fell backwards and slipped, and before I could do anything, he was gone."

"I see, madame." The train manager finished his notes and then bowed. "I think that will be all for now. I can see you are overcome."

She didn't know how she maintained her composure until they left. And then she just collapsed onto one of the benches and buried her head in her hands.

"Have some tea," Con said, groping for the bench opposite her.

"Is the door locked?"

"I locked it."

"I can't forgive myself for this. I couldn't sleep. I was so hungry . . . and no one was there." She looked up at him, even though he couldn't see her. "But this is the lesson I learned: he's everywhere. That man is *everywhere.*"

"He's gone now."

"I don't know that, Con. He fell off the train, but—I can't tell you he's gone." She felt tears on her cheeks and she wiped them away impatiently. He'd scared her again. He'd targeted her this time. She couldn't even think beyond that.

She could feel Con's frustration, that he could do

nothing while she had almost died. But his voice betrayed nothing of that as he said, "Pour yourself some tea, Darcie. Eat something. I've already thought about what to do."

She poured the tea and wrapped her cold hands around the cup. "All right, what can we do?"

"Well, you were right. We're on the most obvious course, and we have to get off of it. We're going to debark at Budapest, and change trains for Belgrade. The line goes straight through to Istanbul. From there, we can disappear, and they'll never find us."

"You're crazy. A blind man and a Western woman. Everyone will know who we are."

"So we'll playact," he said reassuringly. "Just like you said. You've been right about everything; you're much better at this than I am."

But she'd always had to be, she thought. Invariably she and her father had been one step ahead of someone they'd swindled or who had cheated them. She knew all about dodges and disguises. She'd just never had to cope with a sightless accomplice before.

She felt a spark of inspiration. "I think we have to hide. On the train. Do you know when we get into Budapest?"

"Early evening, I think. The timetable should be on the ticket folder. And where might we be hiding on the train?"

"The kitchen. Think, Con. It's perfect."

"We'll get fed, at least," he said dryly.

She ignored that. "We'll steal in after the midday meal, when they're cleaning up and we won't be too much in the way. We'll leave things just as they are here—locked door, curtained windows—pack everything up and maybe stash the suitcases before the lunch hour. That makes sense. Then we won't look as conspicuous when we go to the dining car for lunch, and we can sneak off from there the moment the train comes into the station."

She liked that plan. It felt good to be able to define some action and not to be at the mercy of forces she couldn't understand.

"Doesn't that make sense? We'll be right out in the open. No one can get to us in broad daylight. And by the time anyone tries, we'll be long gone."

It was as good a plan as any, he thought. He was just along for the ride. Helpless. Hopeless. Hapless. He felt like a doddering old man as she helped him along the passageway for the second sitting of the midday meal.

She'd reserved a table very close to the kitchen, and she had managed to get their bags into a storage cupboard in the pantry.

"You need not rush the meal, madame," the waiter told them as he guided Con into his chair. "We will not set another service until dinner since we arrive in Budapest at four o'clock."

"Perfect," Darcie mouthed as Con translated and then asked the waiter to recite the menu. They decided on cream soup to start, stuffed breast of turkey, a vegetable salad, with cheeses and tea to finish.

"We can take the cheese," Darcie said practically. "And whatever vegetables will keep. We ate a lot of that dried meat, and you never know when we might need it."

That, Con thought humorously, should be his line of reasoning. But Darcie had obviously been in that situation as well, in another country, another world away.

They ate in silence, with Darcie packing away the fresh bread and crackers that accompanied the soup.

She hated the fact he couldn't see the countryside as the train rolled on toward Budapest. It was one of the pleasures of the dining car, with its narrow tables, soft lighting, and superbly efficient service.

But at least, they would have one meal, and a moment's peace before the rest of the journey. Sometimes that was all you could expect.

The turkey was rolled and stuffed with a breaded dressing and walnuts, the most luxurious meal Darcie had had since before Roger died. The more so because she shared it with Con, because she could help him by covertly cutting his meat and arranging food, as he directed her, in a way he could manage them comfortably.

She loved his expression, as intent as a child's, as he dug his fork into the turkey—at three o'clock on the plate, and the dressing—at twelve, and the salad, at nine. A very efficient system which diminished his awkwardness and gave him some measure of control.

She picked at the salad, setting aside the lightly steamed and still-crisp julienned carrots to add to the food she had already squirreled away in a spare linen napkin.

They ordered dessert: fruit tart, and chocolate pots au crème. Darcie loved chocolate, he discovered, listening to her sensual moans as she slowly ate the creme.

She packed away the cheese, and poured their tea. "Still another hour until Budapest."

"All right. This train comes into the South station. We'll need to get over the river to the East station in the Elizabeth district. We may have less than a half hour before this train gets on its way again. They'll take on provisions and mail and they'll be gone."

"All right. In a half hour, we'll get into the kitchen. can you make a pot of tea stretch thirty minutes?"

"I can if you can."

More difficult done than said. There was nothing they could talk about in public, so she made light conversation about their fellow passengers until the waiter came to clear the table, after which he signalled that they could remain as long as they wished.

She watched the car clear out. A couple of passengers remained at the far end, reading a paper, or playing cards, or in deep conversation.

She thought the coast was clear. "I think we can do it now." She rose from the table and came around to take his arm. "This way." She didn't look back as she led him through the closer door and into the kitchen car.

It was the most clever arrangement. All the stoves and preparation counters lined one side of the car, with an icebox at the far end, and two chefs in constant attendance.

They wove their way around the assistant chefs and the boys who were washing up from the midday meal, and they pressed forward into the anteroom of the car which was lined with cupboards and closets full of provisions.

"I think they'll let us stay here until we come to the station," Darcie whispered. "Just press back against the wall, and I'll get the suitcases."

She was proud of how she'd managed that, so early in the morning, pretending to the boy on duty that she was taking them to a forward car. It worked perfectly; she'd had time to scout the cupboards, which were emptier now because the train would be reprovisioned in Budapest, and she had found an undercupboard with the requisite space.

And now they waited, as the washer-boys noisily rinsed the luncheon dishes, as the chefs shouted back and forth instructions for the preparation of the evening meal, as the sound of the clacking wheels slowed imperceptibly, and the wail of the train whistle announced they had reached the outskirts of the city.

In the frenzy to get things done before the train came to a halt, no one in the kitchen took notice of them. Or, Darcie thought, no one cared.

She edged her way to a small side window in the pantry. Almost there. Just a few minutes more, and they'd be off and gone.

She turned to Con to tell him—and she saw him out of the corner of her eye: the man with the burning eyes, coming at Con, a knife in his hand from across the kitchen car.

No. No. No. No!

"Con . . . !" she screamed as she hurled herself at him. "Get down . . . ! Damn it, get *down* . . . !"

She rammed him against the opposite wall just as their nemesis threw the knife. It hit a cabinet door, just above their heads.

She heard the babble of voices behind her and shouts and scuffling.

She pulled herself away from Con, and helped him to his feet, just as the train steamed to a jolting stop and everyone lurched off-balance again.

Where was the man? The chefs and assistants had him pinned to the floor, kicking and cursing, and struggling to get free.

She took all that in with one lightning glance, and the lethal dagger just above her head. She didn't even think. She grabbed it, and thrust it into the waistband of her skirt, and then she picked up the suitcases and grasped Con's hand.

"Darcie . . ." *Useless. Helpless. At the mercy of sound.* He held onto her hand like a lifeline.

"Shhh—It was the man . . . and we have to go— *now . . .*"

She picked the first door in the pantry that looked likely, and thanked the fates when it opened onto a narrow passage that led to the loading dock.

She took one look behind her to see if anyone were following, and then she kicked into a run and they were off and gone.

From that point until they reached Istanbul, everything was a blur. They took a cab from the South station to the East. They got second-class passage on a train that left in the morning for Belgrade. There, they connected with the Venice Express which went through to Istanbul.

Everywhere, she looked for the man with the burning eyes, certain he followed them, and that they could never escape him.

"He wants the diamond," Darcie said tiredly, as they huddled against the leather banquette in their sleeping car. She had laid the various foods she'd saved on the table, and she was encouraging him to eat when neither of them had an appetite.

"He wants me," Con said, "dead or alive."

That was worse. She refused to consider it. "Eat something."

"You eat. You need your strength."

"Hogwash."

"And what am I good for, Darcie? All I am is a repository, a map to the location of a legend and a dream."

"How long will it take to get there?" she asked, making a feeble joke.

"You have to fall down a rabbit hole, and hope that the queen doesn't take off your head."

"Lavinia," she murmured. *"She* can't be everywhere."

"No. Only her men."

The man with the burning eyes. The thought pursued them as tangibly as their nemesis, as the train steamed eastward.

Istanbul in the bright white hot light of the afternoon.

She had never felt such heat. It settled on her like a second skin and seeped into her pores. She felt as if she would melt under the relentless sun and that she would just be absorbed in the streets of the city.

It was a place where old and new existed side by side, domes and minarets interspersed with modern European architecture, and ringed by avenues lined with towering palms and enclosed by a wall that seemed to both contain and intensify its contradictions.

The Bosphorus glittered on the horizon, merging with the cloudless blue sky, and the sun beat down mercilessly on whitewashed houses crammed in narrow alleyways that led through the city's native bazaars.

It was here they were headed, after debarking from the train.

"There isn't a vendor in the *souk* who won't bargain and buy," Con said, "and we'll be able to sell some more jewelry. Although—we should register at the hotel first. The Pera Palace will do. It's a little further from the market, but the price is better."

And had she not known she was in heat-drenched Istanbul, she would have thought she was in a luxurious European hotel where they would be waited on hand

and foot and she could have soap and a bath and soft cotton sheets.

And she could have *him*.

They stored the suitcases in the room, and went back out into the sun-baked streets, as visible a target as the sky.

Con told her what they needed: the shrouding tunic and veil of the submissive woman, and the cloak and headdress of the dominating male. Heavy boots for protection and walking. Henna to dye their skin so they would blend into the crowd.

Even dressed like this, she didn't think the disguises would work. He was far too dependent, she was nowhere near enough subdued.

But he knew the language of the *souk,* and the ways of the moneylenders and the thieves. And he knew how to get around the vendors' obvious distaste of showing their wares to a woman, so by the end of the day, he had accomplished all he wished.

Shockingly, converting the jewelry to cash had been the easiest of the transactions once he had garbed himself in desert dress.

He told them he was a trader of white women, and he was taking her to Baghdad, with a dowry of diamonds for which he now needed cash.

Pretend. She had to force herself to act submissive, standing as the moneylenders examined her, with her hands tied behind her and her eyes downcast.

It was enough. "They said you were very beautiful for a Western woman," he told her as they returned to the hotel. "They deeply pitied me for my affliction. They paid me extra in sympathy, the bastards, because Allah would never grant me the blessing of seeing your unusual blue eyes. They envied the man who would buy you. They offered to top whatever his offer might be."

She didn't see the humor. She was sapped by then, utterly wretched in the heat, and the Pera Palace looked like heaven in the sweltering afternoon sun.

They ordered bathwater as they came into the hotel, and dinner, to be brought to the room.

"All I want to do is take off my clothes and lay naked in a pool of water," Darcie said, throwing herself down on the luxurious bed.

It was a very westernized room, designed to cater to travellers on the Orient Express. There was a proper bed, a commodious wooden dresser, two chairs and a table for in-room dining, a cool tile bath, luxurious carpeting, shuttered windows instead of the ubiquitous latticework that could be seen everywhere else; the only thing that differentiated it from a hotel in Mayfair was the godawful heat.

And she supposed, as she watched Con prowl the room still dressed in his *aba*, she might just as well get undressed; there was no question of modesty, there was just the everlasting heat and her feeling that this journey had not yet begun.

She divested herself of everything but her camisole and her drawers, and folded the clothes neatly on the bed.

"This is what we're going to do," Con said, pausing by the shuttered window, and staring out of it as if he could see the streets of the city below. "We're going to disguise you as a man."

"What?!"

"I'd wear women's clothes if I thought I could get away with it, but I'm too tall by Eastern standards, whereas you are approximately the right height for a man."

"And how will we diminish your height?"

"I'm feeling extremely diminished already, Darcie."

Ah! She felt the pinch and emotional sting of those words. Now was not the time to argue with him. And she didn't want to. She wanted something else from him altogether.

"That's a good plan," she agreed.

"It's reasonable, given the circumstances, and it'll allow us to disappear in the crowd. We shouldn't stay here more than just tonight. We'll outfit ourselves for the remainder of the trip tomorrow in the market. We have about another two weeks' journey to Lahore. And I think we'll take the train through to Baghdad."

"But the question is, did *he* get off the train in Budapest and follow us here?"

He sat down heavily in one of the chairs by the window. "Possibly. I keep forgetting Lavinia. Maybe she has operatives everywhere from here to the border. We'll just have to proceed as if she does."

Dinner arrived then, and a queue of servants bearing water carafes on their shoulders, which they poured into the shallow bath, while Darcie huddled under the blankets until they were gone.

And then she immediately darted into the bathroom and knelt by the tub. "Oh God, that looks good," she sighed, trailing a hand in the warm water and then flicking it in Con's face. He smiled, a little.

"Enjoy it. We won't see a bath for another month."

"I'm going to eat first."

"Feast away; you won't get a decent meal either."

She came back into the room and sat down at the table. There was wine and a samovar of tea; lamb in kebobs, rice and beans, a roasted chicken, cheese and fruits. She laid everything out for him, and then poured herself some tea, and some wine for him.

"We can toast the success of the journey," she said. "We're close to the end of the journey, aren't we?"

He didn't answer. He lifted his goblet. "I'll toast to the journey, Darcie. I couldn't tell you where it's going to end."

She didn't like that, but she clinked her cup with his goblet and sipped the tea thoughtfully. There would be an end, she thought, the end *she* wanted, the one that wouldn't have the stamp of her father on it, or someone else's needs or desires. She'd saved him for one reason only, and her life—and his came to that—were worth nothing if they returned to England without *The Eye of God.*

The jewel of power. She knew all about that too— about the dreams that made men kill; the legends for which they died. The man with the burning eyes was counting on that; and Lavinia, so far in the background now as to seem negligible, was gambling on it too.

That didn't mean the threat she posed wasn't there. Lavinia wanted *The Eye of God,* and she wanted Con dead. And she yearned for the child of Roger's blood, and to have Darcie's head.

Two treasures for the House of Pengellis, to bejewel her crown. Time and distance meant nothing to her. However long it took, whatever she had to do, Lavinia would wait the course. Lavinia had patience. Seven years, she'd waited like Lot's wife for Con to give up the prize. What was a half year more to accomplish Con's demise?

But always, when she thought about Lavinia, she felt a sense of urgency, as if the mere conjuring of her name made her a tangible presence to be reckoned with.

A gull screamed outside the window and she felt a chill course all over her body. She pushed away her plate, her appetite gone, and she saw that Con had hardly eaten either.

"If we could leave tonight, I would," he said suddenly. "But it's dark now . . ."

"Yes."

"It's dark everywhere," he murmured. "God, I would give my soul for a moment of light."

"Don't say that."

"Perpetual darkness, Darcie. It's like being dead."

"Not if we bring back the diamond."

"You have no idea what lies ahead."

"I've climbed mountains, Con. I've gone without food. I've shivered in snowstorms. I've been thought buried for good. You were absolutely right. There's no difference."

She watched him wrestle with his anger, his frustration, his need.

"You should have left me at the bordello."

"I was meant to find you."

"Oh Jesus, Darcie."

"Explain why it was me then. Explain all of this."

"I listened to a lunatic."

"I saved you. I brought you back. And now we're both going to be wealthy as kings. What's wrong with that?"

"That simple."

"Absolutely." She knew; she remembered. There was nothing like the feeling of hitting the strike, finding the vein and bleeding the wealth into your pockets as fast as it would flow.

Nothing like it.

"All about the diamond."

"I never lied about that," she murmured. That was skirting it, she thought. That was paring it down to the extreme. She wondered if he'd have been as willing to come with her initially if he hadn't known about the child.

This was meant to be. With every gambler's instinct,

she believed it. She was as bad as Lavinia, she thought. However long it took, whatever she had to do . . . she was going to get him through.

"No. You never did."

"You want it, too."

"It will change nothing for me."

"It will get you back your life, Con."

"And what life was that, Darcie? The one where I spent seven years in a dungeon? Or the years I spent searching for *The Eye of God*? Whose life will be resurrected? Mine? Or yours? I think we know the answer."

"Don't." Oh God, she hated this. She didn't want to hear this.

"Oh, no, Darcie, why shouldn't you live with this too: you may walk away a wealthy woman. But I'll always be in the dark."

Always the dark. It was like the symbol of their quest. She lay beside him in the dark, damp from her bath, naked in the sultry heat, listening to the faint street sounds that echoed up through the open window.

Life in the dark. She heard him in the bath, the soft lapping of the water as he got out of the tub. His hesitant step as he made his way back toward the bed.

In the dark. Always in the dark.

Feeling for the edge of the bed. Feeling for his life. *In the dark.*

How had be survived?

No help wanted or needed. Forever.

No . . . !

She felt his weight depress the mattress, as he settled in beside her.

Wet. Naked. Delicious notions. Luscious words.

But the heat was so oppressive, even in the dead of

night, and the sheen of moisture from her bath had already evaporated.

She didn't want to move.

She wanted him to move, to want her, to take her, and to remove the sting of his ugly words.

In the dark.

Where nothing was seen, and everything could *be.*

Arousing, lying naked and hot next to him in the dark. All she had to do was reach out her hand. She could take him, and he would come.

She lay tense as a bowstring beside him, her muscles as taut as her swelling desire.

All he had to do was touch her, and she would come.

In the dark of the night, when all things were possible, he came to her, slipping sleekly and silently between her legs, embedding himself in her forgiveness and her heat.

It was just the way she wanted it: forceful, hot, focused, and *there.* She cradled him between her legs, wanting to keep him safe and sheltered inside her forever.

But in the dark, she had to learn, nothing was safe, not even her.

He took her with the fury of a sandstorm. He swirled all over her, his mouth, his hands insatiable, primal, raw; his penis centering within her, deep, throbbing, elemental as stone.

And she threw herself against it. She clung to it. She willingly gave herself up to it in a bone-crackling free fall to oblivion.

And that was all it took: a sultry night, a naked man, and the benediction of the dark to cover her, and absolve her of her sins.

Thirteen

They slipped away at the break of day, leaving everything behind that wasn't necessary.

They had arisen early, before dawn, to dress, to pack away their belongings, and by the light of a candle, to remove the stones of the remaining jewelry from their settings which now sat in just one of the pouches that Darcie pinned to the camisole she wore under her tunic.

Everything they were taking with them, they tied under their tunics in bundles made from their underclothing and sheets. It amounted to very little: a change of clothes, soap, the remaining cheeses and breads, the dagger.

She had to carry the dagger. "We will need the dagger," Con told her, even as she recoiled from the thought of touching it again. She had consigned it among her underclothes in the dresser, but in the dim secret light of the candle, as they finished packing, she finally took a good look at it.

It was a good six inches long with a short gold-tipped handle of black obsidian. And it was sharp; sharp as a wound, its tip honed to a fine icy point, as deadly as the man who had carried it.

Reluctantly, she added it to her bundle and tied it around her waist and then they were ready.

They were going one more time to the *souk*, where

they would trade the gold settings for the provisions they needed on this part of the trip.

She made a terrible-looking man, she thought as she caught a fleeting glance of herself in a hallway mirror. Especially when she felt so all-consumingly female. It seemed to her that everyone could tell just by a casual glance at her features, and that the dye she had applied to her skin was not enough to obscure her femininity or her eyes.

But Con was another matter altogether; in his head-dress and cloak, he looked like a desert brigand, born to the saddle and the sand. At the very least, he blended in with the passersby with much more ease than she. It was the unfamiliar feel of the boots, the trousers, and the headdress, set low on her forehead as a precaution to shield her distinctive eyes. And the dagger, bound into its makeshift sheath. Maybe the dagger made her feel the most uncertain of all.

Nevertheless, as they made their way through the narrow streets toward the market, she felt more hopeful than she had in days. It was just a matter of hours now until they were on their way.

He took care of business quickly. Now that she was outfitted as a man, there were no questions asked. As they'd arranged, she communicated with him by signal, kept her eyes down, her senses keen, and counted the money with the skeptical eye of a moneylender.

They came away with hundreds of piastre notes, and food and drink, and he'd bought a revolver, a necessary precaution against desert raiders. After, they purchased third-class seats on the train to Basrah, a two-day journey from there.

From Basrah, they caught the steamer *Magid* for the three-day trip down the Tigris River to Baghdad. Here, there was some luxury, with *hamals* to serve breakfast, and a constant river view of endless muddy brown plains, mud huts and tent villages at intervals in the distance, and strings of camels and horses plodding along the horizon.

They passed a military post and countless marshes, and places with Biblical names, and faster, fleeter sailboats raced the steamer downstream while women and children waved from the shore.

And he could see none of this, Darcie thought, as she walked Con around the deck on the second morning after breakfast. To live a life not being able to see any of this.

She closed her eyes to try to imagine it; but all she could sense was the bright relentless sunlight reflecting off the river, and the presence of people she couldn't see.

Buried in darkness. Walking death. Take back your life. The part you can't see.

She felt someone knock against her shoulder, hard, and she opened her eyes. But whoever had jostled her had merged among the crowd at the rails watching the scenery, except for one lone anonymous figure on the hurricane deck who seemed to be watching *her.*

Baghdad in the morning, under the glow of an orange sun. A panoply of mosques and minarets, bridges and boats, golden domes and orange groves, and date gardens as the boat steamed slowly into the harbor.

A phalanx of officials and porters to greet them. Offers of transportation and guides for hire. A swirl of color and noise and crowds so close-packed, it was impossible to see anything.

"What do we do now?" Darcie whispered under the babble of voices.

"We go to one of the Mission Houses. We'll have a

room for the night, and they'll help with letters of transit and supplies."

They still had to get past the officials who routinely examined the passengers' baggage, that easily done by offering a bribe, and then they were ferried to shore.

They passed through the Custom House with no problem and engaged one of the eager young boys who were hawking their services to take them to the Mission House. There, they were provided with accommodations which were little more than dormitories set up in a basement beneath the mission, and the price of admission was a donation and their presence at the evening service.

In the morning, the mission doctor set about helping those who were travelling to the interior obtain the necessary papers, equipment and guides.

"All of which is very expediently done when you have money," Con said wryly as the number of piastre notes and krans diminished drastically.

"I would kill for a bath," Darcie muttered.

"I warned you."

Their guide, Karun, provided the mules they would need for their journey over the mountains to Isfahan. They scoured the market for trunks and tents, sheepskin coats and boots, *dhurries* to sleep on, cooking apparatus and food.

"But note, everything of value is brought from the market to the home of the prospective buyer," Con told her. "The upper castes do not come out to shop here."

And they travelled, making around fifteen miles a day, over rough roads, camping by the side of mud villages by night, passing caravans of voyagers like themselves, and bedouins seeking rest, walking into the endless expanse of desert toward the mirage of the mountains in the distance.

And Con saw none of it. He felt the heat of day and the cold of night, and he walked quickly and efficiently, for he held in his memory the places he'd travelled all those years before.

They began the ascent of the mountain two days later, and into the rain, and camping in the mud, and making do with little graces, like having water for tea. They huddled at night under their sheepskin coats on their muddied *dhurries*, and they hardly slept at all.

Karun tended mules and set up the tents, took his turn at watch, and was as taciturn as a rock.

They pressed on. Higher and higher, colder and colder, until nothing could be seen but sand and sky, and mud and brush. And onward, over rock and soil, ravines and hillocks, until they breasted the pass that would bring them to the other side and prepared to go over the bridge.

Karun took the mules across first, with their gear. The sun was just setting; he stood motionless at the end of the bridge, his body limned against the purpling light.

"It is safe," he called. "You can come."

Oh, but the fall on the one side was steep, and twilight was coming fast. It was the end of the world. Darcie felt it in her bones. She stepped onto the narrow edge of the footbridge, with Con right behind her, and slowly eased her way along the rocky ledge.

There was brush and scrub to hang onto, but it was even more difficult with Con gripping her hand and slowing her as he felt his way.

And then the wind whipped up with a drizzling rain.

On the other side, Karun waited as they shuffled cautiously across the bridge.

"Only a little, m'em. Just a little more."

She looked up as she heard his voice, and she saw him at the other edge, waiting for them, his eyes burning, his hands tensing for the confrontation to come.

She stopped abruptly. *"Oh my God*—Con . . . it's *him—* it's Karun . . ."

He heard the terror in her voice. "Darcie—the dagger . . ."

"Oh dear Lord, I *can't* . . ."

"You have to . . ."

"He's coming toward us."

"He'll kill us. Darcie—throw the dagger . . ."

His voice was so calm in her ear, as if he had no idea of the danger. As if a wrong step wouldn't hurtle them over into the ravine, and death.

Karun paced slowly toward her.

No words needed. No choices. They couldn't back up, they couldn't go forward. They couldn't escape, one way or the other. It was the dagger or nothing.

She slipped her hand under her tunic and pulled it from its sheath just as Karun lunged threateningly toward them.

She lifted the dagger.

He stopped abruptly, balancing himself against the rock wall with his right hand. There was no doubt he recognized it. "Ahh . . ." His voice was guttural, cruel, different from the tone of sailor and cabman. "But you know—you cannot kill me . . ."

She felt the horror right through to her bones, and she grasped the dagger in her shaking hand by the tip just the way he had on the train. He watched her, with that feral cunning, looking for that telling moment of hesitation, marking her weakness, sapping her fight.

"I can try . . ." she hissed but she couldn't steady her hand; she was never going to be able to use it. Not accurately.

And he knew it.

"Use it." Con's voice in her ear.

Oh God.

"Kill him." The desert bandit, merciless at the kill.

"I *can't.*" The dagger wobbled in her hand.

"Do it, Darcie—or we die."

He couldn't see the man; but he sensed death a foot-step away.

"You are doomed," Karun intoned. "You won't es-cape. Wherever you are, I will come for you." He started toward her again. "I come for you now . . ."

"Noooooo . . . !" she shrieked and hurled the dagger straight at his face, at the burning eyes that reflected the fires of hell.

He stopped short, shocked, and clamped his hand over his forehead, where the dagger protruded like an-other evil eye. He looked at her disbelievingly, his eyes two dark pools of malevolence and hatred, and he stepped threateningly toward her, blood spurting from between his fingers.

"No . . ." the word was a gurgle as blood spumed up from his mouth. "No . . ." as if he were invincible and it wasn't possible. *"NOOOO . . . !"* he shrieked, and then he dropped to his knees and with a keening wail, he pitched over the side of the bridge and into the void.

The rest, after that, was easy. They joined a caravan going through Isfahan to Kandahar, a border town in Afghanistan. They stayed but two days in Isfahan, taking time only to find a place to bathe, to rest their mules, and to buy new rugs, bedding, candles, and a fresh store of food, including tins of preserved meat, tea, flour and rice.

Now Darcie began feeling again that sense of urgency. She had been numb since she knifed the man with the burning eyes. She refused to believe he was dead, even after that fall off the cliff. Nothing was certain, not after everything they had seen.

But surely they were less vulnerable among the travel-lers in the *caravanserai*. Safety in numbers, and among men. The leader of the *caravanserai* thought her an ef-

feminate and managing young man and called her
mast—curdled milk—because she was always sour and
bossed around the tall *malek,* her chief.

It was saner to be in company as they crossed mountains and borders and fended off marauding thieves;
Con knew just enough of the language to have some
conversation, and they found one or two others who
were interested in going on to trade in Lahore.

They stayed three days in Kandahar, and went forward
finally, to Lahore, just inside the border of India.

There they left the traders of the *caravanserai,* and
there, before them, was the end of their journey, and
there, suddenly, they were on their own.

*God's tears. Somewhere it was written that diamonds con-
tained the essence of God, and that when God created man, his
tears of joy embedded themselves in the ground to solidify into
gemstones, superior to any other on earth.*

*Somewhere, in the vast reaches of all the research he had done,
the myths he'd studied, the clues he'd discarded, the theories he'd
evolved, he had determined the location of the fabled Valley of
Diamonds, from which Scheherazade spun the tale of the eagles
and the sheep and valley walls so steep that no man could climb
them.*

*There, on the fringes of the magic carpet of her thousand and
one nights, did she weave a story for the ages, a valley floor
adrift with diamonds and no man brave enough or clever
enough to come and take them away.*

*And then he had come, and he had seen, but he had not been
clever enough to remove them. And because it was a question of
balance, penance had to be paid.*

*The indomitable force and the unspeakable evil . . . perfect
in nature, and blessed in all things . . .*

* * *

They caught him in Srinagar, watching for him, waiting for the moment he must surface to buy supplies. He should have stayed in the mountains forever, Christ in the wilderness, knowing he was about to be betrayed.

But he had thought they were far away, and as a man alone, he was safe.

A man with a secret is never safe.

In the deep of the night, they came for him in the *dak* bungalow where he took his rest. They caught him sleeping, they caught him off guard, and they caught him as neatly as a spider catches a fly.

After that, the days and nights were a blur. They'd planned everything; the hell-hole of his prison pit had been prepared beforehand, and when, after inducements and torture, he refused to reveal the location of the valley, they incarcerated him without a blink.

And then time had no meaning at all.

Somewhere outside of Srinagar. They'd been so wrong.

Now he was here, everything came rushing back like a tidal wave. He needed to think, to eat, to sleep.

And so the tall impassive *malek* and his sour-faced secretary who never looked you in the eye took a *dak* bungalow along the trunk line to Srinagar, to spend a profitable two days in sleep.

Darcie was certain she'd never sleep again, even though the hardships of the journey had taken a toll. She was sunburned, she was aching and sore, and the burden of being Con's eyes had taken a lot out of her and she felt exhausted to the core.

If only she didn't see that man every time she closed her eyes.

Con had no compunction whatsoever about sleeping. He was dead tired, and not even thinking what awaited them. Two rupees was a small price to pay for a measure

of security to obtain some rest. And with that, for a nomi-
nal sum, they were served dinner as well.

Roasted chicken, stuffed eggplant, baked custard—a
feast after what they had endured on the trip.

"How long must I remain *Mast-sahib* then?" Darcie
asked, as she devoured the chicken and custard.

"We'll continue on with it, I think. Along the border,
there are enough traders going back and forth that we
won't be conspicuous."

"And we're going—where?"

"Up into Kashmir, in the Dhambra Mountains."

*Dear God—more mountains. More climbing. More hard-
ships. She was tired of it, suddenly; she wanted desperately to
go home.*

Except there was no home, for either of them.

"When?"

"In a day or two."

She hated those words. She hated the waiting. The
faster they travelled, the sooner they'd get there, and
they'd been travelling for two months at least.

But time meant nothing here. Not to him, in the darkness. And not to her in a place where it was measured
by how many miles you could make in a day.

At least they would be going up to Srinagar by train,
travelling third class, wedged among fifty commuting lo-
cals, assorted livestock and bundles of all shapes and
sizes, going first through Sialkot and along the Jhelum
River up into the mountains to Srinagar in the Vale of
Kashmir.

Srinagar was the land of hills and houseboats, where
the *pukka-sahibs* came to escape the summer heat. But in
the off-season, there were plenty of houseboats available
to rent, and they found one on the Nagin Lake, a short

distance from the town, that came with a house servant, a cook and a *wallah* to drive the *tonga*.

It was Darcie's idea of heaven: the lulling rock of the boat on the gentle tide of the lake. The views, the vista, the weather, the servants, the conveniences.

Con however seemed coiled and tense, ready to spring, primed to explode. "Two weeks," he said. "Two weeks at the most is all we'll be here." He was amazingly calm given how close they were to the objective. It was all swirling around him, the agony and the urgency. The time had come. The balance had shifted. He was meant to be there. She'd been right all along.

"Darcie . . . !" He turned from the window where he'd been staring into his own dark soul.

"I'm here."

"Tomorrow, you will go into town and you will seek out the *box-wallah* called Sidhu Hamil. And you will tell him this: the *Chowkidar* awaits him. He will know what to do."

He was an unprepossessing man, an itinerant peddler, and people in the town called him either a beggar or a saint. He was a man who had given his allegiance to Con Pengellis all those years ago. He knew how to appease the gods of the mountains, how to go, what to take, and Darcie was instructed to expend on him one of the small diamonds so he could purchase their stake.

They were on their way again two days later, up on the snow-covered track toward Gilgit, over the Burzil pass, by mule and by foot, over goat trails and icy rivers, and death defying ravines.

Up up up to the mystical juncture of four mountains, the Hindu Kush, the Himalaya, the Dhambras and the Nanga Parbat, camping under sheepskin-shrouded tents, warmed by two portable stoves, cradled in the howl of the wind.

"Jesus was said to have walked here," Sidhu said in his thin high voice as they drank tea after their meager dinner on the second night, "in the valley, in the grotto where *The Eye of God* rests, and it is said that this diamond is blessed."

"But there's no proof He ever passed here," Con said, his tone dry. "It's part of the legend that just seems to grow."

Sidhu shook his head. "You must believe, *sahib,* and with that belief will come success."

"There's a pass four miles ahead that they call the Top of the World, and from there, you can just see the Panput Valley. It looks inhospitable, impossible to negotiate. A steep fall into a thousand trees."

"The valley?" Darcie whispered.

"The valley. My Valhalla, Darcie. The palace of *The Eye of God.*"

He had marked the place on an outcropping of rock on the ridge at the Top of the World all those years ago. But seven years had effected many changes, the most discouraging of which was that the marking was almost completely effaced. They spent a frustrating half a day looking for it in the midst of the swirling snow. And then, the growth in the valley looked so thick and impenetrable, Sidhu didn't see how they would make it down.

They waited until the snow abated, and then they descended by ropes pulled tight around the rock-bound trees at the edge of the track. Sidhu went first, Con next, and Darcie after.

Slowly slowly down the face of the valley wall, certain no one could follow them, they levered themselves down thick rough hemp ropes, their legs bouncing against the scrub and boulders, sending little rock landslides down into the valley below them.

The sky darkened over, as if the gods were displeased.

Darcie felt her muscles cramp in her legs and arms, and the fear of death invaded her soul. She didn't dare look up, couldn't bear to look down, had no idea whether Sidhu or Con had reached the ground below.

And how would they return? she wondered frantically. *What if they could never get out? Dear God, she couldn't think this way. She would let go and she would die, and someone else would reap the rewards of finding The Eye.*

It was enough to keep her going in the face of her terror, the cold, the impossible descent, with her grip on the rope her sole lifeline. She had nothing else, only this. She *had* to come through.

"Darcie . . . !" Con, below her.

"I'm here . . . !" She wasn't there; she floated above them, lightheaded, surrounded by angels, heading toward the light.

"Come, *memsahib,* come." Sidhu's voice slicing through the icy air.

"I'm coming." She focused on it like a beacon. Just a little bit more. A few feet more. Ever more.

"Come—" Sidhu's thin musical voice pulling her on, "you are almost here . . ."

Almost here . . . she could let go, she had nothing to fear—

She relinquished her grip, her fingers stiff with the cold, and she fell heavily to the ground, she heard Con's voice above her: "Jesus God—the baby . . . !" and she gave up her soul.

Fourteen

Silence. An all-consuming heavenly silence.

She lay cradled in a bed of leaves and scrub at the base of the valley wall, and contemplated heaven. Sidhu knelt beside her, touching her gently in various places.

She opened her eyes in reaction to the pressure of his fingers at a point on her belly. Con stood, leaning against a tree, a couple of yards away, his expression stony.

"An—*memsahib* awakens." Sidhu removed his hand and pulled her coat over her. "All is well."

"Is it?" Con murmured. "Is all well, Darcie?"

Her answer stuck in her throat. She struggled to a sitting position, taking in the details around her: the soft needles on the valley floor; the stones, the trees, the sense of desolation which only mirrored how she felt.

And somewhere, in this witch's forest, riches and dreams. They were that close, and something like this was going to get in the way.

"You didn't jar anything, Darcie? There isn't any bleeding? Any evidence of *anything* wrong?"

She swallowed convulsively. Sidhu must have noticed; Sidhu must have said something. "I'm fine," she managed.

"And how is the baby?"

The loaded question. She could have killed the baby. She had fallen hard, on her back, and all she felt was an ache at the base of her spine. A jolt like that could have injured the baby.

She looked up at Sidhu, whose eyes were sharp and comprehending, and she knew he knew. And something in his expression told her not to dissemble.

"There is no baby," she whispered.

The silence fell like a stone. Sidhu rocked back on his heels and bowed his head. She couldn't even look at Con.

"No baby." He was looking into the darkness, and seeing the limits of her soul.

"There was never a baby," she said stoically. "Lavinia wanted a baby. And I wanted to save my life. The lie kept me alive long enough to escape. And long enough to find you."

He was still silent.

She wouldn't have believed the story either. The whole thing, every detail, true as it was, still sounded like a lie. And the only lie was really the truth.

"Scheherazade," he muttered. "Jesus God—more stories. Do you never end, Darcie? You really are something."

She bristled. "And you are damned fortunate I found you, and even more fortunate that I wanted this . . ."

"This is all you want, Scheherazade, but you've never lied about that."

She supposed he thought that admission gave her something. But it wasn't enough—when she was on the verge of losing everything. "They were going to kill me."

And they'd come all the way to Srinagar to kill him, he

thought. *What wouldn't a person do to stay alive? Who knew better than he?*

He didn't have to be so obdurate. They were rogues, the two of them, and they were not averse to using any weapon they had at hand. He understood that. He just didn't comprehend why the lie was so devastating to him.

But everything was strange. The scents, the sounds, the feeling in the air . . . and the lie. He had no more time to deal with the lie. They could sort all that out later.

"Lavinia could still kill you," he said brutally.

"And she would, after I had given birth to that baby."

That stopped him. There was something about that he knew he should consider, but he couldn't take the time. Time suddenly was more precious than diamonds. He couldn't see the light but he knew it was lowering faster than they had planned.

And they still had to cut through the brush to the excavation.

"We have work to do," he said abruptly. "Sidhu."

"Sahib?" He listened to a barrage of instructions and then turned to Darcie. "Come. I will lead, you will follow. It is but a short distance from here. And we must think about the time—now time is fleeting."

Of everything she had imagined, she could not have conceived of this: one nondescript stone of hundreds, backed up the valley wall.

She couldn't have told one from the other, but Sidhu could. It was the one stone with markings cut by wind and weather, visible only to the knowledgeable eye. Now Sidhu's eyes. And that stone blocked a tunnel cleverly cut into the valley wall.

Uncover the tomb and find resurrection . . .

Together, they rolled away the stone to reveal the gaping tunnel entrance.

Sidhu raised his hand in benediction. "It is good, *sahib*. And now it is time." He handed a lantern to Darcie. *"Memsahib*—please to go first."

"Me?" She was flabbergasted. And scared out of her wits. "But—"

"Sidhu remains on guard," Con said. "He cannot enter a place of the infidel. And we don't have that much time."

So . . . she was going to be first to crawl into a tunnel that no one had breached in seven or more years. She swallowed the clog in her throat. She'd wanted this. And she'd been in tighter places down in the mines in Colorado. What was here that could touch her?

She knelt beside the entrance to the tunnel and immediately a flat musty scent assaulted her nose. She held up the lantern that Sidhu had lit for her. It looked to be a fairly short tunnel. She saw a sharp drop about fifty feet in. And then—what?

Nothingness. Everything about this quest was connected to the dark and nothingness . . .

"I'll be right behind you," Con said. "There's a place about a dozen yards in where the tunnel breaks. You'll see it. I'll talk you through it."

That didn't reassure her.

Going into the dark. Endless dark. On her knees and slowly pushing the lantern forward, the light reflecting back into her eyes. She might as well be blind.

"I'm behind you," Con said as he grasped the hem of her tunic and followed her in.

An awkward eight-legged humping monster making its way through the tunnel . . . and the aura of evil washing over them a dozen feet within the tunnel entrance. Cold. Musky. Murderous.

"Con"

"Keep going—"

Evil wasn't tangible; it didn't whip you in the face. And there was nothing to grasp onto. She couldn't shine her light on it. She wanted to back out of the tunnel and never look back.

"Move, Darcie . . . !"

He felt it too. She heard it in his voice; the evil was immutable, spreading all over and around them like a cocoon.

"I can't . . ." she protested.

"Darcie—we're that close. *That* close."

It wasn't worth it, it wasn't. "But Con—there's something . . ."

"Defeat it."

He knew this thing.

He pushed her forward relentlessly, and she moved involuntarily, creeping creeping forward, with his hand on her derrière, pushing, goading, coaxing, inch by malignant inch.

And only the pulsating dark and the bright glaring light before her eyes.

And that terrorizing evil somewhere in the dark.

"We're almost there," he whispered.

"Almost where?"

"At the drop. Be ready for the drop. Just swing your legs over. It's about four feet, and we'll be able to stand up."

"What aren't you telling me, Con?"

"I'd give my soul to be able to see."

She heard the torment in his voice—and then suddenly, silently, the evil presence laughing at them, mocking them.

"Con . . ."

His voice turned to steel. *"Keep going . . ."*

Her knees turned to jelly. "I can't."

"You will. You *must.*"

She closed her eyes, to close out the presence, to close in his voice and the motivation, the goal. To see what he saw, to know what he knew. In moments, she would see before her eyes the diamond, the mythical, mystical *Eye of God.*

And nothing would prevent it.

But nothing like this lived in a Colorado mine. She had defeated claim jumpers, robbers, outlaws, cheats. Things she understood; things she could see.

She felt the taunting laughter of the presence, and she girded herself, and creeping slowly forward, she continued on. Lantern first, right hand, left knee; left hand, right knee, with Con creeping in tandem right behind her.

She almost fell over the drop. She didn't expect it. Or the presence had distracted her from it.

She put out the lantern and set it onto nothingness, and it fell to the ground.

The presence jeered.

"Quick—over the drop." Con's voice behind her, pushing her on. She swung her legs over and jumped; a moment later he followed her, and they stood crouched, and wary, and determined.

Slowly, she eased into an upright position. The sense of evil was palpable here. She picked up the lantern, relit it, and took Con's arm, and pulled him to his feet.

"Now what?" Her voice shook.

"Straight ahead."

She lifted the lantern. "There is no straight ahead. It's a sheer wall."

"Then we move the headstone of the tomb."

She saw it then, the subtle fit of the stone against stone into the wall.

"Help me then."

The presence was almost unbearable as they each took a side of the stone and pushed and shifted it until it moved.

"It doesn't want us in there," Darcie whispered.

"It has a lot to lose."

They stood at the entrance to the second tunnel, tempted and afraid.

"At the end of this tunnel," Con said, his voice barely above a breath, "is the realization of your dreams."

But even that was not enough to galvanize her. She held up the lantern and swung it around. There was nothing in front of her but darkness, and the heavy sense of evil waiting.

"It's blocking the way."

"We'll pass through it."

"What if it's *him?*"

"He can't stop us. He hasn't yet."

Con leaned against her, forcing her to step over the threshold. And then they were in, past the barrier, into the evil, and moving slowly and hesitantly forward into the dark.

The sense of evil followed, a weight on their shoulders.

"There are stone steps, about a hundred feet down. Watch it."

She held the lantern low to the ground. "All right." She thought she sounded calm, but her voice came out breathless. "Take my arm."

She closed her eyes for a moment, again to try to imagine what he was seeing, what he was thinking. *Darkness. The unending, unnerving silence stretching to infinity. And the air: close, dank, malignant.*

And they were so close. But she hadn't counted on this on-going unspeakable evil. She had thought they'd just walk into a cavern somewhere and pluck the thing up and spirit it away.

Naïve. Foolish. Short-sighted. Dumb. Still hadn't learned that the next big strike never never came easily. That it was always over the hill and the obstacles were almost insurmountable.

And it was always always always buried in the dark.

And for Con, it always would be.

She shivered, in spite of the close musty air.

"Darcie." Con's voice, steely again, set with purpose, his fingers convulsive against her arm. "This is what you wanted. This is why we're here."

"I know." But she'd never felt like this at the kill— wary, reluctant, faltering at the very moment she should pounce.

The evil thing knew it; she felt it all around them, mocking them, provoking them, daring them to go forward and claim the treasure.

"Then *move* . . ."

She moved, holding the lantern in front of her like a shield, one hesitant step at a time with Con draped around her like a cloak. Moved like a snail, moved like a crone who had nothing to live for.

What was wrong with her?

The air was stultifying, the closer they came to the stone steps. She saw them finally just ahead. "We're almost there."

"Go down the steps, Darcie."

She inched toward them, feeling her way in the light as if she were blind. There was something beyond, something below. The thing was waiting. The evil was there.

She paused at the top. The steps descended into darkness.

"Just go," Con whispered.

They fumbled down the steps together. Steep steps, sharply angled, easy to misstep and fall to eternity. She held onto the wall, she held onto him. And she held onto the thought of what awaited them.

"The tunnel veers to the right at the bottom," Con murmured.

She held up the lantern. To the right, into more ominous darkness, and the suppurating evil.

"You'll see columns of rock. Like guardians at the gate," he went on in an undertone as they shuffled on.

She grabbed his hand as they came into view, a horizontal line of thick, coruscated stalagmites, sentinels of the divine.

"The grotto is just beyond."

She felt a chill down her spine. *This close. Almost there. Steps away. She almost couldn't breathe. The strike of a thousand lifetimes . . . and nothing to stand in their way.*

And then she felt it, a violent swirl of malevolence enveloping them, and blocking their way.

She almost dropped the lantern; no—*it* almost made her drop the lantern.

"He's here," she hissed.

"He's dead," Con said, his voice like iron. "Keep walking."

She couldn't. She couldn't move; she felt the evil surrounding her, holding her immobile like the tentacles of an octopus.

"I *can't* . . ."

He lost patience. "Then I *will* . . ." He relinquished her arm, stretched out his arms and pushed forward in the dark.

Immediately he felt the wall of resistance.

"*Con—!*" she screamed as he merged with the fog. *Oh dear God—!* She felt the malevolence drain away from her; her body felt boneless, powerless. But she could move. She took an experimental step after him.

"Con . . . !" But he'd disappeared through the columned portal, and all she could see by the light of the lantern was a swirl of turbulence trailing after him, and the dark unknown beyond.

Her heart pounding crazily, she passed through the stone column, holding the lantern in front of her like a talisman.

There—just ahead of her—light . . .

She moved cautiously toward it, through a natural stone arch that framed the entrance to the grotto. The evil was all-pervasive here, its scent strong, awful, fecund, dead. She felt her throat gag, she wanted to turn and run away, and she resisted the impulse with all her might.

She forced herself to creep through the arch. *"Con . . ."* Her whisper reverberated in the stone. She was in what looked like an anteroom, and straight ahead of her, there was yet another arch, and beyond that, the glow.

She felt the evil trying to repulse her, and she pushed against it, her heart constricted with fear. It was so strong, so wicked, so all encompassing, she almost felt she couldn't defeat it.

And then suddenly, maliciously, it released her, and she tumbled into the grotto.

She was enfolded by the light. It seemed to her that the whole cavernous space was infused with light, emanating from *The Eye of God*. The holy grail of a diamond, placed on a ledge that looked like an altar, side by side with a stone of similar proportions and brilliance that was black like the night.

She stepped into the brilliance of the light, she was

enveloped by it, enthralled by it. She felt shocked that the stone was no bigger than a large jelly mould, and then it didn't matter at all. The stone glowed as if something holy were watching over her. She felt a sense of well-being and saneness, as if everything in the world had suddenly come right.

She moved toward it unerringly as if its power pulled her. And she walked willingly into its light.

Con knelt on the ground before it, and leaning over him, subjugating him was the man with the burning eyes. The sailor, the cabman, the guide they'd called Karun. The personification of the evil that saturated the air.

If she moved one step toward the black stone, it would attack her. It would imprison her as it had Con. It wanted to. It wanted to destroy her for what she had inflicted on it.

But she knew, she felt, all she had to do was stay in the light and she would have the power to do battle with the malevolence from there.

But it went even deeper than that entity called Karun. It felt as if it were thundering in the grotto, waiting to erupt from someplace deep in the ground.

The thing called Karun stood over Con menacingly, with some kind of implements in its hand.

And there was a silence like death as it awaited its command.

"Don't move," Con breathed. "Don't say anything and I will tell you the whole story. This is the altar of the dark and the light. The black diamond is called *The Stone of Samael* after the Judge of the Dead. It sits in balance with *The Eye of God,* and they are never to be touched or moved. They neutralize each other, and bring good and evil into harmony. It is said whoever lays eyes on them will be cursed forever."

"As were you," she whispered, stunned to the bone.

"And now," the entity Karun intoned, "you will be damned to eternity."

He lifted the implements and she was shocked to see he held a cleaving tool and a chisel. He whirled and in a heart-stopping moment, in the blink of an eye, he chiseled into the black diamond, set the angle, and struck it with one sharp, awful rap.

"Jesus God . . ." Con breathed in horror. "Oh my God—"

A dark dense foul-smelling fog spumed into the cavern and enveloped them, freezing them in place. And then it moved unerringly to the entity called Karun, and slowly and completely it devoured him.

It hovered, fetid, putrid, all enfolding, obscuring *The Eye of God* and contaminating the air.

It paralyzed them; it rendered them immobile. Almost imperceptibly it began to re-form, the fog gathering into itself in eddying swirls, solidifying, elongating, transmogrifying itself incrementally before their very eyes.

And suddenly something was there: tall, spare, ascetic, cloaked in black, emanating an aura of depravity and ungodliness from every pore.

It was a man—and it was an entity—possessed of sharp, black, piercing eyes that saw everything and missed nothing.

He lifted his bony hand and Darcie recoiled from the malodorous smell that issued from him.

He pointed at Con, and Con felt the power of his diabolic touch. He reacted violently, pushing up from the floor, and tumbling back down again as the entity lowered his hand.

"Who are you?" he demanded sharply. "Who's there?"

"I am called Lazarin," it said, its words measured, its voice raspy and hollow. "And the power of Samael is dispersed upon the land."

It raised his hand again and pointed to Con, and Con felt the repercussions of the heat and soul-sapping energy through to his bones.

"You have transgressed upon the holy place of Samael, and so you will be judged," it intoned, and then it lifted its leonine head for a moment, as if it were listening to some supernatural power.

And then it nodded and turned its burning gaze back to Con.

"I lay my hand upon you, in the name of Samael, and in his name and in the sight of *The Eye of God*, I offer you the gift of your vision. The judgment of the merciful Samael is as follows: that you may know there is good in evil and evil in good."

It walked toward Con, its decaying essence enveloping them, making them sick.

"The decision is yours, infidel," it whispered, making a sign over Con's head. "The hand of Samael is upon you."

"Don't do it . . ." Darcie whispered. "Con . . . don't— you can't see it, it's a walking corpse . . . a phantasm from the grave . . ."

He felt like he was dying, and like he was being reborn. He'd said it over and over—to see again, he would sell his soul. He felt fractured, the way he envisioned Karun had cleft the black stone. His own depravity cracked within him, splitting him down the middle, and he knew that he had made the decision months ago, and that now he was damned, just as the Karun had foretold.

"I will have my sight," he whispered.

"Con . . . !" Darcie shrieked as Lazarin laid his bony

hand on his forehead. "The will of Samael shall be done," he intoned, sketching the sign with his thumb.

Darcie watched, horrified, as Con slumped over at Lazarin's feet.

And then the fog rose up around them, thick, rank, malodorous, foul. It filled the cavern, penetrating every crevice, every pore. It settled on *The Eye of God,* negating its powers. It rendered her helpless in its wake.

She saw Lazarin's burning eyes, warning her, condemning her, damning her through the billowing vapor, and it was the last thing she saw before she crumpled to the ground.

Fifteen

"Memsahib . . . memsahib—" Someone was shaking her. "Please . . . please to wake, memsahib . . ."

She shook her head groggily. She had no idea where she was or who was calling to her. The hand was gentle, respectful, urgent.

"Memsahib . . ."

She brushed the insistent hand away.

"Please—we must go . . ."

She didn't want to go; it seemed to her she was always going and she was tired of it. She just wanted to lie on the soft ground and fall back into her peaceful dreams.

"Memsahib—the sahib still sleeps . . ."

She opened her eyes. Sidhu! And in this sanctuary. She shook her head again, and then struggled to sit up. Something about that was odd and she couldn't remember what.

And Con—oh God—where was Con? But no, he was right there, on the grotto floor beside her, in deep unconscious sleep.

And there was light—but that came from Sidhu's lantern.

She was oriented now, except she couldn't quite remember what had happened. And then she did. The horror. The evil. The scent.

Oh dear God—The diamonds—!

She jumped to her feet and whirled toward the ledge. *The Stone of Samael* was gone.

Everything came back to her then full force. The fog. The entity. The unholy bargain. Con, limp as a puppet, on the ground. And Sidhu beside him, frantically trying to rouse him.

"Sidhu! When did you come?"

"After a day and a night had passed, *memsahib*. And the sky turned black and the mountain gods became angry."

She was stunned. *A day and a night. They'd lost that much time. Always at the mercy of time.*

She rubbed her eyes. *Her* eyes. What about *his* eyes? Surely they had dreamed everything about the ungodly entity. And where was the black diamond? Or had she dreamt that too?

But no, *The Eye of God* was on its resting place, the light around it extinguished. And something had compelled Sidhu to come.

She got down beside him. "Con—" He was so unresponsive.

Sidhu held up his hand. "All will be well, *memsahib.*"

"How?"

"We will make do. I will make a pallet. Come."

She didn't know what was more frightening: leaving Con or going with Sidhu. "I can't leave him. The thing might come back."

Sidhu considered her words. "This is true. I will find the branches. It is daylight, we have time." He picked up his lantern and with it, lit hers. "Take courage, *memsahib*. I will return, soon."

She wrapped her arms around Con as Sidhu disappeared into the darkness, his lantern a faint glow in the distance.

She huddled closer to Con, avoiding the shadows, staring at *The Eye of God.*

Balanced to neutralize evil. Never to be touched or moved.
Cursed forever—
Samael loose upon the land . . .

She shuddered convulsively. Whatever had happened, the black stone was gone. She wondered if she had the nerve to remove *The Eye of God.*

It wasn't that big. It couldn't be that heavy. She could just tie it up in a piece of her underclothing and hide it under her tunic.

She got to her feet, took the lantern, and went over to the ledge.

There was a scorch mark at the place where *The Stone of Samael* had been. *The brand of the Judge of Death . . . ?* And there was nothing left of the sundered stone except several minute slivers of crystal.

She swept them up onto her fingers. All that remained of a horrible dream. She slipped them into the pouch in which she carried the remaining Pengellis diamonds.

And then she considered *The Eye of God.*

Remembered the enfolding light, the warmth, the sense of well-being . . .

She reached out a hand and touched it. *Cool. Smooth. The object of desire. Wealth and riches at her fingertips.*
Did she dare . . . ?

She took it in her hands and lifted it. Just picked it up in her hands as easily as if she were taking a piece of fruit.

She held it up to the lantern light. Nowhere in its depths could she see the light, the power, or the mystical properties of its legend. It looked like less than it was.

Only Con could tell her. She turned to look at him,

still unconscious on the ground. No help there. And a decision to be made before Sidhu returned.

She held it up to the light again, a stone the size of a pineapple in her hand. And then she set it back on the ledge, and removed her tunic, thankful that for this bone-cold journey, she wore several layers of clothing.

Con had insisted on the trousers, and the sheepskin outer clothes. But she'd also worn a shirt and she reached for her shirttail now, and ripped it into a long oblong piece.

That would do. She placed the stone in the center, and tied the ends of the material over it, around it, and finally around her neck and then tucked it into her bosom, where it hung like a third breast.

And not a moment too soon. She heard Sidhu along the passageway, saw his light before he appeared, and then he emerged from the shadows carrying two thick long branches.

He looked immediately at the altar ledge and then back at her and she felt his tacit disapproval.

"It is not for me to say, *memsahib,*" he said finally. "Come—we will remove *sahib's* cloak, and that, with your tunic, should make a pallet strong enough to carry him."

They struggled through the tunnel to the steps, and there, they hauled him upright and got him up the stairs; and then over the drop, and they were careful to take the time to replace the stone at the entrance to the grotto along the way.

With all that, it took two hours before they set him down at the opening of the crawlway to the first tunnel.

"It will be cold tonight, *memsahib.* We will make a fire, and guard the entrance until daylight."

She unwrapped the tunic from under Con's listless body and tucked it around him. She was shaking with fear again. They'd come down to the valley with so little; they'd expected so much. And they'd gotten more than they'd bargained for.

She didn't know how they were going to last the night.

She huddled close to the meager campfire that Sidhu had made, the lump that was *The Eye of God* pressed between her breast and her knees, and the only warmth she felt emanating from the proximity of Con's body.

But the fire and the two lanterns gave this outer cave at least some semblance of safety, and she was grateful for Sidhu's calm presence and his assurances that Con would recover.

Recover what? she wondered as she stared at the fire. *And how much had he already lost?*

"Beware of useless dreams, *memsahib*. They come back to haunt you."

"What if he doesn't awaken?"

"All will be well, *memsahib*. Sidhu assures you."

Sidhu had brought some food into the Valley with them, and he was stirring up a pot of tea on the makeshift campfire. "You will warm yourself with tea. You will turn your thoughts to the future. For good and evil, you carry *The Eye of God, memsahib*. That alone should bless you."

He poured the tea into a tin cup and handed it to her, and then took one for himself.

"Why did you come?" she asked him. "I thought you were not permitted within."

Sidhu shrugged. "Who knows by what method we are called to do anything, *memsahib?*" He handed her a biscuit. "I heard the call to come."

And what had she heard? The call to greed.

"And before—did you assist him?"

Sidhu nodded. "And I owe *sahib* my life."

She bit into the biscuit. It was stale. Dry. It tasted like manna. They were blessed, alive, and removed from the grotto, and all that remained was to get through the night.

"*Memsahib* should sleep."

"I'll keep watch with you."

"No one will find us."

"But the ropes—"

"No, *memsahib*—" He looked at her kindly, the beggar with wise eyes, and said, "—you can rest easy. The enemy has gone."

Or the enemy was herself.

She cradled *The Eye of God* between her breasts and wondered if she should lie. When Con awakened—*if* Con awakened . . .

The tunnel was blocked now; he wouldn't be able to go back. She could just tell him—it would be so tempting to tell him—that both of the diamonds were gone.

A manipulative slicing up of the truth . . . and not the first time she'd ever done it. The stone was so warm between her breasts, so tantalizing . . . as seductive as a lover.

She never heard Con stir.

She would have sworn she hadn't slept.

And she was shocked to find him kneeling beside her, ruthlessly stripping away her clothes.

"What the hell do you think you're doing?" she gasped, batting his hands away. She reared up, half naked, and lunged at him.

"You're a clever bitch, Darcie." He wrestled her back down to the ground again. "Sidhu told me, you thieving hellcat." He pinned her arms mercilessly. "And yes, I can see."

* * *

She sat resentfully across the campfire from him, eye-ing him warily as he cradled *The Eye of God* in his hands.

His gaze was no longer blank; it was sharp, perceptive, keen. He was a different Con Pengellis from the man she had saved. Everything about him now was focused and contained and she, conversely, felt uncertain and constrained.

She didn't like it. It was like the power between them had shifted and she was standing in quicksand and sink-ing fast.

And she hated the way he looked at her across the campfire.

"And what happened to the *black* diamond, did you say?" Even his voice was different, with a tone of con-fidence and command.

"He had to have taken it." This was the third time she had told him and he still didn't believe her. But then, he thought she'd tried to steal *The Eye of God;* Sidhu told him she'd taken it, and then left her at his mercy to gather wood for the campfire, not betraying by a glance or a muscle any astonishment at the fact that Con had regained his sight.

"He cleaved it into two pieces. And when I awoke, it was gone."

"So convenient," he murmured, turning the dia-mond this way and that in his hands. All he had done, all he had suffered to come to this moment, to hold *The Eye of God* in his grasp, and to see in its depths the power and the possibilities. "The entity took it. I won-der why I don't believe you."

He was sharp as a knife now, she thought, and deft at slicing to the quick. This was the Con Pengellis of the portrait, only more mature, honed to an edge, and fully in control.

"And I wonder why you never mentioned it," she

retorted. "All that mystical mumbo-jumbo about upsetting the balance and the stones neutralizing each other . . ."

He looked at her then, a scathing glance that would have frozen stone. "How can we know, Darcie? What do we know, after all? Well, we know how avid you are to possess this stone."

She didn't know *him*—now. He wasn't in the dark anymore. *She* felt unbalanced and out of control, and like she'd been the one who'd been blind.

"We know," he went on inexorably, "you don't scruple to lie. And we surely know you'll do anything to get what you want."

In the dark.

But now he was in the light, and he didn't like what he saw.

She felt raw, slashed, as if he had drawn blood.

"We wouldn't be here if it weren't for me," she shot back. "I think some gratitude is in order."

"Where is the black diamond?" His voice was calm, neutral and laced with steel.

"He took it." *He took everything, in the name of Samael. And she would never get it back.* She remembered the slivers of black stone, tucked in the pouch at her breast. "Look." She unpinned the pouch. "Hold out your hand." *Oh, his hand . . .* She spilled the five remaining small diamonds and the shards of crystal into his palm. "That was all that was left."

"A careless cut," he murmured, pushing aside the diamonds, and picking up one long shard. He held it to the waning campfire light, staring at it for a long time. "But then—maybe it didn't matter." He gave it back to her. "Put it away."

She was pinning the pouch just as Sidhu returned with an armful of wood.

"Dawn approaches, *sahib*," he said, as he knelt to replenish the fire.

"Good. There's just enough time. Get up, Darcie. We're going down to the grotto."

She got slowly to her feet. He still didn't believe her. He picked up a lantern, grasped her arm and propelled her back into the tunnel.

"What a pleasure to be able to see such treacherous footings."

She wrenched her arm away. "And who got you safely through?"

"Who had her own agenda?"

"We are both still in danger," she said grittily.

"So you say. It occurs to me, Miss Darcie, that yours is the only story we know. For example, *I* don't know that it was Lavinia or Roger who imprisoned me. I don't even know that you were married to Roger. I only have your word for it—watch the drop—" as she almost stepped over it and into oblivion, "and we know how good you are at spinning tales."

"I see," she said angrily. "We're going to backtrack over everything that's happened, and then we're going to call me a liar."

"How about a fabricator of truth?"

"How nice you can see that—now."

"I think I was in the dark about a lot of things, Darcie."

"It's a bargain you'll regret."

"Or you will."

They were at the steps then, and he flashed the lantern downward. "You first, Scheherazade. I can't wait to hear what tale you'll tell."

"I'm not going to say a word. You didn't see the thing. You can't know. You made a devil's bargain with an apparition from hell."

"Or maybe, Scheherazade, that was *you.*"

She descended the steps furiously, aware that he thought her perfectly capable of sending him over the edge, and he followed her, holding the lantern low to light the way.

And then to the right, and into the anteroom, through the stone columns and into the grotto. And nowhere was there any overwhelming sense of lurking doom.

Nor was there that blessed light to warm and welcome them. The grotto was cold and soulless. A pagan altar, eons old.

He stepped up to it, holding the lantern over the ledge. There was nothing to indicate that balanced there had been two mythic diamonds. Only the scorch mark, round, deep, black as a hole.

"He couldn't remove *The Eye of the God,*" Con said, examining the ledge. "There are chisel marks in the stone. He tried to prise it up, and he couldn't move it. Not all the powers of Samael could move it. And yet you were able to pick it up without resistance, without any invocation."

He turned to look at her, an odd look, an assessing look. He hardly wanted to think about it—about her, the Darcie of the dark, the Darcie of the lies, the Darcie of his dreams.

None of that mattered now because, in spite of his plans and regardless of her schemes, they had been deliberately brought to this place, and *she* had been given the benediction of *The Eye of God.*

And he had to live with that. Darcie's dream. Darcie's will. Darcie's desire. And he had no choice but to use her.

He swirled the light around the grotto. "Sidhu said we were unconscious for a day and a night."

"That's what he said."

"What did it look like?"

They were in the right place for ghost stories, she thought. And he would say she was weaving still another tale because it was so unbelievable.

"He looked like a corpse," she told him, shuddering as she remembered the horrific way it formed from the fog. "He looked like a corpse; bony, gray, burning eyes, wearing a long robe like a monk."

"Yes."

He knew this. She saw by his face, by his all-seeing, knowledgeable eyes. He knew all about this, and the unspeakable evil encased in that stone.

"We have to recover that diamond."

"We?" Now she wanted no part of it. She wanted her share of *The Eye of God*—no more, no less. He could pursue his demons on his own.

"We," he said furiously. "We have to stop him."

"Stop . . . ?"

"Lazarin. That's what he called himself, yes?" His eyes hardened. "He has to be stopped, and we have to reclaim the diamond."

"Oh no. Not me. I'll just take my little piece of *The Eye of God,* and go back where I came from."

He ignored her. "We'll be able to move faster this time. We can do more this time. And we'll have to leave soon—he's already had too much of a start."

"Con—you're not listening," she said desperately. "You don't even know where it's gone."

"No—you're the one who doesn't hear. *We* have to do this." He swiped the lantern over the ledge once more but he saw nothing more. "You know, if I had some dynamite, I would blast this place to kingdom come."

He took her arm, and pushed her toward the anteroom. "You don't understand. You have to do this because you've been anointed, Darcie. *You* are the one sanctified by *The Eye of God.*"

"She is blessed."

"So I perceived," Sidhu said. "All is in readiness for departure."

"This place must be destroyed."

"It will be my holy duty to do this for the *chowkidar sahib.*"

"I will be a watchman no more."

"It will be as you wish. Fate has been kind that you could watch over this place even as you were blind." Sidhu bowed. "We must go now."

Con had stamped out the fire, packed the lanterns and removed all traces of their presence there. It only remained to move the stone over the portal to the catacomb of his rebirth, and then they would be ready to make the ascent from the Valley.

They started out in the late morning.

Sidhu shimmied up the rope first.

Darcie watched how he did it, digging his feet into crevices in the wall, scaling his way up hand over hand, cleft by cleft.

I can't do that. I could barely get down.

"I'll go next," Con said, shielding his eyes so he could watch Sidhu's agile body. "And then Sidhu and I will pull you up. I'm going to tie the rope around your waist now, you'll wear the gloves, and you just let us do the work. It will be faster that way."

She didn't think so; she was terrified already of the idea of swinging on the rope with only his ability to tie a knot to protect her. It was a solid knot, though, thick, tight and seemingly secure. She would hold the rope, she would try to get a foothold now and again, and she would be up at the ridge before she knew it.

She watched him doubtfully as he grasped the rope and began to climb. Simple as that, when you could see. You could see everything for a thousand miles, even your destiny.

He disappeared from view, and a moment later, he tugged the rope, the signal that he was about to pull.

She grasped it just at face level and girded herself as she felt herself being lifted off the ground. Like a circus performer, up up up, into the rafters.

She closed her eyes; she couldn't look. To the Top of the World, like an angel. In the dark, like a man who couldn't see . . .

She reached for an outcropping of rock as she neared the top, and braced her leg against it. She reached for Con, as he lay on the edge of the cliff above her, extending his hands to her.

She looked into his dark unfathomable *seeing* eyes and wondered if he would grasp her hands and then just let her go. She saw herself falling down the valley wall, a conspirator who knew too much, and had to be subdued.

She closed her eyes as he took her hands, pulled her up, and swung her onto the ridge.

They stood there, buffeted by the raw mountain wind, at the Top of the World, silhouetted against the sun.

"You don't understand, Darcie," he murmured. "You have all the protection, all the power. *You* are the one."

"I don't want to be any one. I want to go home."

"You said it yourself. Until this thing is done, we can't go home."

"No—I said until we claimed *The Eye of God* . . ."

"You claimed it."

And she carried it still. And she felt the weight of the burden of it.

"We're not selling it, are we? You won't cleave it. What good is it?"

"The good is that we have it, and Lazarin does not. And Lavinia—" he paused, thinking about it a moment; his family hadn't entered anywhere into his calculations to this point, except for the tantalizing feeling that he was missing something about Lavinia.

But his family had nothing to do with their pursuit of the black diamond. And there was no time to consider anything else.

"At this point," he said, "Lavinia doesn't count."

Sixteen

They returned to the houseboat on the Nagin Lake in Srinagar. They came out of the cold harsh mountains from the Top of the World and into the warmth of a hill country spring, where the servants questioned nothing and always were waiting.

"They could be waiting for you in Srinagar," Darcie protested. "They could have followed us this far. They could have followed us to the valley."

She didn't know why she felt so frenzied and unsure. But she really did. It was because she was no longer in command. It was because Con had taken control of everything. Con with his eyes, with his memories, with his past. He was treading on solid ground now; he would make no missteps the way she had while she fought every inch of the way to come this far.

And now she felt as if she had toppled off a mountain.

She didn't like it. *She hated it.*

"They caught me in Srinagar all those years ago," Con said casually, as he divested himself of his sheepskins, his *aba,* and his boots.

It was a revelation that unnerved her.

"Then why are we here?"

"Because we have lodgings, we need some time, and we have a friend."

He rang for the *khansamer* who appeared as silently as air. "Have a bath drawn, will you?" he ordered in Hindi, and translated for her. "And dinner at eight, please."

Dinner. What a lovely word. Not beans, or skewered meat that was raw inside. Real dinner. With Con. Who could see to cut his meat and eat his dessert.

This was a whole different Con. He would never hold onto her again. Never be dependent. Never turn to her in the dark . . .

She shook herself.

She should know better than this. She was a gambler, and one thing always held true: sometimes the rules of the game changed. And sometimes the stakes. And if everything went to hell, you bluffed your way through.

But what did you do when all the boundaries got turned inside out?

You make new ones, she thought. *And you don't let him overrun them and take control.*

She felt him looking at her, as she paced the large front room of the houseboat, and she wondered what he saw under the tunic and cloak and the headdress, and under the henna dye.

She felt uncomfortable suddenly; Con Pengellis knew her too well—in the dark. You couldn't hide from a man when you were naked in the dark.

In the dark, there were no barriers, and no boundaries.

And she saw he remembered that too.

"Lavinia will not rest until she finds you," she said to distract him—no, distract herself. "Wouldn't this be the logical place for her to start?"

He looked so different without his headdress and his paint. Astonishingly different with his eyes. The light in them changed the whole aspect of his face. Made him look hawk-eyed, sharp-sighted, vigilant, keen.

"Maybe. Probably." His gaze swept her, head to toe, missing nothing.

For the first time, she felt the edginess of their enforced togetherness. This was not the same as her taking charge, directing the quest, and fueling it with her hunger and her greed.

In the blink of an eye, everything had passed out of her hands and into his.

At the mercy of Samael.

It was now his jewel. His dream. *His* quest.

She turned her back on him and stalked to the window. It was just coming on twilight, the orange sun sinking into the horizon and reflecting off of the lapping river.

This was a place people came to find calm. To escape the heat.

But the heat was building up behind her, seeping into her pores, stroking her skin.

She whirled to face him. And wished she hadn't. Those eyes grazed her eyes, her mouth, her breasts.

"How can you be so calm?" she demanded.

Those eyes devoured her; those eyes could *see*.

"I can't worry about Lavinia now," he said. "They will not find the grotto. Sidhu will attend to that. They will never have the diamond; it's in your possession now—"

"I hate this," she said fiercely. "I don't want to do this."

"But you've done it, Darcie. You spun your tales, you saved a sinner, and you vanquished a villain. What did you expect?"

"Stop talking like that!"

"Why is that, Scheherazade?"

"It's too mixed up. I don't understand it, and I don't understand you."

He smiled faintly, devastating now that he could see. She could barely stand to look at him. *Only in the dark.*

God, she couldn't deal with this, she couldn't. Or maybe it was the repercussions of the unbelievable things she had seen.

"The only way Lavinia can get to me now is if *you* were the one giving her the lead," he said, his tone gentle, his expression hard.

She felt like slapping him. "Oh! It's just inconceivable you could think that."

"Anything is possible."

Anything. Like Roger might not be dead. And that she was his enemy and no one else. And a white diamond balanced the evil in the world, and Lazarin existed.

"But," he said, "that's not important now—"

"No," she interrupted snidely. "You're going to have us chasing a corpse."

"We *must* recover the black diamond." There was no brooking that tone of voice.

"You must. You can. We're going around in circles."

"Because you're tired; you need a bath. And dinner."

"And sanity," she said stonily.

"And rest."

"Unless Lavinia kills us first."

Lavinia—what about Lavinia kept bothering him? The murderous Lavinia avid for a child—why did it sound so familiar?

"Darcie . . ." he said warningly.

"Con—" she said, imitating his tone.

"*Sahib* . . ." The *khansamer* at the parlor door.

"He says the bath is ready. Go, Darcie. Relax. I'll watch out for Lavinia."

The bastard. "This is *not* a game."

"I never thought it was. You'll give me the two pouches, Darcie. They should never be out of either of our hands from now on."

"And how do I know you won't sneak away with *The Eye of God?*" Oh, she liked saying that; she liked turning the tables on those knowing eyes.

"The stone wouldn't let me."

"Dear God, don't start that."

He held out his hand. "I won't even pursue that. Go to your bath, Darcie. The stone will be here when you get back."

Darcie . . .

Darcie, Darcie, Darcie . . .

What to make of Darcie . . . the Darcie of his dreams?

He knew her intimately and he knew her not at all. He knew the heat of her body, her sinuous curves, the shape of her breasts, her hot greedy mouth . . . and the reality of her was nothing like what he knew of her at all.

She was tall and slender and strong as tempered steel. And the thick silky hair in which he'd dug his hands was as glistening black as a raven's wing.

But it was her eyes that were utterly unexpected: they flashed bolt-blue in her heart-shaped face, smudgy, expressive, derisive, a mirror of her soul. And that mouth— when he looked at that mouth he dreamt of kisses and lies and the succulent moments when it had fully encompassed him.

It was a mouth made for kissing and tasting and passion, wide and full and endlessly fascinating.

Darcie's mouth. Telling tales, weaving lies, enchanting the stone . . .

Maybe she was an enchantress. He was already under her spell. And now, she was possessed of the white diamond; all she'd had to do was take it—and he would never know if it would have come to him.

What had he done?

Tempted fate. Played with destiny. Provoked the gods.

Made his life's work a mythical white diamond—and got Darcie Boulton instead.

And he didn't know—he still didn't know where she fit in the story. But he knew where he was going to keep her: in his bed, under his body, and—for as long as it took—by his side.

She had no clothes. She was immersed in the bath before it occurred to her: everything had been sacrificed for their journey to India. Clothes. Toiletries except a comb and a bar of soap. Maybe if she wished on that blasted diamond, it would provide those things for her.

Nothing seemed real. The whole adventure from England to the desert seemed like a dream. She couldn't believe now, in retrospect, she had done the things she'd done, and with Con's blindness as an impediment.

But they'd done it—they'd recovered the diamond—and he'd known all along that it would have a mystical claim on whoever found it.

She didn't want any part of it. There had to have been something in that grotto that precipitated that nightmare. Entities didn't disappear in a fog; phantasms weren't born out of smoke. It was a magician's trick, engineered somehow by Con, and probably all in aid of keeping *The Eye of God* for himself.

What if his blindness had been a ruse?

A wave of heat washed her body. *All the things she'd done—in the dark . . .*

What was illusion—what was real?

The Eye of God was real. Disappointing, but real. And when they got it back to civilization, where it could be properly cleaved and polished, it would provide her with riches for a lifetime.

That was all she wanted. *All.*

The rest was all a bunch of hocus-pocus, that probably any spiritualist in London could have conjured up.

Exactly. Atmosphere was everything. And where better to perform a mystical sleight-of-hand than in an isolated grotto in the depths of an impenetrable valley?

She was a gullible fool.

It was all about the diamond and its value.

And that was all.

They were going back to England.

And that was that.

She climbed out of the bath and found a towel. It was the kind of seasonal rental that provided those things; so that was good. But something to wear—that was a problem, and the shirt and trousers she'd worn under her tunic for the last month would just have to do.

The *khansamer,* she discovered, had cleaned them as best he could without having the luxury of washing them. That was good too. She began to feel less like an animal rooting in the wild.

She tore a piece of leather from her headdress to bind up her hair, and she shoved her bare feet back into the thick walking boots.

She marched back into the parlor, prepared to do battle.

Which battle—lust or greed? Or were they inextricably entangled?

She found him lounging on a cushioned wicker chair before a table set for dinner. He'd called for a barber; he'd gotten a shave and a haircut while she bathed, and he sat back now, watching her come in, seeing *everything* with those *eyes.*

He looked more like himself now—too much like himself. Like the Con of the portrait. The Con that she'd saved. This Con unnerved her and she didn't know what to say.

"You might want to wash," she said waspishly, pulling up a straight backed chair.

"I've already done so. Gat is waiting to serve us."

Thank goodness. She wouldn't need to talk. She wouldn't need to look at those eyes and wonder yet again how he was seeing her.

He snapped his fingers and the *khansamer* appeared, along with the kitchen boy, and set out the tomato soup which was followed by spiced beef and fried potatoes served with chutney and a red pepper conserve.

She'd never felt so hungry in her life. There couldn't be enough food to fill the void. And Con intently watched her devour every bite.

Her only recourse was a frontal assault.

"So when can we leave for London?"

"We're not going back to England yet." There was infinite patience in his tone.

"Well then, I'll tell you what. Why don't you give me one or two of the remaining Pengellis diamonds, and *I'll* go back to England, and you can go off chasing ghosts."

He ignored that suggestion. "I gave Sidhu another diamond to sell. We're going to need more equipment, and to pay the servants. Clothes. Transportation—"

"Transportation—where?" she demanded suspiciously.

"I think I know where he went."

"He? *He?* That was *not* a *he.* That was an *it,* and I don't care where it went. I care where *I* want to go."

His eyes gleamed. "The stone won't let you go. Don't you understand? Only when the black diamond is recovered will the balance be restored. Now listen. I think it draws its power from the diamond, and that's why it was taken. But since the stone was split, the power must be diminished. So I believe it will seek a diamond field from which to draw and stay at a certain level of energy. I don't think it will go to South Africa. Nor do I think it will stay in India. I believe it will unleash its evil among the furthest known diamond fields in the world."

"The furthest . . ." she said faintly.

"On the Nizmennost Plains of Siberia."

"Oh my God." She closed her eyes. The man was mad. "We—*you're*—going to the most isolated part of Russia on the strength of a hunch?"

"An educated hunch. An educated deduction. Fewer people. A lot of opportunity to wreak havoc. And an untapped supply of diamonds underground."

"Hocus pocus," she muttered. "I'm going home."

"But I have the diamonds," he said gently. "And—as much as you hate it, Scheherazade—I'm in command."

How stupid was she, not to have stolen one of those diamonds as a hedge against this lunacy? She couldn't believe her gullibility. The best she could hope for now was opportunity to rectify that mistake.

She was never going to sleep again. There was only one bedroom in the houseboat, where she'd had her bath. One bed, enshrouded in mosquito netting. One armoire. One washstand. One, one, one.

And two pairs of eyes.

In the dark. What did he see?

She gnawed on the question, as birds as big as vultures swooped outside the bedroom windows and the boat rocked gently against the midnight tide and cradled them in sleep.

He slept. She thought he slept. Or maybe his all-seeing eyes were busy conjuring up illusions.

She was finished playing. She had to find where he

had hidden the last of the diamonds they had removed from their settings. By her reckoning, there should be four left. One would suffice.

She lay stiffly beside him on the bed, having removed only the heavy boots. *In the dark.*

The godawful unholy dark . . .

He couldn't see in the dark—

Unless he was a blasted phantasm himself.

And maybe she'd once thought he was, back when she'd fallen in love with a portrait. She'd thought he was a god, and because he was dead, she could worship him forever.

The reality . . . ah, the delicious reality—when she'd been in control . . .

She most definitely didn't like not being in control.

She had to find those diamonds . . .

She moved experimentally to check if he were asleep. Not a movement beside her. Deep breathing. Deep dark.

She couldn't trust the man. In the dark.

She needed to emulate his thinking. Where would a sorcerer conceal his apparatus? One thought occurred—and she pushed it resolutely out of her mind. But maybe, she thought a moment later, it was not such a far-fetched idea after all.

But it meant she would have to put her hands on him, seduce him and leave herself at the mercy of those eyes.

In the dark.

It didn't matter; it was different, wholly different, because of those eyes. She didn't feel so free now in the dark. Everything had changed and she hated it.

Nevertheless, the objective was the thing.

She was not going to chase a ghoul across two continents just on his whim. She'd had enough of deserts and camps and sultry foreign air.

She moved restively against him. The diamonds

might be in his pockets or in his boots. For all she knew, they were woven in his hair.

What if she just touched him? Just gently grazed his thigh, by his left trouser pocket. She'd be able to tell if there were a bump or bulge. It was just a matter of lightly brushing her fingers . . . there, there—and gently *there*—

She was breathless, suddenly, as her fingers wafted over the firm hard contour of his leg. *Oh God, she wasn't after that . . . not now, not with those eyes.*

Maybe. Maybe . . .

In the dark.

In the dark, he caught her hand and pinned it against her side.

"Darcie, Darcie, Darcie . . ." he murmured, turning and shifting his weight over her. "I was just waiting for you to make a move."

But now—he could see . . .

"You're making more of it than it was," she muttered.

"Ah, Darcie. And you made life so bearable in the dark."

Always the dark—she couldn't get away from it. She couldn't get away from him.

Did she want to ?

He was poised above her, on his elbows and knees; she was surrounded by him, enveloped by his scent, his heat, his desire.

His lips unerringly touched hers; she shook him away.

"Darcie—" a whisper against her mouth. A flick of his tongue against her lips. A questing taste. A further foray, and she didn't resist. He kissed like he remembered her mouth; like he was still without sight and wanted to explore every inch, with hunger, with knowledge, with taste.

No part of his body touched her, only his mouth, yet

the sense of him above her pressed against her; she squirmed beneath him, seeking his weight.

He gave her nothing, except his kiss. He took her with his mouth, thrusting ferociously into the heat and wet of hers.

"Oh God, I missed this . . ."

That firm carved mouth all over, all inside of hers. That long strong body caging hers. Connected to him solely by the lush hard thrust of his tongue.

"Darcie . . ." Breathless, seeking, devouring kisses— in the dark.

It was still the same, in the dark.

He was so strong, so forceful, in the dark. He wouldn't let her go.

"Con . . ."

"No . . . no—"

Swooping down on her again, like those birds out the window, never caressing her, never touching her except by the fierce greedy seduction of his tongue.

He meant to make her crazy; he wanted to make her come by the sheer erotic force of his volcanic kisses.

She felt wet, wild, consumed with wanting him. She couldn't wait to strip off her clothes.

She reached for him, and he shimmied away from her questing hands.

"No fair, Darcie . . ."

"I don't care—"

She slipped both hands between his legs and cupped him. His resolve faltered as he placed himself in her hands.

"Take me," he whispered, and slipped into her mouth.

She tore at his clothes, arching up toward him as he sprang into her hands. She grasped him hungrily, sliding her hands down his jutting length to his scrotum, and under, to the sweet erotic stroke of skin beneath.

There, just there, holding him tightly in one hand and massaging him gently, sensuously between his legs. Just . . . *there.*

And then—

"Don't stop." His voice was shaky, barely above a breath.

". . . couldn't . . ." she sighed, as she alternated the stroking of her fingers with rolling the taut sacs of his scrotum between her hands.

She was avid for him, all of him, devouring the essence of him with her greedy hands.

He held his body away from her still; all she had was the hard jutting length of him and his voraciously demanding mouth, and the erotic sense of his containing her with his body.

All she wanted of him was the hot cream of his desire—and she knew exactly where.

With one hand, she tore open her shirt, and pulled away her camisole to expose her breasts. "I want you here," she whispered. "Come to me here."

He shuddered in her hands. She felt him quicken in her hands.

"I want it on my breasts."

He shoved himself against her encircling hand.

"I want it coating my nipples."

He made a deep animal sound and thrust harder against her fingers. She levered herself up against him, holding one breast against the smooth underside of his throbbing length.

He could feel the hot tight point of her nipple rubbing against him, and the firm massaging of the fingers of her free hand. She was over and under him, writhing against him, massaging him, coaxing him, squeezing and stroking him.

And he held himself back. He wanted to give her what she craved . . . without spending himself on her. And he felt himself coming. That part of him wanted to give her a fountain of cream. Wanted her to swim in it, bathe in it, absorb it into her body. Wanted her never to go anywhere without wearing his scent on her body.

It spurted out of him involuntarily, the magma of the volcano.

She swiped it off of him and spread it on her breasts, covering each hard pointed nipple with his luscious essence.

"Like that," she whispered. "And that," as she stroked the essence of him onto her body. "It feels so good . . . You're so powerful . . ."

He didn't let her finish. He swooped down on her mouth and crushed it, pulling himself away from her hands. If she had so much as moved those hands one fraction, he would have spewed over her, and he wanted to save himself for better things.

He felt her hands reaching for him; shuddered at the tremulous begging moan against his lips, "Don't. Let me . . ."

"You got what you wanted," he growled.

"I love it—I want more . . ."

"No . . . now you wait until *I* want to give it to you."

"You're ready now. I can feel it: if I touch you, you'll come."

"Want to try?"

"I always want to touch you." She reached out her avid hands and caught him hard between them. "Oh God, you're so hot and hard. Let me . . ." She started stroking him, rubbing her fingers along his turgid length.

"You're not getting any more of me."

"I want it. I love it. I'll suck it out of you."

The image of her hot greedy mouth surrounding him shot to his very vitals. He felt himself quickening, rearing back to give her the shot, aching to put himself at the mercy of her succulent tongue and greedy mouth.

He pulled away roughly.

"You can't have it."

"I need more. I want more." Her body undulated beneath him, taunting him, goading him. "You're all ready for it. You're bursting with it. Let me have more. Let me just . . . lick all that deliciousness from right—*there*—" She grabbed for him, and caught him right at the head. "You're an absolute rock," she whispered, as she rubbed her thumb just at the tip.

She felt a drop of it pulse at her fingertip, and she levered herself up and licked it, and then she pulled him into her mouth.

He jerked away abruptly. "I told you—you can't have it."

"Why—?" A cry of pure lust and need, and he loved hearing it.

"Because you want it so much."

"So do you," she whispered.

"But I love making you beg for it—"

"Except you're the one on your knees to me," she taunted him.

"Not for long." With one shocking motion, he pushed her onto her stomach, and his arm snaked under it and lifted her onto her knees so that her bottom canted against his hips. "That's better. Now—" He ripped her trousers away from her buttocks and tore off the thin cotton drawers and exposed her derrière.

She felt him cover her, balancing himself on one hand, and his knees, so that the ramrod length of him rubbed enticingly against her buttocks' crease.

That felt good, and the sense of him enveloping her, but it wasn't nearly as delicious as owning him with her hands. She felt his fingers slip between her legs, feeling for her opening, slipping easily into her wet. Almost . . . he was pushing against her buttocks and probing her with his hand. Almost . . . she was breathless with excitement. Soon . . . she felt the surge of anticipation, the swell of desire.

She pushed against him demandingly.

"What's your problem?"

"Give it to me." Her tone was as imperious as a queen.

"When *I'm* ready."

She felt his one hand on her hip, positioning her. And then his probing fingers slipped away, leaving her empty.

Almost . . .

She wasn't going to beg. She licked her lips, she undulated against him, she pushed against his rock hard length, demanding him. She bit her lips so she wouldn't beg.

She couldn't stand knowing he was behind her, throbbing, naked, ready to explode, and she couldn't have what she most desired.

She broke. *"Do it."*

"You want it that bad." He had to know.

"I want it any way you want to give it to me."

"Good," he murmured in satisfaction, and he reared back and he poised himself just at the apex of her cleft, and slowly, inch by inch, he penetrated her, pushing into her forcefully, a little of his length at a time.

He wanted her to feel it—his length, his strength, his potency. And he wanted to embed himself into her so deeply and powerfully that she would never want it from any other man.

He was getting there. He was loving it, connecting with her solely by the hard jutting length of him furrowing into her. He was almost there, almost buried in her to the root, hip to bottom, his rough pubic hair grazing her tender buttocks, as she bowed on her knees to his virile possession of her.

For a long lustful moment, he let her feel his power and his might, and he slowly withdrew himself from her with the same slow incremental stroke.

And then into her again, slowly, giving it to her so slowly, so lusciously, so forcefully—his stroke measured against her whimpers and moans as he possessed her.

He touched her nowhere else. He took her solely with his penis, methodically and deliberately, giving it to her in short emphatic piston-like strokes that bound her to him as surely as love and kisses.

She wanted this, this rough raw coupling, she wanted his sex, and his power, and he wanted her, and he would use her need as surely as she used his. It was enough.

He wanted to give her everything she demanded. But for now, he was going slow, excruciatingly, heatedly, throbbingly slow, pushing in, in, in; pulling out, out, out. Pushing in to the hilt. Pulling out to the very tip, his penis pulsating to her moans, aching for release, determined to drive her to the very edge so she would never crave another man's sex.

He pushed himself against her buttocks so she could feel his strength.

She moaned against the pillows, begging to feel his length. He was so long and strong, and *there*. He filled her. He lived in her. She'd never known she wanted it like this. She couldn't get enough of him.

He wouldn't stay long enough for her to get enough of him.

His short thrusting strokes drove her wild. She didn't

know what to do to entice him. She wanted to seduce him, to make him stay.

If she could only make him come, he would be hers forever.

He was thrusting into her again when she felt it, fracturing from that sweet spot above her pubis, a spangling glissade of sensation spiralling downward and exploding, with his last throbbing lunge, between her legs.

He buried himself in her, he couldn't get deep enough, tight enough, hard enough for her. And he stayed that way, embedded in her, until the spasms of her climax eddied away.

She couldn't move. All she felt, all she knew was *him*— the pulsating throbbing hard part of him. She had never felt such a vibrant connection before, never felt such a lust to possess anyone. No other man had a penis like this. No one but he knew how to play.

She was aroused by the sheer feeling of his focused force rammed into her like that. She wanted him all over again, and she didn't hesitate to let him know it. She wriggled against him enticingly. She shimmied her buttocks hard against his pulsating length and his churning hips. She arched herself up to him, inviting him like a cat to stroke her and stoke her.

He couldn't refuse her blatantly voluptuous plea. She still hadn't had enough of him. He flexed inside her, girding himself, feeling as potent as a bull, as mighty as a tree.

He took her remorselessly, giving her what she wanted—his long strong pummelling strokes pounding into her, and grinding into her as he finally came, swamping her, drenching her, filling her to the hilt.

Seventeen

She wanted more.

He didn't need words to tell him: her naked body moved voluptuously against his, restive and hot to the core.

He could take her now, he thought, but it was better to wait. Let her need stoke her appetite; let her seethe and writhe and moan. He relished the longing in her that burned with lust for him.

Anticipation was everything. And memory. And the body's hunger to replicate the exhausting, pounding pleasure of their coupling.

And the sheer carnality of her nakedness pressed against his body excited him, and aroused him to a fever pitch, hard as a bone and ready to plow.

But he wouldn't give in to her, not even if she were Eve. Not even if she used all of her erotic wiles.

He loved this moment, in the dark, where he was master and the instrument, and she was the wanton slave of her own desire.

Her body rippled against him, teasing him, torturing him.

His erection elongated still more, thrusting stiffly into the air.

She made a little sound as she felt his covert movement. He grabbed her hand before she could reach for him and immobilized it.

And waited.

She hated him. Why, when he was stone hard and hot to rut in her, was he making her wait?

She wriggled her hips, hoping to entice him.

He held himself tight as a drum as his body betrayed him with an aching, longing surge.

He got it ruthlessly under control. And he waited.

She wedged herself tightly against him, hip to hip, leg to leg, so he could feel the alluring brush of her pubic hair against his rock hard thigh.

She couldn't tempt him.

And he waited.

Aching. Rigid. Towering. Burning to drive himself into her hot tight sheath.

And he waited. He wanted the tension at a fever pitch and her voluptuous need for *him* stoking her as white hot as her greed.

It was unbearable. She lay next to him squirming with lust for him, hot and wet for him, her nipples tight hard points for him.

She didn't understand why she couldn't just climb onto him and ram his desire home.

He was playing some strange game with her. Making her wait like this. Getting her crazy wild and feeding on her hunger for him.

She forced his hand between her legs, and he jerked it away.

"Oh no. No," he growled. "You'll wait until I'm ready."

She went breathless. "I'm waiting."

"Good."

Her body went tight at the sensual implication of that word.

"How good?" she whispered.

"As good as you'll ever get it."

She writhed against his restraining hand. There had to be some way to break him. Some way to make him come. She inched her leg over his, straining closer to his heated body.

Closer still, winding her foot around his ankle and rubbing his skin. And she felt the faintest flex of his body.

Yes.

He waited.

She lifted her foot and stroked his leg. He reacted violently, his hips convulsing at the touch of her toes.

Good. She loved the word. She loved his involuntary response.

She waited, as he mercilessly clamped down on his rampant need.

And she waited, because now she was in control, and she understood about the waiting and the heightening of desire.

Now he was squirming with hunger for her.

Good. That was how you turned the tables. And now—

She lifted her leg and inserted her foot between his legs against the taut sacs of his scrotum. He stopped her there. He kept her there. Her toes flexed against him and his hips moved involuntarily.

"Don't. Do. That." Her voice, ragged and raw. "I want you. *Now.*"

He moved her foot and stroked her toes against the underside of his erection, and then he rubbed the hard throbbing length against her foot.

"There's a part of me that wants your foot, Scheherazade."

"You want *me*," she groaned.

"Let's see. Since you couldn't stand to wait, let's see what it will take to make me come."

He moved her foot to the base of his penis where it jutted away from his body, and he rubbed her foot up up the length of it. "Ummm. That feels good."

Good . . . as good as—

She yanked her foot away, and he caught it back, and stroked himself again. "I like your toes caressing me," he murmured. "The pressure is just right."

"Why are you doing this?" she moaned, frantic with wanting him, willing to take him any way she could get him now. Even with her toes.

"Because you wouldn't wait. I told you it would be good. Better than before because of the waiting. You're hot, juicy, soaking wet; just ripe and ready for me."

"Then take me," she begged.

"Tell me you want me more than your toes."

"I want you."

"Good." *That word, that luscious meaningful, self-satisfied word.*

As good as . . .

He rolled over so that he was poised above her. He grasped her hands and pinned them above her head. She hooked her legs around his thighs, and waited breathlessly for him to mount her.

With erotic precision, he breached her, in one hard soul-shattering lunge, as hard, hot and deep as he could go.

"Yes," she whispered. "Yes." How unbelievably hard he was; how tightly he filled her. She wanted him to stay there forever.

He rocked against her gently, to maintain his fierce control.

"Never, ever . . ." she breathed.

"I know."

"Don't move."

"I couldn't. Not yet."

"The waiting," she murmured.

"I can't move."

"I want you to come. For me. In me."

"Not yet. *Not . . . yet—*"

"Kiss me."

"Not even that. I'm too close."

"Then do it. I want you to do it." She undulated her hips against him, testing him, tormenting him, sensing he was on the edge of his iron control.

Big mistake.

"Tell me a story, Scheherazade."

She made a little sound at the back of her throat. "The story is," she gasped, as she shimmied desperately against him, "I'm . . . going . . . to co-ome—" She broke as her body seized up, spasmed, and began the soft melting slide into oblivion down his long stiff pole.

She toppled into a churning, foaming silence. And then she was complete.

And he waited. Waited. Holding her. Surging incrementally against her hips. Waiting. Sensing. Needing. Needing . . . needing—

He blew. He barely gyrated his hips, and his whole body gathered, he pushed, and he erupted violently into her with one sweet cradling move.

This was a different man, in the dark, now that he had his eyes.

And by daylight—Darcie knelt beside the bed and studied him in the dim dawn light. He was just as she remembered him that first night: long and strong and tempting to touch.

He watched her through hooded eyes as she climbed up onto the bed and buried her face between his legs, rooting for him with her mouth.

"Ah, Darcie . . ."

"I need you again," she whispered, pulling at him, sucking on him until he stiffened in her mouth.

"I have something else for you," he murmured, easing himself away from her. The test was now. The test of his prowess and her need.

"All I want is you," she said, rocking back on her heels.

He leaned over the bed and swiped up his trousers. "But you don't want to go with me."

Her expression changed. "Maybe I do."

He dug into a pocket and handed something to her.

She closed her hand tightly around it: one of the remaining Pengellis diamonds.

"It's yours."

"For services rendered?" she asked, bitterness lacing her tone.

"You're free to make a choice now, Scheherazade." He tossed his trousers to the floor and leaned back with his hands behind his head.

She looked at him, at his long lean body fully displayed for her pleasure. At his thick towering manhood already hard and yearning for her.

And she looked at the diamond.

She got off the bed and took it to the window, holding it to catch the sun to reflect its rainbow light.

"I don't understand."

"Stay or go—that diamond is yours."

"Do you want me to stay?" she asked carefully. It was such a soul-sapping conversation, with both of them naked and ready for other things.

"Don't play games, Darcie. If you stay, there are rules."

"In the dark, there weren't any rules," she said.

"But in the dark, I didn't have any power."

"You had power," she countered.

"I had you."

"Now you don't need me."

He chose not to answer that. "Make up your mind, Darcie. *You* were the one who wanted to go back home."

She vaguely remembered that she had; could barely remember the reasons why: last night had blasted all of that right out of her head.

Oh yes, she'd been rooting around for the diamonds. A stake to get her back home. And now she had it, with no repercussions, in the palm of her hand.

But she wouldn't have *him*. She wouldn't have that body, those kisses, his penis, that lover. And after last night, she couldn't let that go.

"Do you want *me?*"

He gave her a crooked smile and gestured to his body. "Do I, Darcie? I've been in a perpetual state of arousal since you rescued me. And seeing you just makes me hotter and harder for you. Is that what you want to hear? That I'm constantly hard for you? I am. I want to jam myself into you every way I can think of. Every day. Every hour. Every minute. That's your power, Darcie. Your nakedness incites that kind of lust. I'm always rock hard and ready for you. Any time. Anywhere. So you tell me, Scheherazade, what are you going to do?"

She loved that kind of power. She adored his admission that he was always hard for her. She wanted him, and she wanted no one else to have him. And she didn't care how high the price.

It probably started at one Pengellis diamond. She put it on the washstand and sat down on the bed. "I'll go with you."

His eyes kindled. Beautiful, sensual Darcie. He hadn't been sure. He hadn't known if his sex was enough. If she'd said no, he had no idea what he would have done. He'd gambled—and this time he won.

"Good," he said.

Good . . . as good as—in the dark . . .

"Tell me the rules," she murmured, sliding her hands up his hair-rough thighs. "I know one—if you want to wait, we wait."

"Good." He watched her hands and he let her . . . *let her* . . . grasp his throbbing length. "So good." And he let himself—*let himself*—discharge a drop of his essence onto her hand.

She held his eyes as she rubbed it on her breasts. It was so erotic, he almost came; he didn't know which was more powerful: imagining it or watching her do it, and he almost didn't care.

"I want to coat myself like this every morning," she whispered. "That's my rule."

"If you play with me much longer, you'll be able to swim in it," he growled, pulling back from her greedy hands.

She smiled faintly, as mysterious as Eve, reaching for him again. "Tell me your rules."

He envisioned her drowning in his essence, and he spurted again.

"You will never deny me. You will always be naked and willing for me just as I am always hard and ready for you. I could spend my seed on any woman but I'm hard for you. Will you accept those rules, Scheherazade; do you want it that much too?"

Her hands on him had been quiescent as he spoke. But now she stroked him purposefully as she considered his rules.

He wanted her always wet and hot and ready for him. He wanted to give it only to her when he was hard and he wanted it. And that was her power—his lust for her, his need to spend himself only on her.

And she wanted that. She would deny him nothing. She wanted it every bit as much as he did—more. She wanted it now and she would want it ten minutes from now. And this afternoon. And tonight and tomorrow.

Whatever they had done before was nothing compared to the luscious games and the sumptuous couplings of the previous night. What woman would deny herself that? Or the reverberating pleasure of holding him, possessing him, and knowing he was hers?

"I accept the terms," she whispered.

"You want it." It wasn't a question.

She rubbed the thick ridged tip of him. "I want it."

"Take it."

She climbed up on the bed and straddled him, her eyes shrouded in mystery. "Now?"

"Now."

She rose to her knees, and poised herself over him, and then slowly, agonizingly ground her way down to seat herself on him.

And now he was at her mercy. He must wait. She held herself still, her excitement escalating to an impossible pitch, as she watched his face.

But she couldn't help the slight rocking motion. How could anyone keep still when his gorgeous male root was centered in her? She wanted to feel it as completely and fully as possible. She was thrilled that for the first time he could see whose body brought him to this pleasure.

That he could see *her.*

She arched her back against the all-consuming orgasmic sensation of his penetration. It wouldn't take much to send her over the edge. And she could see that he was playing a game: he wanted to wait as much as she.

Just sitting astride him made her hot. The sheer nakedness of her body straddling him like that. Her breasts bare, firm and taut. Her hair, wild and free. She lifted it slowly from her shoulders as he flexed himself inside her.

"No, no, no," she said coyly, wagging her finger at him. "We're going to wait. I'm just going to sit here and feel you so hard and hot inside me and know you're just yearning to explode, and we'll wait. You *do* love to wait, don't you?"

"You'll have to wait too, Scheherazade."

"I'm learning to like it. I get more of you for a longer time between my legs, and I do love that. So—be still. Let me enjoy how hard you are, how stiff you feel."

"What if I can't wait?"

"But I have you rather at a disadvantage. What can you do?"

"Let me show you."

He pressed down on the bed to give himself some leverage to thrust. Immediately, she ground down on him, and smacked him lightly on the thigh.

"That was bad of you—and good for me. Now I've got you even deeper inside me."

"I can't wait, Scheherazade."

"Oh, I see. You wait if it's excruciating for me. And you can't if it's hard for you."

"I can't wait because it's hard for you."

She wriggled tauntingly against him. "You're so right."

"Darcie—" This time there was no playfulness in his tone.

"Yes, Con—?" Her voice was light as air.

"If you push down one more time, I'm going to come."

She smiled, that elusive smile. "Really? You can't wait—? I can't believe it. A man with your rules, your appetites—" She knew it wouldn't take much; she could see in his face that he was struggling to maintain discipline.

It was the last thing she wanted him to do. She began rocking on his erection, slowly, imperceptibly at first, and then with a sensual gyration of her hips that sent him spinning out of control.

He grabbed her hips and pushed her; she bent over him, her hair a curtain around them, as she deliberately plunged back and forth on his shaft.

She looked into his eyes, and it was that knowing, mysterious look of hers that sent him over the edge. He clutched her hips tightly and in one violent convulsive movement, he jammed himself into her and pitched headfirst over the brink.

She was swimming in it. Loving it. Didn't want to move away from it. Loved watching him slide down the tower of his ecstasy to pure soul-sapping completion. It was all she wanted: to be the only one who could bring him to this.

She relinquished him only when his energy and desire were finally manageable and at his command. But until then, she had him, nestled between her legs, fully extended, ridden to exhaustion, and deliciously *there*.

And she refused to let him console her with his hand.

"I'll wait," she said placidly. "I can wait. I'm not the one who couldn't abide by the rules. I'll be waiting for you. And you'll know, all day, that I'm wet and ripe and just on the crest of all that pleasure. So we'll see who really knows how to wait."

"You'll drive me crazy."

"I hope so," she murmured coyly. She wandered around the room, picking up clothes. "I hardly have anything to wear."

"You don't have to dress."

"You're right. One of the rules." She tossed him his clothes. "What about breakfast? I'm starving."

"I'll ring for the house steward. He'll serve it in here."

"And Sidhu is coming today?"

He eased himself up and swung his legs over the side of the bed. "This afternoon."

"Oh good. *Lots* of time to wait."

"Darcie . . ." he said warningly.

"Naked and willing—that's what you said . . . and *ready* . . ."

She watched him as he struggled into his trousers.

"Oh . . ." she pouted. "Not ready."

Depleted was more like it. Drained to the core. Enervated—but feeling his juices slowly heating up again as she sashayed naked around the room, and settled on the bed where she had just lain with her legs splayed.

"Stupid rules," she said, infusing a sulky note into her voice as she wriggled around pretending to try to get comfortable. "But you'll just have to wait."

His body leapt to attention instantly.

"No, no. You promised me breakfast, and I'm perfectly willing to wait."

"You will pay for this little rebellion, Scheherazade."

"I'm looking forward to it, Con."

He sent her a sizzling glance as he closed the door filly behind him and went in search of breakfast.

She turned over and buried her head in the sheets, seeking his sex and his scent.

She had never felt so aroused in her life. She felt like she was riding on it, swamped by it, surrounded by it in a sensual haze that must be obvious to all.

She didn't care. She didn't need love. She didn't need marriage. Those things were not important. All she craved was his unrelenting lust for her body, which bound her to him more securely than any wedding ring.

Already she had turned the tables on his little sensual fantasy. It had already cost her something—but the reward was worth it, even though her body still clamored for release.

She could wait. She wanted him thinking about her all day long, about how she had rejected her pleasure, and forced him to capitulate to his. She wanted him thinking about her naked body still hot and unfulfilled.

And she wanted him stiff as a poker, and bursting for relief. And then she would cuddle him and caress him and tell him to wait.

By the time he returned with a tray, she was somewhat composed.

But he was not. He was furious with her for seducing him and making him wait. He set the tray down on the table with a bang, and roughly pulled the chairs over to it.

"Breakfast, *madame*," he said curtly.

"I *am* hungry," Darcie said. She sat down opposite him, extending her legs. "Ah—tea. So revivifying. Would you like some? And eggs. Fruit. Biscuits. A nice simple meal."

"Quick, at any rate." He took one of the boiled eggs on his place. "I know what I really want for breakfast."

"What's that, Con?"

"Your nipples."

She felt the twinge through her whole body. "Not on the menu, Con." She smiled at him and bit into a biscuit. "I guess you'll have to wait."

Sidhu arrived at tiffin, by which time Con was in a cataclysmic state of arousal, and couldn't have cared less what he brought and what they had to do.

It was Darcie on his mind as she dressed behind closed doors. Darcie, whipping up his fantasies of her waiting for him, ripe, hot and yearning for him to her core.

Darcie, dressing to entice him . . .

"You will go by wagon, *sahib,*" Sidhu was saying, "up through Tashkent and north to Omsk. I have procured money, supplies, clothing for several weeks. You may not be able to track the godless one until you reach Siberia. It is a long trip, *sahib.*"

He spread out the map that Sidhu brought, and marked his way. Through the mountain passes they had already traveled and over two borders. It felt like a lifetime away.

He could barely concentrate as Darcie sauntered into the parlor, dressed in a lightweight shirtwaist and skirt, her hair pulled back in a knot at her neck.

"*Memsahib.*" Sidhu bowed.

She nodded in turn, and sat down at the table. "Let them serve now."

Con clapped his hands—mainly to keep them off of her, and the house steward set out the meal. There was lamb, this time, and vegetables, and the inevitable tea.

And Darcie sitting so composed; she must be squirming in her seat. Waiting, all this time . . . how could she stand it?

Unless . . .

. . . someone else?

In his place. That place. Embedded there, buried there—

He would kill whoever it was . . .

He clenched his hands, dismissing this insane, untenable thought. She was driving him crazy with wanting her, thinking about her. He couldn't wait for Sidhu to depart.

He left just at sundown, after going over every detail of their upcoming journey with a thoroughness that made Con clench his teeth because he wasn't listening.

"Don't get any ideas," Darcie told him as she moved around the room, extinguishing the lights. She was so excited she could hardly stand it, but that was not for him to know. Yet.

"I've got a hundred ideas. Get in the bedroom and take off your clothes."

"No. We have to wait."

He was already ripping off his clothes. "Never deny me."

"That seems contradictory to waiting, Con," she murmured as she watched him. "You can't have both."

"I can have you," he said, pacing toward her. "I'll destroy those clothes if you don't strip now."

"You have to learn to wait, Con," she said chidingly. "A man has to control his urges."

"I'm going to control you," he growled, and he grabbed her; he ripped away the tissue material of her shirt, her skirt, everything, he tore to shreds, and then he pulled everything from the dining table onto the floor. "Now, I feast on you . . ."

And he lifted her onto the table and pushed her on her back, and pulled her toward him so that her pulsating femininity just grazed his penis head. He waited, so that she could feel the jutting force of him poised to take her on.

She pushed up on her elbows to see it, and he held her eyes as he thrust himself into her inch by delicious inch. She almost came then, watching how her body devoured him, how he rotated his hips to push into her, and how deep and far she could take him until he was stuffed to the hilt.

"I've waited all day for this," she breathed, shuddering with excitement. "Don't move." She loved looking at it, the connection between them, solely and wholly to his hard hot sex. But she couldn't stop herself from writhing against it with hot frantic little movements that didn't escape him.

"Beg me for it, you tease."

She groaned. "You know I'm aching for it."

"No one would ever know it."

"You've been thinking about it all day," she accused him, her voice hoarse with need.

"I think I'll let *you* wait."

"Oh, no, don't," she moaned, "don't . . ."

He gyrated his hips. "Like that?"

"Oh yes."

He made a little grinding movement. "Like that?"

"Yes, more—more—"

He drew back an inch and rammed into her. "Like that?"

"Just like that," she whispered.

He drew back again a little further, and drove hard again.

"Yes . . ." she moaned, grasping onto the edge of the table.

He touched her nowhere else. He wanted nothing else, just this erotic connection, her moans, her need, her sex.

He reared back, and took her again.

She arched up violently. "Yes . . . !"

And again.

"Oh God . . . yes . . ."

And again—and again and again in a frenzy of possession, again, like a piston, again, in and out of her again and again, couldn't get enough, not enough, not enough, not her cries not her moans not her spasms not her groans not enough not enough enough . . .

He came . . . like lightning bolting through him, breaking him open sending him skyward like a shooting star . . .

. . . not enough—

They lay languidly entwined in bed. Already he was hot as a poker and thick as a tree and all he could think of was plowing her again. *"Darcie."*

"Ummm."

"Feel me."

"Umm?" She obediently put out her hand. He bulged upward, stabbing the air. "Oh." *Yum.* She smiled to herself. "What do you want me to do about it?"

"I could think of a few interesting things."

"Name one."

"Getting between your legs."

"Oh. That."

"Darcie—"

"I know. The rules." As if she were bored, barely interested when she was trying to suppress her rising excitement. "Do we have to?"

"Never deny me."

"Oh right. That." She put her hand out again. How did he do it, how could he be so rampantly ready two hours later? She stroked him lightly, pausing to play with his head. She loved feeling him elongate in her hand.

"Tease. All you have to do is spread your legs."

"That's the *best* part," she murmured. "And you do all the work."

"I'm ready to work you over right now."

"I think we'll wait," she said. "Somebody once told me something about the heightening of pleasure that comes from waiting."

"You are a witch. You've already kept me waiting too long."

"Let me see." She swooped her hand up the long length of him. "Ooo—you *are* ready." She fondled the bulbous tip, thumbing the ridge. Driving him crazy.

"Who wouldn't want to be possessed by this wondrous thing?"

"Let me guess."

She liked this game, and she loved playing coy.

"How about if I just play with you?"

"I'm not in the mood for games."

She rubbed him lightly, tip to root. "Couldn't I just rub you and stroke you?"

"How about if I rub and stroke you?"

"All you think about is sex," she said, pouting, as she kept her hands extra busy rubbing his length.

"So do you."

"How can I help it? I get to have you between my legs."

"Let me be there now."

"Hmmm . . . I'll think about it." She smiled to herself as he thrust himself into the circle of her caressing fingers. She had him anxious, fuming, and she loved it. "How can I deny you?"

Her tone was getting to him, even in the game. He felt deadly serious as he rolled onto her and poised himself to enter her. He never wanted her to feel lukewarm about their sex and he didn't care if it were a game.

He stabbed himself against her. "Open yourself to me."

He felt her body give—she reached down and guided him, and he surged into her. And into her. Endlessly endlessly into her, as if he'd been waiting to be enfolded by her heat before he gave in to his need and spumed.

The rocking of the boat lulled them into a state approaching sleep, in the dark. Outside the window, they heard the caw of a passing bird. The lap of the water. A mellifluous bell.

"We leave tomorrow," Con said. "Sidhu says there have been questions about us. You were right again. They have come back to look for me in Srinagar. We have to go."

She swallowed. It wasn't for her to protest, when she had agreed to come with him. But oh, she didn't want to go. She wanted to stay here with him and spend their days and nights spending his sex.

He touched her there, as if he knew what she was thinking.

"This doesn't end. It's only begun."

"But it's such a long journey, and you don't even know where to look."

"You look where evil dwells and people are afraid."

"What about your bargain? How can you trust this blessing will last?"

"Truthfully? You can trust nothing, Darcie, not even me."

And who could he trust? He walked on air, with nothing beneath him to cushion his death. They were coming for him. They knew where to find him. No, she knew they would come.

She—sapping his life force as methodically as his enemy. She said there was a child, and there was nothing. She spoke with a different tone, a demoness in his dreams . . .

What?

Demons—surrounding him, tossing him on the ground . . . shifting memories and nothing—until he was found.

Burying himself in her—

Dead dying never see the sun . . .

Evil, black evil, sundered in two . . .

Lavinia, holding in her hand the last stone of the broken necklace. What have you done?

He spiralled downward toward the truth. Lavinia. Roger. The child that never was. Survival. Lust. Dreams. The stuff of myths and death. Somewhere in there truth lies sleeping . . .

Darcie!

He awoke with a start, his head whirling with the imagery of his dream, and the faint apprehension that nothing around him was what it seemed.

Eighteen

Their caravan climbed to the Top of the World and beyond.

Nowhere, on those snow-crested ridges, could they see any trace of the valley or the stone that marked the place.

Sidhu had buried it forever.

"The legend was that the valley was impenetrable," he told her, "and that the diamonds were scattered all over the valley floor. And the only way to recover them was to throw down a slaughtered animal; it was said that the diamonds would adhere to the flesh, and the eagles that nested in the valley would fly the carcasses out and into the waiting hands of the deserving. One of a thousand and one tales, Scheherazade."

But it didn't sound like any tale she could invent, and she infinitely preferred the sensual stories they acted out with each other, in the warmth and in the dark.

On this trip, it was bone-jarring cold and it snowed in the mountains as they headed toward Gilgit and Tashkent. Periodically, there were little cabins, crow's nests they called them, where they could take their rest from the relentless weather.

Sidhu had provided well: maps, directions, the proper

clothes. Provisions. A guide who was known to him and trustworthy.

They had divided the last of the diamonds they had brought with them.

Who can you trust?

She carried two of the remaining diamonds in the pouch, with the shards of *The Stone of Samael*. He had the other two, and *The Eye of God* besides.

She wondered if it were enough. If the quest were worth the reward. If going after the entity was even sane. If she even cared.

"We've let ourselves forget about Lavinia," he said. *Something about Lavinia—or was it Darcie, in his dream . . .* "She took some time to send her operatives to Srinagar, but now they're there. The threat is real, just as you've always said."

But she didn't like being so right and knowing Lavinia so well. And now it would be reported back to her that Con had an accomplice as well—

Her time at Goole Abbey seemed a lifetime ago.

And where he thought the danger was real, she was beginning to believe she had imagined it. Things had changed so drastically. And nothing that had happened to them could possibly be connected to Lavinia.

Except that Lavinia was avid to get her hands on *The Eye of God*.

It was getting complicated again, just when it had become simple. They could have had each other forever instead of a mystical diamond; they could have stayed in that carnal sanctuary in Srinagar forever.

Instead, he had rooted her up so early in the morning, it was obscene, and they had dressed, packed, eaten a rushed breakfast, taken care of the servants, and gone to the house of the guide prearranged by Sidhu.

She hated Sidhu for stressing the urgency of leaving at the early hour.

It was too early up in the snowy mountains they climbed by mule road as they pressed on toward Gilgit. A day and a half later, they camped outside the outpost, and spent the night there.

Their guide, whose name was Naib, arranged a wagon, called a *tarantass,* to take them on to Tashkent.

Nor was there any comfort there; it was a perch and a flat bed on wheels and nothing to cushion the ride. At best, they didn't have to walk or ride the mules. At worst, they didn't have to carry their things. And it was a long journey over weather-rutted roads besides.

A fool's chase . . . and broken dreams.

They came to Tashkent through a large stone gate, and into a city of minarets, walled houses, tree-lined streets and garden greenery. There was a hotel, but it offered no amenities. They took a room anyway, spending the night on an uncomfortable bed before exploring the town.

It was a place that was Eastern and Russian both, with an unexpected level of sophistication. There were long avenues of villas and an old town with a grand bazaar. There was the English Club with a tolerable restaurant, and a reading room attached, that offered books from home and current periodicals.

There was heat and dust and flies, and the ubiquitous women in veils.

"If you don't count the women, it could be a city someplace in America," Darcie said in awe. "It's so much more *green* than I thought it would be, and warmer."

"And English," Con said. "With churches. But probably no one comes here unless they have to. Look at Naib. He's taken the wagon and gone already, even though I offered him a place for the night. I think we'll stay a day—maybe two—and see what we can find out."

But that put them in the position of being outsiders, and they were going to need help. They decided to have dinner at the English Club and see what they could find out.

Con bribed the hotel manager, and they got a bath—lukewarm water in a very small copper tub, but clean water nonetheless, and set before a roaring fire in their room.

Luxury, after a week tramping up and down mountains.

"Imagine squeezing in there," Con murmured, eyeing the tub with real interest.

She slipped her hand between his thighs. "Imagine squeezing *there,*" she countered lightly.

"Why don't we?"

"Don't we have to wait?"

"Isn't five days enough? I've been crazy not being able to have you in this cold."

"It's warm now, Con."

"And I'm damned hot."

"You are stoked like a furnace."

"What are you going to do about it?"

"I'm going to take you in my mouth and make you roar."

She knelt down and began undressing him. God—five days—in the desensitizing cold, as they huddled under sheepskins and flimsy tents, their sensual hunger had been dormant. It was enough to manage to keep warm.

So the minute she unleashed him, she felt her own desire blaze up like wind whipping the embers of a dead fire.

She wanted to devour him, right there, right then.

He had never looked more luscious, more succulent. Their enforced abstinence only made her lust after him the more. She wanted to stuff the whole of him in her mouth, but he was so huge, so long, and he was on the brink of erupting, and she wanted—and she didn't want—to bring him there.

He was ripping off the clothes that he could get to. He hauled her up and away from the taste of him and backed her against the wall. "I can't wait. I want you now."

She held him as he tore away every impediment, and when she was naked, she eased his way. He was meant to be there; he was perfectly shaped and curved to take her standing this way—or lying down, turned over, backwards, forwards, in her mouth, in her hand . . .

She didn't care where, or what he did, only that *he* belonged to *her,* and that he was always aware.

She wrapped her arms and one leg around his hips as he began to thrust—oh, and just the way she liked it: those short hard little thrusts that she felt so sharply. He knew just how to do it, just how to keep himself hard and cocked within her while priming her there.

She felt their coupling keenly, she envisioned it as he drove himself as relentlessly as a piston, hard, hard, hard. Perfect emphatic strokes. Inexorable and strong. Hard, hard, hard. Thick and long. Didn't want it to end. On and on. Breathless and insensate, and climaxing on a moan—long and strong in undulating glistening waves, hot as the sun—until they broke violently over the rock of his erection—and she was alone.

He caught her—he came in her backwash as she rode him home as mercilessly as he had taken her, and still joined, he lifted her in a radiant kiss and brought her finally to bed.

He never broke the kiss. The kiss was the aftermath

that was never going to end. A week's worth of kisses he had to expend. Hot writhing kisses, arousing kisses . . .

And whispers: "I want you again . . ."

Wait . . .

Unending kisses, no beginning, no end. Hours of kisses . . .

"I can't wait . . ."

More kisses, were there ever such kisses . . . ?

"No touching—or I'll explode . . ."

She had to touch. He was rampantly there, demanding her caresses.

He grabbed her hands and pinned them. "You do enough, just with your tongue."

"It's not enough—I need your body."

"Oh, believe me, I know you do . . . but *I'll* say when."

"I don't want to wait."

"Shut up, Darcie," and he covered her mouth again.

She lost track of everything in those lush consuming kisses. He held her hands prisoner so that only her body could move.

Ineffectual body; he didn't want it: he wanted her kisses.

She was soaking wet, her nipples pointed and hard, she was hot for him, aching for him, moaning for him, and all he gave her were those hot luscious kisses.

And a steaming awareness of *him*. Of his heat, his body, his need. His tension and his power. The mastery of his kisses. His red-hot desire. His granite hard erection. His iron control.

She writhed her body, seeking him. He was so close, almost there.

"Please . . ."

"I want to—but not yet."

"I hate you."

"But you love my kisses." He came at her again, stoking her mouth with the same fury he took her body.

She was going to melt from his kisses. She was so hot, she thought she would explode. Or he would. All his delicious essence, all over her.

Yes . . . yes, yes—

He seethed with his lust to possess her. And he loved the waiting. Always he thought he could never get bigger or harder or crave her more. And every time, waiting made everything more explosive.

And he thought, he could insert himself just at the delicious opening between her legs—just there, just the rigid ridged tip of him . . . into her hot velvet just so she was aware . . . He pearled up just envisioning it.

He wanted it. Just the tip coated now with the evidence of his desire.

Still pinning her hands, he straddled her, caging her as before, nudging her, seeking her as she parted her legs to welcome him.

"Please—yes—"

Yes—he found her, yes, he put himself there just as he'd envisioned. Just the tip. Just . . . *there* . . .

She caught her breath. "Oh God—Con-n . . ."

"You like that."

Did she like that? She contracted her muscles in a carnal caress. Just *there.*

Just breaching her, letting her feel him so intensely she thought she'd scream. Rocking slightly against her, letting her know how much more there was to come.

This was enough. If this was all he wanted to give her, she would take just this much. It was all she needed. She undulated against the power of his luscious tip. She was so ripe, so ready; she knew just how to cant her body against him to make the most of him.

It was so erotic, him holding her like that. She arched her back, bearing down on the tip, and riding it high and hard at her center, rotating her hips violently, and gyrating him in turn.

It wasn't quite the same as his full-bore possession of her; it was different—a slow sweet shuddering kiss of a climax as she called out his name.

She slid down into delicious silence. He didn't move. He remained inside her, looking at her with skepticism and disgust.

Seeing eyes—what was he seeing? This was not in the dark, and he could see her now for what she really was: a woman full of sexual tricks and unlimited guile.

She should not have done that. What woman would?

"Well, well, well," he murmured. "You do know some interesting things . . ."

She felt a wave of heat wash over her. "You'd be surprised what those London society ladies have up their sleeves. I was with a very fast crowd that first year."

"But you found me in a brothel, Darcie. It does give me pause."

"It doesn't change anything."

"But it explains a lot."

"Con—don't do this."

"Oh—I won't. I like the idea that you're a whore. It makes everything—simpler somehow."

"Don't—" the word stuck in her throat. "I'm not."

"If you say so." He pulled away from her, still rampant and hard. "I don't have to finish now, Darcie. This time, I'll wait."

"If you feel that way, you should send me home," she said stringently as they awaited the service of the first course at the English Club.

"Let's just say I need a little time to get used to it."

She didn't know what to do. Or what to say. He'd never asked one question about her marriage to Roger or the tenor of their relationship. He'd never been curious even about whether they'd had sex. Never spoke again about the baby that wasn't.

"I loved it," she said finally. "I love it with you."

"You say that to all the men who poke you, Darcie."

She turned her face away. Con with his eyes was as formidable a man as she'd ever met. You couldn't hide a thing from those eyes. Or that body or that mouth. And there were too many things left unsaid. And secrets she'd kept.

"Send me back to England then."

He shook his head. "No."

She decided to be bold; what did she have to lose? "I won't go on if I can't have you."

He sent her a malicious smile. "Oh, you can have me. I wouldn't deny either of us that."

He paused as the waiter served the soup. Good hot thick pea soup, edible with a fork. He felt like smearing it all over her body and licking it off.

He didn't know what he was so annoyed about. Nothing had changed. She was a sexual temptress with an enormous appetite for sex. It should have given him a clue, but instead, he had let himself become immersed in his unending lust for her.

And he meant it: he wasn't going to give that up.

"I had sex with Roger for the first year of the marriage before he went off to the pigs," she said suddenly. "At least he had the decency to wait six months after my father died to publicly rut in the streets. I wanted to know—what did they know that I didn't? What did they do that I couldn't? Why was copulating with a trollop more satisfying than with me?"

"This is a good story, Scheherazade." He motioned to the waiter to remove the soup. "Go on. I'm fascinated."

"We were still living in London. I went to his friends. You know, all those Ladies and Honorables. The ones who, behind their philandering husbands' backs, funded Madame's brothel so that they too could have a place to sport. It was eye-opening. But it didn't answer the question. Because there was nothing I saw there I wouldn't have tried in order to please Roger."

"Well known there, were you?"

"I went a half dozen times with several ladies with whom I would assume you're acquainted. You would not want to know who they are. It would be a terrible disappointment for you to know their lecherous vices."

"And you joined in them, of course."

Her voice went husky. "I watched." She took a deep breath. "A peculiar sort of morality for someone like me. I just wanted to *know*. Not that it helped. In any event, I do know Madame recognized me when I came to her door the night I found you."

He clapped lightly. "That's very good, Sheherazade. Excellent, in fact. The confused and yearning newlywed wife. The horrible husband. The remedy, in fiction, if not life. This is some damned story."

"Any more insane than your accepting your sight and then babbling about the powers of *The Eye of God?*" she shot back. "I thought you'd gone crazy."

"And I have my sight."

"At what cost?" she retorted.

"We don't know yet," he answered quietly. "That's the gamble I took. But you know all about risks like that, don't you, Darcie?"

She stared at him, stony-faced. "Yes, I do."

"We *are* a pair. Today was just a little reminder that this is not a journey to heaven, and you're no angel."

"No," she hissed. "I'm just the woman you have sex with."

"Then I hope we both get what we deserve," he said mockingly, and he motioned for their hovering waiter to serve.

She lost her appetite over that, but she managed to eat some meat and drink some tea, while he devoured everything on his plate.

After, they wandered into the reading room and he struck up a conversation with one of the military men who was looking at *her* with undisguised interest.

He was in his early forties, a veteran of this kind of outpost duty; he was well-fed and had a fleshy face and sharp pale blue eyes.

He introduced himself as Colonel Giles and happy to be of service. And what on earth was a beautiful woman like Madame Boulton doing in Tashkent?

That was blunt and to the point, and the point with the colonel *was* women and sex and nothing else.

"You're looking for *what?*" he asked finally, disbelievingly after the third brandy. "You're wasting all the time of this trip with this adorable woman chasing after who?"

"He's a monk I believe. He might have come this way. I'm looking for someone to translate for us so I can find out."

"Oh hell, you'll always find someone here who wants to earn a few quid. All they have to do is gamble and drink anyway. I'll do it myself, if you don't mind. Can always use a pint and a pound. So tell me about this monk."

"I just want to know if he passed through."

"Is he a criminal?" He gave Darcie a long speculative look up and down. "He hurt Madame Boulton here?"

"No." Con made an instant decision on the basis of his instant dislike of the man *and* the way he was looking at Darcie. "He's a thief. He took something from my family."

"A monk, eh?"

"On the estate," Con lied blandly. "Goole Abbey, in Croxfordshire."

"I see." Giles stroked his chin and looked at Darcie. "Certainly, I'll help you. You want to ask at the church?"

"That's where I'd start."

"All right. These Sarts aren't much for talking anyway. Father Licasi would probably know."

"Is he available now?"

"You're sure in a hurry."

"Tomorrow morning then?"

"He does a seven o'clock mass."

"I'll meet you there."

"Will do," Giles agreed, picking up his snifter and sauntering away. "See you tomorrow. Nice to meet you—both."

"I've never seen you in action before, Darcie. What a treat." He thrust open their hotel door with the force of a bear.

"He's a pig. You'd better go see this Father Licasi without him."

"I appreciate the advice. I know that in your profession you have to be an excellent judge of character."

"Oh you are something, Con Pengellis," she seethed, balling her fists to keep herself from killing him. "The only thing you can hold against me is my making a very bad error in judgment—namely rescuing *you.*"

"Ah, Scheherazade—he was just ogling you."

"But you're the one who spun him that fairy tale."

"Nonsense. I told him all of the truth he needed to know."

"And the rest of it just skirted the edges of being pure fiction. And better than anything I ever made up. Stole something from your family—ha! Diamonds out of a fairy tale . . ."

She swirled around the room furiously because she didn't know what else to do. She felt as if he had left both of them hanging. And he wasn't going to couple with her tonight. She was so annoyed she felt like taking the venal Colonel Giles in his stead.

Just to see what Con would do if he found someone else in her bed.

She ruminated on that satisfying little scenario for a moment. But it wasn't worth the trouble. Once they started on the journey again, there would be no time for all that heat and desire.

But until then—ah! She felt that involuntary sensual twinge. No. No. Not now. But already, she was thinking of the moment he penetrated her earlier that afternoon. All those luscious kisses leading up to that one ravishing crowning of her body.

She had to stop thinking about it.

Suspended by it, dependent on it, yearning for it, out of her mind for it . . . a bare inch of his hard length could make her come . . .

He was right: she was as dissolute as any whore.

They should have separate rooms. Separate lives. She should have left him alone.

"Get undressed, Darcie," he said behind her. "Go to bed."

She undressed behind a screen. That, along with the

bed, a washstand, an overstuffed chair and an armoire, was the only furniture in the room.

And she had very little clothing left; he'd ripped it all to shreds.

I have to stop this. She did have something to wear to bed: an oversized shirt of she'd appropriated from Con. She slipped it on, at once annoyed and aroused by the need for propriety.

Sometimes something covering your body was the most sensual thing of all, she thought, as she crawled into bed. But he wouldn't even give her the pleasure of watching him undress. He waited until he'd lowered the lights, and she knew he was done when his side of the bed depressed.

But he was naked. That was good. And definitely deliciously hard. That was better.

Now she'd just have to make him respond.

"That Colonel Giles *was* very interested in me," she murmured. "English women must be few and far between out here. But surely the men have places they can go to spend themselves. There must be women here who are willing to accommodate a man's lust. Maybe a harem full of women who do it for a price."

Oh yes—this is working. He's steaming already, I just have to pour it on . . .

"Every man must be different, the way he takes a woman. I wonder how a man like the colonel does it. He's a big man. It makes me wonder how big the *best* part of his body is. That's always a sign of a man's potency, don't you think? How big he gets when he's having *social* intercourse with a woman . . ."

She paused coyly, knowing he was seething, knowing she was detonating a bomb. But she wanted it—blasting ferociously deep into her core. And she wasn't averse to lighting the match to send the fire raging out of control.

"I'm trying to remember if I noticed. I mean, why speculate? Of course, I've been concentrating so much on only one man lately. But I'm thinking that I must have noticed *something . . .*"

She felt him lever himself up and climb over her. He grasped her hair and pulled her head back. *Oh yes . . .*

". . . since I can't stop talking about *his . . .*"

He yanked her hair.

"Goddamn you, I'll stuff your mouth if you don't shut up . . ."

"Good," she whispered. "I can't wait."

He felt the primitive roar of absolute dominance explode in his body. Her eyes were his—she'd offered them for life. And her orgiastic body—she would never deny him. And that mouth, that wet, wild, succulently sucking mouth, to live in and die, a thousand little deaths—he wanted it *now.*

With a guttural sound, he came into her mouth, into the wet, the heat, the avid hungry haven of her sucking mouth, her greedy hands, her worship and adoration of the most male part of himself.

She took him, inch by inch, laving and loving him, stroking and caressing the strength and length of him. Pulling everything from him with her lips and her tongue, until he could control it no more, and he spent, in her mouth, all his power.

Nineteen

In the dark, she owned his power and his passion. In the dark, where he couldn't see.

She unbuttoned her shirt and lovingly rubbed the residue of his essence on her skin.

He reached out a languid hand to touch her. "Don't ever do that to me again."

"Do what? Devour you?"

"Bitch. Talk about another man."

"I'm not a whore."

"That remains to be seen."

"Then I guess all observations are fair in this game, Con, if that's what you want me to be."

"At least you don't claim I made you," he murmured, turning on his belly.

"Oh no—" she pushed him. "You don't hide from me. If you're awake and hard, I get to look at you. And if you're asleep and hard—I get to look at you."

"And if *you're* asleep and I'm hard . . . ?"

"Wake me up and take me," she said insolently.

"And if we're having *social* intercourse, and I'm hard?"

She looked at him from under hooded eyes with that elusive, knowing smile as he hardened up before her eyes. "I just know you'll find a way to spend yourself in me."

"You *are* a bitch. I told you I'm hard for you all the time. If you want it, beg for it; I'll stuff you to the hilt, but don't ever *ever* moan and groan about another man's sex to my face."

"Can I moan and groan about *your* sex?" It was thunderously huge now, flexing with all its might, enticing her almost of its own volition.

"No . . . after what you pulled tonight, you have to get on your knees and plead for it."

He rolled over onto his back so that he was poking stiffly into the air.

"At least I can look," she murmured, easing back onto her elbow. "I really *love* looking."

She reached out her hand and stroked him, and he pushed her away.

"Don't try to stoke me, miss bitch. I'll live with my erections. But if you want the colonel, you can't have me."

"There's only one man I want."

He wouldn't be mollified. "You *talked about* his."

She put out a finger and rubbed the underside of his erection. "I don't *want* his."

He caught her finger in his hand. "But you *looked* . . ."

"Maybe," she temporized. "I said maybe I thought I might have . . ." Knowing it was driving him crazy now, and he'd never know if she did or not.

Good. Maybe it would keep him as off balance as she felt.

"You just like looking, don't you? I should just get dressed and never be hard for you again."

"You won't do that. You're about to burst from wanting me. If you just touch me, you'll come like a firecracker. That's how much you want me. You don't care how much I look at you—or any other man—just as long as you're the one in bed with me. You'll probably give

Giles all the details tomorrow so he can salivate over the fact that you're the lucky one. Isn't that what you want? Isn't it?"

"No," he growled, his control slipping. *"You* do—"

All it took were her words . . . and the iron will that held him taut and erect as a pole wavered, and there a drop of his essence pearled up on his luscious tip.

She rubbed it lightly over his head, and brushed her finger over her lower lip. "Take me."

He wasn't giving in.

"Beg me."

"Your body is begging. It wants to come."

His iron will slipped again, and another drop of ejaculate appeared.

"Don't waste it," she cautioned coquettishly. "I need it."

He levered himself up to a sitting position.

"And now you're going to get it. I'm finished playing with you. I'm hard. You're ripe. It doesn't matter where I spend myself. Get off the bed. I want you facedown over the arm of that chair."

She bent over the arm, quivering with excitement. The angle of the arm elevated her bottom and she could feel his length against her crease.

Oh yes . . . yes—all the games and words all to come to this . . . what they hungered for . . . the endless surcease of coupling their bodies . . . yes—

She was canted perfectly to receive him. She clutched the cushion in anticipation as she felt him nudge her just *there.* There was no impediment to his possession. He stood behind, naked, erect, and holding her buttocks to position her, he entered, slowly, slowly, slowly, his body shuddering on contact with her heated wet cleft.

Don't waste it . . .

I need it . . .

He almost blew.

I must have noticed it since I'm talking about it—

His resolve stiffened like a rock.

He would make her forget other men altogether.

He worked his shaft into her an inch at a time. He felt her shivering with anticipation, and wriggling against him, pushing her bottom to accept him, acclimate him and bring him in all the way to the bone.

Don't waste it . . .

The secrets of Eve . . . she knew them all, courtesan that she was. She'd take it any way he gave it, and he wasn't coming till cock crow, and he had pounded her home.

Don't waste it . . .

She was so eager and so wet. She shimmied against him, enticing his thrusts. He gave them to her, hot, hard, emphatic; the same piston-like strokes that she loved, that she begged for. Long steady constant thrusts, in out, in out, holding her hips, in out, absorbing her cries, in out, the center of her world, in out, the core of her being, in out, till she spiralled away, in out, he wouldn't let her go, in out, and she tried to get away, in out, wrenching her body, in out, relinquish his grip, in out, one more thick thrust, in out, pitching them into a storm of sensation impossible to control.

It rammed her dead center, unexpected, unrelenting, pounding her like a hurricane, breaking over her like a dam; he swooped after her and willingly followed her over, and pitched headlong into his wrenching spuming release.

And into silence. That lapping soul-sapping silence, that moment they died the little death.

The only movement, his subtle withdrawal, and they collapsed together on the bed and into the deep swooning silence where nothing needed to be said.

* * *

"I can see Father Licasi alone," Con said the next morning as he sat at the edge of the bed. "There's no need for you to get up."

She stretched luxuriously and reached for him. "I can think of one reason." She struggled to sit up. "In fact . . ." She slipped onto her knees in front of him, and grasped his jutting length in her hand. "I can think of two."

"We don't have much time."

"Then let me coat my nipples with your cream. That's the only thing I want this morning. You can give me that—" She circled his head and began to pump, arching her back to give him an unobstructed view of her breasts. "There—" as he spurted. "There—" as she anointed her breasts, and she took him home.

He left her a half hour later, lolling in bed. She felt pagan, primitive. Curiously sated. She wanted to lie in bed naked all day long, waiting for him. Impossibly, she wanted him again.

Tomorrow, they would start the next leg of the journey, north toward Omsk. Days and days of travel, with no time to give in to their desire. Of course, she wanted to have as much as possible of him now.

She wouldn't let him leave the bed when he returned, she thought. She wouldn't even get dressed. Or pack. She wished she were certain he was thinking about her, that he wanted her.

But there was something in him that enabled him to put all these things into different compartments to be examined one at a time. He could just remove himself from *her,* relegating her to the compartment marked *satisfied for now.*

And now, he followed Lazarin's trail.

When he returned, she would make him forget all that. They had one more day . . .

She awakened to the sound of a knock on the door—and she jumped out of bed. She didn't know how long she'd slept, but maybe that was good because he was back already, and sooner than if she'd spent all that time waiting.

Stark naked, she pulled open the door and jumped back in shock.

"Colonel Giles!"

"Aren't you eager," he said, closing the door behind him as she flew behind the dressing screen. "I love it when a woman is eager."

"What do you want? Why are you here?" She had no clothes; nothing to wear. Frantically, she pulled on the wreck of a shirt and her skirt.

"Don't hide from me, you little tart. I read the invitation in your eyes. I know what you want. I made sure to get your paramour out of the way. We have—oh—fifteen minutes, a half hour at the most." He tossed away the screen. "How much do you want?"

"Are you crazy?" she shrieked. "Get out of here!" She dove across the bed and scrambled to her feet just as he pulled a short fat riding crop out of his boot.

He's insane. Living with this deprivation . . .

He smacked the crop against the bed. "Don't play coy, whore. Looking at me like that. Name your price, I'll pay it."

"He'll be back sooner than that." She needed a story. She was Scheherazade, wasn't she? "He never leaves me alone for long. I swear to you, he'll kill you if he finds you here. If he says a half hour, you can be sure he'll return in ten minutes. He *owns* me."

"Well, I'm going to possess you too, you little hot-tailed tart. Wriggling your bottom at me like you want it." He struck the bed again. "What do you expect a man to do? I can pay for it. But I'd love to force you. It's your choice."

She stood shivering by the window, thinking that throwing herself out and landing on Con's head was easier than trying to reason with him.

And that riding crop was scary. And he *looked* like he loved to use it.

"Colonel, if you just leave this minute, I'll never tell anyone you came."

"You're very very good at this, my lovely, just the right amount of indignation and outrage. Is that your act in bed? But—we're getting nowhere, and obviously—" he paced around to the foot of the bed, "you like it rough." He struck the footboard.

She jumped onto the bed, putting the footboard between them. But that was worse, cat and mouse. Either way she went, he could corner her, and she didn't see anything she could use as a weapon at hand.

"Eager little piece, aren't you? Just lay down and relax, you strumpet, and I'll give you what you want."

She eyed him warily; he just stood there, smacking the crop against his hand, waiting for her move. One way or the other . . . she couldn't just hold him there until Con returned.

She made a feinting move toward the window side of the bed, and he took two steps around to grab her.

She popped off the bed toward the door, reaching to pick up the screen. Anything, anything—too heavy— maybe she could jab him with it.

He vaulted over the bed after her, and she lifted it, with difficulty, and swung it over his head.

Wham! He collapsed on the mattress. *Wham!* To make sure he was unconscious. *Wham!* Her temper got the best of her. She dropped the screen on the floor and knelt beside the bed.

It was a lump of soggy manhood. She debated a moment about whether to search him before she dragged his sorry carcass out of the room.

Why not? He had no business being here. He was supposed to have met Con at the church to interpret for him with this Father Licasi.

She rolled him over, and tapped her hands over his uniform; nothing obvious there. She unbuttoned his tunic, and folded it back to the inside pocket.

Ah! Everything here.

Just not what she expected. No military identification. No letters of commission. Nothing, except a passport in the name of Percival Giles—from a village in Croxfordshire.

Oh, this was getting crazy. They had relaxed their guard too much, never counting on Lavinia's arm reaching *this* far.

They had to have been followed from Srinagar.

But how? Sidhu had made the strictest arrangements. Had buried the grotto. Destroyed the clues.

Had he?

She didn't know what to think. She didn't have time to think. The only decision she had to make was whether to leave him for Con to see.

And that was taken out of her hands moments later, when he appeared at the door.

"Well, well, well Scheherazade; are you telling him bedtime stories too?"

She wheeled around, startled. Thought fast. Didn't want him asking what Giles was doing here in the first place, but that was inevitable. But maybe she could detract from his questions by what she'd found.

"It's worse than that, Con. He lied."

"Oh, he did. He never showed up, and look where he is."

"Listen to me. No more fun and games. He is *not* military." She thrust the passport in his hand.

He scanned it quickly. "Oh Jesus." He tossed it on the bed. "Damnation. It gets worse. Father Licasi speaks English."

"And?" She was pulling out their suitcases as he spoke.

"He probably thought he'd seduce the thing out of you—" Con muttered. "I'll kill him."

"Father Licasi?" she asked, grabbing whatever clothing she found to hand and folding it haphazardly into the suitcase.

"This piece of cow dung." He nudged the body with the toe of his boot. "Not so alluring now, is it? I think it's dead."

She ignored that. There was no time for games. This was serious. "What did Father Licasi say?"

"Father said all Russians are messengers of Death. And many itinerant priests have come through Tashkent because of its direct route to Omsk and the Trans-Siberian railroad. He remembers this one, particularly because he was not travelling to St. Petersburg or Moscow. He didn't know his name. But he told the Father his calling was the Siberian village of Nadyl on the Nizmennost Plains of Siberia."

She felt chilled down to her toes. The diamond was the key. And a sparsely populated area in which Lazarin could unleash its evil powers.

"We can go by wagon and coach to Omsk. But it's a three-day journey. And probably that and more to Nadyl, by wagon or sled."

"But he was here, Lazarin was here. And now Lavinia is in pursuit, sending this piece of offal, her agent."

"Which means—"

"They were in Srinagar," Darcie finished for him. "And they know we're together."

Worse and worse if that were true. She hadn't even considered that aspect, that Lavinia must see them as the guardians of two treasures to confiscate.

She should leave him, she thought. They should separate. He could move so much better, so much faster without her. And there would only be one life and one thing of value on the line.

Her hands trembled as she threw the last of their meager possessions into the suitcases.

"I could . . ."

Con closed the suitcase emphatically. "We go together, and leave him here. You saved me the trouble of killing him. We are in service of the diamond. You are the chosen; when the time comes, you must be at hand."

"It's a lot of nonsense, mumbo-jumbo," she whispered. "Too much to risk when your life is at stake. And I'm scared to death of what the consequences will be of your covenant with Lazarin."

"A devil's bargain," he said, shrugging. "He does give us what we want, but it *was* a gift."

"Or maybe—" a thought suddenly struck her that was the most terrifying of all, "it was the only way for Lazarin to get possession of *The Eye of God.*"

Lazarin had orchestrated the whole thing.

They set off to Omsk with that awful conclusion hovering over them. Everything, from the entity Karun in his original guise as the deckhand, to the moment when they breached the tunnel and entered the grotto, it all had been planned and designed so that Con would come and liberate the stone.

"We could ruminate on this for the whole three hundred miles of this trip," Con said. "There's nothing rational about these events."

"But now it starts to make some eerie kind of sense. You said yourself he couldn't move it. And he gave you back your sight. Why? Because he knew you understood his magic and that it had to be stopped. And how? By the power of the stone that only you could move."

"But now you're in the equation, Darcie. And that's the thing that throws it off."

"And Lavinia." She looked at the desolate landscape without seeing it. "But apart from her desperation to possess the stone and have an heir, where does Lavinia fit?"

"Lavinia wants the stone and wants an heir. And maybe it's as clear cut as that."

"But still—the cruelty toward you . . ."

"I was an arrogant beast, Darcie. But seven years in a dungeon makes a self-centered man angry, hungry, vengeful and mature."

"She'd kill you in a minute, and maybe that was Giles' mandate today," she said thoughtfully. "But how—no, I won't think it . . ."

"I've considered it. How did he get here before us?"

"If Lavinia knows, then she has made a pact with that devil too."

"Or," Con said, thinking the unthinkable, "it was Sidhu."

They stayed overnight at a road inn in Karazhal, one of several way stations on the journey to Omsk, where they shared a sleeping dormitory with a dozen strangers.

In the morning, they were given a breakfast of tea and cakes, and a coach accommodating six arrived there at eight. It left within the hour, and within two, they were acquainted with their fellow travellers: a doctor, an English governess on her way to St. Petersburg after touring the Mediterranean; a banker; and an importer of Russian artifacts, jewelry and gemstones.

Darcie clutched Con's arm. *Dear God—he wasn't saying it but what he meant was—diamonds . . .*

They were everywhere—

But not by word or action did the gentleman betray anything suspicious, and Darcie thought that within such close quarters for so many hours, he would have let slip something.

Maybe it was a coincidence. Maybe they were looking for demons where there weren't any.

It was snowing when the coach rumbled into Omsk down the slushy main street in the center of the city. Here and everywhere, broomsmen worked, sweeping the snow from the sidewalks, dodging sleds and wagons, and passersby. They passed block after block of shops, restaurants and a theater square.

Beyond this was the railway station and a block of hotels, and the coach pulled in front of these.

"Did you arrange your accommodations?" the import merchant inquired. "I can recommend one if you're going to stay a while."

"Are you?" Darcie said. "Staying, I mean."

"Oh no. No." He was a funny little man, plump, stylish and very precise. "I'm heading north in three days' time to the diamond fields of the Nizmennost Plains of Siberia." He leaned toward them confidentially. "I make my best deals with the *natives,* man to man, you understand. My little secret, so I trust you won't tell. But if you're not remaining in Omsk, you'd be just as comfortable at the Hotel Vyatka at the end of the block. I'm staying there myself. Good luck!"

And he was off.

"I don't think we can afford *not* to stay there," Con muttered. "I've got to find out who that man is, and why he's going north to Nizmennost."

And there were other arrangements to be made: money to be converted; registering at the hotel; clothes for the icy climate; the rental of a *drozhky;* horses, furs, a driver who would take them as far as Okrug.

The hotel cost two rubles a night for the most utilitarian room. The transportation, more than a hundred times that.

"It's worth it," Con said.

"I'm impressed at your knowledge of Russian," Darcie murmured.

"Enough to get by."

They went to a nearby restaurant for dinner, tramping in their warm mountain garments through the packed snow. No one looked askance. There were so many travellers passing through Omsk.

And they needed to talk where they couldn't be overheard.

They took a table very far in the back near the kitchen with no one else near, and ordered a simple menu of soup, roast pork, potatoes and tea.

"We don't even know what that man's name was," Darcie fretted.

"I'll find him," Con said grimly, "and I'll find out what he's up to."

"I'm scared."

"We do *not* have a choice. That diamond is already split in two. The best we can hope is that we can recover both pieces."

And he was deadly serious.

"We have no plan."

"Maybe things work better *without* a plan. How could you plan for the appearance of a Lazarin?"

"We must be running out of money."

"We will have to sell another stone fairly soon."

"Perhaps to our friend the importer?" Darcie suggested.

"You mean—as a test? I think he'd call the authorities in the blink of an eye. He's someone who very well might know the Pengellis diamonds. No, *I*—yes, *I'm* going to get into his room and find out who he is, and if he's a threat. And yes, I'll have the revolver, so just keep quiet, Darcie, and eat your soup."

"I have to do *something,*" she grumbled later as they finished their tea.

He sent her a scorching look. "Wait up for me."

Their room was small, with the chimney of a central heating stove radiating a fair amount of warmth. There were hooks on the door for clothes, a wash basin and stand. Two kerosene lamps. A small table and one sagging chair.

It would do. Only she was the one waiting, and there was no room to pace. She sat at the table wearily and waited.

Con and his waiting. A person could die waiting.

She jumped up impatiently. It was a coincidence. It had to be.

Lavinia just couldn't move that fast. *Couldn't.*

And yet—

Time crept by. Con had left her on their return from dinner, and she had no idea how long ago that was. And the room was in the back of the hotel, on an upper floor, and all she could see was rooftops and the sky.

And an occasional light dimming, and finally going out.

How late could it be?

And then, she imagined something happened to Con. The merchant had caught him, abducted him, killed him. Or called the authorities. Or something.

Why wasn't he here yet?

She threw herself across the bed. Better to sleep than make up scenarios that had no basis in reality.

Wait up for me . . .

She thought she would.

She slept.

And felt a hand on her arm, shaking her awake.

She bolted upright. "Con!"

"Shhh."

"What? Tell me!" she demanded in a whisper.

"His name is Kleist, according to the coachman. But he's not registered at the Vyatka. Or either of the two other hotels. Or any of the rooming houses that I found when I was searching out the driver. That precious little man has disappeared into thin air."

Nor could they find any trace of him the following morning. And as far as they could tell, he hadn't rented a driver and sled.

"This is too eerie," Darcie said.

Snow was falling again, and they had come out early to scour the shops for woollen clothing and furs.

"I feel as if we imagined him."

"Or else he's biding his time, waiting until we leave." Con was spending rubles like they were wheat. Two fur blankets; a little heater for coals; sheepskin boots and coats for both of them, and a fur throw.

"You're insane."

"It's cold." He bought woollen underwear and suits for each of them, and mittens, socks and gloves. And some dried fruit and beef; canteens for tea and water and—"I think that's enough."

They needed a wagon to bring it all back to the hotel, but there seemed always to be an *izvozchik* waiting for a fare.

Dinner out again in the hotel restaurant, their table tucked in a far corner where they could talk.

Still, Darcie felt so far removed from the world they were about to breach. She could almost pretend that they were on holiday—or a honeymoon. Oh, but that thought was best left buried.

Especially when Con told her the precautions he'd taken.

"We'll have with us two revolvers and a knife. And I found a small lead-lined container for our trust, which you must wear fastened around your waist. We can't lose it. Or the remaining stones. I plan to sell the next one tomorrow in the market. And then we'll each have one, in case anything happens."

"Nothing will happen," Darcie said, her voice tight.

"We're travelling relatively light so we can move fast and get things done."

"You call that mountain of fur and wool *light?*"

"For the lower reaches of Siberia—yes. You'll be ready to move out as soon as tomorrow morning, as soon as I return."

"And until then?" she whispered.

He sent her a heated glance. "You'll move for me tonight, because, Scheherezade, I'm hot and ready and burning for you."

Twenty

A night of secret pleasures, told in the dark.
Always in the dark. Began in the dark, ended in the dark,
by touch, by word, by feel. Naked in the dark, your sex open
in the dark, with a hunger you yearn to feed.
That way, in the dark, upside down, cradling his sex while
he worships your crown.
The dark passion devours you; you resist, then you come,
in the dark, on his tongue, till he finally sucks you away . . .

He left for the market at dawn, having called for tea,
and bundling himself in the new underwear, suit, coat
and gloves.

She felt leisurely this morning, replete from sex, and
removed from the idea of any threats. She could drink
some tea, pack—it seemed like she was always packing—
and they would get a late morning start.

It was still snowing, and it had drifted up against the
rooftops and the back of the buildings that she could
see. And she heard the unmistakable sound of a cow
mooing in the distance.

Just for this moment, things felt right.

And then she picked up the case in which she would
carry *The Eye of God*—and the feeling dissipated.

She took the diamond in her hands, and held it to the light, and for the life her, she couldn't understand why men risked their lives to possess this large dull stone.

She wrapped it in coarse cotton and tucked it into the case. Then she threaded a belt through an attached loop, and wound it around her waist.

She pinned the pouch with the Pengellis diamond on her camisole between her breasts. Now, she thought, she was ready to get dressed.

She waited a long time—too long—for him to return, pottering around the room; filling the canteen with the remaining tea, rearranging everything in the suitcases—anything to fill the time and ease her fears.

But when he came, the news wasn't good.

"Kleist is still in Omsk. He was at the market, waiting—"

"Oh my God . . ."

"Following me . . . shadowing me—there was nowhere to make a deal."

"What are we going to do?"

"I think I outwitted him for the moment. Our driver is waiting. We're leaving—*now.*"

"Oh God—Con . . ."

"Shhh . . . everything is taken care of. Grab your suit and coat and let's *go.*"

They left by a back staircase, slipping out a side door, into an alleyway. Con took the risk and summoned the driver to pull up there.

She threw everything onto the floor and tumbled into the backseat.

Their driver snapped his whip, the sled lurched forward, and in a matter of minutes, they were one of dozens of conveyances plying the streets of Omsk, until they passed over the train tracks, and down broad avenues to the outskirts of the town, and they were gone.

* * *

She wasn't reassured that they had gotten a head start on Kleist.

"He's coming after us, and not the other way around."

"Probably," Con said. "It's still another chance we have to take." He had tented the blankets over their heads both to protect them from the steadily falling snow, and to give them some anonymity.

"Dmitri, our driver, says he's done it many times," Con said. "One wonders."

"And what if Kleist got to him? What if he's waiting somewhere down the line?"

"We'll do what we have to do. All I care about is if you're warm."

"I'm warm."

"It's damned cold. Your nose is red. Bury it in that fur for a while."

"God, I can't believe we're doing this. All for that stone. Every time I look at it, I see a big colorless rock."

"And yet—" he started to say, and he caught himself. "Maybe not yet. This isn't the time to extol the properties of the stone."

"When will that be? When Lazarin is about to kill us?"

"That *would* be a good time, yes."

"Con—"

"Shhhh. We're going forward, Darcie. That's all we have to know."

But they didn't go swiftly. Several hours into the trip, they stopped to change horses, and replenish their tea and coals. By nightfall, they were ready to stop, and they found a hostel.

Again, they slept in a barracks, wrapped in fur and

heat, among a half dozen travellers who had also sought shelter for the price of ten kopecks.

They were off again in the morning, through a landscape dotted with huts, rivers and mansions, seen through a curtain of diminishing snow.

"Dmitri says—another day, maybe two if the weather keeps up."

"I'm hungry. I *hate* this place."

"We'll find something to eat."

She'd never seen such a bleak landscape. The snow was intermittent and ongoing, constant and white.

Another change of horses at another way station Dmitri knew, and they were able to get breakfast: eggs, meat, tea, water. It was enough. But the lower reaches of Siberia were endless, a horizon that stretched into the night.

They pulled in once again to a barracks for the night.

Dmitri negotiated the price and took off the horses, and she and Con went inside. There were a dozen travellers in the bunks in various stages of sleep.

"Darcie!" Con reached out and held her back. "Kleist . . ."

She gasped. Kleist here, in the wilds of Okrug when Con had outwitted him two days before in the Omsk grand market.

God, there was no end.

They backed out of the room, and into the vestibule.

"I'll get Dmitri." Even he was shaken. He was back in several moments. "Come."

They slipped out into the snow and into the side yard where the sleighs and animals were corralled.

"We have to go *now,*" he said, as they approached Dmitri. But he'd already told him that.

"The horses are ragged out."

"I don't care." What was he doing, arguing with a peasant driver?

"You go at your peril," Dmitri said, and then he started laughing loudly, contemptuously, taunting them with his laughter as he transformed himself, before their very eyes into the plump body and plummy tones of Kleist. Laughing at them, mocking them as if to say he was invincible, and they'd never get away from him.

He couldn't reach a gun; he couldn't pull the knife.

He grabbed Darcie and they ran, ducking behind the sledges and horses, and out of sight of their nemesis.

His laughter echoed into the night.

"I hope . . . I pray," Con muttered, "another travel-ler comes in here tonight."

They merged with the shadows, burdened with their bags. They moved slowly, cautiously, Kleist's laughter fol-lowing them.

"He can't be everywhere, dammit," Con swore, dig-ging for a weapon. His fingers grasped the knife. "Good enough to immobilize Karun. Good enough to under-cut Kleist. Can you see him?"

"I don't think he's moved," Darcie whispered.

"Let's get closer, from his back."

The laughter was impossible, high-pitched, not quite sane.

They crawled noiselessly toward him on the snow.

"It won't work, you know," Kleist called out. "I know where you are. Just give me the woman. And the stone."

Con gestured for Darcie to stay still. They were within feet of Kleist whose laughter echoed into the trees.

"Come out, we'll talk, perhaps we'll make a trade. You've already accepted a gift from Samael—" and he laughed again.

Con crept closer. Closer still.

Aim at the head.

He poised the knife on the tip of his fingers. He gauged the distance to the entity's head. He aimed.

Kleist laughed hysterically, horribly.

He snapped his wrist and released the knife.

It hit Kleist with a sickening thud, and he dropped like a stone.

"Darcie—!" He reached behind him to grab her. "I have to make sure."

Darcie covered her eyes. "I don't want to see."

He inched forward toward the body; it had fallen forward, the shaft of the knife buried in its neck. Blood spewed from the wound, a shocking pool of red on a white ground.

"It's not moving. It's bleeding."

"How much time?"

"I don't know. And I don't know if we should go or stay."

"We can't move anywhere in this snow."

"You're probably right. I'm going to drag him into the trees and cover up the blood. You go inside and get us two bunks."

"I don't want to leave you."

"You're better inside."

"I've never been so scared."

"I'll be in soon." He watched her reluctantly go, and he looked down at the bloody entity. Immobilized for maybe a day.

Or maybe a bloodthirsty man could do something about that.

Silently, with only the snow as witness, he pulled the thing into the shadows, and made sure it was dead.

And now he had blood on his hands, in the name of *The Eye of God*.

He took the reins of the sled the next morning, and they forged ahead; blindly, snow blown, determined, they pressed on toward Okrug in tandem with two other travellers who were going that way.

Blessed be . . .

They could have been attacked by their enemy.

They could have died in the snow.

The power of the stone . . . ?

Buried in the snow, what remained of Kleist, never to be found until the snow thawed . . .

In the name of . . . ?

They raced on through the storm, the whole of their world a white vista before them. Stopping for maps, food, change of horses, sleep.

Through Strezhvoy, Nizhne, Tarko-Selo, pausing only to ask had people seen him, did they know him, the tall ascetic monk with the burning eyes.

They knew of him, they said; they'd never seen him. And it was said he lived in the village of Nadyl on the Nizmennost Plains of Siberia.

And it was there they headed in those final hours, deep on the plain in the near north reaches of Siberia.

The place of diamonds and death.

It was a village of thatched log huts lining either side of the snow-slick road. And then a church, a school-house, a cemetery dressed in white. An abandoned wagon, a lone braying cow, fenced-in yards. And a knot of a half dozen children racing alongside them, throwing snowballs, and calling out questions.

"Where is your village priest?" Con asked them, and they pointed to a large house next to the church. "Where are your fathers?"

They said, "Down in the mines."

"Whom can I talk to?"

"Father Vasili."

They drove into the church courtyard, surrounded by the children.

"We're a novelty," Con said, as he helped Darcie from under the tent of furs in which she'd been wrapped the entire journey. "The priest will welcome us, hopefully he'll feed us, and tell us what we need to know."

He was tall, Father Vasili, and dark, dressed in his robes, and he appeared immediately at the door of the presbytery with a welcoming smile, shooing the children away all the while.

"My son, my daughter—come. There's tea and cakes. Come, get warm."

They removed their coats and their boots in the vestibule, and followed him into the large well-lit room where he motioned them to a table that was set at a right angle to the window, and on either side of which were comfortable upholstered chairs and a sofa.

"Sit on the sofa, do. Manya will bring food. I know you're from far away. Tell me your names."

Con told him, filling him in as best he could with limited language on why they had come.

Father Vasili nodded from time to time and then: "Ah! Here's Manya. Let us warm ourselves before we speak."

They drank, they ate a leisurely meal, by the end of which Darcie was itching to get some answers.

Con sensed her mood and opened the discussion, translating for Darcie as his questions were answered.

"Father, we've come from India seeking some answers. What can you tell us?"

"My son, my daughter, you've come such a long way on your quest. I can tell you, it ends here. Whether it

is what you want to know—well . . . it is for you to tell
me."

"We have heard, along the road and in the villages,
that the man we seek is known by many to live among
the people here in Nadyl. He is said to be a monk, a
man of purpose. He is said to carry a divine stone."

"Ah, the stone. Yes, he is our holy man, blessed is he.
But you mistake, my children; he has been among us
for years."

They looked at each other in shock.

"Oh, yes, he came among us with his talisman stone.
He blessed it to our community; sanctified it to the
blood of Our Father by dipping it in goat's blood; and
in the name of his divine Lord, he cleaved it. A piece
of that stone reposes in the church, and we believe im-
plicitly in its powers."

"And the other piece?" Con asked shakily.

"Our holy man has taken it to St. Petersburg to gift
a part of this miraculous stone to our beloved Father
Russia with the prayer that it will guide his rule and the
country will prosper."

"Oh, dear God," Darcie breathed. "No . . ."

"So . . ." Con went on, pushing aside his shock, "he
is gone."

"But for two weeks, maybe three."

"And a piece of this stone remains in your church?"

"Indeed. Would you like to see it?"

"We would."

"We shall. There is a walkway to the church. I will
take you."

They put on the coats and boots and went out into
the swirling snow.

"So white the landscape," the priest murmured. "So
black the holy stone. This is," he added, as he pulled

open a thick wooden door, "the incantation of our holy man. And in a moment, you shall see why."

He led them from the outer passage into the sanctuary, a simple church for a plain people. Stark white walls, wooden pews, a simple altar, a heavy pine wooden cross over it.

And there, to the side of the altar, displayed in an elaborate sarcophagus, was a faceted piece of *The Stone of Samael.*

"And your holy man, Lazarin, he consecrated this stone to your church?" Con asked, appalled.

"Oh no . . . no. Indeed, the stone was blessed to our church. But our holy man—his name is Rasputin."

They were given a guest room on the first floor of the presbytery. Father Vasili did not want them travelling any further.

They had dinner with him, and pleasant conversation, and then he left them alone.

"What are we going to do?" Darcie whispered.

"We have to steal that stone. Sneak in when the priest is sleeping. And then we've got to get to St. Petersburg, and see what we can find there."

"God, I hate this. I was shocked when he said he's always been among them."

"Power of suggestion, enhanced by the stone. They have no idea what's in that sanctuary."

"I have a feeling they don't care."

"I think you're right."

"I hope we can do this," she fretted. "I didn't expect this, did you?"

"I thought he'd be here," Con said. "But nothing has happened the way I thought."

And they waited. The clock in the presbytery parlor tolled midnight. One. Two.

Darcie took the candlestick and got their boots and coats. And then, like ghosts, they slipped out of the side door and into the snowy night.

The sky was as dark as a tomb. Not a star, not the moon, nothing to light their way but one flickering candle.

"God, this is eerie . . ." Darcie whispered, cupping the flame to shield it from the wind.

"Keep walking."

Their boots made such a loud crunch in the snow, loud enough to wake the dead. All around them, a matte, flat silence. They pushed forward, in the dark.

"We're almost there."

She held up the candle as they reached the doors.

"They always leave them open."

They slipped inside.

"Don't talk; the sound echoes."

Into the sanctuary, the candle flame casting long ghostly shadows in front of them.

Down the aisle they went and up onto the altar, to the shrine where the sarcophagus was kept, closed at night when supplicants were sleeping.

Darcie stood beside him, holding the candle aloft, as Con eased open the cover of the casket. The stone was nestled there, opaque, pitch black, evil incarnate on a pillow of tapestry depicting a biblical scene.

"Now . . ." He took it in both hands.

It didn't move.

"Oh my God . . ."

He tried to prise it up.

It didn't move.

"Darcie . . ."

She set the candle down and together they tried to heave it.

It didn't budge.

"Only Lazarin can move it," Darcie whispered. "Just like he couldn't remove *The Eye of God.*"

"You have it?"

"Yes."

"Take it out."

She saw he was desperate, leeching on to the one thing that had any connection with the stone so far away from its cave of origin.

She tumbled open her coat and pulled open the case. Handed him the wrapped oval of the stone. Grabbed the candle, and then stood back, terrified of what she would see.

He pulled away the protective cotton, and the stone began sparkling all over, radiating like the sun. And then suddenly it shot a fiery lance straight into the heart of the black diamond.

The air crackled above it, lightning bolts shot in the air. Before their horrified eyes, the diamond disintegrated, in the casket, and Con watched, his face impassive, until it was nothing more than a handful of black dust.

"Like a scorch mark," Darcie whispered.

He closed the lid of the sarcophagus. "It is done."

"We should take the casket with us."

He shook his head. "There is no need. Its terrible power is destroyed."

He took one step off of the dais, and stopped. *"Who's there?"*

Darcie slowly lifted the candle, her heart pounding, her whole body shaking in abject terror.

A shadow loomed menacingly at the door, long, lean,

filling the threshold and the whole of the sanctuary with the odor of corruption.

It raised its hand in conviction. Its voice echoed in the darkness, deep, eerie, otherworldly as it paced toward them.

"In the name of Samael," it thundered, *"so shall you be judged . . ."*

And then it vanished into a wisp of smoke that trailed the foul stench of walking death.

They laid everything they had out on the bed: the diamond, now wrapped and in its case; the Pengellis stones, of which there were three; the remaining rubles—of which too little would remain once they gave alms to Father Vasili for the church.

"It was Lazarin," Darcie said. "He is everywhere. We'll never outrun him."

"He is in St. Petersburg, cutting up the rest of that damned stone. And we have to get out of here before the good Father discovers our deceit."

"I think that priest knows everything."

"Anything is possible," he muttered, counting the rubles. "We'll need at least one change of horses as we go through—at least till we reach a place I can barter the diamond."

"This is so crazy." She still felt it—the horror, the terror, the panic. Her hands shook; her heart pounded as if she thought he were standing right outside their door.

Boom boom—at the door—heavy knocking, like doom.

She jumped. Con was more forethinking: he swept their stash into the case with *The Eye of God,* and thrust it under a pillow.

"Open the door."

She swallowed her foreboding, and slowly opened the door.

"Good morning, my children."

Father Vasili.

She let out her breath. "Father."

"Breakfast is served. Already it's dawn. I have a feeling you wish to be on your way."

"As soon as we can, Father."

"So it will be," he murmured, and left them.

Darcie closed the door. "That was odd. He can't have discovered it gone already."

Con stared at the door. "Can't he? We've got to get out of here. Come *on.*"

It took them fifteen minutes to wash, dress and get together their things, and then they joined Father Vasili in the parlor.

"I have had our cook put together some food for you. It's a long journey to St. Petersburg."

That stopped them cold. *How did he know?* Darcie started to ask, but Con shook his head.

"Thank you, Father. You are indeed perceptive in all things."

They sat at the table and ate: coffee, fresh bread and cheese.

"We are indebted to you for your kindness," Con said, as they donned their coats and boots in the outer room.

"Perhaps it is I who must thank you," Father Vasili said.

Con pressed a handful of rubles in his hand. "For your trouble."

The priest nodded. "So it shall be, my son. Your sled awaits you. I have packed the basket inside."

He walked them out into the sun bright morning,

and helped Darcie into the seat. Con spread the blankets, and throw and positioned himself beside her.

"Godspeed, my son," Father Vasili said, making a sign over them and Darcie saw his lips move as if in prayer.

In the name of Samael . . . judge of the dead—

No, no—she didn't see that . . .

Con snapped the whip and the horses took off.

"Con—"

"Shhh . . ." He urged the team faster.

She swallowed her words and, her heart pounding wildly, she turned around.

Lazarin stood at the presbytery door, laughing.

Twenty-one

They were travelling too fast, too long, working the horses beyond endurance, and themselves too. They stopped, first at Nizhne just for the night, and finally, at Tobolsk, the next near-sized city to Omsk.

They had travelled a day and night by then, as fast as if the furies were after them, and they hadn't even touched the basket of food.

Or maybe, Darcie thought, still trembling at the memory of Lazarin watching them depart from the church in Nadyl, they had decided by mute consent, they had better not. That if they opened whatever was packed inside that basket, they might release an unholy host.

"We haven't come nearly far enough," she murmured, as they unhitched the horses in the dooryard of an inn they had come upon just outside the city.

"Far enough for tonight," Con said, heaving up their suitcases, basket of food, and the furs. "We can make one more night on the money we have. Tomorrow, I'll sell whatever I can—even the furs. We won't need them once we reach Samara; we can get the train there."

"It *was* Lazarin in the presbytery courtyard," Darcie said. "What if he turns up, like that awful Kleist, here?"

"I'll kill him again," Con said, with not a trace of

emotion in his voice. "And as many times as it takes to destroy him."

"And if he never dies?"

"He's still not holy enough to redeem the world."

He was dreaming again, on a deep blue sea. Ships, and storms, and diamonds in the rough, and Lavinia, where she shouldn't be . . .

Conscripted—anonymous . . . how he'd come . . . Three months at sea for a cut of the sell. And then something, at docking swung high and struck. All he remembered—but it was enough . . .

Lazarin, laughing . . . and vision gone—

He jerked awake in the dimly lit room to find himself sleeping on a chair, and Darcie curled up on the bed.

Lazarin—everywhere . . .

He'd had an accident on the docks on some voyage over. He couldn't remember it, not what, nor where. Only the sense of injury, and his body falling, almost as if they had disposed of him there.

And then what? Madame came calling, looking for prospects?

"Darcie." He shook her awake.

"Umm. What?"

"It was an accident. The blindness. I don't know where or when. But it was an accident. And they left me for dead."

"So glad you remembered," she muttered and turned back to sleep.

It answered some questions at least. And he could infer the rest. The ship had docked in London, for one thing. And he *had* managed to elude his captors. And he would've gotten home.

Lazarin . . .

On one side, shrouding the powers of The Stone of
Samael. *And Lavinia, on the other, so desperate to find* The
Eye of God *she would kill.*

Why? Why?

Why?

Lazarin, knowing he was powerless to move The Eye of
God.

*Lavinia, searching the four corners of the world for it—to
learn its secrets, to deplete its power?*

*And Darcie, in the middle of it all, with a baby that didn't
exist, and Lavinia avid to possess it.*

*It was as bizarre as anything he'd ever experienced, and he
wouldn't have believed it if he hadn't seen for himself.*

And he knew it wasn't over yet.

"We're not taking the basket."

Darcie dropped it onto the bed. "We're not. All right.
Maybe we should look through it?"

He stared at it, an innocent wooden basket with a towel
laid neatly over foodstuffs for a trip, packed by a consci-
entious peasant cook who worked for the village priest.
What could be in there that wasn't blessed? Breads,
cheeses, a bottle of milk? Some cold meat, fish, eggs and
fruit.

Darcie had seen Lazarin in the dooryard.

"You're right. We should see what's in there."

Darcie pulled away the napkin. The basket was
crammed with shapes wrapped in paper and cloth.

In the name of . . .

"I'll do it," Con said. "I'm the one." He took out
the first of the shapes and unwrapped it. A loaf of bread.
Then, a block of cheese. The next: a bag of apples.
Pieces of cold roast chicken. A jug of milk, slightly sour.

And on the bottom, a piece of paper, folded into a

packet and sealed with a wax stamp marked with an indistinguishable sign.

And writing on the back: "Open in Samara," Con translated.

They looked at each other.

"I didn't even know we were going there," Con said slowly. "How did he?"

"Which *he?*" Darcie murmured, a chill coursing down her spine.

Con rubbed his grizzled face, his tired eyes and made the decision. "All right. We leave everything here."

"Not that," Darcie said slowly. "We have to open that. We have to know what it is."

"Especially that," Con countered. "And I don't want to know."

"I have a better idea. What if we open it on the way?"

"Let's open it now." He held her eyes. "Or do you think for some mystical reason, we have to comply."

He moved to the window without waiting for her reply, and pulled at the seal; the paper ripped and he unfolded it carefully.

She peered over his arm to see what it contained.

A handful of black dust, against the white parchment. Overriding evil, wafting into the air.

"Fold it up!" Darcie cried. "Hurry. Hurry." She grabbed the packet from his hand and threw it into the embers in the fireplace grate.

They flamed up instantly, roaring up the chimney, crackling like a witch's laughter, howling like an animal in pain.

The fire reached out, threatening to consume them.

She grabbed the jar of milk and poured it on. It hissed and spit like a tiger as it burned into the air.

She threw in the bread, the chicken, and it devoured all of that.

And then she laid on the cheese, and it slowly melted over the popping, snapping flames until they diminished and finally went out.

"We would have brought that with us to Samara," she said, her voice suffused with horror. "We would have unleashed the unspeakable evil of Samael in Samara."

He had no answers. "How did you know what to do?"

"I don't know. I just knew."

They looked at each other. No words needed to be said. She wore *The Eye of God*, and she was blessed.

Three days later, they were travelling west toward St. Petersburg on the Trans-Siberian railway. Here, as in the pullman cars of the Orient Express, they had a private compartment with pull-down berths, a folding table, a washroom, and closet. Attendants to make up the beds, and a dining car with luncheon served at eleven, tea at four, and light edibles available into the late hours, and even delivered, if you wished, to your car.

It was pure luxury after everything they'd been through, and Darcie sank into it with a hedonistic sigh. There wasn't enough food to fill her, or water to bathe.

There wasn't enough Con either. He sat silent as a grave.

"Come, eat. We're safe for the moment."

"I'm not so sure." He rubbed his eyes wearily. "I don't even know what we can accomplish in St. Petersburg."

"We can find Lazarin. We can destroy what's left of the stone. Surely that's not so impossible."

He smiled blearily. "It's a huge city, Darcie."

"Someone will know him," she said confidently.

Spoken like the adventuress she was. Nothing was impossible for Darcie. She'd hauled him over continents, found the diamond, foiled the villains. She was heroine for a pulp novel, just as he'd always thought.

The strange thing was having his sight back and participating in the adventure. He wasn't in the dark any longer. And yet, everything was as blank as could be.

"What will you do when we return to England?" she asked idly as she poured him some coffee.

"I haven't thought that far ahead."

"You *must* go back to Pengellis-Becarre."

"Must I?" Even he didn't know, and Darcie, watching him, felt a tremor of foreboding. Once they vanquished Lavinia, the story would be over. What would happen to Scheherazade then?

"We don't need to talk about it now . . ." she started to say and he interrupted her.

"Can we talk about any of it? This far from Srinagar and Nadyl, do you believe *any* of what we've seen?"

"I believe you found the diamond and that Lavinia still wants to kill you," she said gently, worriedly. This kind of thinking wasn't like him; he was usually so sure. "Isn't that real enough?"

Lavinia, he thought. It all came back to Lavinia. All about Lavinia.

And him. He was the source—the connection to everything.

But what was Darcie? Did he truly believe that Lavinia was desperate to get an heir from Darcie? What about that story still didn't fit?

Or was she always meant to be the instrument of The Eye of God?

The questions haunted him as the train bowled down the snow-shrouded tracks, and Darcie set out their afternoon snack just as if she were serving tea at the palace.

That night, they slept on the fur throw on the rolling floor of the car, coupling blindly, heatedly to the rhythm

of the wheels on the tracks, rocking together on soft
radiant waves until they simultaneously climaxed.

And even then, he didn't let her go. He rode her
until morning, cradled between her legs, matching the
pulse of the wheels, the cadence of the track.

"It doesn't matter where I am," he murmured in her
ear, "I love being inside you."

She shimmied against him, enticing him slowly. "And
I love it when you are." She felt the delicious spurt as
he hardened still again.

"You are so wet, so responsive." He nuzzled her neck.

"I can't get enough," she whispered. Stiffer and stiffer.
One more time again. "I love when you take me."

He rocked against her, feeling the expansion of his
power. There was nothing like the dark wet mystery of
her. Everything else receded beside it. He wanted to
live in it forever.

He wanted her now.

He shoved against her experimentally. "Like that?"

"Ummm," she sighed.

Harder. "Is that better?"

"Ah."

A long hard stroke deep into her core.

"Perfect," she breathed, and begged for more.

He pumped her in tight hard steady thrusts, just the
way she wanted it, just the way she craved it. Perfect.
Tight. Hard. Gone. She convulsed beneath him and
around him, and took him along.

They saw Moscow from beside the bridge that crossed
the river, under the threat of snow. It was still another
city of contrasts, ancient and new, its dwellings clustered
near the river that divided the city, and the spires of its
numerous churches soaring against the lowering sky.

Here, Nicholas II's coronation procession down the Tverskaya just a year and a half before. There, the walls of the Kremlin and the vista of Red Square. Market stalls in the Upper Bazaar, and Kuznetsky Street for shopping. They took it all in during the brief two-hour layover, whirling through the city in one of the dozens of cabs that waited at the station.

And then on their way again in the early evening, with the snow lightly falling.

And another night, wrapped in fur and passion and fury, laying on the floor.

They arrived at the Nikolaevski Station in St. Petersburg the following night, and were transferred immediately to the Great Northern Hotel across the way.

The next morning, they were going to scour the churches again as a starting point. The stone could be anywhere.

And, as Con pointed out, maybe not even there.

"No. I don't believe that. It's here, somewhere—probably in some church."

She was determined, fired up. She inquired of the concierge the location of the nearest church, and he directed them down the Ekaterinski Canal to Resurrection Church.

It was a cold day, the snow had abated, but she was thankful for her wool and furs. They hurried down the long residential street divided by the canal, the church in the distance rising up like a benediction.

"We'll find some answers here," Darcie whispered. "It has to be here."

They mounted the steps to the entrance and pulled open the door.

This was a vast church, as different from the plain country church in Nadyl as night from day. The ceilings soared, picked out in gold, with murals and icons all

along the walls. Velvet drapes at the sanctuary, and at
the doors, and two porcelain stoves heating the nave.
The scent of incense permeated the air.

And a feeling of majesty and reverence unlike anything Darcie had ever experienced.

"Have you come for a blessing?"

They whirled at the voice behind them, a young acolyte, dressed in robes.

Con translated and answered, "We come to speak
with your priest."

"Father Cyril prays."

"May we wait?"

The acolyte nodded. "I will tell him you are here."

Darcie sank into a pew and just stared. "He cannot
corrupt this."

"He corrupts everything," Con said. "And he is everywhere."

"We will find him here."

She jumped to her feet, and began pacing restively.

"My children . . ."

Oh no . . . no—no—

The voice of Father Vasili greeted them as he stepped
into the aisle.

"So—you have eluded death and come this far," he
murmured as Con translated. "Blessings on you, clever
ones. I will tell you what you need to know."

"Ask him—" Darcie prodded. "Where is the stone?"

"Listen to me, foolish ones," he answered in response. "There is nothing more you can do."

"I don't believe it," Darcie said adamantly.

"He has been here since the Neva froze over," Father
Vasili said. "He has accomplished much. And there is
still more for him to do."

"What has he done?" Darcie demanded. "What is he going to do?"

"So impatient," Father Vasili murmured. "But that is the way of the chosen. Only, there is nothing she can do."

"Tell us then," Con said, motioning for Darcie to contain herself.

"He has mastered the stone. Samael be with you, as he will be with our little Father the Tsar."

They froze.

"What does he mean? What *can* he mean?" Darcie cried.

"He cut the stone," Con surmised.

Father Vasili nodded. "Our wise and holy man did indeed cleave the stone—into three beautifully faceted pieces."

"No . . ." Darcie moaned.

"And through the auspices of a well-known jeweler, and in the name of Samael, he has presented those valuable stones to our little Father to mark the occasion of the birth of his daughter. One for his sceptre. One for his crown. And one for the Empress to wear on her brow."

"Oh God—"

"And now, he whom you call Lazarin, will make his home in St. Petersburg. He will mingle with all strata of society, he will become a man of holy destiny, as he draws ever closer to the Crown."

"Con—" Darcie said beseechingly, and he shook his head.

Father Vasili went on: "The time is not right, not yet. But soon, soon. This is the judgment of Samael: that Mother Russia shall come into the holy hands of the monk Rasputin."

He looked deeply into Con's eyes. "And so it shall be. All your effort has come to nothing. This is the judgment of Samael: there will be no mercy in any quarter. And *The Eye of God* cannot protect thee. So saith Samael, and so it shall be."

"We can do nothing more here," Con said.

"Kill him," Darcie whispered fiercely. "Take vengeance on him, at least."

Father Vasili looked at her, almost as if he were reading her mind, and he raised his hand. *"No* mercy. This is the judgment of Samael."

And he lowered his hand slowly. "So it shall be," he intoned, and when his hand dropped to his side, he disappeared.

"Oh my God—" Darcie breathed. "Oh my God . . . Where is he? Where did he go?"

"I believe him," Con said. There wasn't any point wasting time on trying to define what you didn't know.

"We have to make sure," Darcie said frantically. "We have to check it out."

"You don't believe it? Believe it. The stone is gone, and there's nothing we can do now. The evil is loose and it goes with the Tsar everywhere he goes. It infects his family. The people. The land. It's too late, Darcie. We got one little piece of it. And it's not enough to stem the rising tide. Rasputin—Lazarin—whatever they will call him—*he* will be in control."

"How can you know that?" she whispered.

"I know. How many times have we faced him, and he hasn't died? You think Kleist is dead and buried a hundred miles from here in the snow. No, by now he's resurrected just like Karun, and he lives in Rasputin's body, and he still goes on. Nor can *The Eye of God* destroy him, or it would have, just like the stone."

"What do we do now?" she whispered.

He gave her a sardonic smile. "Damned if I know."

* * *

It's over. The grand adventure is over. It only remains to return to England so he can reclaim his life.

She didn't want it to be over. Not ever.

How could she tell him? What was she but an opportunist of the worst kind? She'd gotten out of it exactly what she desired. *The Eye of God* entrusted to her like a baby, and nestled between her breasts.

And Con. *Mustn't forget Con.*

And one of the famous Pengellis diamonds. Oh, she'd made out like a thief this time. Sex and money too. She could live like a queen forever, just as she had planned.

They walked down to the frozen Neva River, near the Winter Palace, and watched streetworkers breaking the ice, and over to the Academy of Art, with the two Egyptian sphinxes guarding the front. And across the broad avenue of Nevsky Prospect, and to the Fortress of Saints Peter and Paul.

And nowhere was there any trace of Lazarin. It was as if he had disappeared into thin air. Or it had been he, transmogrified into Father Vasili, just Darcie had seen Lazarin at the presbytery.

And finally, three futile days later, Con told her: "It is time to go home."

They travelled again by the railway, this time going south, from St. Petersburg, to Moscow, Tula, Kursk, Kharkov to the terminus in Sevastopol and, to him, the familiar sight of steamers plowing the Black Sea.

He expended his last diamond in Sevastopol for expenses and passage home. They sailed across to Varna, and it was the last thing he saw.

By the time they reached Bucharest, he was blind again.

Twenty-two

"I don't understand, I just *don't* understand," Darcie fumed as she paced the confines of their sleeping car. They were stranded someplace outside of Bucharest for the moment, the snow being too high and thick for the train to push through.

And here was Con, his eyesight utterly gone, for reasons that she refused to believe.

"The judgment of Samael! Honestly, Con."

"You don't believe it?" Did he? He didn't know quite when he began to notice it: the tired eyes. The blurring. The weariness he just didn't see. *After* their encounter with Father Vasili? Or before?

"You do? I think you're falling for all that flummery far too easily."

"No mercy in *any* quarter," he quoted mordantly. "What do you think happens when you try to destroy a god?"

"That's funny. Why didn't Father Vasili just kill you?"

"For the same reason I didn't kill him, I suppose. You don't kill the messenger."

But there *was* something else. It tickled the edge of his consciousness like a spell. Something he knew. Something he'd even said.

"They used to," she countered acidly. She should

have done it, she thought. She *could* have done it, with the power of *The Eye of God.*

If only she'd taken it seriously, if only she'd really understood that it was hers all along.

And now, he was in the dark again.

"It's ironic," he said. "We begin and end exactly the same."

"No. We don't," she said sharply. "We *don't.* We've crossed continents. We've climbed mountains. We have the diamond. And—" She stopped short. *And?*

The problem was, there wasn't any end. Not until he confronted Lavinia, and took back his life.

"It's *not* the same," she finished firmly. "And we have to figure out why this happened."

"The gift was taken back. It's as simple as that. Penance must be paid."

Yes, he thought, that was familiar too; he'd thought that before, what seemed like a hundred years ago.

She hated the fatalistic tone in his voice. "I'm not going to let you think that way. There *has* to be an answer."

He thought that too, but as with everything else in his life, he'd gambled and lost.

"Darcie, the whole thing was a big vainglorious self-aggrandizing risk. Do you understand that? *I* gave up Pengellis. *I* let Roger just walk in and take it up while I went on my wild-goose chase. I was so convincing everyone thought it was real."

"Well, it was," she interpolated.

"I didn't *really* know that then. I was going to be a hero, all that fame, all that lovely money to be had from splitting a legendary diamond; and that over and above all the other money we made in London and South Africa. Tell me, Darcie, when does a man get smart? How much does he really need?"

She knew the answer to that. "When he makes his final strike."

"Well, we did that, didn't we? And look at the cost. We haven't moved one foot from where we started. And we haven't gained a thing."

"Except the diamond," she said. *And each other, she didn't say.*

"We haven't gained a thing," he repeated. "But we *have* unleashed something unspeakable on the world. *The balance must be kept.* I knew that. And I arrogantly walked in and changed it. You don't think that calls for a cosmic punishment, Darcie?"

"I think something's going on that's closer to home."

"You're so practical. So sensuous and beautiful. How lucky I am you found me." But his tone was bitter. Mocking—and she didn't know if he were ridiculing her or himself.

Neither was acceptable.

"Sometimes you can't choose, "she said. "Sometimes things are meant to be." But that sounded fantastic, and fatalistic too, and it wasn't quite what she meant to say.

"Well, there you go," he murmured derisively. "It is the judgment of Samael: that he shall from this time forth walk in darkness. And so it has been."

She wouldn't let it be, she thought fiercely. She would not let him believe in the vengeance of an entity that didn't exist.

"I wish we had kept the dust," she said suddenly. "Maybe it could have worked for you like what you said about Lazarin—his drawing his power from the diamond fields . . . Maybe if you still had a part of the stone . . ."

Yes . . . that shocked him into awareness. She had defined his elusive thought: but not the dust—the shards. The slivers of black diamond he'd carried with him

from the Valley to Tobolsk. Where he'd sold the second
to last diamond, and discarded the pouch.

Where they'd burned the dust.

"Jesus, Darcie . . ." His possession of the shards had
preserved his sight, and not the capitulation of his soul.

She wasn't aware of them in Budapest, but she was
certain by the time they reached Vienna, Lavinia's
agents were after them. Almost as if she had blanketed
every train station of every possible route.

They were at every stop where crowds swarmed, and
they were passengers on the train. They ate in the dining car, and paced past their door, and there was no
way to escape.

She cursed fate that they were burdened by his sightlessness. How did you save a blind man from disaster
when it surrounded you like air?

It was coming, as surely as the dawn. Lavinia hadn't
given up on claiming her treasures. Or killing Con.

This was just a different kind of evil. Maybe one from
which they could run. They might even have a chance—
in Paris—if she could keep them at bay.

She didn't tell him, at first, but she was so tense, and
so unresponsive, he prised it out of her.

"Lavinia's people are on the train."

He thought that was interesting. Everywhere she'd
seen Lavinia's *people,* he'd had only her word. And now,
when he was doubly dependent on her, they were all
around again.

Darcie had the diamond . . .

Darcie had the answers.

*Surround him with the enemy, and kill him with what he
couldn't see . . .*

Was *that* what it was really all about?

Whom did *you trust, when a fabulous diamond was at
stake?*

*And how much was spit and fairy tales to take advantage
of his dependence?*

He felt like he was falling in the dark. It rose up to
meet him, slamming him in the eyes.

Darcie the trojan horse.

Darcie's allegiance to—who?

*The body that launched a thousand mile quest had seduced
him royally. He had fallen like a shooting star.*

*And all to return to the crux of the matter, except that Darcie
had accomplished exactly what she'd set out to do.*

The last big strike.

And he'd handed it to her too.

. . . dear God—

*Lavinia was just the diversion so he wouldn't perceive what
was going on. And just like any other man, he'd let Darcie
subjugate him with his heart.*

Goddamn, damn, damn—

"Con? I'm scared."

Was she?

He girded himself to amplify the deception, remembering the journey out. What was real, what was the lie.
"You're not scared of a thing, Scheherazade."

She looked at his stone carved face, his blank eyes.
I'm scared of you.

"We might be able to elude them in Paris."

"Why?"

"More ways to escape; more routes we can take. We
know the city. You know the language."

"You're right," he murmured, "that does make
sense." She was masterful, he thought. He had named
her exactly right. "But for now, what do you want to
do?"

She'd be a stranger in a strange land, so she wouldn't

leave him now. But in Paris—she had the means, the motive—she'd abandon him like a sack of rotten wheat.

"We have to keep to the car. I'll get our food—"

"Just like last time," he murmured. Was she that clever she thought she could replay the same scenario and he would still bite? "But you shouldn't be carrying the diamond—if the threat is that pervasive."

"And you can't see our enemies," she retorted. "We're some fine pair. I think I'm better off holding it."

"And if they attack you—?"

She didn't like saying it. "It's gone."

Very good, he applauded silently. *Just the right tone.* "I can think of maybe one place no one would think to look. Do you want to risk it after all we've been through?"

"But I can *see* the danger," she argued.

"Not from behind. And not if they grab you from both sides. Not if they immobilize you."

"All right—all *right*. You have a point. Maybe the thing is, we can't protect it to the extent we should right now. We can only do what we can do."

"Well then—you must leave it here when you see to our meals. We'll have a password or something and I won't unlock the door unless I hear it."

He thought that sounded reasonable, and not as if he were suspicious of her at all. A compromise of sorts that for the moment he could live with.

"All right. I won't gamble with it. Choose your password."

"Why don't you?" he said.

"Our enemies know everything about us," she muttered.

"Then let me suggest—they can't know this—*penance must be paid.*"

* * *

He held *The Eye of God* in his hands—in the dark. A rough eight-sided stone that felt and looked like less than it was.

Yet men had killed for it; women had lied.

And because they had taken it, the balance had tipped to the other side.

It wasn't easy to hide either. Darcie had drawn the shade on the door window, and doused the lights since he sat in the dark anyway.

He ruminated on her cleverness.

Probably this would be the only time he'd get his hands on the diamond. Probably, she'd never let it out of her sight from now on.

Probably. And she'd look for somewhere neat to kill him, like that attendant she'd thrown off the train.

Oh my good goddamn. All the things Darcie had done in the name of protecting him and sustaining their quest. It made him queasy, remembering.

For all he knew, she was a professional thief and this was an elaborate hoax solely to get possession of the diamond. She wouldn't scruple to kill him then. And blame it all on Lavinia.

And there! The other thing that niggled at him: the woman Darcie described was not the mother he'd known.

Lavinia was a hard-headed businesswoman, pure and simple. She coveted The Eye of God *because of its value split into individual stones, and what it would add to the bottom line. And the public notice it would bring to the firm. Lavinia had known just how to merchandise those things.*

If she couldn't have the diamond, she'd publicize the quest.

And she had been a damn sight better at it than he had been. And a gentle mother when he was young . . .

There was a knock at the door, two short raps, then one, repeated twice, as prearranged. He pocketed the diamond and moved to the door.

"Who's there?"

"Con—it's me. *Penance must be paid.*"

He slipped the locks and she eased in.

"I guess that worked," she murmured, "but you have to pull down the table so I can see to the lights."

He knew his way around the car by then, and he got the table, she groped for it, and set down the tray, and then she turned up the lights and locked the door.

"We'll leave on the lights next time," she said, slipping onto her bench. "Well, it's chicken again. The usual accompaniments. I hope you're hungry."

She didn't say a word about the diamond as she arranged his plate, and they ate in silence, as they usually did. And then she would leave the tray outside by the door.

"Con—I should hold the diamond. That only makes sense."

He knew he couldn't stop her, except by force. And he weighed, in that split second, where that would leave him. Give her the diamond, and she could abscond forever. Keep it himself, and he might have to hurt her.

Either way, he could be left dependent on strangers, with no way to know who was an enemy or a friend.

Blast the power that had taken his eyes!

"Maybe not," he temporized. "Especially if you'll be going in and out two or three times a day just to feed us. Maybe it makes more sense in my hands."

"There's something weird going on here," she said suspiciously.

"No, we're just being supremely cautious. Now that Lavinia's after us, I mean."

He heard the rattle of the china as she cleared the table. Pulled the locks. Opened and closed the door and locked it again. Like she was using motion to cover her frustration, her anger, her dismay.

Or else she was planning her next move.

Either way, he was keeping the diamond.

He heard her fold up the table, and pull down her berth. They'd agreed that no attendants would make up the beds.

"Have it your way," she said finally, and there was a shrug in her tone.

"It makes sense," he said, and he too lay down.

She lay angry and seething in the dark.

He was acting so odd, like he didn't trust her. After everything that had happened, and all they'd been through. She felt like shaking him.

But as she lay sleepless across the room from him, she understood that things were very different this trip. Now they had the diamond. And he had again lost his sight.

What man wouldn't be bitter alone in the dark?

She wondered why she thought they had forged any bond. She'd been nothing to him but a whore, in the dark.

Now his attitude finally made sense. She already had her tithe and he was finished with her. When he claimed Pengellis-Becarre, he'd take a *worthy* bride, and *The Eye of God* would be the centerpiece of his return.

And he wasn't giving it up, even to save his life.

She couldn't believe everything she'd done for him, but that was the risk an adventuress took. Had she thought he'd be dependent on her forever? Or fall in love with her unceasingly demanding body?

She didn't know what she had thought, except that she couldn't bear the idea that the thing was over—in every way.

But not yet. They still had to get to Paris. Make their escape. Return to England and successfully make their claim.

His claim.
Damn. Damn. Damn.
Blessed be . . .
There was still that—and what it might mean.
And they'd yet to confront Lavinia.
She took a deep steadying breath.
One thing at a time.
The story still wasn't over.

The train passed through Munich, with a brief stop. Darcie reconnoitered the dining car and brought back lunch. She felt like a servant, a waitress. Less than her worth.

Like the stone, with its hidden power that she'd seen.

Maybe she too had covert powers she hadn't yet tested.

She felt the evil eyes of their enemy watching them. "Con . . . ?"

He was looking at the window, seeing nothing. She felt an abject wave of sorrow wash over her. What *would* he do, once they returned to London? He'd *have* to give over the running of the company to someone else. He could still be the hero, the figurehead. The blind Con Pengellis who'd once been a god.

How did a man fall so far from grace? This was such unjust punishment. It wasn't fair. And it couldn't be fought on any terms that made them equals.

She was the daughter of an itinerant miner, and he was the son of a wealthy diamond merchant, and a honorable to boot.

Damn. Those discrepancies didn't matter in a desert. They mattered on a train going back to civilization. *His* civilization. She had been an interloper there.

Oh, God—it was so complicated. The truth of it all

was she'd been nothing more than a camp follower trying to get rich quick.

And while she supposed she had rights as Roger's
wife, Con probably wouldn't want her anywhere near
him when they returned.

"Con?" she tried again. She hated these silences. This
was not a man on a mission. It was a man who was
thinking too hard and making assessments she was not
going to want to hear.

"Yes, Darcie?" Polite. Calm. Raging inside probably
at this awful turn of fate.

"It will be all right, when we get to England," she
said. She didn't know what to say; he was such a stranger
and now she walked in a strange land. And there was
nothing she could say to crack his impassive mein.

"You'll be safe," she added, hearing the desperation
in her tone. "I'll make sure we're safe there."

He smiled faintly, and she didn't like that smile. "I'm
sure you will."

Paris!
A half hour to arrival at Le Gare du Nord.

The conductor's voice echoed all up and down the
sleeping cars.

Make ready, all who will depart at the station . . .

She was the one who packed. She felt his helplessness,
his fury. And something else contained that she
couldn't define.

This was it, the moment. "I think we should get out
as far from this car as we can."

"You lead the way."

He was too agreeable, too amenable.

He didn't believe her—

No! There was too much at stake. He *had* to believe her.

She had two valises, wrapped in the fur and strapped together, so she could manage them with one hand.

And she had him.

"Do you need help, madame?" She jumped. An attendant? Or an enemy?

"Non, merci." She needed it desperately. She held Con's hand as they shuffled to the next car, squeezing by irate passengers trying to debark.

"Go on, Darcie, it doesn't matter."

"I *hate* this new sensibility of yours. Why aren't you fighting? Why don't you believe me?"

He supposed he shouldn't have been shocked. What could he hide from the Darcie of the dark who knew him so well?

"Don't you *dare* not fight—" she said fiercely. *For this—for us, she didn't say.*

"I feel like we can't escape it. I feel like I cheated fate and now—penance must be paid. What do you feel, Darcie? Triumph? That you've won?"

"I just feel like getting out of here before they get us."

"Right—*they* . . ."

He didn't believe her. He didn't *believe her!*

She pulled him violently down the passage, not caring who he slammed into in her haste. Damn him. Damn him, damn him, damn him.

She managed to get them three cars away from where watchers would expect them to emerge.

Managed that, with all his reluctance and the passenger herd.

And then the train whistle blew, and they had to get out.

She stepped down warily at the next exit, peering out from the protection of the train.

"Oh my God," she breathed. "Oh dear God— Con . . ."

They were waiting for them. They were right in front of the car she had chosen to exit.

And, she thought, she shouldn't have been surprised. Anything was possible. Con had said so, all those months ago, and they'd seen it time and again in the succeeding months.

Anything was possible, and so there they were: Roger and her *father*—the living dead.

"Welcome, my dear," Roger said. "Do hand over the diamond—or I will shoot you dead."

Twenty-three

The train whistle wailed. The engine started up in a huge cloud of steam.

"Run . . . !" Darcie screamed, dropping everything and pulling his hand.

"Jesus, Darcie . . ."

"Shut up . . . !" Even though she knew it was futile, they ran, knocking into passengers, tripping over baggage.

Roger was right behind them; her father pawing through their luggage.

They just might make it, they just might . . . if only Con had his eyes.

She felt him fall behind her, heavily, pulling her down flat on her back.

Roger had tackled him, and now he stood, covering them with his gun.

"Resourceful, Darcie. You were ever that. Get to your feet, both of you. We won't make a scene."

She had gambled on the fact he wouldn't. She scrambled to her feet.

"Con? Are you all right?"

"Yes." *And humiliated. And a fool.*

Roger.

And his accomplices.

Including Darcie.

It made such sense. And Darcie had the diamond.

And she told such wonderful stories, even the one about pretending to try to escape from Roger.

So good. Good as it gets . . .

He wanted to kill them all.

"My father is here," Darcie whispered.

"How neat," he murmured. It just tidied things right up. They'd used him, all of them; he was the dupe, the gull, the tool.

They were all going to share in the cut from the diamond.

Darcie too.

By God . . . penance was being paid—

"Come now," Roger said. "Lavinia awaits us."

"It was all an elaborate hoax, wasn't it?" Con said. "From the moment I escaped, you had the thing planned."

"More or less," Roger said. "Of course, Darcie's father conveniently *died* to give her an urgent motive to seek the diamond. There's nothing like greed. We had you covered on all fronts, until you escaped. And then of course, I had to *die*. We thought that might get you back to Goole. But in any event, things have worked out. You have the diamond, and we'll just cleave it tidily and sell it at a profit."

"And Lavinia?"

"Ah . . . Lavinia. She's getting old, Con. She's a little dotty. Keeps talking about its powers. Nothing worth listening to. A few million pounds ought to quiet her down. Then of course, we do have the birth of the child to look forward to. Except"—he took Darcie by the elbow and turned her around— "I don't see any evidence of it, do I Darcie? There never was a baby, was there?"

He shoved her away from him and she fell against Con.

"Aren't you the sharp-witted bitch, my darling. Mother bought it, whole cloth. She'll be so disappointed. I don't *think* there's anything else. So that should answer your questions for now."

She hated him. She despised Roger with a killing fury. A man who looked so much like Con and who was such a liar and a cheat.

"What happens now?" she asked, barely able to contain her rage.

"Why, we'll go back to Goole, my dear. And we'll sort out our lives."

It rose up before them in the twilight, stark and eerie, a pile of stone and secrets, shrouded in silence.

The trip had been excruciating. She had to face her father, face her own sins. The man she depended on, loved, cared for and carried, had been seduced by the stone.

His big strike. She was to have been his foil. Hadn't he hammered it into her, the legend of the stone: And made her feel responsible for getting his share?

Oh yes, he'd primed her well for the task. She'd had everything at her disposal: he'd bought her entree to the castle, outlined the quest, and gave her the mission. And then he'd perished, to enhance her mandate to carry out the task.

Treacherous! Such a betrayal—of her love, her belief in him, in them—as partners, as a team.

Her whole life was a lie, she thought, beginning to end.

Or maybe her life had begun the day she rescued Con.

She had no other allegiances here.

"You will give up the diamond," Roger kept telling her. "It will be mine."

"Ours," Leonard Boulton added. "Such a clever Darcie, finding Con, and getting him there."

Her heart was stone; he couldn't touch her anymore. She did not know this man he had become.

"My dear," he chided. "There's no difference between this and what we did to gain possession of the Colorado mines."

She turned her head away. That was a long time ago. A long long time ago. It was the deal that had given him the wherewithal to come to England and instigate this plan.

An uncut diamond worth a fortune in gold . . .

She didn't want to think about it—any of it—or her part in it.

She hadn't thought about it at all from the day they'd left Colorado; she'd never looked back.

The mark of a gambler, depending on luck.

"I know Darcie has the diamond," Roger went on conversationally. "There was never any doubt once we knew you two were together. She's very good at what she does, isn't she, Con?"

"Most excellent," he said dryly. *And oh, what she does . . .*

He felt the impotence of a man abandoned by fate. He'd lost everything. He couldn't defend against Roger and Darcie, who still had their eyes.

Such a clever Darcie . . .

And he hadn't believed in the danger.

He just hadn't thought it would come from his heart.

"Are we there yet?"

"We're in the park," Roger said. "You remember the park?"

And all the dead trees, their branches begging heaven . . .

"Almost there. Mother will be waiting."

Ah yes, Lavinia, the other part of the equation.

What about Lavinia?

The carriage lurched to a stop.

Coming home again, blind. Always blind to what was around him, even when he could see.

Hands helping him out. Not Darcie.

Roger's rough hands, pushing him. And the distinctive scent of the air, dry as dead leaves. Goole was dead. He'd never seen it, but it had always been so.

"Clever of you to have brought him to Goole after you found him," Roger murmured to Darcie. "I'm utterly taken by your ingenuity. I had a treasure beyond price and I never knew it."

"You should have stayed dead," she spat.

Good, Darcie. Good. That sounded so protective, so combative. Darcie to his defense, white knight to a man immured in an endless night.

The air changed as they entered the hall.

Thick, stuffy, redolent of spices, bringing back the moments and memories. The portrait—that everlasting blasted portrait that made Darcie fall in love—it was in front of him, over the stairs, haunting him, the ghost of his former life, because he knew it was there.

He heard footsteps. And then the starchy tones of the butler, as he took their coats.

And then he heard a lighter step running along the balcony above him.

And *her* voice: "Where is it? Where's the diamond?"

Roger, speaking first. "Mother—"

"I don't give a damn about anything else. *Where is that stone?*"

And finally, a puzzle solved. He couldn't see, but he knew, and he wouldn't pretend, so he said it boldly, out loud.

"That's not my mother's voice."

* * *

They froze.

Darcie plucked his sleeve. "Con, that's your mother."

"That isn't she."

"Roger, where is *The Eye of God?*" Lavinia was tired of games, tired of waiting. Darcie could see it in her face, in her eyes. The lines were deeper, the cruelty more apparent. She was a woman on the edge of a precipice, struggling not to fall over.

"*She* has it." Roger gestured to Darcie.

"Give it up, girl. Grab her, Roger."

Immediately, he clamped his hands across her shoulders, pulling her tightly against him. She kicked him, bit him, stomped on his foot.

"Oh, she's a one. Look at her—fighting like an animal. She's wreaked enough havoc on this family. I'm tired of her. She took damned long to get the thing. And now—it's *mine* . . ."

Lavinia reached for her, her fingers clawed; Con jumped, toward the sound of the voice and the threat to Darcie, and knocked her down.

"*Who are you?*" he demanded, his hands at her throat.

She choked, fighting him with what seemed like superhuman strength.

Boulton wrenched him off of her, and held him back.

She made a guttural sound. "This is no son of mine. Roger—tear off her clothes if you have to. *I want that stone.*"

She backed up against the staircase to watch the melee.

Right under Con's portrait, Darcie noted with one part of her consciousness, as she wrestled with Roger. There was nothing she could use as a weapon. This was a sparsely furnished hallway. Rugs. Paintings. A trestle table covered with a tapestry. A suit of armor. An ax.

"Darcie . . . !" He was on the floor with her father. ". . . don't . . ."

"I . . . won't . . ." she panted as she shoved Roger, hard, and wrenched away. She ran down the length of the reception hall to the pedestal with the suit of armor.

"No you don't—" Roger, two steps after her.

Frantically, she pulled and twisted the long handle of the ax, forcing it free.

"Stay back!" she commanded, brandishing the thing in his face.

"Darcie . . ." Roger, conciliatory now.

She took a quick glance over his shoulder; her father had gotten Con down and he was sitting on him.

Damn them all.

"Back up, Roger, or I'll take off your head."

He raised his hands and stepped backward.

"If you know anything about our little adventure," she continued conversationally, following him down from the pedestal, "you know I've done a fair amount of . . . interesting . . . shall we say? things along the journey. I won't scruple to do what I have to now. So—" she turned to her father in a vicious movement, "get off of Con, or I'll slice you to pieces."

"Ah, that's my Darcie," her father said, climbing to his feet.

"Over to the stairs," she ordered, as Con got to his knees. "You traitor. I know which part of *him* I'd butcher. Are you all right, Con?"

He nodded. "Are you?"

"I found a nice medieval weapon just down the hall, Con. Not quite as efficient as a knife, but I see a few parts I could hack off with ease."

"For God's sake," Lavinia spat. "The thing's as dull

as a dish." She advanced toward Darcie. "I want that stone."

Darcie held her eyes as she swung. Rounded, dark, vicious eyes like an owl. The Lavinia she had known— and not.

"Who *are* you? Why are you so desperate? What do you really want—a baby or the diamond?"

"I'll have both," Lavinia sneered.

Darcie shook her head. "Neither. There was no baby . . ."

Lavinia's face changed, transformed into something evil and beyond human. "You lie!" she shrieked, charging toward Darcie.

Darcie swung, and nicked her shoulder.

Lavinia howled: "Leonard—she's your daughter. *Get her . . . !* Roger—*kill her . . . !*"

They started toward her menacingly, and she swung with all her might. One by one they dropped to the floor.

"Darcie . . ." Con behind her, listening to the chaos. "You have to cleave the diamond."

"Oh my God, are you crazy?" She poked the ax at Lavinia who made a movement toward her.

"Don't touch that diamond," Lavinia screamed.

"You're the only one. You have to do it. It's the only way to stop them. She is *not* my mother."

She swallowed hard, swinging the ax again as her father approached.

"Don't do it, daughter. What do you know about cutting gems? You'll destroy it, the legend of a lifetime."

"Darcie . . . you have the power. It's the only way."

"Why, Con, why? Who are they?"

"They are acolytes of Samael, possessed by the evil. We cannot give them the diamond."

She groaned. "Con . . . I can't. I won't destroy the diamond."

"You have to, Darcie. It was meant to be."

"Don't listen, don't do it!" her father shrieked.

"We have to defeat him. We have to destroy *her*, she is the most dangerous of them all. We must right the balance, Darcie. Penance must be paid."

"Yes—" she whispered.

"*NOOOOOO . . . !*" Lavinia screamed.

"*Yes!*" Con decreed. "This woman—this *thing*—the shell of the woman I called mother. She is possessed, her body inhabited by the entity Lilith who walks the earth in the company of Samael, whose stone we destroyed.

"Lilith, the first wife of Adam, who was condemned for her disobedience, and for her voracious appetite for children and men. It is said, because of this, when she went to heaven to beg for the oil of mercy, she was turned away, and that only when she finds a body to inhabit may she try again. No wonder she was avid for your child, Darcie. The love of a child begs mercy.

"But now we know: Samael is among us, seeking the diamond. You *must* cleave it and destroy *her* forever."

"DON'T LISTEN TO HIM!"

Her father, this time—or maybe not . . . who knew what entities were among them—and she couldn't take the chance.

"I will—I'll destroy it—"

"Better than this wickedness . . . I'm *telling* you— even though you know her as my mother . . . it is *not* she—and it *must* be done . . ."

She backed up toward the table, and they followed her, almost as one body—her father, Roger, Lavinia.

"He's lying," Lavinia said, reaching out her hand.

Whoosh. Lavinia jumped back.

Tears streamed down Darcie's face. "Are you *sure*, Con?"

"It was my dream, my quest. I knew there was something—something about Lavinia, and I'm telling you now—you have the power . . . kill the evil—*cut the damned diamond!*"

Whoosh—another warning, as Roger lunged toward her.

Con heard it all, and he couldn't do a thing. Darcie had to believe him. She had to keep them at bay. And she had to achieve a cut.

God, he would kill to have his eyes back . . .

Darcie felt his anguish; she had to be strong, for both of them. They were watching her—those eyes, those flaming dark, looking into pools of hell eyes . . .

Con was right. She *had* to do it.

She slipped the stone out of the leather pocket and set it on the table.

"That's it . . . ohhhh—that's it . . ." Lavinia whispered, reaching out her hand.

Whoosh . . . the blade sliced the air, just nicking her hand.

"Bitch," Lavinia screeched.

"Oh God. That's it," Boulton muttered. "Like dross before it becomes gold . . ."

Whoosh—she'd kill him too if she had to . . .

Whoosh—Roger jumped backward as she sliced at him.

She held their eyes. She watched them. They were all looking for the moment, the chance when one—or all of them—could dive for the diamond.

She had one chance, one choice, no niceties. She didn't have to understand angles or fractures. All she had to know was if Lavinia possessed the diamond, everyone's life would rupture.

She poised herself, swinging the ax toward them, aiming at their necks. Their necks were good—tender, vulnerable, pulsing with lifeblood.

And they knew it. They weren't going to rush her. She could do serious harm.

But it was just in that moment, when she lifted her arm upward, and before she sliced down—

And it could pop out from under the pressure of the blade, she thought.

Then they might get to her . . . and pull her down.

"I'll hold it," Con said calmly, as he sensed her frenzy.

Oh God, worse and worse. Con could be killed.

"Angle it over the table, and I'll stand on one side."

"You're crazy," she muttered.

"Do it."

Do it. She'd been doing it, one way or another, her whole life.

"All right. Take the stone and position it where you feel comfortable."

He groped his way to where she was standing. "You don't want your back to them."

"A good point."

Whoosh—as they saw this conversation as an opportunity to move.

Now he was at the head of the table, between them and the stone.

"That's good, Con."

He balanced it on the tapestry cloth. "I'm ready."

I'm not . . .

She couldn't swing from full high—they'd get her first. It had to be a short, sharp, emphatic swing, right to its heart.

Her hands were icy cold, her heart pounding. She poked at her father as he started to move.

"You know, maybe I ought to practice this—get a little twist in there where I could kill someone who tries to get in my way."

Her father froze.

"That's better—*daddy.*"

Now . . .

She chewed her lip. Con stood there like a statue, his hand balancing the stone. One chance. One swing.

She held out the ax so that the blade touched the stone. Thank God the thing was big.

She turned to look at them. They cursed her to hell.

She lifted the instrument and chopped it down on the biggest, most legendary diamond in the world—

Lavinia screamed as the blade connected—

And she cracked it—

Roger roared—

And she pounded it—

Her father moaned.

And she split it in two . . .

Liquid spumed out—great globs of thick clear liquid—she heard Lavinia scream, and she looked at Con, and the liquid was all over his face, and the way he was staring at her, and she could tell—he could see.

And Lavinia howling . . . shrivelling before their very eyes into a sharp-beaked gull, and then transforming into an owl, a vulture—swooping up into the air suddenly to attack Roger.

Roger! Pushing at the thing, beating it away, and it flapping its wings, shrieking, screaming, biting him with its beak and suddenly, there was an explosion and—nothingness.

And both of them—gone.

Everyone else—frozen in place.

Con, dumbfounded; Darcie, transfixed. Her father, utterly bewildered.

And then her father moved. He leapt for the table and grabbed one piece of the diamond. And then he sprinted for the door.

He never made it. The liquid enveloped him like lava,

foaming out from the center of the diamond, and adhering to his skin.

He died on the spot.

Darcie couldn't look. She looked at Con. *Con with his merciful eyes.*

Blessed be . . . meant to be—

Alone with the diamond and all it had wrought.

It looked like two halves of a broken stone. No luster. No sparkle. Nothing to distinguish it from a rock on the sand.

And this had been *The Eye of God*. And now that it was sundered, the balance would be maintained.

"How did you know—all of that, about the possession, and *the oil of mercy?*"

"*The oil of mercy* is legendary; I've studied the lore of every culture in search of clues to the whereabouts of the diamond. There had to be a link to Samael to explain why she was so desperate for the diamond. It meant something for her. Not just the riches from splitting it up. Something deeper.

"Some property of the diamond was essential to her. And then something about her obsessiveness about the child struck a chord. I remembered the legend of Lilith's demand at heaven's gate. And the old story about Samael accompanying her. We *had* to know what was contained in the diamond, Darcie. We had to make things right."

"Your eyes are healed. Nothing could be more right," she said.

He nodded. "And the enemy vanquished. The judgment is: from this day forth, he who had been blind, now can he see. And that which must be done, will be done. The power *was* yours, Darcie. The evil is dispersed, but now there can be remedy. We will split *The*

Eye of God, into as many pieces as we can, and we'll gift it where its power will counteract the evil. Penance *must* be paid, Darcie. That is *all* we can do."

After all that, she thought. And in the end, the cost was too great. The diamond would be cleaved because penance must be paid.

And greed and cupidity rebuked and given into the service of good.

Epilogue

Kisses. All he could think about was kisses.

Darcie's kisses.

And diamonds. He was drowning in diamonds since he had taken back Pengellis-Becarre. His return caused a sensation. Everybody wanted to see, to touch, to hear Con Pengellis who had returned from the dead.

Con, who only wanted to see, touch and hear Darcie. God, he wanted Darcie. There wasn't a waking moment he wasn't thinking about Darcie, and the quest, and all the luxurious hours of their lovemaking.

Darcie!

And where was Darcie? Darcie was living the life of a profligate wealthy widow in the Mayfair Hotel.

Darcie said, they had to wait. How would it look, if he were living with his brother's widow?

Very biblical of Darcie. It tied right in with everything. He *really* appreciated her concern for his character and morals.

He *really* did.

Was there ever a woman like Darcie?

He sat at his desk and looked over papers, and budgets, and drawings of new faceted cuts, and all he wanted to do was deck Darcie from head to foot in diamonds. He wanted to deck Darcie altogether.

He played the perfectly proper suitor, willing to wait.

He *hated* waiting, and he cursed the day he ever made Darcie wait. She knew just how to use it like a club and he had taught her how.

Of course, that didn't stop her from attending a whirlwind of events. He read about them now and again in the gossip columns because *he* wasn't allowed within a block of her. *Not* good form, said Darcie, pursuing your dead brother's wife in public.

He wanted to pursue something else, but even that was denied to him. He couldn't make the rules now. She could—and did—deny him *everything*.

And he wasn't sure how long he would put up with it, but it did add spice to things—for now.

And in the meantime, while he was *waiting*, he put his time to excellent use—when he wasn't daydreaming about Darcie. He was planning their wedding—although she didn't know about that part yet. He was designing her ring—but she didn't know about that either.

And he was constructing their life—but he hadn't gotten around to mentioning it.

He planned to inundate her with diamonds. It was the only proper gift for a heroine.

But he was annoyed to see he was not the only one who thought that about her. There was Darcie, her photograph in the paper, the lovely widow Pengellis, the story said, enjoying the races on the arm of the Earl of Fotherington.

That got his juices up.

He called on Darcie the next day.

"Con, you *cannot* visit me like this. It's not good form. I've been learning *all* about good form. There are *rules*, you know."

"I remember rules," he muttered. "I'm coming in."

"This isn't right," she fumed. "I'm trying very hard to live down all those stories that circulated about me after you announced your return and Roger's death. I have the Pengellis name to maintain now."

"And you're doing a right and proper job of it too, Darcie. At the theater last week. At the races Saturday. Church on Sunday. And all on the arms of three different men. My brother, if he hadn't been such a swine, would be turning in his grave. Besides which, I'm tired of waiting."

"Oh, but Con—people just won't understand about your brother's wife. Those are the *rules.*"

"I'm sick to death of rules and waiting."

She considered this for a moment. "Oh. Well. All right. Was there anything else you wanted to tell me?"

"Who the hell is the Earl of Fotherington?"

"A *very* nice man," she said earnestly. "He'd love to get married and set up his nursery . . ."

"Oh? Is he lined up behind your other paramours? Or are you keeping them all *waiting*?"

"Of course he doesn't have to *wait*. He's not my brother-in-law."

"Darcie—I swear . . ."

"But Con, I don't understand why you're so annoyed. What do you have to do with the Earl, or anyone else? I mean, you know I can take care of myself. And now there's money, and time, and . . ." her voice trailed off.

He looked into her deep blue eyes, and he saw the eyes of a gambler who knew when to cut her losses. And that was just what she had been doing with him, and it struck him like a blow to the gut.

This was no game.

"Are you jealous, Con?" she asked.

"I will kill the man who gets hard because of you. How about that, Darcie?"

"How about you?" she asked challengingly.

"Why don't you see?"

She held his eyes and bit her lip. She didn't know what he wanted from her now. She had thought that now he had reclaimed his life, he would want to stay as far away as possible from the Darcie who had destroyed his family. He wouldn't want an adventuress who was out for what she could get. He wouldn't want someone he knew too well.

Now that he was the Honorable Connack Pegellis, Bart., he would want a *lady*, born to his social set.

And then she had thought if she made herself into the kind of woman he would pursue, he might come for her—eventually.

The problem was, it had taken too damned long, and she had just been on the cusp of giving up on him altogether.

She wanted him so badly. If she touched him, she would set off a conflagration. She'd go to a place from which she'd never come back.

It was a moment to weigh the risks. She would either come away with what she wanted; or take home a different pot.

She almost thought it was worth it and that her ploy to keep him dangling was working.

"What's in it for me?"

His expression set. "Me."

"That's tempting, Con."

"I rather thought it was."

Arrogant beast. "But of course the Earl . . ."

"You've been *noticing* the Earl, have you?"

"Well, really Con—I'm free to *notice* whomever I want. We're not in the middle of the desert, you know."

This was getting ridiculous. "Darcie, come kiss me."

"I can't do that either, Con. You know where that will lead."

He was tired of this game. And it *was* a game. He liked their other games better. And he wanted her. He swept her into his arms and crushed her mouth under his.

"Darcie, dammit . . ."

"Very romantic," she whispered against his lips. Oh, how she'd missed his lips. "More."

That was better. That was Darcie.

Kisses and diamonds . . .

Proper dresses—proper hair . . . he pulled at them as he kissed her—Darcie in diamonds, Darcie bare . . .

Darcie's hands slipping in and cupping him between his legs.

The feel of her fingers, explosive *there.*

"Hurry." Darcie's voice, breathless with need.

"God, Darcie—all this *stuff."*

"I know." Her voice was tremulous. "I hate it."

"Don't wear it." He had off her shift, her corset, her camisole. "Always be naked for me."

Her eyes closed and her knees went weak. "Always be hard for me."

"Am I not? I've been hard for weeks waiting for you to finish playing merry widow. God, Darcie . . ."

They sank to the floor naked.

"Oh, Con—let me see you." She grasped him tightly, and all her intentions went out the window. Whether she would be a brother's widow or his whore, she wanted him. She needed him. And she wasn't too proud to beg.

"Take me."

She kissed him there, on the tip, the head, up and down the shaft. Kneeling to him, worshipping him, never enough of him—*there.*

"Darcie—" he murmured, pushing her to the floor almost too late.

He opened his hand, and diamond dust swirled all around her, all over her body, glittering like paint.

"Let me adore you."

His hands all over her then, all over, and she felt him press something against her skin.

She lifted her head to look, and she saw he had set a diamond in her navel.

"Con . . . !"

"We cut the diamond, Darcie. We made a dozen stones. Two of them will be set among the Crown jewels for the protection of the King. And we will present them in court, you and I, at the end of the month."

Balance. It was all about balance.

And there was only one more thing he had to do for balance to be restored.

He spread his hand over her belly. "Isn't there something biblical about a man cleaving to his brother's widowed wife?"

"Is there?" she asked barely above a whisper.

"And that it's a blessing if he marries her?" He touched the stone in her navel. "This is a fragment I cut and shaped for you. Let it be your engagement stone."

She caught her breath. "Yes."

"You'll marry me."

"Yes. But only because it's a blessing."

"No waiting."

"I promise."

"No rules."

She smiled. "Only if you make them."

"Forever?"

"More," she promised, she asked.

He kissed her deeply, in token of *his* promise, and

then he lifted the stone to the light and rainbows shot out, striping her bare body in liquid color.

"And in honor of our love," he murmured, setting it again reverently in the hollow of her navel, "this diamond shall be known forever more as the Eye of Heaven."

Darcie levered herself up on one arm and touched it. She felt a trembling deep inside her, a quickening just beneath the stone, and she looked at him with wondrous eyes.

He held her gaze as he shifted his weight so that he was over her, and poised for the moment of possession. "This is the judgment of the stone," he whispered. "You are *my* chosen one, Darcie. You are my heaven," and with a triumphant thrust, he brought them both home.